BE SURE YOUR SINS

BE SURE YOUR SINS

HARRY FISHER

This edition produced in Great Britain in 2021

by Hobeck Books Limited, Unit 14, Sugnall Business Centre, Sugnall, Stafford, Staffordshire, ST21 6NF

www.hobeck.net

A CIP catalogue for this book is available from the British Library.

ISBN 978-1-913-793-43-2 (pbk)

ISBN 978-1-913-793-42-5 (ebook)

Cover design by Jem Butcher

www.jembutcherdesign.co.uk

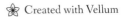 Created with Vellum

ARE YOU A THRILLER SEEKER?

Hobeck Books is an independent publisher of crime, thrillers and suspense fiction and we have one aim – to bring you the books you want to read.

For more details about our books, our authors and our plans, plus the chance to download free novellas, sign up for our newsletter at **www.hobeck.net**.

You can also find us on Twitter **@hobeckbooks** or on Facebook **www.facebook.com/hobeckbooks10**.

In memory of my mother
Christina Fisher

CHAPTER ONE

When Celia Fraser, who only had one arm, had left her Edinburgh home that morning with her granddaughter and her dog, she could never have imagined that only one of the three would return home safely.

Now, the corner shop's doorbell was dinging in her ear as she battled to keep the door open using a combination of her remaining elbow and her not inconsiderable backside, while manoeuvring two heavy shopping bags through the rapidly reducing gap.

She had lost her right arm in the motorcycle accident that claimed the life of her first proper boyfriend forty-five years ago come June. So, not for the first time, she cursed the shop-keeper for fitting a self-closing mechanism 'that would crush a bloody hippo', as she told anyone willing to listen.

Celia blinked against the sparkling spring sunshine as she scanned the wide pavement for her granddaughter. Neve would be twelve next week but her tiny cartoon-kid frame and freckled button nose rendered her way too small and innocent to be moving up to high school in August. In Celia's eyes, at least.

'Grandma!' came the shrill call from her left, followed by an over-excited yelp from Maddie. The golden retriever's tail swished a perfect hemisphere in the dust as she fought against her training and Neve's valiant efforts to keep her anchored. Celia had rescued the two-year-old when she was little more than a pup. Maddie's totally unconditional love always gave Celia goose bumps, and she wondered what had possessed her previous owners to give up on such a gorgeous puppy.

Two days later, once Celia's shattered pelvis and fractured left femur had been stabilised and she'd recovered enough to give a statement, she struggled to recall in which order she'd registered the raucous amalgam of sounds: child screaming, dog barking, tyres squealing, trainers slapping on paving slabs, doors slamming and engine racing. She couldn't say when Maddie's leash had been ripped from her grasp, and even through the dregs of the anaesthetic she was utterly shocked to be told that the rear wheel of the stolen, scruffy, off-white van had driven over her as it accelerated away.

As soon as she was lucid enough to comprehend, her son had reassured her that Neve was unharmed. But he couldn't bring himself to tell his mother about the emails he'd received containing videos and stills of her beloved Maddie cowering in a rusty cage while two snarling, slobbering pit bulls battled to get at her through the grid.

Unfortunately, his insensitive idiot of a wife let that fact slip while Celia was still in hospital.

CHAPTER TWO

'How was it?' says Andrew.

Detective Constable Andrew Young is my sidekick, my sounding board and the person in Police Scotland whom I trust above all others to watch my back. His name's Andrew, never Andy, and I'm Melissa Cooper. Detective Sergeant Cooper. Mel, to practically everybody. If I hear 'Melissa', I'll expect to see my mother, who will likely have a bee up her bum about something.

I shrug. 'Same old stuff, only more of it.'

I'm talking about our daily ops meeting, which is where I've been for the last half hour. It's a resource management forum but it also gives us the opportunity to share information and maybe even a lead or two that will help us catch the bad guys as quickly as upstairs demand we should.

I don't usually attend but my boss, Detective Inspector Jeff Hunter, is keen to expose me to the wider machinations of the service. This is for when, God forbid, I'm ever up for promotion. He's one of the good guys, Jeff, bless him, but I'm a detective because I want to be. I love my job, being immersed in the nitty-gritty of crime down here in sunny Leith and I have no desire whatsoever to be in police management. I'd rather solve crimes. Because every step up those slippery rungs means your head pokes further into the political murk that, in my humble and probably ignorant opinion, gets in the bloody way of solving crimes.

'You'll never guess what, though,' I say. Andrew arches an eyebrow. He can be a man of few words when it suits him. 'Frosty Knickers was there.'

Another eyebrow. 'Why?'

'Beats me. She had her inscrutable face on, which is almost as ugly as her normal one.'

'Says the oil painting.'

I should probably glower at him or chuck something mildly dangerous at his head but I have to admit he has a point. I could claim to be tall, blonde, with a face and a figure that would turn a stone gargoyle's head but regrettably, I'd be lying through my teeth. Make that middling height and brunette. And short skirts with high heels aren't really my thing.

But, returning to the subject: Frosty Knickers. Real name, Deirdre Keown. Like me, she's a DS. Her preferred persona appears to be 'total bitch' and, straight up, it beats me where she gets her energy from. As you might have gathered, we don't get on. It's not that we were best mates and have fallen out. She's hated me since the minute we met. I've no idea what I ever did to the woman and actually, I don't give a toss.

Keown – no one calls her by her first name – didn't contribute to the meeting and departed with her nose in the air while everyone else was still shuffling papers and closing notebooks. Jeff didn't comment, he's too much of a gentleman but he kept an eye on her as she left the room as if he needed to be convinced she was gone for good.

'Did you mention our blackmailer investigation?' Andrew

flicks something invisible off his sharply creased trouser leg, which is paired with a blinding white shirt. The knot in his tie could have been sculpted by laser. Dark brown hair, designer stubble and a healthy suntan all combine to make him more GQ model than police officer.

'I did. No joy. No one had even heard of the guy. Or these con artist sisters, if that's what they were.'

This is the strange case of Rhys Harding, an elderly gentleman who limped into our HQ in Queen Charlotte Street about a fortnight ago and said he wished to confess to a serious crime. Now trust me, this chap looked like no criminal I ever met. More like a cross between Father Christmas's kindly older brother and an e-fit of Grandad of the Year. He had a deep Welsh accent that would give warm maple syrup a serious run for its money. He said he was sixty-eight but if he'd upped that by ten I wouldn't have been surprised. He had charcoal half-moons below slightly rheumy eyes, a sallow complexion and two walking sticks that he laid carefully by the side of the table. He didn't find it easy to straighten up again. Not a well man.

Leith Police HQ is a rather grand four-storey sandstone terrace that sits on a busy crossroads with tight streets and similar height tenements all around. It's almost two hundred years old and at various times the building has housed the town hall, sheriff court and a jail. We're not far from the docks and all that that entails, but the ongoing gentrification of the area has pushed the seedier elements into small pockets of misbehaviour that keep us on our toes. Inside, the place is a hotchpotch of spaces; some big enough for a bus and others, hardly a pushbike. There's also a double basement where it's wise to leave a trail of crumbs if you ever want to be seen again. I've been stationed here for ten years and the refurbishment never stops.

Andrew had interviewed Rhys Harding in one of our less dilapidated ground floor rooms and I tagged along for the ride. At that stage we didn't know if we were dealing with a crank or a senile pensioner acting out a misplaced memory. But the tale he told was more than a little surprising.

A widower for half his life, his wife died of cancer when they were both in their thirties. They'd no kids and he never remarried. About twelve years ago he volunteered for a local charity that supported homeless and vulnerable people. He befriended two young women, clients of the charity. These days they're called service users. They claimed to be sisters. Ill-advisedly and against all the rules, he invited them to his house for a few days over Christmas. He told us it was a brutal winter, the hostels were full and they looked like they could do with a decent meal. Long story short: big mistake and the first of many.

Rhys was under the impression they were just having a good time. Drinks, laughter, music, and larking about with his camera. He'd been sure all three of them had over-indulged but, in time, he realised it was only him. When he woke up in the morning, they were gone and so was his camera.

He never saw those women again but a couple of days later he received a visitor at his house. Once this man explained why he was there, Rhys had no choice but to allow him inside. He dropped a buff A4 envelope on the kitchen table but Rhys wouldn't even look at it, never mind pick it up. So the man shrugged, ripped open the seal and fanned out a dozen photos printed on poor quality computer paper. The images weren't pin-sharp but they didn't need to be.

Evidently Rhys wasn't the women's first patsy. Friendly cuddles on the sofa had been cleverly orchestrated to appear significantly worse. Nothing too explicit, a bare thigh and a glimpse of underwear here and there. His hands bordered the danger areas but when we studied the images closely, it was clear the women were holding them in position.

The coffee table was strewn with empty bottles, glasses and cigarettes. Another image showed a credit card, a rolled up piece of paper and a dusting of white powder. Rhys swore there were never any drugs in the house and crucially, he wasn't in this picture. Whatever, the effect was damning. Older man, young women, sex, drugs and alcohol. The only thing missing was the rock band.

My extremely poor poker face must have put in an appearance because he addressed me directly. 'I've regretted that night ever since. I didn't just let myself down, I let my wife down and my friends down. And then there's my colleagues at the charity. I was weak and pathetic and stupid and ...'

He stopped speaking and shook his head. He sat for a while, staring down at the backs of his hands. They were trembling. I began to wonder if he thought that by eventually telling his story, the ton weight he'd obviously been carrying all this time would be lifted. Nothing we could say would change anything so we gave him time to compose himself, and he picked up his story again.

The man had produced a data disk from a jacket pocket, tilting it so the light glinted off the surface. He explained he was a journalist, working on a feature about homeless siblings and how it was almost inevitable they would end up as prey to some *lowlife scum on the make*. If Rhys didn't pay him £10,000 for the disk, he would publish the images and brand the Welshman as a predator who had exploited his position to take advantage of two vulnerable young women at a particularly emotional time of the year for them.

Rhys's first reaction was to tell the journalist to go to hell but the photos weren't even back inside the envelope before he folded and asked how he should pay the money.

He said, 'I panicked at the thought of what this man could do with the story. I could see myself losing my job, my work with the charity, even ending up on the Sex Offenders' Register. I know what I did was stupid but I just prayed the whole thing would somehow go away.'

It was no surprise to hear that after Rhys had paid, the journalist produced another disk and a different set of images. These were on offer for the increased price of £20,000. The silly old fool – his words, not mine – coughed up.

Now, I don't know what they teach people at journalism school but clearly this particular student paid close attention at the *Being a Nasty Unscrupulous Bastard* lectures because he double-crossed Rhys and kept copies of the disk. At the last count, the old man had handed over about £70,000. He had no record of the transactions, they'd all been in cash and no emails or texts had ever been sent.

Andrew asked why he hadn't contacted the police. Rhys admitted he'd been on the point of reporting it a number of times. But, 'I didn't have the guts.' His gaze was permanently downcast and his posture slumped even further.

So we asked, why now?

'I'm terminally ill. I've been given six months, tops. There's nothing more this blackmailer can do to me but I can't rest until I clear my conscience.'

Then he handed us a letter to his GP, giving his authority to check he actually was terminally ill. If he'd stuck out his wrists to be cuffed I'd quite possibly have made a proper exhibition of myself and burst into tears.

The charity is still operating so we asked them to check the dates Rhys gave us against the names of these so-called sisters. Nothing came up. So either he was lying or they were. My bet's on them. As Andrew said later, 'Poor bugger. Those pictures were so inconclusive, if he'd called the guy's bluff we'd have struggled to prove a crime was committed.'

Andrew was right. Rhys had wasted his savings and a big chunk of his life. On the plus side, he's finally shifted an enormous burden from his shoulders that just might make his last few months a little more bearable.

I can't be sure but I'll be surprised if we invest much more police time on this poor, sick old man, who's suffered a punishment that far exceeds his so-called crime.

However, I do intend to develop an unhealthy interest in a Mr Iain McLure: journalist, extortionist, and utter bastard of this parish.

CHAPTER THREE

Detective Chief Superintendent Mark Thornton posed in front of the full length mirror. He straightened his tie, buttoned his jacket and studied his reflection. Then he sucked in his stomach.

Better.

He lifted his coat off the bed then picked up a decorative pillow from the floor and tossed it towards the padded headboard. It balanced upright for an instant before toppling over. He flapped the top sheet and turned it down. Then he glanced at the crumpled half-made bed and wondered briefly why he'd performed this utterly pointless ritual. He checked around the room to make sure he hadn't left anything but as he had no luggage, and his keys and wallet were in his pocket, there wasn't much chance of that.

Thornton's position in the upper echelons of Police Scotland brought intense pressure and he thrived on that. It made him feel alive, buzzing. But something had just happened that he hadn't seen coming. It had left him with an uneasy feeling.

Mark Thornton had been having affairs for years. His wife

knew but didn't seem to care, therefore neither did he. That suited him fine. His women always conformed to a particular type: much younger than him. Meaning early to mid-thirties, definitely no older. The reason he had affairs was for the sex, nothing more. He could put up with some small talk over a quick drink before the main event. But long soulful post-coital discussions? Definitely not. Similarly, no quasi-romantic dinners in off-the-beaten-track restaurants. He didn't worry about being caught, he simply couldn't be arsed with all that nonsense. He'd taken women away for the weekend a couple of times but if they weren't screwing, or sleeping, he used work as an excuse for paying them as little attention as possible.

So this latest one? They'd only been at it for a couple of months but he would be telling her enough was enough. Because no woman had ever dumped him. Not once. It was another one of his rules.

About five minutes earlier he'd come out of the bathroom. She was dressed, about to head back to her office. She didn't look like she'd just had sex. A quick shower, make-up refresh, and when she flicked her fingers through her hair it fell naturally into shape. Perfectly suited to a lunchtime quickie.

When she said she wouldn't be able to see him again for a week or two, he told her flat out they should call it quits. No weasel words, straight between the eyes as he always did. Normally the shock was enough to send them packing. Sometimes they blubbered; he thought that was pathetic. Occasionally they shouted and screamed. Still pathetic but understandable. Either way, it was over and on his terms alone. No way back.

But her reply smacked him between the eyes. 'I don't think so, Mark. Not yet. I'll call you.'

He blinked. She smiled, and sauntered out of the room.

He stared at the inside of the door as it closed behind her.

Her reaction didn't concern him too much. When she called, if she called, he wouldn't answer. And if he couldn't avoid speaking to her then he'd be busy – for the foreseeable future. Eventually she'd get the message.

Thornton was an arrogant, conceited man, totally used to having his own way. Always in control. Always called the shots. But he was completely unaware that his current lover's apparently insignificant act of defiance was simply her opening play.

Because she intended to screw him over. Big time.

CHAPTER FOUR

The treasurer of the church hall redevelopment committee scanned the quarterly bank statement for a third time before lifting her head. 'Like I've already said, I have no idea what these debits are.'

'But *you* are the treasurer, Dr O'Keefe. It is *your* responsibility to be fully cognisant of every transaction related to church funds. It is not acceptable for you to declare you have, if I may quote, "no idea".'

Emily O'Keefe was exhausted. She'd entered that state where her legs were uncomfortable no matter how she arranged them and her eyes itched like she'd wandered into a sandstorm. She pushed her glasses up into her hair, a heavy bob of dark-brown-going-grey, closed her eyes and pinched the bridge of her nose. She shook her head slowly. Any faster and the jetlag she was suffering made everything feel a little disconnected.

It was Saturday morning and she'd just flown home from what was supposed to be a relaxing two week, all-inclusive family holiday at a five-star hotel in Mexico. She knew now why all the photos on the resort's website had either been shot from 'creative' angles or filtered artistically. All the better to disguise the cracks, the grime and the decay. Then when their flight home was delayed by twenty-two hours, when the refreshments ran out mid-Atlantic and when all her complaints fell on profoundly deaf ears, the term 'relaxing' was about as accurate as next year's weather forecast.

And then, *then*, you're five minutes in the door when the complete nonentity of a chairman phones to say there's an emergency committee meeting at the church.

And ... breathe.

The committee room was an austere, bland place with no natural light. The long, pale refectory table was useless for meetings, people had to lean back and forth to talk to colleagues on the same side of the table. But Emily had a clear view of Kenneth, the pompous old git who'd lectured her on her treasurer responsibilities. She'd never liked the man and didn't know anyone who did. She regretted that she was a devout Catholic and a GP to boot, or else she'd have slapped him about his wizened ginger head for speaking to her in such a condescending manner.

Note to self: way overdue a visit to the confessional. Better add that to the long list of uncharitable thoughts and deeds I've stockpiled in the last two weeks. Apologies, Lord.

She turned to the chairman. 'Look, I'll phone the bank on Monday and sort it out. There's bound to be a simple explanation.'

Kenneth interrupted. 'You could call now. We *do* have telephone banking after all.'

Emily scanned the faces of her fellow committee members, searching for even a morsel of support. She didn't expect any, and she wasn't disappointed. *And as for this ineffectual sap in the chair, he could say something positive. Couldn't he?*

She exhaled. 'If it'll keep you happy.'

While she was on hold, she studied the figures again. Fifty-two thousand pounds, in six separate transactions, ranging from two thousand to twelve thousand, all in the last two months or so. She'd balanced the previous quarter's statement, and was absolutely certain there were no unauthorised debits in that period.

'Put your telephone on loudspeaker would you, *Doctor* O'Keefe?' said Kenneth. 'I do believe I speak for everyone when I say we're all entitled to hear both sides of this conversation.'

There were nods, albeit some were reluctant, from round the table. Kenneth smirked and whispered to a man on his left. Emily wasn't keen on him either. *This is my last year. Definitely my last year.* She tapped the speaker symbol on her phone and pushed it away from her.

Emily couldn't handle the tension. She stood and paced up and down the length of the table, fists clenched, looking down at the gnarled pine floorboards. She wondered how old they were.

It was several minutes before an adviser came on the line. Emily explained the issue, answered the security questions and was put on hold.

'Hello, Doctor O'Keefe. I'm sorry to keep you waiting there. I can see the transactions and I can confirm these payments were made to an account in the name of a Mr Jackson Craddock. Is that name familiar to you?'

The banking adviser's voice echoed in Emily's head as if it were a special effect from an Eighties' synthesised pop song. *Familiar to you? ... Familiar to you? ... Familiar to you?* She wondered for a moment if her phone actually *did* have an echo setting.

Now her eyes were locked onto said phone, willing it to

switch itself off, explode into a thousand pieces, fly out of the window. Anything.

'Hello, Doctor O'Keefe. Are you still there?'

Kenneth leaned forward and spoke directly to Emily. His sneer would have cut granite. 'Jackson Craddock? Can't be too many of them about.' He sat back and folded his arms. 'In fact, isn't that your husband's name?'

Emily stared at the chairman. His expression suggested he'd swallowed a pint of emetic. He was as beige as the wall behind him.

Why does jetlag make you feel so dizzy, so nauseous?

Kenneth snatched up the phone and, still on loudspeaker, barked at the adviser, 'Thank you for your assistance, young lady. We'll take it from here.' He slung the phone across the table and only Emily's reflexes stopped it sailing off the edge.

Kenneth grinned like he'd scooped the Euro-Millions. 'Well, isn't that interesting? I know GPs earn a good salary but now we can all see quite clearly how you can afford all-inclusive holidays to Mexico.' He turned again to the man on his left. 'And business class too, I expect.'

Emily was sure she was about to throw up. Leaving aside the account holder, Mr Jackson Craddock, her main problem was the sort code. She recognised it as belonging to the bank her family used. The account number wasn't theirs, she knew that because it had three sevens in the middle. But to paraphrase the old Meatloaf hit: this time, two out of three *was* bad.

But if she thought she'd reached rock bottom, she would soon be disabused of that notion. She called her husband and asked him to come over to the church. They only lived a few streets away and although he was undressed for bed, she made it abundantly clear that she needed him 'right now!' So he came.

Twenty minutes later most of the others had left but unsurprisingly, Kenneth wasn't for shifting. No, the little creep wouldn't miss this for the world and although Emily wanted to object she had no stomach for the fight. The chairman was still here too. *He* could hardly bale out.

Jackson was a triathlete and ultra-marathon runner and not much fazed him. So although he was as mystified as his wife, he was calm and immediately offered to call the bank. He was confident this could all be sorted out quite easily. Kenneth snorted at that but for once he was completely ignored.

Jackson made the call and explained the situation to an adviser, who adopted a brisk let's-see-what-I-can-find-out attitude. The first sticking point came when Jackson said this was an old account he never used so he didn't know the answers to the security questions. But the adviser explained that as it was in Jackson's name, and all accounts in his name were linked, the security questions were the same as for the others.

Within seconds, the adviser confirmed the amounts were credited on the dates matching the church's bank statement. Jackson was relieved, as was Emily. Kenneth's expression would have turned milk. Unfortunately, these positions were about to be reversed.

Prompted by his wife, Jackson said, 'Right. We'll worry about how this happened later but in the meantime can you transfer the entire £52,000 back to the account it came from?' He smiled encouragingly at Emily. *Nearly there.*

'Ah, no,' came the prompt reply. 'I'm afraid that as soon as these transactions were credited, they were immediately transferred to a different account in a different bank.'

'Which bank?' Jackson asked, about a millisecond before Kenneth.

'It's an international transfer to a bank in Switzerland.' Emily and Jackson stared at each other, confused. 'But there is a payee reference, and it's the same reference for all the trans-actions.'

'So who's the payee?' asked Emily. She had her fingers clasped, forehead resting on her thumbs, eyes closed. She was dreading the answer but also desperate to hear it in the hope it would offer her a last-minute reprieve.

The adviser hesitated before he spoke. 'It says "Life Choice".'

Jackson turned to his wife. 'Life Choice?'

Emily tried to answer so only he could hear. But her voice caught and she spoke far more loudly than she'd intended. 'Euthanasia.' She cleared her throat. 'It's an organisation that promotes people's right to end their lives.'

The chairman of the redevelopment committee for the church hall at Our Lady and All Saints was the last to speak.

'You've donated £52,000 of the church's money to a euthanasia practitioner?'

He glanced up as if the off-white ceiling would offer divine providence.

'Holy fuck!'

CHAPTER FIVE

——————

It was early evening and not yet dark. The rays from the setting sun illuminated only the top floor of the four-storey building on the north side of the Grassmarket, a large rectangular open area which nestled below the castle in Edinburgh's old town.

The young woman loitered on the other side of the street. She was mid-twenties, long dark hair and dressed provocatively. Deliberately so. She stood for a few minutes more. The shadows at ground level held her in their grasp, protecting her, making her feel secure. The building opposite had a pair of automatic sliding doors onto the street but the one on the left only swished open partially, catching out many of the people who passed through.

She became aware she was shaking. If she'd been holding a full glass of water in her right hand she'd have spilled at least the top two inches. In her head, she gave herself a serious talking to.

You can do this. You must do this. Because if – make that

when – you come out with the right result, your life will change. And definitely for the better.

The woman was imagining a brighter future. Perhaps not Swarovski-sparkling but certainly with a sheen to it.

She stood a little taller, shoulders back, chest out. She smoothed down her dress, gripped her bag to stop it bouncing off her hip and crossed the street just as the lights changed. She jogged the last few feet to avoid being mown down. A crowd of students, maybe six, maybe seven, jogged onto the wide pavement in front of her. She paused to let them go ahead and, despite being so tense, she smirked when one of the men clouted his shoulder off the door frame. There was a lot of swearing and giggling as they funnelled through before fanning out.

She drew in a deep breath and followed them inside.

———

AT THE SAME time as the woman passed through the doorway, a few miles away in the north of the city a girl screamed. And because she screamed, her younger brother screamed too. And much louder. So the girl screamed again, not louder but certainly at a far higher pitch. Then their father told them both to put a sock in it.

But he wasn't angry. He was trying desperately not to laugh and so was his wife.

They'd packed the car. Two medium-sized wheely cases, two smaller cases, one in a migraine-inducing shade of pink and one with a *Toy Story* motif. Plus, two travel backpacks jammed to the gunnels with the things his wife couldn't fit into her case.

While his family belted themselves in he set the house alarm, closed and locked the front door and scanned the windows one more time. He thought briefly about checking the whole house but that would have been overkill. Both he and his wife had already done that from the inside. They'd even sent the kids round too but that was in a vain attempt to use up even a tiny percentage of their surplus energy.

Finally, he thumbed his key fob to open the driveway gates. He glanced to the right and left as he rolled the Range Rover out onto the street before accelerating away. The gates slid closed behind him.

Tommy Jarvis was a builder who owned a construction company specialising in house extensions. Few of which were completed on time, on budget or to his customers' satisfaction. He wasn't a spy, nor an undercover police officer. Nor was he a neurotic gangster in an American movie so he paid no attention whatsoever to the rusting but perfectly serviceable twelve-year-old Ford Mondeo that peeled away from the opposite side of the wide tree-lined avenue and tailed the Range Rover until it reached the crossroads about three hundred metres further along.

The builder was indicating left as the other car pulled up, parallel to his right.

The Mondeo driver and his passenger wore dark hoodies, and stared straight ahead as the cars set off on different routes. The Mondeo didn't have to follow the Range Rover, the two men knew precisely where the family were heading. So they drove quickly, nipping along as opposed to booting it, and reached the passenger drop-off point at Edinburgh Airport while the builder was still loading his family onto a car park shuttle bus.

The Mondeo's passenger, who sported one of those long wispy beards that lacked an accompanying moustache, found himself a seat in sight of the Jet 2 check-in desk for TFS: Tenerife South Airport. He pretended to read his newspaper while the builder handed over their cases in exchange for boarding cards before he and his wife shepherded their two near-hyper children towards security. Next stop: a fortnight at a family-friendly resort near Los Christianos.

Bearded-man stayed where he was until after the flight took off with dad, mum and kids safely aboard. While their offspring sat, zeroed in on their tablets, mum and dad were dreaming of kids' beach clubs that lasted all morning, allowing them at least two extra hours in bed. Dad was hoping for lots of sex. Mum knew that but was far more concerned with catching up on her beauty sleep. The kids had been a handful in recent weeks.

Not long after, the Mondeo pulled up outside a dodgy locals-only pub in the Niddrie area of the city, where the two men nursed lager shandies until closing time.

They sat in the car for a full hour before they drove back to the tree-lined avenue. They thought it ironic that even in this relatively affluent area, two street lights were out of commission within spitting distance of the builder's detached sandstone villa with its driveway, two-car garage and workshop. Still with their hoods up, they pulled two heavy rucksacks from the boot and marched quickly and quietly along a lane that led to the rear of the house, where they scaled the six-foot stone wall without undue difficulty.

Even with the alarm set, accessing the house wasn't going to be a problem. They'd broken in a few months previously during the Christmas holidays. On that occasion all their client required them to do was retrieve an envelope that had been posted through the front door. Their task tonight was significantly more complicated.

———

A FEW HOURS LATER, at the same time as the builder and his wife were trying to convince their two desolate children that the pool and all its waterslides would still be there when they woke up in the morning, two thousand miles away a young woman sat on the edge of her bed. The tears had dried on her cheeks and the space between sobs was lengthening.

Her dress lay in a heap on the floor. The rip down the front meant she'd never be able to wear it again. It had been forcibly stripped from her. Her pants had also been ripped off, her attacker had taken them away. He'd told her exactly what he was going to do with them. The woman pulled a bedsheet into her lap, as if that would offer some protection. In her right hand, she was holding her phone. She blinked as she attempted to focus.

As she waited for officers to attend she pulled on her robe and stood by her open bedroom window. In the distance she could hear the klaxons and sirens of what sounded like several fire appliances all heading in the same direction.

But the relationship between her allegation of rape and a building in flames in a different part of the city would never become apparent to her.

CHAPTER SIX

JUST DESERTS. *Or, a taste of your own medicine.*

Two idioms, there must be others which accurately describe what this lazy, self-centred GP is hopefully suffering. But I don't care. If she had shown more compassion to her patients this would never have happened to her.

Rumours spread through the congregation at Sunday Mass like waves washing over pebbles. The queen and three of her entourage are absent. Whispered conversations over the backs of pews and across the aisles are followed later by murmuring huddles amongst the weathered headstones at the front of the church.

I am not involved. I do not care for the self-appointed and self-important hierarchy of this supposedly Christian establishment. I am not tall enough to enter their field of vision. But as I watch and listen, rumour is elevated to fact. Glee outnumbers sorrow by four to one.

Then today, Monday, I call my GP Practice at precisely 08:15. My intention is to be concealed in the mists of dozens of calls the practice receives in this first hour of the week. I ask for an appointment with our family doctor.

A tiny sparkle of self-satisfaction warms my cheeks when I am told I will have to see a different GP. I politely ask why, and the harassed receptionist explains that my doctor 'Is not in'. I feign concern and express a sympathetic wish that she will return to work tomorrow. The receptionist declines to comment on the doctor's state of health and I wonder briefly if they have their own version of the Hippocratic Oath, perhaps an administrators' omertà. But she does say, 'We're not sure when she'll be back.'

I accept an appointment with an alternative GP to maintain this charade. It's on Friday, four days away, but I'll call again tomorrow to cancel. I am in robust health.

I am now free to indulge in a delicious period of schadenfreude as I consider the virtually endless repercussions the O'Keefe-Craddock family will undoubtedly be suffering.

Because it will not only be Dr Emily O'Keefe who is in misery. No, there will be collateral damage to her husband, their brats, their extended family, and however many friends and colleagues who remain loyal. Hopefully they will be few.

My musings bring to mind a biblical saying. I am no scholar so I look it up. It's from the book of Numbers: Chapter 32, Verse 23. I clap my hands in wonder when I notice a curiosity relating to the chapter and verse numbers. The first two numbers multiplied together equal six; the last two multiplied together equal six; and the sum of the first and last numbers is also six. Considering the project upon which I have embarked, the reference to six-six-six is more than a little coincidental.

But to return to the saying, it reads 'Be sure your sin will find you out'.

I am delighted to point out, Dr O'Keefe, in your case it most certainly has.

CHAPTER SEVEN

'What do you mean, I'm not covered?'

Tommy Jarvis was speaking to an insurance agent, from the balcony of the family's holiday apartment in Tenerife, the morning after their flight from Edinburgh.

The woman spoke with a soft Northumberland accent but she was confident in her response. 'It's as I've explained, Mr Jarvis. You *did* have a buildings and contents policy with us but it was cancelled in December.'

'*Cancelled? In December?*' Tommy's tone and volume were about as aggressive as he felt right at this moment. 'Are you having a fuckin' laugh?'

His daughter, Phoebe, gave her mother a wide-eyed stare and whispered into her ear.

'I know, sweetie. He shouldn't have but Daddy's a little bit upset.'

Joanne Jarvis was just about holding it together. Her blonde hair was still damp following her shower and she hadn't yet put makeup on. Truth be told, she didn't need it. On top of her pyjamas she wore a white towelling bathrobe. She hugged it around her daughter, as much for her own benefit as for the six-year-old's. Her son padded about on the balcony poking his teddy through various holes in the stone balustrade so the bear could roar at the people below. Those who understood English were in good humour but not because of the boy. They were enjoying the cabaret being provided by his father.

'But *why* is Daddy so upset? We're on our holidays. He said it was chill-time.'

Joanne kissed the top of her daughter's head. How do you tell your child her house has been all but gutted by a fire that probably started not long after they landed in Tenerife? Worse, how do you explain all her toys and books and games are gone? And even worse, if that's possible, about the loss of an enormous white fluffy toy pussy cat Santa had given her the previous Christmas. Phoebe immediately christened it Scooby but nobody knew why.

When their neighbour had called with the news a few minutes after nine, Tommy immediately phoned the insurance company's emergency line. Joanne was desperately clinging on to the fact that everything important to her, that could never be replaced, was safe: her kids, her husband and her engagement, wedding and eternity rings. But how on earth would they recover from the loss of their home and most of their possessions? She could only hear Tommy's side of the conversation but clearly something was terribly wrong.

'Listen to me. I'm telling you I didn't cancel the policy. Why the hell would I?'

The agent sympathised but she remained professional while she negotiated the call. 'That's not for me to say, sir. All I can do is repeat the facts. You took out a Platinum Level buildings and contents policy with us last July but you wrote to us in December to inform us you were cancelling it.

Tommy Jarvis was a hard man. Nothing and nobody scared

him. Utterly ruthless in business with a reputation for a neck of solid brass, he was blunt beyond the point of rudeness and took no cuttings from anyone. Especially customers. Despite all this, he was nervous now.

But whatever his faults, Tommy was smart and he switched smoothly into polite and conciliatory mode. 'I'm sorry, I didn't catch your name.'

'It's Lynette.'

He was standing in the doorway to the balcony, the lintel was only a few centimetres above his head. His belly hung over the waistband of his shorts. He traced a big toe along a join in the ceramic tiling then drew in a breath. 'Okay, Lynette. I'm sorry I lost the plot earlier but I've just found out there's been a terrible fire at my house. I'm away on holiday with the family and I don't even know how much damage there is. So we're all upset and that's why I shouted at you.'

'That's okay, sir, I do understand and I'm extremely sorry you've suffered this loss. But, I repeat, your property is not covered by a current buildings and contents insurance policy with us.'

One of the key attributes of a successful negotiator is the ability to remain calm so Tommy bit his tongue. He disregarded Lynette's statement. 'You say I cancelled the policy. Do you have a letter from me to that effect, with my signature on it?'

Lynette confirmed she did.

Damn!

'But I'm telling you I didn't write it. And anyway, the policy is for well over a million, so don't you send out some sort of confirmation?'

Lynette told him yes, that was standard procedure. She gave him the date on the letter and a window when he should have received it. Finally, she confirmed they had a signed policy cancellation form, dated 29th December.

Tommy shook his head. 'I didn't see that letter either but ... actually, can you hang on a minute?' He pressed the phone against his chest. His skin felt clammy. 'Jo-jo, when did we go to Majorca?'

'Christmas holidays. Why?'

'Exact dates, Jo-jo!' He snapped his fingers three times. 'Come on, come on.'

His wife ignored him. He always shouted at her when he was stressed. She checked her phone and gave him the dates.

'Ah hah! Lynette, we were on holiday at that time. No way could I have signed it.'

'Wait one minute, sir, while I discuss this with my supervisor. Do you mind if I put you on hold?'

Tommy winked at Joanne. Things were going to work out after all. He glanced outside as raucous laughter echoed around the pool below, mixed with the sound of a ball slapping off water.

Lynette came back on the line. 'Mr Jarvis. I've spoken to my supervisor and our position remains unchanged. We cannot accept liability for your loss as you are not covered by one of our policies.'

Tommy was momentarily stunned. He was down, but not yet counted out. 'That's just shit. Let me speak to your supervisor. Him, her, whoever they are.'

'I'm sorry, Mr Jarvis. I can't do that. He will simply reiterate what I've said.'

Phoebe ducked her head deeper inside her mother's bathrobe as her father yelled, 'Fuck's sake. My house and my business have been insured with you for years, and now you wash your hands of me. Typical bloody insurance company!'

There was a brief silence on the line. 'Actually, Mr Jarvis,

I've checked. We first issued the policy last July so you were only insured with us for a little over five months.'

A couple of summers back, Tommy had completed a parachute jump. For charity, if you can believe that. Right now, his guts were churning like they were before he jumped out the plane. He recalled his secretary coming to see him about nine, twelve months earlier. She was reviewing all their service providers and other agencies because she reckoned quite a few weren't providing value for money. And Tommy remembered she'd specifically mentioned buildings and contents insurance for the house.

Tommy laid a hand across his forehead, covering his eyes. He was fucked.

Royally fucked.

CHAPTER EIGHT

THE JUDGE BRUSHED a miniscule piece of lint from his right sleeve before returning his attention to the woman standing about six metres away from him. She was impeccably dressed in a navy business suit and her hair appeared as though it had been styled that morning. But her complexion was devoid of colour, which spoiled the overall effect.

He studied the papers in front of him before speaking. 'Emily O'Keefe, you are accused of embezzling the sum of £52,000 from church funds at Our Lady and All Saints. You then distributed that sum onwards to an organisation, in Switzerland, that specialises in euthanasia. How do you plead?'

Emily strained to focus on the judge but her vision wouldn't clear. Her legs were shaking and if both palms hadn't been planted on the table in front of her she would surely have keeled over. She made an attempt to answer but nothing came out of her mouth.

The judge leaned forward, squinting at her.

'Come on, Emily,' murmured her solicitor. 'All you have to say is not guilty.'

She swallowed but the handful of gravel lodged in her throat wouldn't budge. She tried again. 'Not guilty.' But it sounded like 'noggily'.

The judge raised an eyebrow and noted her plea.

Now her solicitor was able to put in his tuppence worth. 'Your honour. My client is a respected doctor, a GP with an unblemished record, and a reputation for actively engaging with the community. The practice is severely understaffed while she is absent so we have asked this case to be expedited in order that we can quickly prove her innocence to enable her to return to caring for her patients.'

The judge swung his gaze over to the prosecuting counsel. 'Do you have any objections?'

The prosecutor raised himself into a half-crouch for long enough to say, 'No, your honour. Apart from the term *innocence*, that is.' He kept a straight face as he sat down.

The judge banged his gavel at the precise moment Emily's legs gave way. Her solicitor helped her into her chair but after only a few seconds he gathered his files into the crook of his left arm and knelt down beside her. 'Emily, we have to leave now. We're only keeping the seats warm for the next plea.'

She tried to summon up a smile but instead she broke down in tears. The solicitor put his hand on her forearm and gently tugged her to her feet. He did a terrific job of manhandling her out of the courtroom.

God, he thought. *What the hell will she be like when she's convicted?*

Of course he would do his best but the way it was looking, 'when' was beating 'if' hands down.

CHAPTER NINE

I WHEEL my chair over to Andrew's desk. 'What's the story with our alleged blackmailer?'

The latest refurbishment programme has reached our office. Above my head, skeins of new cabling sprout from holes in the ceiling and walls. If they're still here at Christmas we can hang decorations from them.

Andrew's notebook is already open. I glance at the pages and smile. It's beyond me how anyone's writing can be so neat. But my expression morphs into a frown. I see he's recorded *some* notes but far too few for my liking. Not much more than a page of A4.

I'd directed Andrew and two other DCs in my team, Steph Zanetti and Tobias Hartmann, to investigate McLure. They've researched his history, family, talked to people who know him, checked out his finances and his electronic footprint, trying to find any evidence the man is a blackmailer.

'Headlines first,' he says. We've worked together for about six years and he knows to get right to the point. But I don't expect his summation of about three man days' work to be quite so succinct. 'Iain McLure is either the worst blackmailer in the world or he's a modern-day Robin Hood who gives away every penny he extorts.'

I glare at him. Then I look down at his notebook, go back to my glaring and spread my hands. My expression has WTF written all over it.

This cuts no ice with Andrew and he continues with his report. 'Iain McLure, no middle name, age forty-eight. Free-lance journalist, graduated from Warwick University in 1994 with a degree in politics. Based in Edinburgh since '96, single, no long-standing relationships we can find. Owns a one-bedroom, top floor flat, in Dalmeny Street, Leith. Lived there since 2002.'

The address screams bog-standard. The tenements in this area of Leith contain a blend of owner-occupiers, rentals and youngsters whose parents have given them a leg-up on to the property ladder. Like about a dozen other streets, Dalmeny Street runs at right angles off Leith Walk, a wide thoroughfare that connects Leith to Edinburgh. This road comprises several different streets along its length but generations of locals have always referred to the entire thing as Leith Walk. Or often simply The Walk.

The 2008 property crash, followed by the absolute bollocks that was the Edinburgh Tram Project, decimated the area. I grimace at the memory. Main routes right through the centre of the city were severely affected while the tram construction works dragged on. Leith Walk was excavated, there isn't a better word, for about four years. Property prices dropped through the floor. Small businesses suffered because entire carriageways were ripped up so cars and delivery vans weren't able to park and people couldn't cross the road to nip into their preferred newspaper shop or whatever. The businesses that survived, and many did not, did so by the skin of their teeth and usually through sacrificing jobs.

The project staggered on for years past the due date and overran on budget by hundreds of millions. And the bitter irony for traders up and down The Walk was that, after all the carnage, the tram route was terminated before it reached the area. In fact, construction work has only recently restarted, bringing yet more traffic chaos to the community. Bloody council!

But gradually, despite this debacle and boosted by an influx of European émigrés, Leith recovered and is now vibrant and regaining its prosperity. But if McLure has owned a flat there throughout the period, he probably bought at top dollar then saw his investment trundle along the sea floor for a long time before the value headed skywards again. If he's lucky, it's likely worth whatever he paid for it twenty years ago.

Andrew moves on. 'He had a few jobs after he graduated but all of them were short term. I've contacted four ex-employers in the East Midlands but no one can remember much about him. Then he got a job up here but was let go within a few months. According to his boss, McLure didn't deliver. His articles and features were nowhere near incisive enough. Just not cut out for investigative journalism. Print media was beginning to struggle so it was an easy decision to let him go.'

Andrew pauses to give me an opportunity to drill down but there's nothing there for me so I wave him on.

'He doesn't have much of an online presence. He's on Twitter but only about three hundred followers. Not on Facebook or Instagram though, which is a surprise. Does have a website: Iainmclurejournalist.co.uk. Fairly basic, hasn't been updated in years.'

My mouth is drooping at the corners due to the sheer

banality of this man's life. A blue cable disappearing into the wall behind Andrew catches my eye. I wonder why it's not light grey like all its chums.

'Next, finances,' says Andrew. 'He has a savings account with a couple of thousand in it and a current account with a few direct debits and standing orders. Standard day-to-day income and expenditure, no loans or credit agreements apart from his mortgage.' He pauses. 'Payments up to date, and six years to run.'

I ponder for a second then give him the nod to continue.

'There are credits to his bank account every now and again. Probably commissions.'

I rock my head from side to side. 'I guess if he's been a free-lance journalist for this long he must have contacts who give him enough work to keep him going. Were you able to trace the payees?'

'No.'

I didn't expect anything different. When we make initial enquiries like this, the bank will usually clarify at a headline level but without the proper authority they're within their rights to refuse more detail. At this stage, we have no grounds to request that authority.

'So he doesn't have a steady job but he pays his mortgage on time. Do the figures stack up?'

'I've only gone back three years but yes, they do. He's financially stable but far from flush. Minimal outgoings, few major purchases. So, all fairly modest and considering his bank and credit card statements, a lifestyle to match.'

'Does he own a car?'

'No. But he hires from Budget relatively frequently. Spoke to them too. He always deals with the Seafield franchise but they have such a high turnover of staff nobody knows him well enough to comment.'

I tap my pen against pursed lips while I consider McLure's financial position. 'All fairly modest as you say, Andrew.' I sit back. 'And nothing that strikes you as suspicious?'

He shakes his head. 'No. Nothing.'

'Okay. Moving on. Family?'

'That's an easy one. Parents deceased, a long time ago. Council tenants their whole lives.'

My sidekick's not being a snob here. He's telling me there probably wasn't much spare cash kicking around so there was no silver spoon for Iain McLure to feed from.

'And,' says Andrew, 'one older brother. Also a journalist, Paul.'

It takes a few heartbeats but I get there in the end. Paul McLure, far-travelled BBC trouble-zone correspondent. Some nights he's on every TV news bulletin, wearing the latest trends in Kevlar. Pops up in the sorts of places I wouldn't go near without an SAS platoon guarding my butt.

'Any chance of speaking to him without tipping off McLure junior?'

Andrew scratches at his cheek with the end of his pen. 'All the BBC will tell me is he's on assignment. But I'll keep at it.'

'Good man. What else is there?' I ponder my own question. 'Neighbours?'

He consults his notes. 'There are seven other properties in the tenement. Apart from McLure there's only one owner-occupier, an elderly gentleman on the ground floor. The other six are tenants. We've spoken to five but none of them are more than passing acquaintances and they only see him once in a blue moon. Funnily enough, the one party we haven't managed to trace yet are the people in the top floor flat next to McLure's. I had a peek through both letter boxes. His is neat and tidy but next door's a dump.'

I smirk. I've been in Andrew's flat. Even the spiders leave

their shoes at the door. 'Is it possible he doesn't actually live there?'

'It's possible.'

'Recent transactions on his accounts?'

My colleague shakes his head. 'Apart from direct debits his last cash withdrawal was £200, and that was over three weeks ago. But, I guess, even that's not particularly outlandish. If he genuinely does live a frugal life a couple of hundred pounds could last quite a while.'

He closes his notebook. That's all, folks.

I push my chair back and consider the ceiling. There's a blue cable up there too. It goes into a junction box but doesn't appear out of the other side. Curious.

'So, if I can summarise, here's what we have.' I refrain from saying *Bugger all.* 'It seems Iain Ordinary Journalist isn't particularly successful in his chosen profession, and not a lot of excitement going on in his life. But our Iain has a world famous brother in the same line. Could Paul McLure be a factor? Did Junior decide blackmailing people was an easier way to make money than having his arse shot off in the Middle East?'

Andrew doesn't answer. He lets me work it through.

I come to a straightforward conclusion. 'Keep digging, my good man. I am not ready to let our Mr McLure off the hook quite just yet.

'And now,' I wave my hand mock-dismissively as if I were some regal personage, 'be off with you. My two children await and I am certain they will benefit from stern maternal guidance.'

Andrew bows. 'As you wish, your ladyship. We shall reconvene on the morrow.'

CHAPTER TEN

Adopted Son of City Philanthropist Charged With Assault and Rape

THIS IS a headline I've been expecting. I have mixed feelings about it because I know this man to be a kind and generous person, one who helps others. But he has been charged with this appalling crime and it remains to be seen how the case against him will proceed.

Even if the charges are considered not worth pursuing, the problem for the accused and his family is that mud sticks. And despite the work they do to support the community, they may never be able to cleanse themselves of it entirely.

Only time will tell how this will all pan out. I pray for a positive outcome.

I snip the article carefully from the newspaper and smooth it out with the flat of my hand before placing it in a dark grey box file along with others of similar ilk. The remainder of the newspaper including the weekend supplements is consigned, unread, to the recycling basket.

Standing at my kitchen window, I gaze out into the garden and think for a moment.

Whatever happens, I must not forget that I am not the only person who is responsible for all this.

CHAPTER ELEVEN

WHEN TOMMY JARVIS returned from Tenerife and saw the state of his house he was ready to kill. But he'd grabbed hold of his rage and throttled it. Now it was bubbling under, more intense. Cold.

He'd pissed off plenty of people in his life. The sensible ones backed down but it looked like someone had retaliated. The question was, who? And once he found that out, he'd be asking why. And not politely, either.

The previous day he'd left Joanne and the children at the resort. Leaving them there meant he wouldn't have to worry about them and, after all, they'd paid good money for the holiday. But he knew she'd be under a lot of strain, keeping the kids entertained and under control. Never an easy task at the best of times.

He went to stay with his dad, who knew the questions he shouldn't ask and when to keep quiet. Tommy didn't have a bit on the side, which would have been convenient in these circumstances. But in his world, love and honour meant precisely that. Not love and honour until a new model caught his eye.

He was interviewed by a police sergeant. Tommy told him he didn't know anyone who might bear a grudge against him and certainly not to the extent of burning his house down. Not strictly true, but no way would he admit it.

They sat in Tommy's office. It was a warm day and the room didn't have air-con. The sergeant ran a finger round the inside of his shirt collar as he read from the fire service's report. Although wilful fire-raising hadn't been entirely ruled out, early investigations suggested it was unlikely. The cause wasn't an explosion or a candle left burning, it had definitely started in a section of ceiling. Probably due to an electrical short that had sparked and set alight to discarded materials left in the ceiling void by the kitchen installers.

Tommy bit his tongue. He could see himself sweeping rubbish under a floor or behind a section of wall panelling, out of sight and out of mind. But his personal litany of failings included being a world-class hypocrite so if the sub-contractor, even inadvertently, had placed Tommy's family in danger through such a practice there would be hell to pay. And then some.

But the sergeant was beginning to enjoy himself. 'It appears the builders have definitely cut corners. Was it your company who did the work, Mr Jarvis?'

Embarrassed, Tommy had to confirm it was. The officer stared at him, askance. *Hoist by your own petard, matey-boy?*

As far as Tommy was concerned the conversation then spiralled through the floor but the sergeant could barely suppress his mirth when he asked about insurance, including Public Liability and Professional Indemnity. 'Sounds like it'll be an interesting conversation indeed, sir. Substandard work by the builder, but you're the builder so how is the insurance company going to take sides for you against you?'

The police officer flicked through a different report. 'And then, Mr Jarvis, you say your house insurance policy was cancelled. By person or persons unknown, it says here.' He grins. 'That would be classed as fraud, you know.'

Bastard is having a right laugh now.

So, yes, Tommy was angry. And cynical. There was much more to this than the eye could see.

Which is why he was currently deep in conversation with his office manager, Gary Dempster. Gary had been with him for a long time and Tommy trusted him like a brother. And the gist of this conversation was, 'Get out there and speak to everyone we know. I want you to find the bastard who attacked my family. And when you do find them, they will bloody suffer.'

Tommy stood up and looked down at Gary. 'Suffer like they wouldn't fucking believe.'

CHAPTER TWELVE

When Detective Chief Superintendent Mark Thornton heard the voice on his phone a belt of adrenaline sluiced into his gut.

'You know who this is?'

It had been a long time since the Chief Super had spoken to this despicable human being but he'd always known the man was only a phone call away. He glanced up to check his office door was closed before answering.

'Yes.' No need for elaboration.

The man's next statement made Thornton close both eyes.

'I have learned that a Detective Sergeant Melissa Cooper and her underlings have been asking some, how can I put it, "uncomfortable" questions about me.'

Thus far, the caller's voice had been calm. Accepted, there was a distinct edge to it but still, it was on a relatively even keel. That was about to change. Drastically.

'Now. I do not give a tinker's shit how you do it but *get that fucking bitch off my back*. Right a-fucking-way!'

'But ...'

'But. Fucking. Nothing!' Each word escalated in volume and stridency from its predecessor.

Thornton removed his glasses before laying them carefully down on his desk blotter. 'It ... it'll be difficult for me to interfere in a DS's investigation. She's a long way down the chain of command.'

'Don't care. Not my problem. Yours.'

'I'll see what I can do.'

Calm again. 'No. "I'll see what I can do" is what a helpdesk tosser says when your phone's not working, or some such shit. This is not "I'll see what I can do", this is "I'll fucking fix it". *Immediately!'*

Thornton remained silent. It wasn't down to him to terminate the call, no matter how desperately he wanted to.

'Because, Detective Chief Superintendent Thornton, if you don't fix it your fucking career goes down the pan faster than a greasy shite.'

It's not possible to slam down a mobile phone but if it were, Mark Thornton would be down to one functioning eardrum.

CHAPTER THIRTEEN

THE GUY whose backside I'm admiring is framed in our kitchen window. I'm trained in covert surveillance techniques so he hasn't spotted I'm there. Or more likely he has and he's just letting me have my fun.

This is Callum, love of my life, father of my two teenage kids and a significantly better cook than I'll ever be. His culinary skills date back to when he was a stay-at-home dad, who declared his children would never eat reconstituted chicken or anything with a dodgy-looking seafarer on the packet. They're teenagers now but he still takes classes and I put myself through purgatory at the gym twice a week to counteract the effects.

I've met his 'cooking ladies' at one social event or another and, by and large, they're lovely. I have spotted the occasional fluttered eyelash and casual toss of expensively highlighted locks but they were probably more for my benefit than his.

That said, I'm not concerned in the slightest because I trust Callum one hundred per cent never to stray. 'Better the bunny-boiler you know,' he'd commented one day. As backhanded compliments go, that one earned him a sharp dig in the ribs.

I stroll over, reach my arms around his waist, tuck one cool hand in the gap between two of his shirt buttons and stand on tiptoe to press my nose into the little hollow behind his ear. I stretch a little further to kiss his cheek then drop onto the balls of my feet, resting my chin on his shoulder.

'Hiya Toots,' he says. 'How's my favourite crime fighter?'

'Pooped. And looking forward to a quiet night in.'

My head starts to vibrate. He's doing the fast choppy thing on a pile of green stuff with a black-handled kitchen knife. It's a skill I've never possessed and I don't have enough fingers to learn. I watch as he scoops up the choppings and bungs them into a pan, where a creamy substance is bubbling away. I don't ask what it is. It's not that I don't care but he loves to do the whole describe, flourish and dish-it-up-at-the-dinner-table pantomime and it's a shame to deny him his little triumphs.

'I walked home from school with Conor this afternoon.' He's talking about our fifteen-year-old.

'What, none of his mates around?'

'Yeah. Three or four. But when he saw me, he dissed them and crossed over to my side.'

This is nothing earth shattering, he and his dad are like two peas. But the fact that Callum's mentioned it means my follow-up question is straightforward.

'Anything new?'

'There were quite a few, ah, silences.' He bashes me aside with his hip and uses a paper towel to wipe away something I can't even see.

I smack his bum as I turn away. 'Back soon.'

———

48

I RAT-TA-TAT my knuckle on a door that displays a sign: *Sisters Welcome. Yeah, right!*

'Open up!' I call. 'It's the Feds.'

'Hang on a minute while I stash my gear,' comes the corresponding yell.

I walk in. 'Too late, buddy. It's a bust.'

'Got a warrant?' A disembodied voice floats out from within the depths of a black and red gaming chair. The monitor facing him is eye-wateringly emerald but the headphones on the floor tell me he's playing the machine, not some kid in Paraguay.

I kiss him on the top of his beautiful blond head, then flop down on a beanbag with my back to the wall and casually fold a discarded school polo shirt as I settle in. I devour him with my gaze. Many moons ago I did that a lot while he slept but these days it's rare for me to outlast him of an evening.

I don't bother asking him to stop playing so he can have a cosy little chat with his mum. He's a Millennial. He can hold a perfectly lucid conversation while he's making his electronic Lionel Messi lookalikes turn their opponents inside out.

'How was school today?'

'School ... was school.'

'What did you learn?' Years of practicing with villains and witnesses have honed my open questioning skills until they're almost good enough to handle two teenagers.

'I learned Mrs Mellis must be pretty stupid if she thinks shouting at us for an hour will make us listen.'

I smile despite myself. 'Anything else?'

'I also learned I stand a much better chance of Karen Forrester fancying me if I ignore her completely.'

He pauses for a second to raise a fist. A goal, I suppose.

'And how's that coming along?'

He wrinkles his nose, which is super-cute when you're fifteen with spikey hair and freckles.

'If she hasn't texted me in a week, she's toast.' He nods, satisfied he's set this arbitrary deadline.

Times change. In my day you asked a pal to make the initial contact, while you skulked round a corner waiting to hear if you'd pulled.

I reach over and lift a discarded sock from underneath his desk. I can't see its mate so I drape it over my thigh. 'What about, oh I don't know, something academic?'

'Maths was okay.'

I sigh, and we lapse into a short period of companionable silence. I love that. I watch all his involuntary twitches and jerks as he manipulates the controller at a speed faster than the eye can follow. Well, my eye at any rate.

Then he drops the controller into his lap. He stretches his arms above his head, grabs hold of the headrest and peers down at me from aloft. 'How may I help you, mother?'

Damn. That's me on the back foot. I lock eyes with him but this ceased being an effective tactic when he was about ten.

'Anything bothering you, son?'

He pretends to think but only for an instant. 'Nah.'

'Everything is good?'

He doesn't do the thinking bit this time. 'The Karen Forrester situation aside? Yes, everything is good.'

Ace interrogator that I am, I can't figure out where to go from here. So we smile, serenely, at each other.

Then. There it is. The tick. The tell. The tiny clue that I have a glimmer of an opening. His gorgeous, fresh faced, plook-free cheeks – turn pink.

'Ah hah!' I point, and my smile escalates into full blown grin.

Now he glowers at me. Not happy. Busted by an involuntary physical reaction. He folds his arms.

I fold mine too.

He continues to glower. Then breaks eye contact. 'I need some space to think.'

Take your time, sonny boy. I'm in no hurry.

Eventually he makes a decision. I see it in his face but it still takes a full minute before he can spit the words out in the right order.

'You see, Mum. I think ... I have ... a problem.'

I know he's desperate for an escape route but I keep that door firmly closed. It's his turn to sigh.

His eyes are everywhere but on me. He addresses his next statement to Messi and Co. 'You always told us we should never break a promise. And by "us" I mean *me* and *my sister*.'

He's talking about his older sister, Lily. 'You don't want to break a promise?'

He shakes his head, still avoiding my gaze.

'Concerning your sister?'

He nods.

I say. 'Don't worry, son. You haven't.'

He grins. It's a grin of relief. Détente is maintained.

'Dinner's ready!' comes a shout from below.

I lean forward and slap his thigh. It makes a resounding *thwack*. He squeals and I chortle.

'Come on, kiddo. Let's eat.'

CHAPTER FOURTEEN

'DID YOU KNOW,' I say, 'bookkeeper and bookkeeping are the only words in the English language that contain three consecutive sets of double letters?'

Andrew wears an expression of profound regret as if he were pronouncing the last rites. 'I must add that to our useless pieces of information database. I can leave the author field set to the default: Mel Cooper.'

I put on a wounded expression but he ignores me. We're tramping along a narrow corridor, heading for an interview room. We meet a chap wearing dark blue overalls and have to walk like crabs to avoid the enormous toolbox he's hefting. His contractor's badge has spun round on its lanyard so I can't see his name. I should probably check but I don't. Slap my wrists.

Once we're past, Andrew tells me about the woman we're going to meet. 'Her name's Rebecca Michaelson. She's Iain McLure's bookkeeper, and has been for about four years.'

'How did you find her?'

'I didn't. Steph pointed out that if McLure is freelance, he'll probably be a sole trader so he'll have to file accounts.'

I've admired Andrew since he joined Jeff's team as a DC about six years ago. I had just been promoted to DS and it won't be long before the boyo follows suit. He's held in high regard by anyone who matters and this is a good example why. He's made it clear Steph deserves the credit, which is great for her especially as she's relatively new to the team.

Before he opens the interview room door, he adds, 'From Michaelson's knowledge of McLure's accounts, the lifestyle he portrays matches his earnings.'

We enter the room, me first. This is an internal room, the only window is high on the wall and gives out to the corridor. It has a grey venetian blind but for the life of me I can't imagine why. If a basketball player passed by you might see the top of his head. Rebecca Michaelson is leaning against the opposite wall, one foot crossed over the other. She's wearing skinny jeans and a casual jacket over a white tee shirt. She's tapping at her phone but as soon as she sees us, she holds a side button and drops it into her handbag. I hear a faint buzz as it powers down. She saunters over and I'm immediately struck by how open she is. She sticks her hand out and introduces herself then adds, 'But Becca's just fine.'

No nonsense. Immediately trustworthy. Excellent.

Andrew had briefed her earlier so I can jump straight in. 'What's your impression of Iain McLure, Becca, based on your dealings with him?'

'Hmmm.' She ponders for a second. 'He's not a high flier, that's for sure.'

I sit back. 'Tell me more.'

'On average, he probably only pulls in one or two contracts a month. And he does have real fallow periods.'

'Which last how long?' asks Andrew.

'Oh, six to eight weeks sometimes. If I were him I'd be concerned but it doesn't seem to bother him in the slightest.'

Me again. 'And these contracts, are they lucrative?'

She makes a face. 'Far from it. Three, four k. Sometimes a wee bit more but not often.'

'Anything unusual about his accounts?'

'For instance?'

'Have you seen any larger amounts going through, which are unaccounted for?'

Becca looks straight at me. 'You've studied the accounts?'

'Of course.'

'In that case, if there *were* any larger amounts not accounted for, you'd have seen them.' She cracks a smile. 'Money laundering's a crime, DS Cooper.'

A fair point, I have to admit. My gaze flits around the room while I'm thinking. That venetian blind catches my eye and I notice the adjustment cords are missing, so it's even worse than useless.

We talk in general for a while about the accounts but nothing of any importance crops up. This man McLure appears to be completely unremarkable. How can he possibly be a blackmailer?

While I'm cogitating, Andrew steps in and changes tack. 'What sort of person is he?'

She shifts to face him dead on. Tugs at her earlobe. 'It's quite hard to say. I don't have much contact with him apart from when his accounts are due. I email him a reminder, he sends them back. He's always on time but they *are* pretty straightforward. Once I've completed them, we usually have a quick catch up to talk them through. He signs them, I file them, job done for another year.'

Becca shrugs as if to say, *And that's that.*

'And you don't speak at any other time?'

'There's never any need.'

Andrew again. 'And you've been doing his accounts for what ... three, four years?'

'The next set of accounts will be the fourth.'

'Due when?'

'November.'

Andrew checks his notes. 'Do you happen to know the accountant he used before you? Bruce Milligan?'

She adjusts her position, crosses her legs, runs a palm along her thigh. 'I do.' She hesitates. 'I mean, I did. Bruce passed away. Heart attack.'

Andrew gives me the slightest of nods, he's done thrashing this particular horse. I step in with one last question. 'You've maybe already answered this but do you get any sense he has other funds squirreled away?'

'Well, no. Not as far as his accounts are concerned ...'

This catches our attention. For the first time she appears uncomfortable. 'It's just ... it might be nothing but ...'

Oh spit it out, woman.

I prompt her. 'But?'

She fiddles with an earring. 'Like I say, it could be nothing but I did see him driving a flashy sports car.'

Andrew and I don't actually sit up straighter but it feels like we do. My sidekick's a petrol head so he steps in. 'What type of car?'

'Em, it was black.' I'm surprised, I didn't have her down as girlie but at least she has the good grace to be embarrassed. 'I'm not much up on cars. I don't drive you see. So I was on the bus.'

'Where about?'

The street she names has been for decades one of the most heavily congested, highly polluted urban stretches in Scotland. 'St John's Road. Near the roundabout at the foot of Drum Brae.'

'In which direction was he travelling?'

55

'Towards town. I was on my way to work, out at The Gyle.' It's a business park on the western perimeter of the city, at the junction of the Edinburgh bypass and the Glasgow road.

'What time was that?'

'About nine o'clock. I start at half past.'

'And what day?'

From her expression I guess she was hoping we wouldn't ask that question. 'No idea.'

Andrew says. 'Maybe it wasn't *his* car.'

'I think it was. He was smoking.' She looks at us in turn. 'People don't smoke in other people's cars, do they?'

That's another good point.

Andrew flips open his iPad. 'I'd like to show you pictures of some cars but first, can we clarify what you meant by "flashy" sports car?' He taps away at the screen before angling it towards her. 'For example, this is an Audi TT. And this ... is an Audi R8. Are they both flashy, as far as you're concerned?'

Becca laughs, swipes the iPad and points at the TT. 'Even to me, this one isn't flashy. But the other one? Yes, that's more like it.'

Andrew pulls up a selection of sporty cars: Porsche, Lamborghini, Maserati, Aston Martin. You name it, Andrew shows her. But she says no to all of them, laughing at herself because of her total ignorance of all things automotive, before admitting, 'They're all beginning to look the same to me now.'

No matter, at least we know which segment of the market this car fits in to. Before she leaves, I ask her to keep an eye out for McLure *and* the car on the same stretch of road. I'm hoping she might be able to identify the make and model next time. A photo would be brilliant but I realise I'm being a tad over-optimistic.

Andrew and I chat afterwards. He's already confirmed

McLure doesn't own a car but he'll run another check, against him as an individual and also through his company.

But going back to this sports car, even with only a flimsy description it's possible we *could* track it down. No question it's the longest of shots. There are ways and means but we need a little more. The problem is a search will consume an enormous amount of already scarce resources and I'm not ready to commit them. Yet.

But, there's a tiny foreign body roaming around my intestinal tract, prodding at me with a sharp stick.

And what this means is I'm not quite finished with you, Iain McLure. Because I do believe you have secrets that are there to be winkled out.

And, as winkling goes, I'm right up there with the experts.

CHAPTER FIFTEEN

'TWENTY-EIGHT.'

This is Lily's answer. She's my daughter. We celebrated her seventeenth birthday last month.

Now, twenty-eight is a perfectly reasonable answer if I'd asked: 'Which bus are you catching into town?' And twenty-eight is an amazing answer to: 'What was your mark out of thirty in the biology exam?'

But twenty-eight is a totally shit answer when the question is: 'And how old is this new boyfriend *exactly*?'

I look at her. She looks straight back. It's as if I'm studying my own reflection. Now of course Lily is beautiful, she's my daughter and naturally I'm biased. She possesses a fabulous smile, has dark blonde hair with the figure and the bearing of a confident young woman. But there's a danger this confidence will spill over into challenging because she's just stated, without any qualms at all, that her new boyfriend is eleven years older than her and she's waiting to see exactly what I have to say about that.

At this point what I desperately want to do is press her

pause button, rush downstairs and scream at her father, 'Did you know about this?' Please note the terminology here: 'her father', not 'my husband'. Important distinction.

But I don't do that because Callum would have told me if he'd known. Definitely.

Getting back to Lily, here's my problem. The standard follow-up questions if this guy was a similar age to her are no bloody use. Like, what school is he at? Or, is he going to university? The guy's twenty-eight, for Christ's sake!

Instead, I'm desperate to find out: how long ...? Where did ...? And the unaskable, Have you ...?

But I swallow them all down and do what I always do when an adolescent crisis arises. I say, 'Come on. Let's go for a walk.'

Then I notice Lily has already picked up her fleece. Dammit! A goal down in the first minute and a mountain to climb.

As we wander the streets, arms linked, she tells me the good news first. He's not one of her teachers. The crowd are on their feet at that one. Then she follows up with the whole story and I try my hardest simply to listen.

They met in Starbucks a couple of months ago. Lily and about six of her girlie mates were crammed into an alcove for four. The soon-to-be-boyfriend, Kevin, was across the aisle in one of those comfy armchairs. He was on his own. Lily's pals were blabbering on at top volume about boys, some celebrity's wedding and how Tanya Wotsername in the year below is, like, a *total* bitch. Lily sees Kevin is earwigging, he rolls his eyes, she rolls hers, they laugh in unison. And the rest, as they say ...

'So why was he in the coffee shop on his own?'

She jams on the brakes. 'Mu-um!'

I grab her arm and haul her along. 'Sorry. Sorry.' I don't want to be *that* mother. You know, the ultra-paranoid version, the freak-out-if-your-kid-farts model. 'Sorry,' I say again, and give her a hug and a wee kiss on the cheek. We have to squeeze up close to the wall as a small boy comes hurtling along the pavement on his bright blue scooter. A man comes jogging along behind him so we stay where we are to let him pass. But he doesn't say thanks. Ignorant peasant.

Lily's in a minor huff but it won't last long so I use the time to think. I've never met him but why, why, why does a man of twenty-eight want a girlfriend of seventeen? Put your hands down everyone, I'm ahead of you. I was, once, that age myself. And I'm not stupid.

She asks how I knew. I hesitate. 'Conor!' she says.

I put her brother in the clear by explaining that I'd applied some pressure, but he hadn't actually shopped her. Lily is somewhat mollified but she might still kick his arse.

'But how did Conor find out?' I ask.

'Spotted us in town. We were kissing.'

That's Lily. No beating about the bush. No weasel words like smooching or cuddling.

She waits as I struggle to format a suitable response. Then, 'Just ask your questions, Mum,' and links her arm a little tighter in mine.

I don't cut to the chase. She'll tell me the main answer in her own sweet time. We had the S.E.X. discussion last year. There was a boyfriend she was dead keen on, and asked my advice. In the end, I don't know whether they did or they didn't but the relationship didn't last. I tied myself in knots. She wouldn't have sex with him so he dumped her because he didn't get what he wanted. Or she did have sex with him and he dumped her once he'd *got* what he wanted.

It's the age difference that's most vexing but I force myself to stick to the wider issues. 'Where do you see this going?'

'I don't know if it's "going" anywhere, Mum. I like him. He

60

makes me laugh but for now we're just keeping our own company.'

'Where do you go? Does he have his own flat?'

'At the moment he's sharing but he's looking for somewhere else, says it's a dump.' Then a sideways glance. 'And before you ask, no I haven't been there.'

Small mercies. 'And what does he do for a living?'

'He works in an office.'

'Doing what?'

She shrugs. 'Not sure.'

I don't want to push it but what sort of answer was *that?* We stop at a junction, do the old Green Cross Code bit then walk on.

Then I ask about their social life. 'Will you be hanging out with his friends? Have you met any of them yet? Because surely your pals are all too ...'

'Immature?' She laughs.

'I was going to say young.'

She laughs again. 'Like hell you were.'

I think for a minute. 'Honey. If your dad was ten years older than me, the age gap wouldn't be such an issue. But seventeen and twenty-eight?'

I leave all the points hanging, like his friends are too old for her and her friends are way too young for him. Lily will be going to college, possibly not even in Edinburgh. She has no income, he does. Culture? Boy bands versus, oh, I don't know, rap or grime or some shite like that. The list would reach China if I rolled it out.

I can sense she's thinking along similar lines so I give her space. But then she changes the subject and it's not my call to drag her back. Soon we're approaching the house. At the front door she stops and clamps a hand on my wrist.

'Are you going to tell Dad?'

'I have to, honey. It's the way we work, you know that.'

She knew what my answer would be before she even asked. She nods, this time to herself. 'I'll tell him.' A much better idea.

She moves to put her key in the lock then half turns towards me. 'Just one more thing, Mum.'

'Go on then, Columbo.' But that one flies right over her head.

'Can you please be a mum about this, not a copper?' Another pause while she switches from question to direct instruction. 'No checking him out.'

I don't even cross my fingers behind my back. 'It never occurred to me, honey.'

And if you believe that my trusting little darling, you'll also believe Father Christmas is a fat guy with a white beard who spends half his time in chimneys.

CHAPTER SIXTEEN

I'M NOT sure what I expected but my initial reaction is disappointment.

I've come to see for myself how badly the builder's house is damaged. This contemptible man who cares so little for his fellow human beings that he will cheat, lie and swindle entirely for his own gain.

I'm not the only person here. A dozen or so people have gathered including two small children and a Red Setter enthusiastically sniffing the smoky air. Burned wood is the principal ingredient but there is also a chemical tinge. From materials that were part of the house, I suppose, and perhaps some generated by the fire service in their efforts to extinguish the blaze.

I stand on the opposite side of the street; from here I have an unobstructed view. An elderly couple walk slowly by. She passes comment but I am wearing headphones and I pretend not to hear. The phones are the type that cover the ears, with a band across the head. They are large, white and silent. The music isn't necessary, only the effect.

I try to assimilate the scene slowly, rather than consume it *as if I were ravenous. It occurs to me I should take photos but I hesitate. It wasn't part of my plan. Then I relent. I can always delete them later.*

The electric gates have been cast aside by the firefighters. The entire house and its grounds are cordoned off by protective fencing, meaning I cannot easily see what damage the rear of the building has sustained. Although if the condition of the right hand gable and the roof are any indication, I imagine it's significant. A chimney stack has toppled through the slates, charred joists are open to the elements and most of the upper windows are either shattered or scorched. The front door is boarded over but the flames don't appear to have reached there. Perhaps this is to prevent access.

I know it started in the kitchen diner, which is to the rear right. I discover that if I walk slowly back and forth, and peer carefully through the neighbouring gardens, I can see the two recently added extensions have been virtually destroyed. One of them was a family room or sunroom, the other was a small workshop that backed onto a garage. The planning department's pages on the Council's website truly are a remarkable fount of knowledge.

Before leaving, I reflect that if this builder used the same shoddy materials and substandard components on his own house as those he inflicted on his customers, it is somewhat ironic that they have fed the flames that have so injured, hopefully fatally, the mother ship.

As I return to my car, parked several streets away, I wonder why I am suffering this lingering sense of disappointment. I visited Berlin not that long ago when times were considerably better. I was there with my intended, who was soon to dump me in the most callous manner when my personal struggles intensified to the point that most aspects of my life were disintegrating. We were in the Kaiser Wilhelm Memorial Church, just off the

Kurfürstendamm, one of the city's most elegant boulevards. The church was badly damaged in a bombing raid in 1943. Photographs on display showed the area at the time when the war was turning in the Allies' favour. Entire neighbourhoods were a flattened, smoking ruin yet miraculously the spire survived. Berliners have nicknamed it 'der hohle Zahn'. It means 'the hollow tooth'.

But the builder's family home hasn't suffered intensive strategic bombardment by hundreds of Lancaster bombers. No, it is one sandstone building and one internal fire set carefully to appear as an accident. No accelerants were employed. The fire investigators would easily detect those, which would perhaps sway the builder's erstwhile insurance company to uphold his claim.

But as these thoughts play through my head, I become satisfied that Tommy Jarvis now has his own hollow tooth and perhaps he may eventually reflect that the financial and emotional impacts on his family are no different to those he has imposed on many other families, mine included.

I look forward to reading the newspapers over the next few days. Surely there will be tasty cuttings to enhance my rapidly swelling collection.

CHAPTER SEVENTEEN

It's time for home. I move to switch off my computer but hesitate. I allowed Lily to believe I wasn't going to do this but come on, talk about false promises?

Kevin Moffat, aged twenty-eight. Lily's boyfriend. We've still to meet him. My daughter's not yet given us that pleasure. Little minx.

If he were eighteen I wouldn't bat an eyelid. Girl of seventeen, boy of eighteen, that's normal. It's those extra ten years on the male side of the equation that make me pause.

Then I close the PC down. But I haven't gone all soft, I *will* be checking Kevin out but not on my office computer or using police systems. These days, annoyingly, that's illegal.

So I leave the office, walk to my car and switch my phone over to my personal account.

I start with Google, search Kevin Moffat & Edinburgh. Several relevant results pop up. A solicitor, with links to his Facebook page and LinkedIn profile. A body fitness coach. Links to other references for both of these men. I see other results further down the page but the word Edinburgh is scored out meaning these Kevin Moffats are most likely based elsewhere.

Google was the easy option, now I'll have to dig a bit deeper.

Since the proliferation of social media, and Joe and Joanna Public's apparent desperation to broadcast every aspect of their miserable little existences to the world, specialist search engines have been designed that allow me to browse publicly posted information across social networks like Twitter, Facebook, Instagram and Snapchat. And there's nothing to stop me logging into these as plain old Mel Cooper.

Genuinely, I hope that whatever I find is innocuous. So I click on an icon, search again ... Now we're talking.

First thing to say is he doesn't look his age. Kevin is fresh-faced, fair haired and thin. He's posted dozens of images in the past few weeks but only a few that include Lily. And none of them together. Not even a bad selfie. I see two that he's obviously cropped, leaving only himself in the picture. His arm is around a girl's shoulders but all I can see is she has long red hair so it's definitely not Lily. An ex, perhaps? I check the dates and these ones are only three or four weeks old. As first impressions go, this isn't brilliant.

He's also posted images taken at gigs. There are captions but the bands mean nothing to me so I google them. Heavy metal? Lily *hates* heavy metal. The photos are mainly selfies, and our Kevin is with some highly suspect characters including possibly the same redhead. She's hanging all over him. I zoom in to focus on his eyes and, bad selfies notwithstanding, they appear to be more than a tad glazed over.

Okay, Kevin my man, you're not covering yourself in glory so far.

But now I'm stuck. If he was linked to one of my cases, I'd

be able to run a search for him on our systems. But he isn't, so I can't.

I drop my phone into my lap while I think. The car's clock reminds me it's home time but I want to set one or two hares running first.

I search for a contact and hit dial.

'Dave Devlin speaking.'

'Dave. It's Mel Cooper here. Do you have five minutes for a chat?'

———

IT'S NOT QUITE nine in the evening. I'm flaked out on the sofa in our living room reading a trashy chick-lit novel. I hear our front door closing. Lily's home, and she's early.

Not slightly early, you understand. We're talking a couple of hours before the deadline we eventually agreed upon before she went out. International peace treaties take less time to negotiate.

So an alarm goes off and I'm upright and feeling around with my feet, trying to locate my slippers. I can only find one.

Lily appears in the doorway, nearly holding it together. But as soon as she sees me, my beautiful baby girl breaks down. She stands there, arms out and I catch her as she threatens to slump to the floor.

My first uncharitable thought is *bastard boyfriend. I don't know what he's done but he's going to suffer for it*. I'm about to discover I should bark up a different tree.

It takes about twenty minutes but eventually, interspersed between the sobs, hiccups, sniffles and wails, she tells me the full story. No wonder she's a mess.

Lily's best pal, Paula, has been dating a sixth year boy, Luca Contini. I'm trying to tie this in to the state Lily's in and figure out she probably had the hots for him at one time. The doe eyes tell me I'm not far wrong. *He's blind, honey. That's all.*

Apparently this lad was arrested a few weeks ago, accused of peddling drugs to younger kids at school. *He's a sleazeball, honey. Forget him.*

'But Luca would never do that, Mum. He's so ... sweet.'

A sweet, blind sleazeball? This is becoming a bit mixed up.

'Anyway, he's ... he's ...'

We're back to the sobbing again.

'He's what, honey?' My arms are around her shoulders and I'm attempting to peer into her eyes meaning my head's sideways and our faces are so close I can't actually focus. Never mind, I'm here for her. 'Just tell me. Things'll be much easier after that.'

But I'm wrong. Things won't be any easier at all because the words my darling girl is struggling to spit out are: 'committed suicide'.

Luca Contini. Sweet, blind, sleazeball.

And dead.

But as I hold on to Lily, doing my best to comfort her, I can't shake the feeling that I've heard the name before.

———

THE FOLLOWING MORNING, Andrew comes up with the answer.

It transpires Luca is ... *was* the son of Leo Contini, Procurator Fiscal. To explain, the Scottish legal system is different to our English counterpart. The independent public prosecution service for Scotland is the Crown Office and Procurator Fiscal Service, or COPFS. There are offices of the Procurator Fiscal in every major population centre. They receive and review reports of criminal offences from the local police and determine whether there is enough evidence to press charges. Deeply ironic, therefore, that Leo Contini's office was responsible for deciding whether or not his son should face criminal charges. That is, if the poor boy hadn't died.

Last month, Luca was done for drugs because based on information we'd received, officers were monitoring a dealer who we know is one step down from the top boys in Edinburgh, with strongly rumoured links to Merseyside gangs. His name is James Kilbride, known throughout Leith as Spider. One lunchtime, we followed this arse-wipe to a row of shops near Luca's school, where he and Luca met. They had a short conversation outside a bakery while a couple of other hoodies hemmed them in, partially obscuring our view. Their behaviour suggested they'd conducted some form of transaction.

As the saying goes, we followed the money and tailed Luca to the school. Just inside the gates he stopped to speak to another pupil, a boy of similar age. We moved in, stopped Luca and asked to search his backpack. He agreed without any argument so we were surprised when we found a sizeable bag of cannabis and, in a side pocket, two baggies containing traces of cocaine.

The other boy was aghast when we asked if Luca was supplying him. Luca denied all knowledge of the drugs but they were in his bag. So ... done deal.

But things changed from bad to worse for our Luca. Turns out he had an unconditional acceptance for Strathclyde Uni to study, wait for it ... law. If it had been a poncey non-degree like International Philosophy with Byzantine History, the Uni might have acted differently. But because professions like law, healthcare and education fall under the Home Office guidance on Common Law Police Disclosure, Strathclyde suspended their offer pending the outcome of the court case.

Tragically, it appears Luca couldn't handle either the shame or the disappointment. Maybe both. Three days ago, his mother wasn't able to rouse him for school. She found a litre bottle of vodka next to his bed with only a few centimetres left in the bottom. His phone revealed browser searches for how many paracetamol constituted a lethal dose, which he'd have discovered wouldn't kill him. Not immediately at any rate. But there were similar searches for vodka and the irony is that although he probably didn't drink enough of the stuff to kill himself, it was enough to render him unconscious. Tragically, he choked on his own vomit and died.

My colleagues were virtually certain Luca Contini was innocent. Naturally, the dealer clammed up completely and without any evidence of wrongdoing on his behalf there was no way to force the issue. Or, indeed, prove Luca was set up.

According to his father, the boy worked hard at school, wasn't stressed about exams and was looking forward to uni. Far from doing drugs, he didn't smoke or vape, didn't have much of a taste for alcohol and although he was going steady with Paula neither of them were huge party animals. They preferred to socialise with a small circle of friends. Including Lily.

So, all in all, things are just not stacking up here.

But, and this is a monster of a 'but', Lily's final words in our conversation last night were, 'Mum. You'll be able to find out what *really* happened to Luca, won't you?'

The correct and proper answer should have been along the lines of: I'm sorry, darling. I can't interfere in another team's investigation without good reason.

But naturally, I'm a complete soft touch when it comes to my kids so what I actually said was, 'Of course I will, pet.'

CHAPTER EIGHTEEN

CAROLE CRICHTON STOOD by her office window, three floors above the car park. For some unfathomable psychological reason she'd always found that difficult conversations, even those she conducted over the phone, were much easier to handle if she was standing up. And as difficult conversations go, this was a belter. Even for an HR Director of over thirty years' experience.

Down below, the driver of a big white Lexus was making a complete tit of their attempt to reverse park but as much as she'd have loved to watch the cabaret unfolding she couldn't afford to be distracted.

DS Mike Rutherford placed his copy of the documents on the boardroom table and looked up at the three other people in the room. 'I have to say, this seems to be a terminally stupid thing for the manager of an IT department to do.'

Nobody disagreed.

'I mean, surely someone with his expertise would know this was bound to come to light eventually.'

Carole squeezed her ample frame into the chair and

studied DS Rutherford over the top of her black-rimmed glasses. The company's Operations Manager watched her expectantly and thanked his lucky stars she was in the firing line. While no doubt thinking, *Hey. That's why you're paid the big bucks, lady.*

'Derek Parsons isn't an IT expert, per se,' said Carole, which drew *How come?* reactions from Rutherford and his colleague, DC Paton. She leaned forward and put her pen down. 'He's only covering the post temporarily because the substantive IT manager is off long-term sick. We put Derek in there because he's an excellent man manager with strong leadership skills. Which is what that particular team needs right now.'

DS Rutherford leaned back and moved his tie aside so he could scratch his belly. 'And you're certain this isn't a mistake?'

Carole deferred to the Operations Manager. 'We've tracked everything to his laptop, his user ID, his profile. There's no mistake.'

DC Paton spoke up. 'Could someone have hacked it? Stolen his ID?'

'No. All the laptops have retinal and fingerprint scanners.'

Rutherford jotted that down and returned to Carole. 'And no other issues with him? Performance? Conduct?'

'No. Nothing. He's one of the good guys.' Everyone heard the pin hit the carpet. '*Was* one of the good guys.' She closed her eyes for a moment. 'What happens now?'

Mike Rutherford gestured towards the documents. 'From the data you've gathered, there doesn't appear to be any doubt he's either committed, or he's in the act of committing a criminal offence. If he *has* been posing as a young teenager in these chatrooms then he could be grooming or attempting to groom a minor. So we'll want to speak to him, most likely caution him and take him away to be interviewed. He's in the building, yes?'

'Definitely.' Carole glanced at her wrist. 'He's in a management team meeting that can't be far off winding up.'

And so it was that Derek Parsons' vehement protestations of innocence were witnessed by several eavesdropping colleagues, who found many and varied reasons, none of which were even borderline legitimate, for hanging about outside the meeting room before rushing back to their desks to gleefully dish the dirt.

CHAPTER NINETEEN

A FEW DAYS have passed but I can still feel Lily's sobs and shudders against my body and the insides of my arms as I attempted to console her following the tragic death of her friend, Luca. When you add in the ill-advised promise I made to find out what *really* happened, this is why I can't shake the sensation that there's definitely something iffy about this wretched case.

I squeeze behind Andrew's chair and mosey on out to the office kitchen. The water dispenser gurgles and half fills my plastic cup before beeping and declaring itself dry. I step back into the corridor intent on catching the lazy inconsiderate reprobate responsible for this most heinous of office crimes but all I can see are tightly closed doors.

I know from bitter experience that the refills are heavy but today that's not a problem for me. That's because there are none. Bastards! A collective description for both lazy inconsiderate reprobates and water dispenser refills.

I sit down at the less sticky of the two tables and swirl my half cup, and as I consider why this young man took his own life the utter tragedy of such an unnecessary and stupid waste catches me unawares. Tears brim then roll down my cheeks. I don't wipe them away. I need to suffer a little, to imagine how I might possibly feel if I were Luca's mother. I picture Lily and Conor, both separately and together. I see their happy smiling faces at different ages, in their school photographs, in their beds while they sleep, as they run around playing, and as they fight and squabble and cry and complain and refuse to do their homework.

Thankfully, I catch a break and no one comes in to disrupt my self-indulgent reverie. After a couple of minutes the sorrow lifts and I stop crying. I don't wear mascara so I don't have to worry about cascading black streaks turning me into Alice Cooper, and because I didn't rub my eyes I should look relatively normal when I go back to my team.

Now I can think clearly, here's what I don't understand. You're a clean living, apparently well adjusted, intelligent kid. You're about to go off to study law, and your old man is a Procurator Fiscal. Seriously, would you peddle drugs to kids? Worse, would you peddle drugs to kids at your own school? At the front gate? At lunchtime?

No. I don't think so. You cannot have been that naïve, that stupid. I squeeze the sides of the clear plastic cup and it makes a satisfying crack. I lean over and drop it in the recycling bin.

So, Luca, what else is there?

Leaving aside the not inconsequential fact that you had a sizeable bag of blow on your person, you had no connection to anything narcotic. Not nicotine, and rarely alcohol.

According to your dad, you didn't need money. You definitely weren't spoiled but you don't even burn through your monthly allowance, paid directly to your bank account. My colleagues had checked; there was a healthy balance sitting there so a lack of cash is not the issue.

Were you being pressurised? Mixing with a bad lot? No, says your girlfriend, Paula. And your other friends back her up. Not Luca. No way.

Which kinda leaves Leo Contini. Father, Procurator Fiscal, scourge of the local bad guys. So far we haven't found any link, nothing to substantiate the suggestion that Luca was set up in a tit-for-tat revenge motive. Sins of the father, and all that.

But I still can't shake the feeling there's definitely something not quite right about all this. I certainly won't be stepping on any toes. Not yet anyway. But I will leave this on a slow burn and see if anything new crops up.

I stand up just as a PC walks up to the water dispenser. She finds out the well is empty and glowers in my direction. I consider glowering right back but settle on the sweetest of smiles instead.

Far more satisfying.

CHAPTER TWENTY

Son of Procurator Fiscal Found Dead at Home

THE CUTTING *from the daily paper trumpets news I hadn't anticipated. The boy has died and I am forced to consider: how do I feel about that?*

Thinking rationally, I refuse to become emotional about a person I care nothing about. I did not, literally or figuratively, pull the trigger. Therefore, what I feel is ... nothing.

It is unfortunate, of course it is. The boy himself did no harm to me or to my family. But that is not the point.

The article is brief. It doesn't state what caused his death but the phrase 'no suspicious circumstances' suggests natural causes or an accident. It's even possible he took his own life.

No matter. There will be an inquest that I will attend if at all possible.

The family requests privacy to grieve for their son...

THIS SENTENCE EVOKES *a sensation in me. It could be humour, it could be anger. I can't be sure. I give it no more thought but am momentarily annoyed that this undesired emotion has used up one iota of my energy.*

I place the cutting in the box along with its friends. Take all the time you need, Mr Contini. Because your destiny is that your pain will be a constant companion, as if it were a heavy brocade cloak nailed to your shoulders.

And that ... is just as it should be.

CHAPTER TWENTY-ONE

'Morning, Dave,' says Steph.

DC Steph Zanetti was seconded to my team a few years ago while she recovered from a broken ankle, sustained while 'Chasing some ned' through a building site. She's extremely tenacious, bright and she works hard. A real pocket rocket. Steph's late twenties, keeps her blonde hair tied back and comes in every day upbeat and positive. She can be uncomfortably direct, but it doesn't half cut through the crap.

I glance up from my desk, she's speaking to PC Dave Devlin. He looks over and we exchange smiles. I've a lot of time for Dave, he's an excellent copper. He's based in Leith too, so we come into contact all the time.

I'm only half listening as Steph carries on. 'That was a belter of a post you put out this morning. What an amazing coincidence, eh?'

'It was indeed,' says Dave. 'What are the chances?'

Personally, I don't do Facebook or Instagram. I'm only there because the kids are, but bearing in mind Lily's news about this new boyfriend, a fat lot of good that did me. But professionally we have embraced social media so I'm guessing Steph's spotted an item on the Police Scotland newsfeed. I'm busy and their conversation probably has nothing to do with me but I'm a nosey old bat and I can't stop myself.

'What's this, then?' I ask.

'You tell her, Dave. It was your *collar* after all.' Steph slaps her thigh and cackles out loud. Clearly she's cracked a joke because Dave's laughing too. I'm beginning to wish I hadn't bothered.

He comes over and leans against a pillar next to my desk. A painter sanded it down earlier this morning so Dave will be covered in dust. He's as bald as a bowling ball, wears glasses and sports a moustache he's always shaving off. I'm honoured by its presence today, though.

He says, 'You maybe heard about this but a golden retriever was stolen from a pensioner down in Portobello recently. She was out shopping with her granddaughter.'

I adopt an *Oh, really?* face. I do like dogs, it must have been a terrible shock for the woman but come on, hardly a week goes by without this sort of thing happening.

Clearly Dave reads my expression because he jumps in quickly. 'I know, but this one was different. The woman was seriously injured trying to protect her dog. The thieves were driving a stolen van and she was caught under the rear wheels.'

Now I feel bad. 'How is she doing?'

'I haven't seen her recently but not long after the incident I discovered she's Bryan Fraser's mum. Apparently she's recovering, but it's very slow. Fractured pelvis and broken leg, terrible injuries for a woman her age.'

Most coppers in Edinburgh will know Bryan, he's a sergeant in our Custody Suite at St Leonard's station on Edinburgh's South Side. I lay my pen down on the desk. 'I know Bryan's a laid-back kind of guy but wasn't he jumping all over the investigation as soon as he heard about it? Especially with it being his mum and all?'

'Too right he was, practically had to be dragged away from it. And then some cruel bastard sent him a video of the poor dog in a cage, with two pit bulls desperate to get at it.'

'Jesus! Really?' Then I see a glimmer of a smile on his face and I remember how this all started. 'So what did you post?'

Dave smooths down his moustache. 'It was about the retriever. Weirdly, it showed up safe and well a couple of days ago. Not a scratch on it. Turns out an old chap out in Danderhall, whose own dog had recently died, was given the animal to look after. This was only a couple of weeks after it was taken. His family don't know who gave it to him but they didn't push for any details because he was so chuffed to have the company, and the family had enough on their plate. It's a shame but the old chap had been poorly for a while and now he's in palliative care. The family couldn't keep the dog so they gave it to a friend and the first thing this woman did was take it to a vet.'

'Chipped?'

Dave nods.

'But why,' I continue, 'didn't the old man have it checked out?'

'The family said he'd owned dogs his whole life, knew exactly what he was doing and had absolutely no time for vets. So they left him to it.'

I look up at Dave. 'You're right, that's totally weird.' My eyes flick away as I work my way through this rather strange tale. 'So somebody in a stolen van snatches a dog off the street, runs over its owner, badly injures her and drives off. Then her son, who's a police officer, is sent a nasty video that makes it look like the poor thing will be bait for fighting dogs. And, after all *that*, it turns up safe and well with a pensioner in Danderhall?'

'That's about it, Mel.'

I'm shaking my head. 'Did we ever find out who stole the dog?'

'Nope. We didn't.' He sighs. 'Anyway, I'd better scoot. But before I go ...'

He leans over and pops a piece of paper on my desk. He's scribbled 'Re Kevin Moffat – will have news for you soon'. I give him a nod and a smile in return.

As Dave heads away he spots the white dust from the pillar on his upper arm and bats at it with his hand. I can hear him tutting from here.

Thinking about the tale he's just told, I'm still puzzled. At face value, Mrs Fraser's dog is home safe and it's nothing more than a strange coincidence that her son's a police officer. But nothing's ever that straightforward, is it?

Then my phone rings. A woman. She introduces herself as Dawn McDermott, a solicitor. The bells remain silent.

'DS Cooper, I've been instructed by one of my clients to call you. A Mr Rhys Harding. I believe you and one of your colleagues interviewed him recently.'

'Ah, yes, we did. How is he?'

'That's why I'm calling. I believe he told you he was suffering from terminal cancer.'

A tiny trickle of iced water runs all the way down my spine. 'That's right, he did.'

'Unfortunately, I'm calling to say Mr Harding died a few days ago.'

I'm stunned. 'But I'm sure he said he'd been given six months.'

There was a slight pause. 'Yes. Regrettably, he didn't get that long, I'm afraid.'

There's no point in saying much more. After I hang up I try hard to feel worse about poor old Rhys Harding dying than the fact that I've lost my key witness against Iain McLure.

Regrettably, I fail.

CHAPTER TWENTY-TWO

WHAT ARE MY CHANCES, do you think?

That was the question Emily O'Keefe was desperate to ask her solicitor. But she didn't see the point: she knew the answer already.

Her day in court was over. The legal teams had done their bit. The witnesses to fact and character had testified, some more eloquently and truthfully than others. And the judge had summed up. In truth, she lost any hope when four prosecution witnesses including a fellow doctor and the Practice Manager all testified Emily was irritable and snappy for a period of several weeks that coincided precisely with the dates the amounts were transferred from the church account.

To counteract them, her solicitor had done the best he could to shore up her character. He wheeled out several people, all prepared to sing her praises. Highly respected GP, unstinting contributor to charitable causes and a hardworking, kind and loving mother to boot. He emphasised her unblemished record and also rubbished the notion that Emily had embezzled the money to donate to an organisation that promotes euthanasia. Why would she do that? What did she have to gain? And Emily a good Catholic girl, too.

Emily had been desperate to explain about the ridiculous number of hours she had been working, about how many doctors had taken time off in that period, about being so anxious she cried most mornings before heading off to work, and about the back injury she'd suffered the day she helped a nurse lift an elderly man who'd fallen in reception. But her solicitor had strongly recommended she didn't take the stand because, 'Everything you put forward in your defence will sound like an excuse. Let's not give them that on a plate'.

And the only thing that bothered Emily about that was, *He's absolutely right. Damn him to hell and back.*

A major plus point was that Kenneth the Weasel wasn't called. Emily was sure he'd have been gutted to miss the opportunity to sprinkle vinegar on her wounds and despite the circumstances, she found that amusing.

Now she was in the hands of the jury, a motley crew; none of them even remotely resembling Henry Fonda. She was doing everything she could to keep things light but she knew she was inches away from breaking down. Again.

Her husband, Jackson, had been in court. She hadn't wanted him there but he'd insisted. She would have preferred to be on her own with no one around to dish out meaningless platitudes. As the jury shuffled out he smiled across at her. Doubtless, he intended to transmit positivity and encouragement but by dint of the fact his smile never touched his eyes, it simply said, *You're totally screwed.*

Her solicitor had gone off to 'touch base with the office' but before he left she'd asked him the same question she'd asked first thing that morning: how long? His first answer was, 'Probably eighteen to twenty-four months,' but she'd glared at him until he blinked and upped the ante. 'Two to three.'

And he clearly didn't mean months.

Then the door swung open and the man himself stood in the gap.

'We've been called back.'

CHAPTER TWENTY-THREE

It's mid-morning. I stop by Andrew's desk and ask, 'Ever heard of a builder in town by the name of Tommy Jarvis? Company name's TJ Construction.'

Andrew thinks, shakes his head. 'Nope. Sorry.'

But I can see there's something rumbling about in there so I wait. A few seconds later he snaps his fingers. 'Cancel that. The company used to be Jarvis Construction, Tommy's father started it. They build extensions, mainly. Had a deservedly bad rep for shoddy workmanship, treating customers poorly, things like that. They changed the name but people still know who they are.'

He's drumming his nails so there's more to come. Luckily I'm a patient girl.

'I seem to remember they featured on one of those TV programmes about cowboy builders. Tommy came close to being charged for pushing a reporter around.'

Beats me how we moved like lightning from 'no' to all that background detail but that's Andrew for you. Memory like a steel box.

I jump as a throaty reverberation rattles through the ceiling directly above my head. 'Jesus! What the bloody hell is that?'

Andrew is nonplussed. 'Drilling. It started while you were out. They're putting in a new raised floor in the room above. They'll be at it most of the day, apparently.'

'How the hell are we supposed to work with all that racket?'

'Anyway,' he says, totally ignoring me, 'getting back to Tommy Jarvis, why do you ask?'

I glower at the ceiling but whoever's using the drill is clearly enthusiastic in their work. 'His name cropped up at this morning's ops meeting. Apparently his house caught fire about ten days ago, big sandstone villa off Claremont Road. I heard it might even have to be pulled down. Worth over a million, probably.'

'Goodness!'

Andrew has to be seriously provoked before he'll actually swear. It's amazing we get on so well. What he says next is the very definition of ironic. 'Here's hoping he's insured.'

'Ah. A few of our colleagues were having a giggle at Mr Jarvis's expense because, as it turns out, he *isn't* insured. He thought he was but apparently, the policy was cancelled and he didn't know anything about it.'

I don't laugh. Losing all your possessions isn't exactly amusing.

Andrew whistles. 'Jeez, not insured and a million down on the deal. How did that happen?'

I swivel my seat from side to side. 'Who knows? It's more than a bit odd, though. Don't you think?'

Then I toss him a look he's seen before.

Andrew sighs, puts his PC to sleep and sits back. He knows what's coming. 'Let's hear it.' Then he lifts his voice a little. 'Steph. Tobias. Listen up.'

Steph pulls her chair over, grinning at Andrew. Tobias, pronounced Toe-bee-ass, is German. He's on an exchange transfer to Jeff's team from Cologne and he's been doing crime analyst work with us for about three weeks. And compared to the perceived and possibly outdated Teutonic stereotype, Tobias is the polar opposite: black, not particularly tall and borderline portly.

Addressing him at first, I explain I have this thing called the rule of threes. It's referenced in many other walks of life, like speechwriting for example. But this is my own personal version.

I tick fingers off. 'One. In our job, bad stuff happens every day. Lots of it, single things, unconnected. And most of them fall under the heading: shit happens. Two. If two things happen that appear to be connected, they might be and they might not. But usually, it's nothing more than coincidence. Then there's three. And in my world if three things happen that might be connected, again, they might be and they might not. But we've reached a tipping point. A critical mass, if you like.'

Tobias raises his hand, bless him. 'What are these three things, boss, and what is the connection?'

An officer from another team sticks her head round the door, can't see the person she's looking for, glances up at the racket still coming down from above, grimaces and leaves. As the door is closing I answer Tobias's question.

'One. This dog that Dave Devlin told us about. Now, unfortunate fact of life, dogs are stolen every day. Could be for resale, could be for breeding. All these cockadoodles that people pay thousands for. Worth nicking, aren't they? But there's more than one odd thing about this theft because it's *not* a fancy breed, it's a bog-standard retriever. So what made those thieves so determined to steal that particular dog, that they were willing to put an elderly woman's life in danger. The poor woman could easily have died under that van. No, I just don't get it.'

I'm on a roll now. 'And then there was the threatening video that Bryan Fraser was sent. Sounds to me like it was intended to imply the dog was either going to be bait for pit bulls or it would actually be fighting them. But thankfully, it turns up safe and sound. Not a mark on it. Maybe it killed all the pit bulls, I don't know. But here's the thing. Why steal a dog, threaten the family then go to the trouble of rehoming the poor mutt?'

I look at my three colleagues. 'Tell me if you think differently but in my book the whole thing's definitely unusual.'

Nods of heads all round. No one disagrees with the 'unusual' classification.

I glance up. The driller has stopped for a tea break. Thank the Lord!

Steph speaks, *without* putting her hand up. I really must have a word. 'Going back to the dog, if they actually *were* ruthless they would just have cut the chip out of its neck. Gyp ... I mean travellers, do it all the time. Nick a dog they fancy, rip out the chip, tape up the wound and Fido has a new home. Bob's your uncle.'

'Making it all the more likely the retriever was stolen for a different reason,' says Andrew.

'Precisely my point.' I'm glad they're on board with my cockamamie theory. Now there's a cracking name for a dog breed.

'Now, two. Leo Contini's son.' Any levity in the room vanishes. 'No way was this kid involved in drugs. Doesn't stack up at all. Almost certainly a set up. But why? Tragically the boy's dead, meaning there's no crime to answer to, so we all move on. Except his poor family, of course. Anyway, we've stopped investigating. Appears we've forgotten it looked like a setup. But assuming it was, who would go to those lengths and why?'

Still no dissent in the ranks so I keep going. 'And then we have number three. This builder's house burned down and his insurance was mysteriously cancelled. Are those two events related? And is it beyond the bounds of coincidence that we've had three cases on our doorstep within a relatively short time period that are all a bit fishy?'

'Boss,' says Andrew, 'I'm trying not to burst your bubble because I do agree with you that these cases are a bit strange but what makes these three stand out as being markedly different from any number of cases that come across our desks?'

'In *my* head, do you mean?'

He grins, unabashed. 'I was leaving that part out.'

I shrug. 'It's a fair point, and I'm not sure I can justify it.' I point at my stomach. 'But it's nothing to do with my head. There's something in here and it's niggling at me.'

I run a final check round the room for doubting Thomases. Andrew's wearing his best waiting patiently expression. Steph is mildly excited. And Tobias? Well, poor old Tobias looks bewildered. Clearly he's struggling to make any sense of my rationale. He can come and sit next to me on that one.

'What's next, boss?' asks Steph.

I ponder for a second but I've already made my decision. And bugger me, the drilling starts again.

'I'm off to have a blether with Jeff,' I shout over my shoulder as I head for the door.

———

AN ACCURATE DESCRIPTION of my boss, DI Jeff Hunter, would be angular. If you scraped all the fat off him there wouldn't be enough to fry an egg. His face is an assembly of several different angles and planes, all of them severe. His nose hooks at about ninety degrees and the bump halfway down supports wire framed glasses. He stretches out his lanky frame until he's diagonally rigid in his chair. He must be about nine feet from end to end. Gradually, he reacquaints his bum with the seat.

'Mel,' he says. 'This is more than a bit tenuous.' The look he's giving me adds on, *even for you.*

And the truth is, I can't disagree with him. Tenuous, it most certainly is. But what I'm banking on is that Jeff trusts me. We've worked together for seven, eight years and he knows when to give me my head and when to rein me in. This latitude means I don't often push it unless I'm on solid ground. But at this moment, the terra firma feels more like terra swampy.

'Apart from the whole *unusual* thing,' he says, 'is there anything else linking your three cases?'

I wince. 'I wish the answer was yes. But no, nothing so far.'

'Tell me what you're planning to do.'

Ah hah! Not quite go ahead, but not 'take a hike' either.

'Andrew, Steph and I are all fairly committed just now but Tobias'll have space once he finishes the background work on the Hamilton case. I'll be asking him to scrutinise recent ops meeting records for anything particularly unusual, accusations not proven or totally refuted. Where it appears like there *might* be a setup or where there might be a third party pulling the strings.'

A smile is playing tag with Jeff's lip so I bash on.

'I know, boss. I know. If Tobias draws a blank, I'll drop the whole thing. But hopefully he won't because something is bugging me about all this.'

Jeff moves his head around as if he's checking it's not about to fall off. He reaches a decision quickly. 'Ok, Mel. Keep me posted.'

I'm halfway out of my chair when he asks, 'Any movement on your blackmailer?'

I shake my head. 'Nope, nothing. Unless we can track down Iain McLure and this mysterious black sports car, this case could go tits up before we're even started.'

CHAPTER TWENTY-FOUR

EMILY SAT IN COURT, waiting to be told her fate.

Everything seemed to take an age. Even at the death, the whole announce-the-verdict pantomime, which she thought was an incredibly apt word, was unnecessarily protracted like the worst, the very worst form of reality TV. All that was missing was the break for commercials in between 'we find the defendant' and 'guilty'.

'Guilty,' said the jury.

Guilty?

Voices crashed around the courtroom. People were speaking. The judge, her solicitor, a woman over to her left. If any of it was directed at her, nothing registered.

Someone took her arm, her feet transported her body out of the courtroom, down two flights of stairs, along an interminable corridor, through a door and into a chair. The crotch of a pair of trousers loomed in front of her. She thought it must be a security guard. It was her solicitor.

He was speaking.

'What?' she said. Had that come from one of her children

she would have replied, 'It's not "what", it's "pardon"'. So she changed it to, 'Pardon?'

'The judge is going to take time to consider your sentence.' He stopped there.

'But?'

He drew in a deep breath and blew it down his nostrils. 'But you should expect jail time.'

'When ... when will I hear?'

'A week.'

'A week,' she repeated. Flat tone, totally without modulation.

Inside, she was bursting to scream, *How can this possibly be happening to me?*

CHAPTER TWENTY-FIVE

THE PUBLIC GALLERY *is sparsely populated, something of a surprise, but it means I am able to make my exit quickly and don't need to push past anyone.*

O'Keefe's family were present, as you would expect, but their sniffling little huddle was a few rows down from where I chose to sit.

I suppose my gleeful anticipation would have been in stark contrast to their high anxiety, but when the verdict was announced I was already steeling myself to remain stiff, to display zero emotion, as if I were a completely neutral observer.

I descend the stone staircase outside the courtroom, trying to keep alive the more delicious aspects of the hearing. How O'Keefe virtually collapsed at the word 'Guilty'. Her family gasping as one. How quickly she was removed, and my all too brief view of her back as she disappeared.

I had been watching her solicitor closely. Did he expect that result? He didn't seem even slightly surprised but that could be a stoicism that comes with his profession. Perhaps it's simply a case of move-on-to-the-next-job.

Outside, in a fine drizzle, I move well away to one side. I keep my shoulder to one of the pillars that guard the steps in front of the building, poised to move behind it if anyone even looks like they will glance in my direction. My arm fits neatly into the vertical fluting. The surface is cool, but strangely comforting.

Ah, there's Jackson. What does he think of his wife going down? Will he worry at all about what will happen to her while she is incarcerated? Surely the woman who comes back to him will be a very different person. I am intrigued by the potential changes to her personality and behaviours and I look forward to being able to observe and enjoy these at my leisure.

Then there are her offspring. Her parents. I know she has a sister.

But then, what do I care?

She deserved it. They deserve it.

All of it.

CHAPTER TWENTY-SIX

'But why the hell would Kevin say that?'

PC Dave Devlin shrugs. 'Beats me, Mel. It's a strange one.'

'And your mate, Elliot, he's sure about this?'

'Certain. He collared the lad for speeding. There were six of them, on four motorbikes, all doing fifty-five in a thirty. Then Elliot discovered he and Kevin lived on the same road so he had a quiet word with his stepmother. Suggested it might be a good idea if the lad found some new friends.'

'But Kevin didn't listen?'

Dave takes a gulp of his coffee. 'Seems not. He was done not long after for breach of the peace, then shoplifting. Still running with the same crowd.'

'So what changed?'

'He was badly beaten up by a rival gang. Came to his senses, in more ways than one. After that he sorted himself out, got a job, moved away from the area. No trouble ever since.'

'And that was when?'

'Just over four years ago.'

'When he was ...'

'Nineteen.'

I sit still, attempting to make sense of Dave's story. I'm confused, puzzled, mystified. I twirl my coffee cup as I ponder my earlier question. Why is my daughter's boyfriend pretending to be twenty-eight when he's not even twenty-four?

So, Mister Kevin Moffat, between lying about your age and having a police record, squeaky clean you are not.

But now I have to address my biggest problem: how to explain all this to my darling daughter, who is not going to be impressed when she finds out what I've been up to.

CHAPTER TWENTY-SEVEN

'NOTHING, BOSS.'

Tommy Jarvis necked another two inches of his pint. He was sitting at the bar, facing the gantry but the bottles and their labels held no interest for him.

The man who'd spoken was Gary Dempster, his office manager. In a totally legitimate organisation Gary's job description would be obvious, if perhaps a little generic. On the surface, TJ Construction might appear to be legitimate but poke about in the sawdust and you'll find rusty nails.

In Tommy's company, office manager meant *fixer*. Gary made things happen, and made other things go away. He'd been in the job for over fifteen years and, even including Tommy's wife and his father, Gary knew more about his boss than anyone. He knew people who liked him, and people who definitely did not. The latter group dwarfed the former. He knew the customers Tommy had cheated, sub-contractors and suppliers he'd short-changed, planning officers he'd bribed and documents he'd had altered. And he knew where TJC had cut corners.

Almost a week had passed since Tommy demanded Gary find out 'what bastard' was responsible. He'd driven round all their sites and a few of their competitors'. He spoke to men, and women, who knew people, who knew people. Gary asked his questions and he relied upon the fact that most of these men and women were wary of Tommy so he didn't have to tell them to keep schtum. He also visited a variety of pubs, betting shops and cafes where he might find out what he wanted to know. He struck out in all of them.

So either they knew and were not inclined to help Tommy out, or they didn't know. He strongly suspected the former but there was absolutely no way of proving it.

Gary was what you'd call wiry. Even a strand of his hair, greying now, looked like it could be used to repair a fuse. There was no chance of him turning bald any time soon. He kept an eye on Tommy's reflection in the mirror that was set in the gantry. 'Younger's Fine Ales' it proclaimed. The rust spots and cracks on the glass, and the gouges out of the heavy wooden frame gave a clear indication not only of the age of the mirror but how many decades had passed since Archibald Cuthbert Younger's brewery ceased trading.

Having given his all too succinct report, Gary thought there was a fair chance Tommy might go off on one. Even if he did, the denizens of this bar likely wouldn't notice, never mind react. Gary had witnessed his boss in a rage often enough, but it was water off the proverbial duck as far as he was concerned.

But Tommy just finished his beer, spun round on the stool and slipped to the floor.

'Keep looking, Gary. And come back to me when the answer's not nothing.' Then he headed for the outside. He'd promised his dad he'd be home in time for dinner and he'd cop an earful if he was late.

Gary watched him leaving and ordered another beer.

Although he'd admitted to Tommy that after several days he'd come up with Sweet Fanny Adams, he hadn't exactly told the truth. He'd found out a little bit more than that.

But no way on earth was he telling his boss that certain police officers had found a dodgy builder with a burned out shell of a house and no insurance one of the funniest things they'd heard in a long time.

CHAPTER TWENTY-EIGHT

MARK THORNTON's call was answered but no one spoke.

But he knew the man was there, listening, waiting for him to speak. He'd have sighed loudly but that would antagonise, the last thing he wanted. Thornton was far too tense to play stupid power games. 'I've talked to DS Cooper's boss. They have nothing on you apart from the word of an old man, who died recently as it happens. The investigation's going nowhere.'

'For your sake, it had better stay that way.'

'I'll keep an eye on it.'

'Do that.'

The line went dead.

Thornton rubbed his eyes. He wondered how long it would take for the other shoe to drop.

CHAPTER TWENTY-NINE

'BECCA MICHAELSON PHONED while you were out,' says Andrew.

I don't catch on immediately. There's a man in blue over-alls standing on a stepladder, poking about in the ceiling above my desk. He's holding a screwdriver between his teeth and he has a loop of cable round his neck. He glances down and sees my expression. 'I'll only be a minute, dear. Just checking a connection.'

I sigh. He's only doing his job. But ... *Dear?* Calm down, Mel. You've been called a damn sight worse.

I turn back to Andrew. 'Who did you say phoned?'

'Becca Michaelson.'

It takes me a second. 'McLure's bookkeeper? Has she spotted him again?'

'She has, but don't get all excited. We still don't have a make or model.'

'Bloody hell! Why not? Is she blind?'

Andrew smiles. 'It was on the same stretch of road, a bit

closer to town. She was on the bus but she didn't have a clear view. A van was passing and it blocked her line of sight.'

I'm disappointed with that; my face must show it.

'But,' he says, 'she was fairly certain it was the same car.'

'She thought it was probably his car because he was smoking. But could it be a hire?'

'Almost certainly not.'

I'm about to ask why he's so sure when I realise he's way ahead of me. I raise my eyebrows.

Andrew waits while the electrician climbs down off his ladder, folds it away and wanders off, studying the ceiling as he goes. 'I've called all the specialist hire companies within a fifty mile radius of the city and there aren't that many black sports cars to choose from.' He flips open his notebook and thumbs through the pages. 'Of the two that are currently out on hire, one's an Aston Martin being used to film a commercial in Glencoe, and the other's a BMW Z4 convertible. It's currently somewhere on the North Coast 500, being driven by two women on their honeymoon.'

'Two women?' I'm incredulous. 'On their honeymoon? In a two-seater? Jeez, they must be travelling light.' I think about the holdall of toiletries I lug about, even on a weekend away and shake my head at the prospect. 'Anyway, good work. But it doesn't look like we're any closer to finding him.'

Steph pipes up. 'Not necessarily, boss.'

I swivel through ninety degrees. 'Go on, then.' The way she gathers herself before speaking tells me this is likely to be complicated. Normally I'd tell her to cut to the chase but this time I bite my tongue.

'I was speaking to one of the crime analysts, chap called Aaron, about something called QUEST. Stands for Queries Using Extended Search Techniques.'

Our ability to analyse law enforcement data has come on

leaps and bounds in recent times. The main source of that data is the Police National Computer, or PNC. When I first learned about it I imagined a single entity, some great electronic behemoth whirring away in a cavernous warehouse just off the M25. The reality is the PNC is a network of several databases containing national and local information that we can all access. What's made a huge difference is we now have civilian and police crime analysts, like Tobias, who are able to interrogate the data in a far more sophisticated manner.

Going back to QUEST, the key words are Extended and Search. Our analysts can download masses of data and then run detailed searches, known as queries, against the data based either on facts or in our case assumptions.

Once Steph can see all my cogs are whirring in unison, she carries on with her explanation. 'McLure was driving a black sports car, make and model unknown, heading towards town on St John's Road this morning, about 09:10.'

I perform some mental geography. 'So he crossed the roundabout at the foot of Drum Brae?' I'm stating the bleedin' obvious, I know, but my job here is to sense-check Steph's thinking and ask the occasional stupid question. Which I'm highly qualified to do.

'Correct. If he came in from the north, he could have started his journey from South Queensferry or even Fife. If he joined from the south, he probably travelled from somewhere in the city. Or from the west, he drove in off the Glasgow Road or he came round the bypass.'

Steph whips a map off her desk and lets us study it. The route options she described are highlighted. She doesn't talk us through them, we're all familiar with the area. I have them fixed in my head but then I point at a blue dot. There are several, one on each of the highlighted routes. 'What do these signify?'

'ANPR cameras or their equivalent.' Steph's talking about cameras that were installed as part of the original Automatic Number Plate Recognition or ANPR network, the blue ones that are on all the trunk routes in the UK. But there are many other types of camera that can read number plates like local authority CCTV, garage forecourts and average speed cameras. ANPR gathers data from all of these and many others besides.

'So, all these routes coming into the city converge at St John's Road and the blue dots are the last ANPR cameras that McLure would have passed assuming he made that journey. Yes?'

'Yes.'

'And the times next to the blue dots?' She's annotated the map with various times ranging from o8:25 to o8:50.

'According to traffic control, for a vehicle to reach St John's Road at about o9:10 it would've passed each of the cameras at approximately those times. I've included a tolerance of fifteen minutes either way in case he stopped en route or was delayed for some reason.'

I give her a pointed look that says, *Okay Steph, you have my attention, keep going.* So she does.

'The analyst, Aaron, will run a query for all the cars that passed all those points, at those times. And again with a tolerance of plus or minus fifteen minutes.'

We pause while I think about the logistics. I count seven blue dots, all on Edinburgh's arterial routes then can only imagine the number of cars that would pass each camera in a half hour time period during the morning rush to work.

Andrew says, 'So what did Aaron think? Can he do it?'

'He's confident it'll work.'

I'm nodding and thinking. 'Talk us through what happens once you have the results.'

'Assuming it works, the query will generate x number of cars—'

'Where x is a variable between huge and astronomical,' says Andrew. That raises a titter and Steph carries on.

'Then for all the cars that meet the flashy sports car criteria we feed their registrations into PNC and run more queries to extract data about these cars. That'll pull out stuff like make and model, the owner's details and crucially, the colour.'

'Neat.' Andrew makes tiny clapping motions and nods in congratulation to Steph. In return, she blushes and glowers at him but it's obvious she's chuffed.

'And,' I say, 'all you have to do is match the data against a master list of high-end sports cars.'

She flaps a sheet of paper at me. 'Got it here.'

'And then?'

'Grunt work, I'm afraid. We'll have data on the cars and their owners but I'd be amazed if McLure himself is listed. So I'll have to check all the owners to see if they have any links to him.'

'What about his brother, the war correspondent or whatever he is?'

'I've checked him too. Doesn't own a car either. Too busy being shot at.'

Andrew taps the table and holds up his pen. 'I'm just thinking, if McLure started his journey from a point *this* side of the cameras, the car won't appear in Aaron's data. So why don't we simply gather data from the first camera on the city side of St John's Road?'

'Because,' says Steph, 'if I can find out which direction the car came from, I'll be able to cross-reference his journey against owners' addresses. If I strike out, I'll move on to the city-side cameras, and the only problem is if his entire journey was in between the two sets of cameras. I think that's unlikely but I'll cross that bridge ... etcetera etcetera.'

I nod, in full agreement with her rationale. 'Well done.' I'm beaming. 'In fact, extremely well done, Steph. That was good solid investigative work.'

'Thanks, boss.'

I stand up. 'Right. Let's wait and see what your man Aaron comes up with and we'll take it from there. When will you have the results?'

Steph pauses while she's gathering her paperwork. 'Hopefully later today or first thing tomorrow.'

Back at my desk I open a drawer, lift out a folded sheet of paper and study the brief jottings from my chat with Dave Devlin yesterday. I haven't talked to Callum about the Kevin situation but that's only because I haven't yet figured out how I want to handle it. I'll let it rumble around inside for a while yet, there's no real urgency as far as I can see.

CHAPTER THIRTY

TODAY HAS BEEN A BITTERSWEET DAY. *Highs and lows. Peaks and troughs. Positive and negative. Rough and smooth.*

In a matter of hours I have received two items of news. Good news and, just to balance things up, bad news.

Good news first. I know the outcome of the sixth and final element of this project, assuming six is where it all ends. The man with the job of managing an IT department and who demonstrated a total lack of common courtesy towards a fellow citizen in obvious distress, has been apprehended. He is accused of grooming minors on internet chatrooms and through contact by email and Messenger. That is the upside.

But it is the downside that disturbs me. The golden retriever that was taken from its owner has been returned to the family. The old woman is still in hospital, I don't know how she is and neither do I care. Leaving her aside, I'm sure the rest of the family would have suffered while their pet was away from them, especially when they believed it was intended as fodder for fighting dogs.

But they certainly did not suffer for as long as I intended. Nothing like it, and that is disappointing.

But what is more of a disappointment is that the lowlife whom I charged with the responsibility for making the animal disappear, permanently, and who promised me he had completed this fairly straightforward task, has screwed up. I have yet to decide whether or not he will pay the consequences for betraying my trust.

But no matter. Six people. Six events. Six lives either ruined or at the very least seriously affected. And not only six individuals but hopefully six families too. For the moment, I can celebrate. Job done.

But this euphoria is likely to be short lived. The police aren't stupid. There's a lot of information out there and too many people have been involved for it to remain a secret. So I'm sure the police will come. In fact, I am certain of it. But I must do what I can to delay that inevitability for as long as possible.

CHAPTER THIRTY-ONE

I'm on the sofa watching the news but I can't concentrate. I glance at the clock. Twenty past ten.

'She'll be on the next bus,' says Callum.

'She bloody well better be.' I'm trying to sound gruff but only to disguise my escalating panic. Lily is late home, on a school night. She'd gone up town to meet Kevin. They were going to the cinema and she was catching a bus home afterwards.

This is a recent addendum to the terms of the Lily Cooper Social Freedom Treaty. When she's out in the evening she doesn't *have* to be collected by Mum or Dad. Naturally that clause is automatically revoked if it's raining, or cold, or she has chums to be dropped off all over town. No, that's a different kettle of ball games. But tonight she said she'd definitely come home by bus, and she'd be on the 21:50.

She wasn't.

We live at the end of a cul-de-sac that slopes up from the main road. From a window at the top of our stairs we can see the bus stop so I had taken myself up there just in time to spot the 22:10 sailing by without stopping. That's when my nerves kicked in and when I discovered her phone was switched off. This isn't like her, she's normally good at keeping in contact. I look out the window one last time. It's one of those clear nights where the streetlights are on but there's still a fair amount of light in the sky so my level of anxiety backs off a little.

'If she isn't on the next one we'll have to go out and find her.'

My husband doesn't reply, he just nods. He doesn't come out with anything stupid like *Where would we look?* It's a sensible question but I'd take his head clean off if he even thought about asking it.

I bring up an Edinburgh transport app on my phone. It shows the buses in real time, as little rectangular blobs edging along their routes. The next bus is three stops away, the other side of a double bend where the road goes under a bridge. As I watch, the little blob passes the bridge and stops. I hurry upstairs to my vantage point and focus on the road end.

The bus passes a gap between two houses, and stops at the shelter. Two passengers disembark. They walk off, hand in hand, in the opposite direction.

I'm freezing cold and roasting hot, both at the same time. I stand there for a few seconds but there is little choice, I have to discuss this with Callum. He's been quiet for the last fifteen minutes or so, which shows how anxious he is.

I'm about to move away from the window when halogen headlamps catch my eye. A dark coloured car turns into the street. It's a taxi. I watch, willing it to drive all the way up the slope. But it stops three or four houses down on the other side of the street. My stomach is doing backflips; I'll have to visit the bathroom before I talk to Callum.

Then I spot a blonde ponytail bobbing about as my darling daughter appears from behind the taxi and scurries across the road. She has this odd habit of rising up on her tiptoes when she wants to move quicker than a fast walk. At most times it's amusing, even cute. But not tonight. Definitely not tonight.

I close our bedroom door behind me and wait a few minutes. The alternative is to stand at the front door, arms folded, foot tapping, eyeballing my watch. But no, I'll have to be cooler than that when I listen to what she has to say for herself.

———

In the living room I'm treading a fine line between being relieved that Lily's home safe and wanting to strangle her for worrying me half to death. The former wins out by a short head but that doesn't mean I'll be going easy on her.

'You gave us a big scare, young lady.'

She's cuddling up to her dad on the sofa – probably thinks that's a safe haven. 'I'm sorry, Mum. I missed the bus, I think it was early.'

'Even so, why didn't you call? I tried ringing but your phone was switched off.'

'I know. I forgot to charge it and it died while I was out.'

I make a face. '*Barely* plausible, Lily. When I was young my excuse was my watch had stopped. Funnily enough, *my* mother didn't believe me either.'

She starts forward as though she's about to protest but clearly thinks better of it. She gathers up her stuff and says, 'Time for bed.'

She kisses her dad, then me, but as she turns away I notice something about her. Something different. I don't know if I spotted it because I'm a detective or because I'm a mum. Maybe a bit of both. Then Callum gives out a little cough and I glance at him. He aims his eyes at our daughter's retreating back and flutters his fingertips near the base of his throat.

I nod. 'I'll speak to her. Better if this comes from me, I think.'

———

LILY OBVIOUSLY HURRIED up the stairs because her door is already closed. I tap on the doorframe but only out of habit: I certainly will *not* be waiting for permission to enter. Not for this. She doesn't say anything, just blinks a couple of times. Then she frowns, which I daresay she's entitled to do.

'Lily, your father and I think it's about time you brought Kevin over to meet us.' Be fair, I don't see why I should take *all* the blame. 'Oh, and while I'm on the subject, I'd like his address and phone number please.'

She huffs. 'It's a bit soon for that, Mum. We haven't been going out all that long.'

If it were possible to categorise a smile, the one I give her would be labelled: *Nice try, dear.*

'But long enough for you to have ... how to put this delicately ... taken your relationship to the next level.' She has the good grace to blush. 'So we'd *definitely* like to meet him. I think sometime over the weekend will be fine.'

She shakes her head and makes to speak but I reach out and place a fingertip gently on her lips. 'Lily. Apart from your father the one person you should never tell fibs to ... is your mother.'

'But ...'

I indicate her little backpack, she dumped it on her bed as I came in. 'Is it in there, pet?'

'Is what in there?'

She knows exactly what I'm talking about but I say it anyway.

'Your pink tee shirt. You know, the one you were wearing under that top when you went out?'

I kiss her still frowning forehead. 'This weekend, Lily. I'll let you know when. Make sure you tell Kevin.'

CHAPTER THIRTY-TWO

GARY DEMPSTER WASN'T A CRIMINAL.

A bump in his dad's car a few months after he passed his test as a teenager earned him a careless driving charge and a small fine. As records go, his was a blip but recently he'd certainly been *thinking* like a criminal. Because despite Tommy's many flaws, he'd always treated Gary well, so if some bastard had cancelled the insurance and torched the house then Gary would be trying his damnedest to find out who it was. He'd leave the why to Tommy. And what happened to them afterwards.

Criminals always revisit the scene of the crime. Gary wondered if that was just a TV or film cliché so he googled it. He was gratified to read 'Although it's not true in all cases, there is evidence to suggest that it is true when the crime is fire raising. The criminal may take pleasure, even sexual gratification, from watching the flames especially if they are causing the damage he or she intends'.

Gary was an avid viewer of wildlife documentaries and that gave him an idea. A quick trip to the nearest electrical supplies outlet, a few straightforward purchases, and within a couple of hours he'd set up motion detecting cameras in Tommy's front garden on three trees that bordered the pavement.

He was standing back, admiring his handiwork when his phone rang. He didn't recognise the number but he accepted the call. 'Gary speaking.'

'Gary, this is Detective Constable Andrew Young from Police Scotland. I'd like to speak to you about the fire at Tommy Jarvis's house.'

Gary whipped round in a full circle and back again so quickly, he practically turned himself inside out. There appeared to be no one there but he checked out all the parked cars, and every tree, fence and hedge. Nothing.

'Gary? You there?'

Was someone watching him right then? Or did a TJC van drive past and he hadn't noticed? They'd seen him putting the cameras up and they were pulling his plonker. Bastards!

He spoke into the phone. 'Is this a wind-up?'

'No Gary, it's not. This is DC Andrew Young. I was given your number by the office at TJ Construction. You can contact me through 101 if you like.'

Gary hesitated. 'No. You're ... em ... okay. What did you say you wanted to speak to me about?'

'The fire at Tommy Jarvis's house. But actually, I need a bit more than that. I'm part of the investigation and I'd like another look around. I understand you have keys so can you meet me at the house?'

Gary almost blurted out he was there already but he bit his tongue. Then he imagined this DC whoever-he-said-he-was could instantly trace his van but he told himself not to be so bloody paranoid.

'Aye, when?'

'Just as soon as you can make it. An hour, say?'

Gary tried to think of a reason to turn the police officer down but drew a blank. 'Okay, I'll see you there.'

'Thanks. One more thing, though. I know TJC built the extensions at the rear of the house so could you bring the plans with you. There's a few things I'd like to go over.'

'Yeah. Can do.'

Nobody jumped out from behind a tree and yelled, 'Gotcha,' so Gary climbed into his van and drove off.

———

ANDREW ARRIVED HALF an hour early and fished a white hard hat and yellow hi-vis jacket from the boot of his car. He'd suggested an hour to Gary, but he wanted time at the site on his own. Technically, the building was classified as 'Dangerous – Do not enter' but he was there with Tommy Jarvis's permission, as the owner and the contractor who would be repairing it. Or flattening it.

Given Tommy's reputation, he and Mel reasoned that it was way beyond the bounds of coincidence for the house to spontaneously combust within hours of the family going on holiday so, most probably, someone had broken in and set it alight. The problem was, so far the fire service had no proof it had been set wilfully. For example, they found no evidence of forced entry.

But they didn't know then what we know now, mused Andrew.

He walked up the lane that led to the rear of the building. People who break in to houses rarely kick down the front door to do it. There were footsteps in the mud, of course, but probably from local residents who used the lane as a through route. He scanned the rear wall, definitely a potential point of entry.

He hoisted himself up onto the top and sat there side-saddle for a minute, imagining climbing over it while carrying a toolbox or something similar.

'Easy if there were two of them, or maybe they were carrying their tools in backpacks.'

Andrew was relaxed about talking to himself. He found it easier to work stuff out. He dropped down into the garden and after twenty minutes wandering around, had a proper sense of what he was searching for and was hopeful the architect's drawings would show him what he needed to know.

He heard a van door slam and walked round to the front to find Gary unlocking a padlock on the chain-link fencing over the driveway. They introduced themselves and Andrew asked to see the plans. Gary spread them out on a picnic table, one of those slatted efforts where the seats and the table are all part of the same unit. They put stones on the four corners to stop the paper flapping about in the breeze.

Andrew compared the plans with what was left of the rear of the house. He could see that both extensions had been devastated, they had been opposite each other to form a small courtyard. The kitchen diner faced directly onto the courtyard and was linked internally to the extensions. Two enormous gaps in the rear wall were boarded up, and the rooms above each hole were also affected. The overall effect resembled a scene from a Middle Eastern warzone.

Andrew asked if security lights had been installed. Gary raked about in his pockets for a pen and circled them on the plans. There were three. One shone onto the rear of the house from the right hand extension, the other two were situated to illuminate a wide arc that reached out beyond the courtyard.

Andrew moved over to where the kitchen window would have been and scanned the surrounding houses for any with an unimpeded view. Apart from a few windows scattered around, a couple of which were sixty or seventy metres away, none of the houses had a clear line of sight that wasn't interrupted by trees in either their gardens or Tommy's. He was now firmly of the opinion that, to a determined thief, the lights would only have been a mild deterrent.

He could see Gary keeping a close eye on him from over by the picnic table, but at this point Andrew wasn't particularly bothered.

'Where would I have come over?' he murmured, turning to his left. 'Over the wall near where it meets the neighbour's garden, round the perimeter behind those bushes and pop out directly below the security light.' He pushed his way into the undergrowth and smiled when he found footprints in the earthen border that ran towards the house from the end of the wall. He dropped down on his haunches and traced his finger-tips across an imprint. He'd arrange for a crime scene tech to examine them later but he doubted if they'd produce much in the way of evidence. Eleven days had passed since the fire so the prints were far from clear. The weather, foraging animals and dropping foliage had seen to that. But they were there, and that was good enough for Andrew.

The ground immediately behind the house was a mess of broken glass, splintered window frames, charred wooden facings, jagged shards of broken slate and numerous other materials that had once combined to form the rear of the building and its contents. Gary watched as Andrew began raking about in the debris near to where the lights had been. He had no intention of helping the officer, but he *was* intrigued. He took a few steps towards Andrew but the DC held out a flat palm without lifting his head. Gary stopped, feeling like a schoolboy who'd been told not to cross a road. But he didn't go back to the table. He stood there, arms folded, not happy.

Eventually Andrew found what he hoped he would. He dropped a piece of black glass, about the size of a two pound coin, into an evidence bag and stuck it in his pocket. It wasn't the fire that had rendered the glass black. It was paint, probably from a spray can. He expected the sensor had also been blacked out but that had been plastic and wouldn't have survived. No matter, he had evidence that strongly suggested a possible break-in. They'd ensured they were working in darkness but now for the next question, how did they bypass the alarm?

Andrew wasn't a professional housebreaker but he'd arrested a few who were, and some were only too keen to brag about their craft. So he knew where to check first. As he walked past, Gary asked, 'Find anything?' Andrew nodded but didn't reply.

His next problem was how to reach up to a diagonal soffit that formed an inverted 'V' at the front of the building.

'Gary!' The office manager looked up from his phone. 'Got a ladder in your van?'

'Nope.'

Andrew stood and pondered. 'Did they *really* lug a ladder to and from their vehicle?' He shook his head. 'No way. Too bulky, too noisy, and bloody suspicious if anybody had spotted them carting it about at that time of night.'

He scanned the grounds. The neighbouring house had a rickety old garage at the back of the garden, adjacent to the stone wall between the houses. The wall was only about five feet high. A mess of weeds and brambles poked out over the top from the other side but only towards the front of the building. He leaned on the wall and peered down into the gap at the rear.

'Ah hah! You stashed it here, you clever little housebreakers you.'

A few minutes later, Gary helped him prop up the extending ladder against the front of Tommy's house. Andrew climbed up to the alarm sounder box. Although he preferred to keep Gary at a distance he had no choice but to ask him to act as safety man.

Again, Andrew's perseverance paid off. *Sneaky buggers muffled it.* He dropped a wisp of loft insulation and a few crumbs of white polystyrene into evidence bags. Gary did his best to see what Andrew was up to but the DC was careful to keep his body in the way.

Back on the ground, Andrew pondered the burglars' next steps. 'They knew if they broke in through the patio door, the intensity of the fire would smash the remainder of the glass and destroy any evidence. And the muffling meant no one would hear the alarm when it went off.'

Andrew had his arms folded, staring up at the sounder, trying to work out a sequence of events that made sense. 'They blacked out the security lights, muffled the alarm, broke in then switched the alarm off. That means they knew the code. Then they set up something in the kitchen to start the fire. But they had to make it appear like a fault or bad workmanship. These guys knew the insurance was cancelled, so as long as the cause wasn't seen to be malicious Jarvis couldn't make any claim against criminal damages.'

He paused there, happy with his rationale so far. But what happened next?

'So everything's ready to go. They can take the insulation off the sounder box and dump the ladder over the fence. They set the fire, reset the alarm and scarpered out the front door, locking it behind them. It catches hold and burns through a sensor, which sets off the alarm and that's when the neighbour hears it. But by the time the fire engines get here, the house is well alight and the bad guys are miles away.'

He moved a few steps, studied the boarding over the front door. He shouted to Gary. 'I want to see inside the vestibule. Do you have keys for those padlocks?'

Gary let them in and wandered off, through to the ruins of the kitchen and sunroom, while Andrew poked about in the vestibule cupboard. It contained an electricity meter, a few small tools, lightbulbs and an old black rubber-encased torch. He switched the torch on but the insipid glow was lucky to reach the glass. The cupboard was unharmed by fire so both the sheet of paper torn from a notepad and the empty brass hook on the back of the door had survived unscathed.

'Tommy, Tommy, Tommy. You complete and utter muppet. Talk about making things easy for them?'

Andrew was still shaking his head when he heard Gary cursing. He picked his way through to the kitchen and found the office manager standing below what had been a lowered section of the ceiling. He was holding a short length of charred cable, which had a lump of melted plastic component on the end. It was about the size and shape of a Mars Bar. He ripped the cable away and dropped it at his feet.

'What's up?' asked Andrew.

Gary glared at the police officer. His expression would have terrified anyone he directed it at. 'Cheap crappy Chinese transformer!' He waved the item under Andrew's nose. 'We'd *never* have specced this for the boss's house. I wonder what else the cheating money-grabbing bastards skimped on.' He hurled the piece of plastic onto a pile of rubbish before charging off in the direction of the front door.

Andrew picked it up and followed the other man out of the house. Despite the seriousness of the situation, he was chuckling.

'*Now* we're getting somewhere.'

CHAPTER THIRTY-THREE

TOBIAS IS BECOMING MORE familiar with our Scottish idioms and slang but this time he doesn't require a translation. Apparently there are needles and haystacks in Germany too.

He's been working on the task I set him, which was always going to be a long shot. I'd given him systems access so he could trawl back through daily ops meeting agendas and fair play, he's done a terrific job so far.

Tobias may be a little bit of an oddball but he's a good fit in our team. He's a grafter: organised, meticulous, enthusiastic and as it transpires, artistic. Based on the data he extracted, he's drawn a comprehensive mind-map that, at first glance, includes most of the crime categories we investigate. He's labelled each of these categories as either common law or statute crimes.

To explain, some countries have a Criminal Code, which places most or sometimes all of their criminal offences together into a single document. Scotland doesn't have one. A crime, or offence, in Scotland can be classified under two broad headings: common law offences and statutory offences. 'Common law' crimes like theft, murder and breach of the peace have been around for ever. They weren't created by Parliament, and as such are not defined in legislation. But any crime that *has* been created by Parliament is a 'statutory' crime. Rape, for example, was redefined by statute in Scotland in 2009 to take account of the changing circumstances surrounding the offence, and particularly certain defences adopted by the accused. A good example concerns the issue of consent.

Tobias's mind-map depicts a series of major strands spiralling out in clockwise fashion from the hub, each one representing a crime category. He's ordered them alphabetically beginning with Assault. The other strands include Breach of the Peace, Fraud, Sexual Assault and Threatening and Abusive Behaviour.

Most of the strands have sub-branches hanging off them. For example, the Fraud strand sub-divides into Embezzlement and Extortion. Then, scattered all over the mind-map and next to the appropriate branches, he's recorded every case of potential interest as individual items. Some of these have symbols next to them, and related items are linked by dotted red lines.

I point at one of these lines – there appears to be a duplicate entry. 'Quick question, Tobias. How come the case involving Celia Fraser's stolen dog is mentioned in two places?'

'Ah. Because the crime was originally a theft I logged it as such, but given that Mrs Fraser was subsequently dragged under the van I also placed it under Aggravated Assault.'

I nod. 'Makes sense.'

As I study the data more closely, I find Tommy Jarvis listed under Wilful Fire-raising. Luca Contini's supposed crime is part of the Misuse of Drugs strand, on a sub-branch labelled Possession With Intent to Supply.

Tobias stays silent while I work my way round the map.

Since he joined the team he's caught on quick. He understands, or more likely was tipped off by Andrew or Steph, to get to the point quickly. No faffing about. So he waits for my questions, answers them briefly then lets me move on.

As I delve more into the detail, I notice he's appended a coding to all of the items and a few also have descriptive words taken from the agendas. It's quite a creation and seems to make perfect sense but it'll be interesting to hear his thought processes. 'Okay, Tobias. Talk me through it.'

'I started the analysis from two months preceding the earliest of our three cases. That is the stolen golden retriever. If I go back much further, the task may become too big. But I will review older cases if necessary.'

He indicates various elements of the mind-map as he's talking. 'Next to each item is the date of the crime, the name of the accused and also the investigators.'

I see what I suppose is a code at the end of each item. 'These letters, what do they mean?'

'To concentrate our investigative efforts, I have classified each case against your "unusual" criteria. So the letters NL mean the case is "not likely" to match the criteria, and P means it will "possibly" match.' He taps his finger on a case with PM. 'This stands for "probable match" so it is a case that I believe we should give further consideration to.'

I run my pen along a couple of the codes. 'And the numbers at the end?'

'Priority. Number one is high, number two is low.'

'Fair enough. How did you decide which cases were high priority?'

Tobias leans in closer and points out a few specifics. 'You might expect that I would have classified every PM, or "probable match" case, as high priority. But when I examined them I found that some cases involve criminals who are well known to us. In general they still meet your "unusual" criteria but I think the fact that they are known to us makes them ... *less* unusual. Therefore they are low priority.'

He can see I appear doubtful so he pushes on. 'This could be coincidence but when I looked at the three parties whose cases you brought to our attention – the dog owner and our sergeant, the PF and his son, and the builder – no one in their immediate families has a criminal record. They all said they didn't know why they were targeted, and none of them are violent.'

'Not even Tommy Jarvis, the builder?'

'No. There are rumours and accusations but that is all. We know he has fallen foul of the council authorities, particularly planning regulations, but he has no record.'

He slides the paper over and indicates the bottom right corner, where there is a neatly scribed list. 'These are the high priority cases. I studied the criminal records for everyone who was accused, charged or convicted of these crimes, and attempted to classify whether they are likely to commit a crime in the future.'

I glance up at him but he has anticipated my question.

'I checked what age they were when they committed their first crime because, as we know, this is an important predictor of a person's criminal career. And I also took into account factors such as their gender, their employment status, and family or lifestyle influences.'

I'm impressed. 'Good thinking, Tobias.'

'I also reviewed, briefly, our investigations into each of these cases to establish whether there might be scope for wrongful arrest or perhaps requests from the Fiscal for more evidence. Because if your *feeling* is correct and this *does* involve a setup then we are searching for an accused person who, despite the evidence, is a poor match for the crime they are supposed to have committed.'

I stand up and rest my forearms on the back of my chair. 'So, let me get this straight in my head. Your high priority cases will involve people with no criminal record, their profile suggests they are unlikely to commit a crime in the future, and our investigations may have been flawed. Correct?'

'Correct.'

'All of which, as you say, makes those people a poor match for the crime they're accused of. And therefore, it makes them an excellent match for further investigation.'

'Also correct.'

I lean forward to scan the list. 'So how many are high priority?'

'Nineteen.'

I smile. Most other people would have said about twenty, but not Tobias.

Now, I'm a bit of a girl for systems and spreadsheets, so I ask him why he's stuck to pen and paper.

'You only allocated me two days to complete this initial analysis. I believed I could see the wider picture quickly and more easily on paper. If we decide to investigate these in more detail, it will not take long for me to build a database.'

'Fair enough.'

Tobias has made a tremendous job of this preliminary stage and I tell him so. His eyes stay down on the papers but I can tell he's pleased.

I check my watch, just after three.

'Right, Tobias. I'm sure there's much more detail but I imagine it's mostly in your head.' He nods in agreement. 'But I need hard data I can study. I understand why you didn't start with a database but I'd like you to create one so we can sort and filter the results easily. What's in your diary tomorrow?'

'Nothing until the afternoon. The morning is clear.' He pauses. '*Was* clear.'

See? I told you he catches on quick.

CHAPTER THIRTY-FOUR

I'M in the station sharp this morning but Steph is already beavering away. I stop at her desk with my coffee and ask, 'What were the numbers then?'

She takes off her glasses and knuckles her eyes. I wonder how late she worked last night. She picks up a notebook. 'Aaron's search showed almost nine thousand cars passed the cameras in the time frame we identified. Fifty-nine were black sports cars and thirty-seven of those are what we've classified as high-end.' She hands me a printout. 'This is the PNC data associated with each car.'

I put my coffee down so I can study the report properly. Starting from the left hand column, it reads: Registration Number, Make, Model, Year of Manufacture, and Colour. The key field is next. Registered Owner. I scan down the column. McLure's not listed and none of them are Leith addresses. I don't fall off my perch.

Her ponytail bobs about, reflecting how animated she is. 'My plan was to contact all the people on the list then I thought, what will I say to them? Excuse me, Mrs Smith, I'm a police officer, do you know an Iain McLure? Because, sure as hell, if they do and they're acting as a front for him, they wouldn't bloody tell me, would they?'

That makes me laugh. 'Unlikely. So what's your plan?'

She scratches at her ear. 'I'm not sure yet. I'm working my way through the data, searching for inspiration.'

'Okay. Give me a shout if I can help.' Then I lift my coffee off her desk and wander off, leaving her to crack on.

———

'ARE YOU WINDING ME UP?' I had asked Tobias, once he summarised the filtered data on his spreadsheet.

'No. Why would I do that?' he replied, a little puzzled. It's a semi-permanent state for our in-house German. Tobias is by no means humourless, he can share a joke with the best of us but team banter can, understandably, throw him.

'Frosty Knickers?'

'I'm ...'

I stick my hand up before someone plants potatoes in the furrows on his brow.

Tobias's more in-depth analysis of his data has thrown up six cases that fit both the probable match *and* the priority one criteria, including the three we've already identified. But it's the last one that's caught my attention.

This case concerns a man who's about to go on trial for assault and rape. He is Kim Seung-Min: South Korean, aged twenty-five and a successful businessman. He owns an extensive chain of beauty salons called Boutique KSM all across Edinburgh and the Lothians. And before you jump to conclusions these salons are, as far as we know, perfectly legitimate enterprises. They're not a front for a more sinister female-oriented 'service' industry.

Furthermore this individual's adoptive father, Sir Robert Parker, is a popular Edinburgh philanthropist, champion and principal sponsor of several local charities including those that support abused women and disadvantaged children. Tobias explained it's common knowledge that Kim works hand in glove alongside his father and although he shuns any media attention, is frequently seen actively supporting the charities' efforts. We also know that he drip-feeds women into jobs in his salons to help them regain their self-confidence and to put much needed cash in their pockets.

So far, so squeaky clean. I'm beginning to wonder if there *is* a chink in the armour of this case.

'Why should we be looking at this again?' I ask.

I've already noted the name of the investigating officer, my nemesis in Police Scotland, Edinburgh. It's DS Deirdre Keown, who I know as Frosty Knickers. But Tobias hits me with his ace of trumps. He scrolls along the data and points at the Reason column, where he's typed 'Sub-standard Investigation'.

───────

WHICH IS why I'm sitting here, chilling to the marrow as the permafrost from the pants of DS Keown fills the void between us. It's a hell of a convoluted metaphor but you get my drift.

'And what does my investigation into this case have to do with *you*, Detective Sergeant Cooper?'

Oh, shit. In for a penny ...

After I've explained, she sighs and comes over all dramatic. 'So, let's see what we have here. On the basis of some half-arsed theory about, what, fake crimes dreamed up by your "team" ...' She does the quotes thing with her fingers here, which seriously pisses me off, but I manage to refrain from slapping her stupid sneering face. 'You want to reopen *my* investigation? An investigation, I might add, that satisfied the Procurator Fiscal, who intends to prosecute a dangerous *foreign national* for attacking and raping a defenceless young woman who was, I might also add, a visitor to our fair city. Have I got that right?'

She's daring me to reply but I sense she's not quite finished with her tirade. I don't have to wait long before she's off again.

'Oh, and by the way, I hope said same foreign national goes down for a long time and is then deported back to whatever paddy field his obscenely rich adoptive daddy fished him out of.'

She folds her arms tight across her admittedly impressive bosom and hits me with the latest in an incessant stream of acidic glares. I reorganise the troops and make an attempt to regain lost ground.

We're in a briefing room where one wall is stacked from floor to ceiling with cardboard packing crates. Some lucky sod's moving out of this dump. I adjust my position to avoid a shaft of sunlight that's found a mangled slat in the venetian blind. There are plenty to choose from.

'Deirdre ...' The mercury plummets another few degrees. 'DS Keown. We now have four "crimes".' I do the finger waggling bit too, hoping it'll bring her a little bit onside. If nothing else it might show her how stupid she looked a minute ago.

I repeat all the reasons why these four crimes don't stack up. But as I'm speaking I realise that of all the people I've explained this to, she's the only one who is downright hostile to the theory. And I know it's weaker than a baby's bicep but there's no point in running away with my non-existent tail between my slightly dimpled thighs. So I take a breath and go on the offensive, as reasonable negotiation has thus far proven to be a waste of time.

'I don't necessarily want to *reopen* your investigation, I'm simply asking your permission to look at it again.'

'Why?'

'Because although I can't prove anything yet, I have a strong feeling that—'

'Feeling?' she snorts. 'We didn't cover that particular module at *proper* detective college.'

Okay, I've officially taken enough shit from this ... what's the female equivalent of 'wanker' anyway? On another day, this might provoke amusing existential debate but I'm totally fed up of this arrogant cow taking delight in pushing my buttons.

'Don't tell me you never act on feelings, Deirdre. Or gut instinct. Because you do. All cops do at one time or another. So what I'm *telling* you is I *think* something is a bit smelly about four recent crimes in our jurisdiction, including this *alleged* assault and rape.'

At this point a Mexican stand-off ensues, involving two possibly premenstrual women with arms tightly folded and stares set at dismember. But I tell you what, I sure as hell don't intend to blink first.

Eventually her eyes drop to the table. *Ha! Take that, bitch!*

She makes a big show of closing her notebook and putting her pen away, which is no mean feat when you think about it. She fixes me with another glare but it's down at the insipid end of the scale. 'Normally, I'd fire this up the line and have you sorted out. But not this time. It'll be entertaining to watch you make a complete tit of yourself while you waste our limited resources. And the boss, that's Detective Chief Superintendent Thornton to you and me, will have your guts. So carry on *Melissa*. Reopen a perfectly good investigation, why don't you.'

And with that she marches out, belting the door practically off its hinges.

I said all I wanted was her permission to look at the case again. But I lied. I completely agree with Tobias's analysis. Perfectly good investigation?

My arse.

CHAPTER THIRTY-FIVE

It's approaching G&T time when Steph lets out a whoop. I look up and she's sporting a grin wider than my backside. 'You'll never believe this, boss. The bugger drives a McLaren!'

Andrew, Tobias and I drag chairs over to her desk and she explains to us mere mortals how she found out.

'I didn't expect McLure to be listed as a registered owner, and he wasn't. But PNC also holds each vehicle's current insurance details and I'd hoped I might find him listed as a named driver.'

'I'm guessing that was too much to hope for,' I say.

'It was, yes. So I called all the insurance companies just in case the details for any of the cars on my target list had changed recently, meaning PNC might be out of date, and I was able to confirm that most of them are owned and insured by individuals. All bar three.'

An omnipotent being pulls a big lever and we collectively lean forward.

'One is a Maserati GranTurismo,' she says. 'It's owned by a car club.'

Tobias and I adopt dumb expressions but Andrew nods as Steph explains. 'Members shell out several thousand a year for the privilege of borrowing a wide range of vintage, classic and other desirable cars, with the odd Morris Minor thrown in. I spoke to the secretary of the club and he confirmed there were no members called Iain McLure. He told me their vetting process for applications is ultra-rigorous simply because a few of their cars are worth serious amounts of cash. So it's extremely unlikely McLure could have joined under an assumed name.

'Then there's a Mercedes AMG-GT. It's owned through a shell company by a wealthy solicitor who uses it to entertain, and scare the shit out of friends and clients by the simple expedient of hammering it all over the Highlands on roads that aren't much wider than the car itself. His PA told me her boss is well over seventy and every time he goes away on one of his "trips" she's convinced it'll be the last time she sees him alive.'

Andrew and I both laugh at that but Tobias doesn't join in. I suspect he'd prefer not to picture the poor old chap ploughing off the road into a loch.

Then Steph tells us about the third car, a McLaren 720S.

'The registered owner is a company called Cross Leisure. Its only other asset is a pub on the east side of Glasgow. It's called The Cross, funnily enough. The landlord, also a director of Cross Leisure, is one Francis or Frank Crolla.'

'Where exactly in Glasgow is this pub?' Tobias's question catches us by surprise.

'Dalmarnock,' says Steph. 'Have you heard of it?'

Tobias nods. 'Yes. I read about it in an economic report recently. It is not an affluent area.'

I glance at Steph for confirmation. 'He's right, you know. And without being judgemental, the published accounts do not suggest either the company or Mr Crolla can afford such a car. In each of the past five years the turnover was consistently low and it barely scraped a profit.'

'The car thing strikes me as odd,' I say. 'Back in the dim and distant, people put their cars through their businesses so they could benefit from tax breaks. But over the years HMRC have tightened up the rules and it's not tax efficient to do that now.'

'That's true, boss. It isn't tax efficient, doesn't mean you can't do it though.'

I have to concede that's fair comment. 'If the McLaren's registered to the company, are there payments for it showing on the bank statements?'

Steph opens a ring binder and flicks through the pages. 'Yes, monthly instalments of £1900 to a finance company.'

My gaze wanders off into the distance. An expensive car, registered to a business that hardly turns a profit, and possibly being driven by McLure, who appears to have no connection to Cross Leisure or Francis Crolla. So far, this isn't making any sense at all.

I shake my head and change tack. 'But why would the owner of a pub in Dalmarnock be driving into Edinburgh at that time? And twice, at that.'

'Ah, but here's the thing. According to ANPR logs that car hasn't been anywhere near Dalmarnock.' I'm still processing that when Steph says, 'But, I also checked out the company's accountant. Transpires it's Inglis Bruce-Mair and that's when alarm bells started going off all over the place.'

'Why?' says Andrew.

It's not like him to be so far off the curve. I stay quiet because I know the answer and I wonder how much Steph knows. Plenty, as we're about to find out.

'Inglis Bruce-Mair are two women,' she explains. 'Alice Inglis and Phyllis Bruce-Mair. Launched their company in the eighties and called it IBM. It wasn't long before the computing IBM threatened to sue, citing trademark infringement. Back then, the behemoths were fond of throwing their weight around and attracting loads of publicity at the same time. But Phyllis told them to get lost, it ended up in court and the judge threw it out. Said that if those initials are your names, you're perfectly entitled to use them. The big IBM were at it, of course, but this time it backfired and it was Alice and Phyllis who lapped up the headlines. Then, as soon as the fuss died down, they changed their logo to IB-M. Stuck two fingers up, basically.'

Andrew folds his arms and gives a few slow nods. Steph continues her story.

'The two women began to cultivate a corporate image that motored along on just the right side of the tracks. Some of the clients that comprised their portfolio, if not out-and-out crooked, were ever so slightly unsavoury. Other accountancy firms with stronger principles than IB-M's shied away from those clients, even if their profits were high. These days Alice keeps a low profile but Phyllis still likes to rattle cages for a hobby. And the bigger the cage, the louder the rattle. Oh, and they only employ women.'

Andrew doesn't often harrumph but he does this time. 'How the hell do they get away with *that*?'

Steph's on a roll. 'The story goes, they don't actually break any rules. Their recruitment ads are always worded perfectly. Blokes who are familiar with IB-M don't even bother applying, it's a complete waste of time. But men who aren't in the know don't ever make the shortlist. And if anyone complains, it's always dealt with properly ... but never successfully.'

I'm impressed too. 'How do you know all this, Steph?'

'My dad's an accountant. They were all in the same year at uni and although he wasn't exactly friends with them, IB-M has a fairly high profile in Glasgow so word gets around. It's common knowledge that the company's struggling. They're locked in to a fifteen-year lease on offices in the Merchant City. They're trying to sub-let but no takers so far. *And* they're beginning to discover their women-only policy is fatally flawed because it's reduced the quality of job applications.'

'No shit,' says Andrew, which earns him a quizzical look from Tobias. 'I bet they've discovered the best women wouldn't take a job there even if they were desperate.'

'You're probably right but Phyllis Bruce-Mair doesn't appear to want to move with the times.'

'So, Steph,' I say. 'We have a pub in an area of Glasgow that's not particularly well-to-do. It doesn't make much money but it's paying for an expensive car, and the company's accountant mainly services less than legit clients. Are we on to something here?'

'I'm pretty sure we are, boss, but here's another thing. Cross Leisure actually has two directors, Francis Crolla and a woman called Elaine Bartley.'

'I'm guessing from the expression on your face that this woman is important to the case. Who is she?'

Steph's practically grinning. 'I'm not sure who she is yet, exactly. It's the letters after her name that are interesting.'

I'm expecting these letters to be LLB or MRCVS or some other professional suffix so my gob falls open when Steph spells out: 'D E C E A S E D.' Then she qualifies that by adding, 'And furthermore, deceased since 2002.'

————

I DECIDE this evening's G&T can wait a while. 'How do these pieces all link together, Steph? Iain McLure, the McLaren,

Francis Crolla's pub in Dalmarnock, IB-M and the not-even-recently-deceased Elaine Bartley.'

'I said the McLaren hadn't been anywhere near Dalmarnock but twice recently, ANPR logs show it was on the same block in Glasgow as IB-M's offices. Even better though, we've tracked several journeys beginning and ending in Fife. The village of Kinghorn, to be more precise.'

'Have I missed something?' says Andrew. 'Why is Kinghorn in Fife "even better"?'

Steph's eyes are twinkling so much we practically need sunglasses. 'Because Elaine Bartley, ex of this parish, owns a house there.'

The three of us gawp at her then Tobias breaks the ice. 'Can dead people own houses in Scotland?'

As questions go, that was a belter. I wait until the laughter subsides. 'Have you been able to trace the car directly to this house?' I ask.

'No, but there's an ANPR camera in a garage forecourt about two hundred metres away. So if McLure *is* driving the McLaren and it's been logged in Kinghorn several times, I'll eat my hat if he doesn't live in that house. Oh, and by the way, I sent Becca Michaelson some stock photos and she's sure it's the same car. She remembers the rear light clusters, reminded her of a big game cat. Safe to say she was stunned when I told her how much it was worth.'

'Aye,' says Andrew. 'They're not cheap. North of £200,000 before you start adding extras.'

Or about five years of my salary, which just proves there are far too many rich bastards in this part of the world for my liking. 'Okay Steph, your call. What do you think we should do next? And by "we" I mean you and Tobias, naturally.'

Steph taps her pen against her lips for a few moments then places it carefully on the table. 'I want to talk to Frank Crolla ...

but not yet. There must be a link between him and McLure and I need to figure out what it is before I go blundering in. McLure has no idea we're tracking the car or that we know about the house so I don't want to tip him off. Phyllis Bruce-Mair's also on my radar because I think she can answer the main question.'

'Which is?'

'Why is McLure driving a car *and* living in a house, both owned by directors of a Glasgow pub, one of whom has been dead for about twenty years? But going back to the pub for a minute, it might also be relevant.'

'Why? What are you thinking?'

'I'm thinking this pub is in a less than affluent area, where cash is probably still king. It doesn't *seem* to turn much of a profit but if there's a lot of cash flowing through the business then maybe it's not all legitimately accounted for.' She checks her wrist. 'So it might be worth having a chat with IB-M.'

We're all pulling on coats and half listening while Steph makes her call. It's obvious she's talking to reception. After a few moments she sits a little straighter and adds an edge to her voice. 'I *understand* she may be busy but this is a police investigation into a serious crime. So the *minute* she's finished talking to her client, please tell her to contact me immediately.' A pause. 'I'm Detective Constable Zanetti. Stefania Zanetti. I'll spell that for you.'

She catches Andrew digging me in the ribs and mouthing *Stefania?*

Fortunately the daggers she slings in our direction are of the visual type.

CHAPTER THIRTY-SIX

'Mum, you promised.' Lily's tailgated me on my way into the kitchen.

'Promised what, dear?' I fuss around, arranging snacks on serving dishes.

'That you wouldn't ask Kev loads of questions.'

As per the three line whip I dished out the other night, Lily's brought her new boyfriend home so I can see the whites of his eyes. She might think it's none of my business but if my teenage daughter is having a sexual relationship with a man over ten years her senior then, rightly or wrongly, I want to meet him. She's maybe exaggerating about the level of grilling but the poor little darling doesn't know what questions I still have up my sleeve. The opportunity for those hasn't been quite right so far but the night is young.

I decide my best defence is to act the ditzy mum, I'm rather good at that. I pick up a couple of dishes and thrust them at her. 'Carry these through for me, would you?'

She takes them from me and fails to notice I've deliberately distracted her. I grab three more dishes and angle my head at the door. 'Now come on, while these are still hot.' Then I advance on her, giving her no choice but to retreat. She hits me with one final glare before turning on her heel.

Back in the living room Callum and Kevin appear to be talking local politics, the disastrous impact of the Leith tramway construction project on small businesses in the area. This is a surprise. I expected cars or sport or some other boring male domain.

I lay out my spread on the coffee table then lift my head. 'Did we miss something interesting?'

Callum replies, 'Kevin was just saying his dad ran a hardware shop on The Walk for years but he lost so much custom he had to close down.'

'That's a real shame, Kevin. Did he start up again somewhere else?'

'Don't know. He moved away.'

Kevin's tone makes it clear that this line of conversation is now stone dead but Lily comes to the rescue by wittering on about a reality show they're both into. It means nothing to Callum and me but we make an excellent job of faking enthusiasm. I don't *think* they spot any of the looks that pass between us.

The chit-chat meanders along while we tuck in to the food. Eventually I decide to raise the ante a bit, my first venture away from neutral territory. 'So Kevin, Lily tells me you're sharing a flat. Is it your flat or ...?'

I feel my daughter tensing up beside me. Interesting; I thought it was a fairly mundane question.

Before he answers, Kevin glances at Lily but she doesn't notice. Too busy transmitting death stares at her mother. I aim a warm smile at him but actually it's for her benefit.

'No,' he says. 'I can't afford my own place yet. I'm sharing with a guy from the office but I'm moving out soon.'

146

'Oh? Why's that?'

He shrugs. 'I think I can probably do better.'

Okay. One door closes ...

'Will that not make it awkward if you work with the guy?'

Lily puts a half-eaten piece of quiche on her plate, normally she'd scoff it in two bites.

'Not really. We're in different teams so I hardly ever see him.' He leans forward and spears a piece of cold chicken with his fork. 'Anyway, he'll soon find another tenant.'

'Any idea where you'll be moving to?'

'I'm checking out a couple of places. Nothing definite.'

I catch my husband's eye. Give him a look that says, *Over to you. I'm getting nowhere here.*

He picks up the baton as I snare the last piece of chilli cheddar from the plate. 'What is it you do for a living, Kevin?' he says.

'Insurance. I'm a trainee claims investigator with Scottish National.'

'Sounds interesting. Do you enjoy it?'

Kevin shrugs again. 'It's okay. I might not stay.'

That's the third or fourth time this evening he's shut us down, so now my hackles are definitely raised. I go quiet for a while. My inner demons are wrestling with the major question of the day: I want to bring up the subject of Kevin's age.

But I don't.

Better make that *can't*.

Maybe I'm not particularly discreet, and I'm not certain I care too much about that, but I watch him closely while his attention is elsewhere. I know Lily's desperately trying to catch my eye but I don't bite. All the time I'm evaluating him I wonder why he's pretending to Lily, and to us, that he's four years older than he actually is. Because he certainly doesn't look twenty-eight and he doesn't have the bearing of a man approaching his fourth decade. As the evening wears on, Callum and I fade into the background for longer periods and the conversation skews more to what Lily's been up to and what she might do with her life. Which, I note, Kevin appears at ease with.

Now I study my daughter, who's given up glaring at me. *Do you believe he's twenty-eight, Lil? And if so, why? Because you're not talking to him as if he were, are you?*

Is it that we cannot judge other people's age accurately when we are young ourselves? Or has age not yet assumed any relevance to my daughter's generation?

So I leave the question unasked, the issue unexplored. But I certainly will discuss it with Lily once Kevin has gone home. I don't know how I'm going to bring it up but as things transpire, I don't have to.

———

Callum and I are in the kitchen, tidying up while Lily walks her boyfriend to the bus stop. My husband leans over and pecks me on the cheek. 'Congratulations, darling. Tremendous self-discipline.'

I lean against the edge of the worktop while he stacks the dishwasher. He's turned this into a black art, adjusting the positions of numerous items before slotting in the final dish. I have to admit the whole thing's beyond me.

He casts an eye around the surfaces, declares himself satisfied with his efforts. 'Are you going to leave it? This thing about Kevin's age.'

'Do you think I should?'

He scratches at his cheek. 'Probably not.'

The front door opens and closes, and I hear Lily flipping off her shoes. I follow her into the living room, where she's deposited herself in a corner of the sofa. She pulls a cushion onto her lap and stares at the TV, which is switched off. The buttons are on the floor next to her phone but she makes no move towards either of them. I sit down at the other end, facing her, my feet tucked underneath me. Upstairs, I hear the bathroom door opening, the click of a light switch and Conor's bedroom door closing behind him. Callum glances in before taking the stairs two at a time. Think I'll be handling this all on my lonesome.

Lily turns round, sits cross-legged. The cushion stays on her lap, I don't know if its role is comforter or barrier. I can see she has something to say so I give her an encouraging look then wait. Eventually she works out her opening line.

'You were watching Kev a lot tonight, Mum.'

I say, 'Hmmm,' and she raises an eyebrow. Now it's me that has to search for the right words. I'll have to tell her Kevin's not ten years older than her, that's a definite. Of course, I'm pleased he's not twenty-eight but I don't know why he led Lily on like that. And should I explain about the misdemeanours he committed as a teenager? About the beating he suffered, which appears to have been the catalyst for a reformed Kevin? If indeed he is reformed.

I hoped I'd like him. I wanted to like him but I'm not sure. When I asked Callum he wobbled his hand from side to side. Not one for rushed decisions, is my darling husband.

I smile. Just a little one to myself. Because I know the reason I'm hesitating is I'll have to admit to Lily how I found out. Then there will be fireworks.

Oh well, in for a penny. I take a breath. 'Honey. If Kevin were only a couple of years older than you, maybe even a wee bit more, we probably wouldn't be having this conversation.'

'No. But he's not, is he? He's ten years older than me.'

'No, he's not.'

She pauses, narrows her eyes. 'He's not what?'

I scoot along the sofa until I'm right in front of her. 'Lily. You're probably going to be angry with me but you're my daughter, you're only seventeen and it's my job to keep you safe.'

She pulls the cushion to her chest. 'You checked him out.'

'Not exactly. All I did was ask around, put out feelers.'

'You checked him out!' I get the full petted lip. 'And I specifically asked you not to.'

I spread out my hands. 'I'd no choice, Lily. Ten years plus, it's a huge difference at your age.'

Then she remembers why we're heading down this path. 'Wait a minute, you said he's not.' Her expression switches from anger to confusion. She stares at me. 'He's not twenty-eight?'

'No, darling, he's only twenty-four.'

She raises her palms to her cheeks, pulls them down a bit which makes her eyes go funny. Moves a hand towards her phone but thinks better of it. 'Did your ... feelers ... turn up anything else?'

I make a quick decision. 'No. Nothing.'

She jumps to her feet, slings the cushion back in its place. 'I'm not pleased you did that, Mum.' The briefest of pauses. 'But I'm glad you did.' She picks up her phone, weighs it in her hand. 'I wasn't planning to see him tomorrow, but I am now.'

Then she leans over, kisses me on the forehead and storms out of the room. I can't be certain but I think I hear the word *fucker*.

I trust she isn't referring to me.

CHAPTER THIRTY-SEVEN

THE AFTERNOON SUN *is filtered by the cobwebs and crusty bodies that form a second skin on the inside of the window.*

I'm standing at the worktable in my garage. The door is closed so my nosey neighbours can't see in. I love it in here, I don't ever allow anyone else into my sanctuary. I have spent countless hours inside this relatively small space. I can, and do, potter to my heart's content.

But today I'm not frittering away time. Tidying, or rearranging, or throwing stuff out. No, I am here for a purpose. In front of me are the newspaper cuttings I have been collecting. I've read them all several times so, really, they no longer serve a useful purpose. But, with my pragmatist hat on, if they were discovered I would be in trouble.

Although there isn't even a suggestion thus far, the police will eventually want to speak to me and if they were to come armed with a warrant they would surely find my little hoard. That would be damning so I must get rid of them.

I have carried the shredder in here. I feed in the clippings, and it does its job. But I have heard it is possible to reconstitute shredded papers so there is a second stage to their destruction.

I prise the lid off an old tin of emulsion paint, not without some difficulty. It crackles and creaks before giving way, dropping small shards of dried paint onto the floor. It is not quite half full and I have to puncture the skin with the blade of a screwdriver. Then I use two hands to lift the shreds and stir them into the off-white mess. As I fill the tin it becomes more difficult to move the mixture around but a few minutes later all the shredded newspaper is enveloped in White with a Hint of Apple.

For good measure I pour some white spirit on the top, and stir the mass once more before jamming the lid back on and hammering the crumpled edges down until it's properly sealed.

Then I conceal the tin in a black refuse bag and drop it in my landfill waste bin. It's due to be emptied tomorrow morning.

That should help to keep the wolf from the door, for a while at least.

CHAPTER THIRTY-EIGHT

I GLANCE up as the door swings open and Steph strides in with Tobias in tow. She's in a chirpy mood but that's normal. It'll be a sunny day in hell before our Steph's grumpy.

It's late in the afternoon. They've been in Glasgow, questioning Phyllis Bruce-Mair about her pub-owning client, Francis Crolla, and his sleeping partner, Elaine Bartley.

She drops her bags on her desk and Tobias lays a printer paper box next to them. They both pull up chairs. My never-reducing pile of emails can wait. 'How did it go?'

'IB-M are definitely in trouble,' says Steph. 'And after I had a chat with the NCA on the way back, Phyllis herself will probably be in similar shit.'

I blink a couple of times. 'Well, that all sounds extremely interesting. And you've been speaking to our friends in the National Crime Agency? Do tell.'

———

Phyllis Bruce-Mair had kept Steph and Tobias waiting in IB-M's reception area for almost quarter of an hour before putting in an appearance. But Steph wasn't too bothered, she'd used the opportunity to have a good scout around.

IB-M occupied the ground and first floors of a five-storey office building in St Vincent Street, a few blocks west of George Square. The term 'occupied' was relative. The ground floor wasn't exactly a hive of bustling activity and the receptionist didn't field a single call the whole time they were there.

Steph spied a 'For Lease' sign through the window and noted the estate agency, just in case. The room possessed high ceilings, cornices and deep skirtings but the paintwork was hacked and the wallpaper, as a minimum, needed a wash down. The balding grey carpet tiles sprouted a few curled corners, deep indented scars indicated where filing cabinets had once rested.

Steph strolled over to the reception desk. It was configured for two people but only one woman sat there, eyes glued to the screen, her hand resting on the mouse. The spare place to her left was covered in a layer of general office crap, and the monitor was missing. A dusty keyboard lay upside down, the battery compartment open and empty. The lid was nowhere to be seen.

'How's business?' asked Steph.

The woman glanced up. 'You see it all.' Not even a smile to dress it up.

Just at that, a slender blonde dressed in a royal blue suit appeared in the doorway. The woman was probably early fifties. She looked Steph up and down, but completely disregarded Tobias. 'Come this way,' she barked, and turned on her heel.

The two officers made eyes and followed her upstairs to the first floor. The décor on the stairs was, if anything, a class down from reception. As they reached the next level Steph noticed all the doors bar one were closed and saw no light or movement behind the glass panels.

Phyllis Bruce-Mair swept into her office, waved a hand in the direction of two chairs and positioned herself behind her desk.

Steph started to introduce herself but Phyllis shook her head. 'I know who you are and why you're here. So get to the point quickly. I'm in between appointments at the moment so I don't have much time.'

'As you wish, Mrs Bruce-Mair,' said Steph.

'It's Ms, actually.'

'Ah, yes. Of course it is. I do apologise.' Steph didn't sound even slightly apologetic. 'As I explained when I called you, Detective Constable Hartmann and I would like to review the accounts for ...' She flicked open her notebook.

'Yes, yes. Cross Leisure.' Phyllis moved her mouse and stared at her monitor but the screen remained black. She tutted. 'I'm afraid that will not be possible.'

'Why not, *Ms* Bruce-Mair? Because that's *precisely* the reason we've driven forty miles to see you this morning.' Steph paused. 'And you were fully aware of that.'

'They're stored in our archive facility. It's on the other side of town and I haven't been able to arrange to have them brought over.'

'The most recent financial year is archived already?' said Tobias. 'Why would you do that?'

A door banged shut somewhere along the corridor, and the sash window behind Phyllis rattled in its frame. She jumped a little in her seat. The woman's fragile bubble was close to popping. 'Um, yes. I mean, no. They'll still be on file here, naturally.'

'In that case, please show us those because they will

include the previous year's figures, will they not? And while we are examining them, please ask one of your people downstairs to collect the earlier years from the archive.' Phyllis opened her mouth but Tobias was in quickly. 'After all, they don't appear to be particularly busy.'

He looked her straight in the eye. 'We will wait.'

———

PHYLLIS BRUCE-MAIR COULD NEVER BE MISTAKEN for a fat lady. But boy, did she sing. She was clearly rattled, decided it was prudent to cooperate and cancelled her other appointments for that day. Steph and Tobias leafed through the accounts to see if anything obvious jumped out. They ignored more complex items like depreciating assets, leaving those for the police forensic accountants.

But they did notice several payments to an electronics and security firm that appeared overly expensive and when they asked Phyllis, it was obvious from her expression they'd hit a nerve.

She studied her palm for several seconds. Steph could see the woman's hand was trembling.

'I told him,' said Phyllis.

'Francis Crolla?' asked Steph.

The accountant nodded.

'Told him what, Phyllis?'

'That those items would stick out like a boil on the end of his nose. A small business like his, supposedly spending all that money on electronics. Bloody ridiculous.'

'Did you raise a SAR?'

If an accountant believes a client has submitted inaccurate figures in their accounts, including omissions, or if they suspect the client is engaged in money laundering activity the accountant is legally bound to file a Suspicious Activity Report, or SAR, with the National Crime Agency. Every accountancy practice has a Money Laundering Reporting Officer and for IB-M, Phyllis Bruce-Mair was that person.

If a practice has these suspicions and doesn't file a SAR, they are deemed to be complicit and the reporting officer can end up in jail. When filing the SAR, the accountant is under no obligation to inform or tip off the client; indeed that is also a crime and may result in similar consequences. Added to that, the client doesn't enjoy the equivalent of attorney client privilege so, should they be investigated by the NCA, they would not be told their accountant filed a SAR.

Steph tidied the paperwork in front of her to give her time to formulate her next line of questioning. 'Phyllis, you believed Mr Crolla had submitted inaccurate accounts information and was involved in money laundering. Is that the case?'

Phyllis sighed. 'Yes.'

'And not only one time, a few years in succession?'

'Again, yes.'

'Each time, did you file SARs?'

Now Phyllis's attention was on the backs of her hands. 'Yes, of course. But ...'

'You understated the severity of these inaccuracies?'

She hesitated before answering. 'I'm afraid I did.'

'So were you thinking that if you kept the SARs at a low profile, the NCA would be unlikely to investigate Mr Crolla?'

Phyllis remained silent.

'And,' said Steph, 'the added benefit would be to keep the regulatory bodies off your back.'

The accountant lifted one shoulder, said nothing.

Tobias leaned forward. 'Ms Bruce-Mair, have you done this with other clients?'

Phyllis glowered at him. 'Do you *really* think I'm going to answer that?'

'We don't,' said Steph, 'but there are two other questions you *will* have to answer.'

Phyllis raised an eyebrow so Steph asked her questions.

'One: how is it possible for a business the size of Cross Leisure to purchase a car worth upwards of £200,000? And two: are you aware that Mr Crolla's co-director, Mrs Elaine Bartley, has been deceased for about twenty years?'

Phyllis Bruce-Mair didn't reply to that. It's incredibly difficult for a person to speak when they are running for the door with a hand jammed over their mouth.

Regrettably, a few seconds later, the somewhat tired décor on the first floor landing of IB-M's offices was further spoiled by spatters of undigested food of indeterminate provenance.

———

THE TWO DETECTIVES had a decent view of the front door of The Cross from their parking spot on the opposite side of Dalmarnock Road. The pub was a single width unit in the ground floor of a scruffy tenement. It sat shoulder to shoulder with a newsagent and a tanning salon. None of the three was likely to win industry awards for their shopfronts.

The car's clock read 14:10. They'd watched the front door for about twenty minutes and it seemed the pub had been relatively busy this lunchtime. A group of four men, sharp suits and shaved heads, came out and chatted on the pavement. Then one shook hands with the other three before they separated. Several more customers left in ones and twos but only one middle-aged man went in. His jeans were hanging off him and his Man United top must have been through the wash about a thousand times. Across the back it read 'Cantona'. He flicked a cigarette end into the gutter, pushed against the front door with his forearm and disappeared from view.

'Exclusively male so far,' said Steph.

'I don't think it's a place for ladies who lunch, that is for sure,' said Tobias, pointing at signs on the window that listed the televised sporting events for that week. There were three or four a day, minimum. They checked for a website but the pub didn't have its own. Only generic listings, and nothing on Tripadvisor.

'It would be good if we could see what the place is like from the inside but we can't run the risk of bumping into Crolla.'

The Cross accounts strongly suggested the pub was a gold-mine, filled to bursting seven days a week with punters able and willing to pay premium prices for their preferred tipples. From where they sat, Steph was dubious. She knew that even a quick visit would give them tangible evidence that Crolla's figures were worthy of further investigation. But given the clientele they'd spotted so far, there was an excellent chance that if she went inside, everyone would make her in less time than it takes to call 'last orders'.

They discussed it and Tobias reckoned he was a far better bet. 'I will simply be a tourist, who has walked along the river but has taken a wrong turning. I will have a beer, I like football, I support FC Cologne and I will ask for directions to Celtic Park. I don't wear a suit or a tie, and how many black German police officers work in Glasgow?' He jerked a thumb at his chest. 'I hardly resemble authority, do I?'

Steph agreed that Tobias had a point. Although your average Scottish cop wouldn't get the gig as a model for Armani, her colleague had elevated untidiness to a higher plane.

She held her hand out. 'Okay, but give me your warrant

card. Now you're formally off duty and there's no harm in you having a pint.' She hitched round in the driver's seat to face him. 'Let's be clear. You are *not* going in there to investigate a crime or to pull a trick on anyone. The information you will be gathering is not confidential or sensitive, it's in the public domain. So what's the place like, how much is a pint, what's on the menu? Things like that.' She faced him dead on. 'Fair enough?'

Tobias laughed. 'Jawohl!'

———

STEPH KEPT a casual watch from over the street. As spying missions went, this one was as straightforward as they come. She'd worry if her colleague was inside for any more than half an hour but her fairly arbitrary deadline was still ten minutes away when Tobias pushed the door open and headed off down the street, zipping up his leather jacket as he walked. Steph waited two minutes as agreed. No one else came out so she drove after him. A few hundred metres further on, she passed him as he crossed a side street.

She pulled over and he climbed in. The corners of his mouth were turned down.

'What's up, Tobias?'

'When my girlfriend comes over from Germany, I do not think we will go there for a night out.'

———

TOBIAS HAS GIVEN Andrew and me a detailed description of The Cross. More substantial inside than it appears from the street, prices on the cheap side, more beer and whisky than dry white wine and cocktails, a basic snacks menu, scuffed dark red vinyl underfoot and the Formica tables are bolted to the floor. On the entertainment front, two pool tables in constant use, more TVs than your average electrical outlet and a juke box permanently stuck in a sixties and seventies time warp.

Time to delve into the accounts. 'Steph. These payments that Crolla made to the electronics company, what were they for?'

Steph's marked the key places in the accounts with small Post-its. 'Security reviews, internal and external CCTV, alarm systems, web-cams and laptops, TVs and broadcast licenses, music systems. And new cash registers in the past year.'

'Any sign of all that expenditure, Tobias?'

He shakes his head. 'No. There were televisions on every wall but they were not new. I did see a basic alarm system but no CCTV and definitely no web-cams. And I think these new cash registers must still be in their boxes.'

'Faked invoices, then.' No one disagrees.

I study the next page. 'Over £240,000 for staff costs? That has to be about twelve or fourteen full time. Is that realistic?'

I glance up at Tobias but he shakes his head again.

'And the cost of stock might be okay for an upmarket boozer in the Merchant City, but seriously?' I push the paper-work away.

'The only wine I saw was on draught. There were many different brands of whisky, vodka and rum but only two different gins, maybe three. It is very much a man's pub.'

I turn to Steph. 'This is a dangerous balancing act Phyllis is performing here. She's filing SARs to keep the regulator off her back, and understating them in the hope the NCA don't act against her client, or even other clients for all we know. How does she get away with it, eh?'

'Because there are tens, maybe hundreds of thousands of SARs generated every year and the NCA only have resources to act on the ones that are the most serious. But if her clients genuinely *are* bent, you're right, it's a dangerous game she's playing.'

'And you think she genuinely didn't know Elaine Bartley is dead?'

'You can't fake puking up all over your office, boss.'

I screw my face up at the prospect. 'Right, being serious for a minute, it appears we have several links to Iain McLure. We haven't proved it yet but it's likely he drives the McLaren. Cross Leisure is the registered owner of the car and Elaine Bartley, deceased, is a director. And before you ask me, I have no idea how a dead person can own a property but apparently she does. The property is in Kinghorn and ANPR logs tell us the McLaren stopped somewhere nearby. Therefore, reasonable to assume McLure's living there. Maybe temporarily, maybe permanently, who knows? IB-M are the accountants for Cross Leisure, and Phyllis Bruce-Mair has all but admitted their accounts are not accurate. Tobias's view of The Cross is that the recorded accounts don't tie in with the style of the pub or what they have on offer but we'll have a better idea once our forensic accountants have been through them. All with me so far?'

A general nodding of heads says they are, so I press on. 'Now, here's where we don't have any answers. Where does Frank Crolla fit into all of this? If the pub's accounts have been falsified does Crolla know about it?'

'Impossible to imagine he doesn't, boss,' says Steph.

It's hard to argue with that so I don't. 'We know the McLaren and the Kinghorn property link McLure with Cross Leisure, and possibly with Elaine Bartley. But we don't yet have any connection between McLure and Frank Crolla, or McLure and IB-M.'

That was quite a speech so I stand up and stretch, walk

about. Three pairs of eyes follow me around, waiting to hear where we go now.

I sit down and think. 'McLure probably thinks he's been smart but, luckily for us, not smart enough. It looks like he's set things up so one company owns the car and the deceased Elaine Bartley owns the house. He could have made things more complex, built in more layers, but he didn't. He's off-grid but he hasn't burrowed too deep. So why not? Probably he's not expecting people to be digging. Or maybe it says more about his arrogance, he's assumed he can't be found.'

I check my watch. 'Right. That's enough for today, I think. Terrific work, you pair. Steph, before you knock off contact the NCA again. Ask them for advice on how we should proceed with this. But make sure you explain it's all part of an ongoing investigation so they shouldn't even be thinking about moving on Crolla or IB-M without talking to us first. And definitely *not* until we bring McLure in.'

I nod to myself. We're done here. 'Let's reconvene tomorrow and decide how and when to pay McLure a visit. And Frank Crolla too. But McLure's the priority.'

CHAPTER THIRTY-NINE

I PASS Lily as I'm driving up our street and give her a cheerful toot of the horn. She waves back, a big grin on her face. As usual, she's not bearing a grudge. We meet on the driveway, where I sling an arm round her, squeeze her shoulders and plonk a big wet kiss on her cheek.

She squeals. Yells, 'Get off, Mum,' and tries to wriggle free. Honestly, she's acting like a little kid and I love her for it. She cranes her neck to see if there's anyone around to witness this dreadful level of child abuse but we're all alone. She detests it when I do things like that. For example when she has friends over, and I wander about the house singing off-key at the top of my voice. That's when, apparently, I'm 'like a total embarrassment, Mother!' But who cares? It's great fun winding the kids up every now and again, keeps them off balance.

'Thought I'd better tell you, Mum. I've had it out with Kev.'

I feign nonchalance. 'Oh? How did that go?'

'Men!' She sighs. 'Turns out he was just trying to impress me, pretending he was older than he is. But it got out of hand,

and he didn't know how to admit it. Said he didn't know how long I'd go out with him and if I'd dumped him, the age thing wouldn't have mattered. Unfortunately for him, my mother's a nosey interfering old policewoman.'

I don't take umbrage at her description of me. 'So everything's okay?'

'Yeah. But I told him if there was anything else he'd like to admit to, he should do it while I was in a forgiving mood. One-time opportunity.'

'And was there?'

'No. But I told him if he lied to me again he'd be my latest ex-boyfriend.'

I stretch out an arm to give her another hug but she dodges away and does her tiptoes running thing.

I wince as she crashes through the front door, bouncing it back off its hinges. 'Hey, Pops,' she yells, 'hope my dinner's ready.' And disappears into the kitchen.

I grab my bags and blip the car locks. *She* might have forgiven him but I think I'll be keeping an eye on our Kevin for a wee while yet.

CHAPTER FORTY

'I'M SORRY—'

'Sorry doesn't FUCKING CUT IT.'

Iain McLure knew he was *that close* to losing it. He drew an enormous breath in through his nose and forced his clenched fist to relax. He examined his palm and the four livid marks his fingernails had left behind. No, the time for screaming and for swearing was over. It was vital he remained calm. The line crackled with latent tension as Mark Thornton waited, dreading McLure's next words. He didn't have to wait long and he was quite right to be fearful.

'Do not speak,' barked McLure. 'Just listen.'

Thornton didn't even say okay. He figured he knew what was coming next but he figured wrong. As McLure began to speak, the DCS experienced a brief jolt of relief. He anticipated the worst but the first few words he heard, for some bizarre inexplicable reason, didn't sound all that bad. Then things changed.

'You said the investigation into my "activities" was going, quote, "nowhere". But I have been told that is not the case therefore you *lied*. And as a result there will be consequences. So I've sent you an email, copied to Mrs Thornton. It's time she heard, officially, about your young bits on the side.'

Thornton closed his eyes. His wife already knew. He was in the clear. *Thank you, God.*

Then *God* kicked him in the nuts.

'Oh, and I've copied it to your daughters too. The little darlings deserve to know just what a self-centred turd their father is.'

Thornton's phone pinged but he kept it jammed up against his ear. He didn't know what McLure had sent and right now, he didn't have the balls to find out.

McLure spoke one more time. 'This is your last chance. Definitely your last chance. No more warnings. Make sure the investigation's stopped, right away, or I'll be dropping a bigger bomb.'

———

THORNTON WAS SITTING on the edge of the bed, naked, cradling his phone between his knees. He blinked several times in a vain attempt to stop the tears falling.

The woman slid over from the centre of the rumpled queen-sized bed and knelt behind him. She wrapped her arms round his body, squashing her breasts against his upper back.

'What was all that about, Mark? Who were you apologising to?' She leaned over, peered into his face. 'Are you crying?'

Immediately, he broke free and stood up. 'Mind your own damn business. It's bugger-all to do with you. In fact, put your clothes on and fuck off out of my sight.'

She remained kneeling, palms on her thighs, head tilted. Her expression suggested she was amused by his outburst. She was cooling down rapidly as the perspiration dried on her body. She could have pulled some bedding around her but she chose not to.

'Actually, Mark, you appear to have forgotten that I paid for the room this time so unless you're coming back to bed for, hmmm, unfinished business,' she patted the sheet beside her, '*you're* the one who'll be leaving.'

She waited for a few seconds but he stood there as if he were calcified. Then she shook her head, slipped off the bed and padded past him into the bathroom.

———

THE MILLENNIAL GENERATION weren't actually born with mobile phones welded to their palms but for some, they might well have been. Yvonne Thornton was a classic example. Twenty-four years old, but only twelve when her parents bought her a Sony Ericsson, which was superseded by her first iPhone two years later. Scarcely a new model launch went by without her upgrading. Her younger sister, Nicole, was the beneficiary of her sibling's cast-offs and became even more of a phone geek than Yvonne.

And so it was that within minutes of Iain McLure issuing his final warning, a horrified Mark Thornton and his momentarily confused daughters were all watching the same video clip. For the life of him, the police officer could neither recall the name of the naked young redhead straddling him, nor the room in which the act was taking place. The irony of the film's subject matter compared to how he'd spent the last half an hour wasn't lost on him.

Nicole, whose hair was a similar colour and length to the woman on top of Thornton, suffered a fleeting instant of panic before she realised it couldn't possibly be her on the screen.

Yvonne however, wasted no time on the woman. She fully expected the supine man to be her father and wasn't in the least surprised when she was proved right.

Thornton was still staring at his phone. There were several things he couldn't understand. How had he been stupid enough to miss a camera focused directly on the bed? How on earth had McLure gotten hold of the footage? Had McLure engineered it? Had the woman duped him deliberately? He studied her again but her long hair hid her face. As he watched the film more closely he realised the angle was designed to identify him, not her. He supposed that was the point.

Meanwhile his daughters' calls to each other were clashing in voicemail hell. Yvonne messaged her sister:

Please call me now, line clear.

She had to wait for a full two minutes while Nicole stopped crying long enough to explain where she was.

Half an hour later, on a bench in a quiet corner of a city park, Yvonne explained to her little sister that she'd known about their father's affairs ever since their mother had slipped up a few years earlier, confessed how much she knew about her husband and 'his sluts' and stated that she had long since ceased to give a shit.

In the hotel, Thornton was desperate to phone Yvonne and Nicole but couldn't dredge up the courage. He sat with his elder daughter's photo on the screen but he couldn't make his finger tap the call icon. Eventually he sent a bland WhatsApp:

Hi sweetie, is it okay to give you a call?

Then he hesitated for an age before adding:

Luv u, Dad xx

He prayed they hadn't seen McLure's email but he wasn't fooling anyone, both girls were normally lightning fast with their responses.

His phone remained mute. He had no choice but to try again.

I'm so so sorry, Yvonne. Please call me so I can explain.

He considered and immediately rejected all manner of message endings, and finally hit send.

He refreshed the screen repeatedly but the two grey ticks stubbornly refused to turn blue, which would have indicated his daughter had read the message. He didn't know she'd read it on her home screen without opening the app so gradually he became more optimistic.

Then a message arrived from Nicole's number and his heart bounced. But within seconds his smile more resembled a rictus grin as he began to register what it said.

This is Yvonne. You are a BASTARD. You better tell Mum about this IMMEDIATELY or I will. Nicole is moving in with me and won't be going back home until YOU MOVE OUT. The slut in the video is probably younger than me. You are DISGUSTING and we both FUCKING HATE YOU.

CHAPTER FORTY-ONE

I HEAR feet crunching along the driveway. Andrew appears round the corner of the house.

'Anything?' I ask him.

We're in the small seaside resort of Kinghorn, Fife, situated on the opposite side of the Firth of Forth from Edinburgh. King Alexander the Third died here in 1286. Fell off his horse on the beach on his way to see his new wife. Not exactly a heroic way to go, and I'll wager she was a bit miffed at only being Queen for five minutes.

My overall impression of the place is manicured, kept neat and tidy for tourists on day trips from the capital and wealthy American golfers working their way round the dozens of courses in the area.

The description also suits the detached white bungalow we're standing in front of. Technically, it's owned by the late Elaine Bartley and is no more than a short fairway from the nearest ANPR camera at the local filling station. We believe this to be Iain McLure's bolthole and if he'd only answered the doorbell when Leith's finest came a-calling, the question would have been resolved.

Things are rarely that straightforward.

Andrew had checked the rear of the building while I stayed by the front door. He shakes his head. 'All the blinds are closed. No sign of life.'

'Garage?'

He nods. 'There is a window but it's covered up from the inside so I can't see in. And the doors are locked.'

I make a face then I turn full circle, checking out the garden. It's neat, tidy, grass cut, bushes trimmed. The odd weed here and there, but clearly it's tended frequently. However, I dismiss the thought that McLure is a keen gardener. It just doesn't fit with what we know of him so far.

'May I help you?'

The gentleman is on the driveway of the adjacent house. Probably late sixties, a straggly band of white hair at ear level and wire-rimmed glasses. He has a cardboard box balanced partly on the bonnet of his car and partly on his hip. It's that type of place, I guess, where two characters mooching about in a neighbour's garden receive a polite welcome, not a 'What are you up to?'

We move over to the fence and I explain who we are. 'We're looking for the person who lives here. Iain McLure. Do you know him?'

'Is that his name?' I'm momentarily confused, wondering if McLure might be using an alias. 'Because he's lived next door for over ten years and I haven't a clue who he is or anything about him.' He shifts the box over a bit and pulls a bunch of keys from his pocket. He peers at a car key and blips the locks.

I see he's wearing a wedding ring. 'Might your wife know?'

He lays the box on the back seat of his car, then straightens up. 'I'm afraid not.' He gives me a small smile. 'My wife died about fifteen years ago, long before the chap – McLure did you say? – moved in.'

I reach my hand out towards his arm but stop short of making contact. 'Ah. Sorry about that, sir.'

But he waves away my apology. We chat for a minute or two, ask him a few more questions before talking to several other residents of the street. The gist of the plot is this: nobody knows anything about McLure because he never talks to anyone. He blanks people if he meets them in the street, but that's rare because he takes the car everywhere. He does drive a McLaren. When he passes anyone he never waves. Nobody can tell us when he's likely to be home. And, as I thought, he does have a gardener but the man's not local.

The responses became slightly more positive when I ask if McLure lives on his own. The couple opposite tell us, 'We think he did have a girlfriend. She stayed over quite often but she was like him, never took you on. Well suited, they were. She drove a little blue car. A Hyundai or a Kia. Something like that. And no, couldn't tell you the registration number.'

I hand out my cards and ask people to call me if they see him. I reassure them that no, he's not dangerous at all.

We take one last tour round the house but no joy. Once we're in the car I say, 'I suppose if he doesn't talk to the neighbours, he'll never know we were here.'

CHAPTER FORTY-TWO

On our way back from Kinghorn, Andrew drops me off at Leo Contini's office. The room is lined with books relating to the law, hundreds of them. I wonder how many he's read. Or even opened.

In theory we're supposed to be talking about his son, but there have been a few periods of silence. Some were awkward, some companionable but, fair to say, it's not been easy getting to the point.

I try again.

'Everybody knows your boy was set up, but now he's gone there's no one working the case. However, I'll be doing my damnedest to prove he was innocent and I'm slightly surprised you're not doing the same.' I keep my voice gentle. 'So my question is, Leo ... why not?'

His eyes are brimming so I give him space until he's ready.

'It's ... I don't know, easier somehow.' He stares out of the window. 'Had Luca been convicted I would be all over it and I wouldn't rest until he was cleared.' He gathers himself and turns to me. 'But he wasn't convicted and as you say, no one actually thinks he did it anyway so it's better to let it all slip away. People will forget.'

He lowers his gaze.

'Okay, Leo, and I do apologise for pushing it, and this is me being Devil's Advocate to a ridiculous degree but ...' I leave a clear pause until he looks up at me. 'Convince me.'

His head snaps back and his eyes narrow. 'What?'

'Give me something you haven't told anyone already. Something new that'll encourage me to keep going. To prove beyond all doubt that your son was innocent.'

'I can't, Mel. I've said everything I could possibly say.' He sighs. 'It would simply be the same words in a different order.'

Leo appears to have collapsed into himself. Defeated.

Then, a spark. His eyes brighten, and not through tears. He reaches for his phone. 'Could you wait outside please? Hopefully I won't be long.'

———

An hour has passed and I'm with Paula, Lily's best pal and Luca's girlfriend. I hate to think of the prefix 'ex' but tragically, that is the case.

I've known Paula since she joined Lily's class, aged seven, part way through a term. A tiny wee thing with a shock of thick black hair. She's a grown woman now but she doesn't seem to be any bigger today. Not to me, at any rate.

Lily told me that Paula has cut herself off. She hardly ever leaves the house and shuns visitors. But her mum lets Lily in and the girls sit together. They cry, they hug, they talk. But they *never* discuss Luca or what happened. That'll take time. But time is in short supply if I want to keep the investigation moving.

I explain that Leo suggested I talk to her, and repeat the

spiel I gave him. Finish with, 'Convince me, Paula, that Luca wasn't involved with drugs.' I lean towards her, pick up her tiny little hands from her lap and add, 'Please.'

I have to wait a while but once she starts talking, it all comes tumbling out. And she is surprisingly calm.

'You know I'm an only child. We're a very small family. I have an aunt and an uncle here, and another aunt in New Zealand. She emigrated there before I was even born. She's a widow, her husband was an alcoholic. I have two cousins over there but I've never met them. Except on Instagram, obviously.' She offers up a small smile, and I send back a similar-sized one. Baby steps.

'I also had two cousins here but the older one died from a heroin overdose about five years ago. And her brother is an addict too, so ...' She swallows, hesitates and carries on. 'My aunt, who's their mother obviously, has terminal cancer. We don't know how long she ...' Paula's jaw wobbles. 'Well, you know.'

Her voice regains some of its strength. 'Losing one of your kids to drugs must be incredibly stressful. But worrying about losing the other one as well? I'm not stupid, I know stress itself doesn't cause cancer but I really do believe that if your body's defences are down, surely it's easier for a disease like that to take a hold. So, one way or another, drugs and alcohol have taken almost half my family.'

She alters her grip and now she is holding *my* hands. 'Trust me. If Luca was involved with drugs in any shape or form, I wouldn't have touched him with a bargepole. Or, if he'd gone anywhere near drugs after we started dating, I'd have dumped him in a heartbeat.' She makes a slicing motion with her right hand. 'No second chances. Finished!'

She looks at me from below her coal-black fringe. 'And you

must believe me, I loved him to bits. So, Mel,' she'd dropped the Mrs Cooper when it was no longer cool. 'Convinced?'

I give her an enormous rib-crushing hug, and leave.

CHAPTER FORTY-THREE

'You wait a minute please. I tell my daughter to watch shop then we talk.'

Steph and Tobias moved off to one side of the counter, while the corner shop owner vanished through a door marked *Staff Only*. Steph half turned as the bell behind them tinkled. A young lad wandered in, spotted them, about-faced and marched straight back out.

She laughed. 'Fair to assume he's not on Britain's Most Wanted list?'

'Probably,' said Tobias. 'But he is guilty of something, I think.'

The shopkeeper, Samir, and a young girl appeared behind the counter. She didn't seem much older than fourteen. He spoke a few words to her, pointed at various things near the until then hurried over to them.

'If customer wants alcohol, I must go. Otherwise, pfft!' He rocked his head from side to side as if that explained 'pfft' then looked at them expectantly.

Samir was Punjabi Sikh. He wore a stylish burgundy

turban together with black dress shirt and Levi's. Behind the scenes, his English was practically flawless and accent-free but for some reason known only to himself, he felt the need to put on the immigrant-Asian-shopkeeper act. His wife and all four of his daughters had been pleading with him for years to cut it out but he'd played the part for so long he couldn't change, even if he wanted to.

'We'd like to ask you about your customer, Celia Fraser,' said Steph. 'She's the woman whose dog was stolen from outside your shop.'

He hit the police officers with a full set of gleaming white teeth. 'Mrs Fraser. Very nice lady. Customer long time. Very funny.'

Steph was a little surprised. According to Bryan Fraser, his mother didn't have a decent word to say about Samir. 'A nice lady? Very funny?'

Samir did the head rocking thing again. 'She make me laugh. Best laugh any customer. Always try wind me up. Complain all time, especially about door. She very funny. I put angry face on with her. You know, like this?' Samir screwed up his face but it appeared more as if he were suffering from indigestion. 'But I like her. I am so sorry she was injured by men driving van.' Samir had adopted a glum expression but it didn't last. 'I very happy dog is home. Why people do things like that? They are scum!'

'We don't know,' said Tobias. 'Do you know anyone who dislikes Mrs Fraser? Who might want to do such a thing?'

The shopkeeper shook his head several times. Steph could have sworn his turban moved. 'No! But you find them, you kick fucking arse!' He brandished his fist for emphasis. 'And throw key away.'

It took a monumental effort for the pair to maintain any composure after that one.

Outside, they stopped to compare notes.

'So,' said Steph. 'Neither Celia, nor anyone we've spoken to, knows why she was targeted. She admitted to Dave Devlin she can be annoying sometimes, but Dave thought she was playing her old lady card.'

'But not annoying to the extent of someone stealing her pet, being willing to risk dragging her under a van, and sending threatening videos to her family.'

'Definitely not. Let's go and talk to Bryan Fraser.'

———

THEY FOUND Custody Sergeant Bryan Fraser on a break, nudging the contents of a blue plastic box around with a fork. As they approached, he speared a piece of greenery, regarded it as if it were a form of contagion, and shook it into a bin he'd moved to the side of his chair.

'Not a word, Steph.' He pointed the fork at her. 'Not a word.'

She held up both hands and eyeballed a bar of chocolate lying on the table. Bryan ignored her completely.

Steph sat down opposite him, and Tobias pulled a chair over beside her. Steph made the introductions then said, 'Sorry to disturb you, Bryan. How's your mum, by the way?'

The custody sergeant laid his fork down, shook his head. 'Not doing too well I'm afraid. Her leg's giving her a lot of pain but because of the fractured hip she can't get up and about. She's trying to put a brave face on it but every time she thinks about what happened and how badly things could've turned out, she gets all upset again. I thought with Neve being safe and Maddie appearing without a scratch on her, she would perk up. But not so far.' He sighed. 'It'll be a long haul, I think.'

'And your daughter?' asked Tobias. 'How is she?'

'Not good, mate.' Bryan's voice caught for an instant. 'People will tell you kids are resilient and most of the time it's true. But seeing her Grandma hurt like that has hit her hard. Nightmares. Terrified if she sees a white van. Doesn't want to go to school. All sorts of stuff, really. She's having counselling but progress is slow so far. But thanks for asking. Appreciate it.'

There was a brief silence then Bryan spoke. 'Anyway, what can I do for you?'

The remainder of their conversation was short, simply because Bryan agreed with everyone else's assessment of his mother's character. He finished with, 'Yeah, she can be a grumpy old bat but she doesn't have a bad bone in her body.'

And when Steph asked him if *he* might have been the reason his mother was targeted, he snorted. 'If you're planning to make a list of people with a grudge against me, you'd better order a fresh notebook.' He shovelled the remaining contents of the blue box into the bin and ripped the wrapper off the chocolate. 'And make sure it's A4.'

CHAPTER FORTY-FOUR

GARY DEMPSTER WAS BEGINNING to think using motion sensitive cameras to find the person who'd tried to destroy Tommy's house was ill-advised at best. He'd borrowed the idea from watching wildlife programmes, but capturing images of solitary snow tigers on a high Himalayan pass could hardly be compared with monitoring pedestrian traffic on a busy residential street.

Every evening after work he reviewed the footage from that day. He misguidedly assumed he'd be able to watch it in fast forward but then discovered he spent more time rewinding to watch segments again. And all the people he thought might be of interest turned out not to be. Workers, kids wandering along to school, posties and of course, dog walkers. All innocent.

People checked out the damaged house as they passed but no one paid it undue attention. Sporadic bursts of work were carried out to clear the site and make it safe so there was usually something to see, but not much that would keep a person hanging about for long. That would change if they began pulling it down but as Tommy and the insurance company were still at odds, that wouldn't be happening any time soon.

Dispirited, Gary thought he'd give it a couple more days before admitting his idea hadn't worked. He'd continued to ask around, trying to unearth any nuggets of useful information. But time was passing, the fire was old news and lips remained tightly sealed. For good, by the look of it.

Gary would never say so, but Tommy hadn't helped himself by his actions and how he'd treated people over the years. He was feared, disliked. Often both. Not the best combination when you're asking them for help.

After an hour, falling asleep, Gary gave up. Ironically, had he watched for only another ten minutes or so he would have found what he'd been searching for.

CHAPTER FORTY-FIVE

Iᴀɪɴ McLᴜʀᴇ sᴛᴏᴏᴅ outside the pub, a few metres upwind of the smokers. His hands were shaking so much it was surprising they were able to hold his phone. He tapped the screen and studied it for several minutes. His gaze was locked on.

When the video stopped he dropped the phone into his shirt pocket and massaged his temples with the fingertips of his other hand. He lowered his head and closed his eyes. A passer-by wondered if he was crying, but didn't stop to ask.

He looked up a contact and stabbed the Call icon. It rang five times before it was answered. McLure didn't even attempt to remain calm. 'Thornton! Police officers have been at my house, ferreting around. *How do I know?* What sort of stupid fucking question is that? I have security cameras and an app, you complete fuckwit.' Then he paused. 'Ah, wait a minute. Jesus! Stay off that phone 'til I ring you back.'

He cancelled the call then tapped and scrolled and swiped. And watched. And swore. He searched around for something to kick that wouldn't hurt his foot.

He selected a file from his Dropbox and messaged it to Thornton. Then he waited a few seconds before redialling. This time the call was answered on the first ring.

'Not only were Cooper and one of her goons at my house, they've checked out my flat in Leith. So you're out of warnings. That file I've just sent you, I *will* be making it public. Your problem is, you'll never know when I'm going to do it. Your only chance is to stop Cooper, and stop her right now. Or I will. Because I know what the bitch looks like and where to find her. And if she has family, I'll find them too.'

McLure was composed again. Tirade over. He didn't give Thornton any opportunity to respond, he simply ended the call.

Then he marched back inside and swiped his jacket off his chair. It was a black leather biker jacket, and heavy. The trailing sleeve caught his beer glass, sending it crashing to the tiled floor. A woman at the adjacent table moved smartly to avoid the spray of froth, and several others twisted round in their seats to see what the commotion was about.

McLure ignored them all. The situation was critical. He couldn't risk returning either to his house in Kinghorn or his flat in Dalmeny Street. No, there was only one place where he'd be safe.

He had no idea what he would say to her after all this time but he'd think of something.

———

MARK THORNTON STARED at the jpeg symbol on his screen. He was terrified of what it contained. He ran a hand through his hair, hesitated then tapped the icon.

'Oh my god! Where the *fuck* did he get this?'

The image showed Thornton at a table in a pub. He knew

exactly where it had been taken, in an old coach house tavern about ten miles south of the city. He was hemmed into the corner against a traditional stone wall. He recalled a collection of decorative porcelain plates that hung from hooks all the way round the room.

At the time, Thornton was a brand new DI. Two men had driven him to the tavern, where they joined two others. The photo showed the table was laden with drinks, and Thornton appeared to be having a jolly old time. He was laughing and had his arm slung around the shoulders of the man sitting on his right. No one who saw the photo could ever be persuaded he'd been coerced into being part of this merry little band.

One of the men was facing away from the camera, another was side on. The other two had made sure they were in full view and they were the damning ones. Their trial for drug-running and other ancillary crimes had collapsed that same day. They were free men, and the DI was the man to thank for that.

When McLure had called him, Thornton was in his car. He'd pulled over when 'McLure' flashed up on the multi-media display above the centre console. Now, sitting there with the engine ticking over, he put the phone face down to avoid looking at the image but he might as well not have bothered. Every detail remained as clear as day.

Iain McLure had been blackmailing him ever since he was a sergeant. He'd not long been promoted and although positive behavioural culture change in the police was well under way, Thornton's DI was only a few years away from retirement and was one of the worst examples of old school. He had no time for this 'touchy-feely shite', as he called it and came down hard on any of his subordinates who tried to embrace the new regime. Of course, the smart ones did change but were savvy enough to keep their distance from the DI's bad example.

They knew his day was past and it wouldn't be long before his bosses would be moving him on.

Thornton was a different type of smart. He knew the DI was on the take but he could foresee an opportunity looming up where he'd be able to step into this particular dead man's shoes. But, as always, his all-consuming arrogance would become his downfall; he'd completely discounted the possibility the crooks in the picture would stitch him up. He *thought* he was their ally, the man who would grease their wheels. He was actually their pawn, and pawns for the most part are utterly dispensable.

At the time the picture was taken, McLure was still clinging on to the notion that he could become a successful investigative journalist. He was working on a feature that brought him into contact with Edinburgh's drugs underworld, and met one of the key players in the photo. Long story short, McLure was able to help this man and in return was given the photo on the understanding that either could release it as and when it became necessary. But the crook didn't ever need to and that was why the DCS was now seeing it for the first time.

Thornton knew nothing of this unlikely alliance but it was crystal clear that McLure had left him absolutely no choice: he could *not* leave Mel Cooper running free on this one. He'd been thinking about it and had come up with a solution, relatively straightforward but it would take a couple of days to put in motion. Until then he would be on tenterhooks, but there wasn't a way around that.

As he drove off DCS Mark Thornton realised that yet again he was not in full control, and he didn't like it.

He didn't like it one little bit.

CHAPTER FORTY-SIX

I WONDER what they do with people who are claustrophobic.

Emily O'Keefe examined the tiny space she was sitting in. White laminate panels in front of her, behind her, to her right and to her left. This last one was the door. None were even a couple of feet away. A tiny frosted glass window high up to her right, a single fluorescent light in the ceiling, and the floor was a hard vinyl that would withstand a power-hose. The cubicle reeked of disinfectant.

The prisoner transportation vehicle idled in the compound for another ten minutes before it began to move. It wheezed and jerked back and forth as the driver manoeuvred it in the tight space. The journey took over an hour, giving Emily plenty of time to think.

Two years. Probably reduced if she behaved and met all the criteria for early release at the twelve month point. She'd asked her solicitor if she would be eligible for electronic tagging, formally known as a Home Detention Curfew. He'd said it was possible she could be released with a tag as early as six months into her sentence but that depended upon her behaviour. One of the conditions was that she would have to stay at an agreed address between the hours of 19:00 and 07:00 every night. This was such an incentive that Emily vowed she'd be the model prisoner. She'd attend every class and rehabilitation session on offer, she'd work hard, keep her head down and stay out of trouble.

But for her mental wellbeing, she thought it best to antici-pate being incarcerated for twelve months, minimum. In that year there was so much she would miss. Birthdays, Christ-mas, the kids' exams, to name but a few. Her daughter was fourteen, she'd need help and advice with her emotions, maybe even relationships. Her husband was completely useless in that regard. Her son was a year older; how would all this affect him? She had no idea, he was such a closed shop.

Would she be able to rejoin the practice? She'd contacted the senior partners but they were typically non-committal. Would another practice take her? Would her family have to move house? City? *Country?*

She didn't even consider if they could go back to their church. She knew these people inside out. Catholic they may be, but Christian? Not a chance.

As the vehicle swayed along, her head nodded. Sleep would have been easy. But she sat up straight, shook herself out of it but couldn't erase the one thought that constantly danced round her brain.

I'm innocent. I didn't take the money. I know I didn't.

And of course she hadn't. But not many people believed her. Her husband, kids, parents, sister; they knew she would never have done it. But the people at the church? Her boss? Colleagues? Even some of her friends? 'She's guilty'.

At the first meeting with her solicitor he'd asked her outright and looked her straight in the eye at the same time.

She'd said, 'No. I promise you, I'm not a thief.' He appeared to accept that.

Their problem was she had no real defence, whereas the prosecution attacked her story from several angles. She was the treasurer; she had access to the church account; no counter-signature was necessary on electronic transfers. The destination account was in her husband's name, in their bank. And then there was that damned all-inclusive, business class holiday *to fucking Mexico.* And all she could offer in return was *I can earn that amount in six months. Tops. Why would I steal it? And why on God's green earth would I donate it to promote euthanasia?*

Easily countered, of course. Wealthy women will shoplift nonsensical items like a pair of tights and it's nothing to do with whether or not they can afford them.

The vehicle slowed, turned sharply to the left, bumped over a sleeping policeman then stopped for a few seconds before moving on. Emily strained to see out of the window and could just make out the tip of a yellow barrier, blurred by the glass.

The last thing she considered before the engine was switched off was this. *I didn't do it, so who did? And more importantly, why?* This question tormented her every day. Kept her awake night after night. *Why? Why? Why?*

She'd given up on *How?* That was beyond her. But it had to be complex, and therefore expensive. Someone disliked her so much they'd paid a lot of money to make this happen to her. And she hadn't a clue who that was. None whatsoever.

In the last couple of weeks Emily had developed a morbid fascination for TV documentaries about prisons. UK, all-female prisons in particular. These programmes often adver-tised companion websites containing detailed information on police, court and prison procedures so everything was out there.

As a result, when she and four other prisoners were processed nothing was a surprise to her. The female prison officers were firm but essentially kind. That was until a young blonde, about nineteen, mouthed off at them. The officers' response to the woman was harsh and instant, leaving Emily and the others in absolutely no doubt they were not to be messed with.

They took her clothes away except her underwear. Emily had known to wear plain white cotton, anything else she would lose. Then the officers told her to strip, the intimate search was the first real physical indignity she had experienced.

Emily had this misconceived notion of spending her day helping her fellow inmates. She was a doctor, an experienced GP. They would come to her with their ailments and concerns. She'd dole out comfort and advice and send them away feeling a lot better about themselves. They would look up to her, respect her, appreciate everything she did for them.

But once she was installed on the wing her crashing naïvety was punctured in less than an hour.

Unfortunately for Emily, the other inmates didn't give a toss that she was a doctor. The jungle drums were beating; she was a thief. Furthermore she was a successful electronic thief, who'd embezzled over £50,000. And if she could steal that amount, she could steal more. Much more.

She was surrounded that evening by four inmates who were outwardly friendly, they wanted to know how she'd done it. When she explained she hadn't stolen the money, that she was innocent, they laughed at her. 'Course you are, doc. Now spill the beans.'

'No, honestly, you have to believe me. I didn't steal the

money and I've no idea who did. Or how they did it. I was set up.'

In an instant, the women's attitude changed. Their previous good humour vanished. Stony expressions, dead eyes. As one, they turned their backs on her. It was as if she'd ceased to exist.

The following morning Emily was in her cell trying to concentrate on a book. Two inmates appeared in the doorway. Neither was particularly tall but they carried themselves like boxers, light on their feet, hands loose and ready to move. They left a small space between them. Emily's cellmate immediately rose from her bunk, hurried forward and slipped sideways through the gap, eyes on the floor. A heavier woman with short red hair pushed into the cell, her two lieutenants followed her in and just before they obscured her view Emily noticed three or four others blocking the doorway. They were all facing out into the wing, but their role was clear, block anyone from seeing inside.

Later, curled up on her bunk, her hands jammed between her thighs in an attempt to salve the pain, Emily was down to the occasional sob. The redhead's words looped round in her head. 'Tell me how you did it, doc, and we can be partners in future "transactions". Then you get protection from all the other nasty cows in here who'll want a taste of what we've just had. Otherwise, this happens again tomorrow, and every day after that until you do tell us.'

The woman kept her promise. It didn't matter where Emily was in the wing, they isolated her. They were extremely clever about it, there was never a prison officer in sight. Other inmates immediately switched their attention away or became strangely preoccupied. Emily knew better than to shout for help or create any commotion.

But on the fourth day she was ready for them. She stayed

in her cell all day until they came for her. As the redhead was pushing her way into the cell, Emily stood up and in a couple of fluid swipes her tee shirt and trousers hit the floor. She wasn't wearing underwear. She leaned back against the table and lifted her arms way out to her sides. 'There's nothing I can tell you because like I've already explained, I didn't steal that money. So whatever you're going to do to me, get on with it.' Then she turned, bent forward, placed her palms flat on the bunk and moved her feet until they were wide apart.

Nothing happened.

She glanced over her shoulder to find the redhead giving her a ferocious glare. Nobody moved for a couple of seconds until the woman sniffed loudly. Then she wheeled away and the three of them barged their way through the startled group outside. One of them looked back just in time to see Emily pulling on her trousers. She picked up her tee shirt and stared at the other prisoner, who immediately dropped her gaze. Before the shaking became uncontrollable she put her clothes on, sat down on her bunk with her back to the wall and pulled her thighs up until they touched her chest. She hugged her shins and laid her forehead on her knees.

'Three hundred and sixty-one days to go, Emily. Only three hundred and sixty-one days.'

CHAPTER FORTY-SEVEN

*T*HE DOCTOR HAS BEEN SENTENCED *to two years behind bars.*

Only two?

It's hard to take in. I'm livid.

Had it been four years reduced to two for good behaviour, I could have accepted that. But two, down to one, and possibly another few months off while she is at home with a tag on her ankle. She could be free in only six or eight months.

I am close to punching something but I reign in my anger and clear my mind. I know now that the blame for my overblown expectations lies with the pompous know-it-all egotists at the church. Barrack room lawyers, all of them. I should never have listened. But I did, and that was my own stupid fault. I will not be caught like that again.

So, it is fortunate that I have a backup plan. A final step I can put in place to ensure, as best I can, that Doctor Emily O'Keefe serves her full sentence.

No remission. No license. No tag.

No freedom, and definitely not before it's due.

I pick up my phone, perform a number of Google searches. In minutes I have all the information I need.

Two full years, Doctor. That's what you will serve.

It means running an almighty risk, but it is certainly one I am willing to take.

I have no choice.

CHAPTER FORTY-EIGHT

Anyone in Leith who's familiar with the dodgy side of the local tracks knows where this drug-dealing little scrote drinks. So we walk into the pub, spot him at the bar and march right up to him.

As we approach, a woman standing next to our target lays her drink down on the bar and moves off in the direction of the toilets. I hear heels clicking on the floor until the loo door swings shut behind her.

'Hello Spider.' I hold out my warrant card to confirm what he already knows. The filth, that's me and Steph, have invaded his inner sanctum. Steph's about eight stone soaking wet but I've seen her taking down six-foot nutcases so I'm quite relaxed, despite the alien surroundings. We're here because the aforementioned scrote was the guy our colleagues spotted in earnest conversation with Luca Contini just before they lifted the teenager for possession with intent to supply.

I check the place out. It's as black as the Earl of Hell's waistcoat, mainly because all the windows have been blocked up to provide as much wall space as possible for the televisions that encircle the walls. There must be at least twelve, some of them practically butting up against their neighbours. Every sport imaginable is being broadcast, although why the patrons who frequent this dump would be remotely interested in cricket is way beyond me.

When I'd said 'Hello Spider', a titter rippled through the bar but when the subject whipped his head round it stopped dead, as if someone had pulled the plug. The choreography was impressive.

Spider. It would be neat if he'd been given this nickname because his surname was Webb. But sadly, no. When he was but a nipper, still a wannabee scrote, his cruel, cruel mates discovered he was petrified of the eight-legged variety and the name stuck. These days, not many people risk calling him that to his face, but by far and away it's the easiest way to get under his skin.

I smile. I'm not exactly sure what beatific looks like but I give it my very best shot. If I keep this up my cheeks might split so I address him again. 'I need a word, Spider.'

He sticks his neck out and exposes the full panorama of his disgusting teeth. 'My name's James Kilbride,' his eyes track up and down, '*bag-lady*. You'd be smart to remember that.'

'Ouch, Spider.' I hold my hand in front of my face like a fan, and flutter my eyelashes. 'I know I'm not exactly Kate Middleton material, but "bag-lady"? That's gotta hurt.'

He whirls a hand around in a *whatever* gesture and spins back on his bar stool. I notice he has to perch right at the front of the seat or his wee legs would be left dangling. He jabs a finger at a beer tap and although the barman moves towards it, he doesn't shift quite as quickly as I thought he might. Perhaps James Kilbride isn't as big a man as he imagines he is. Or used to be.

As Spider sups the head off his beer, I move into his eye

line. 'I'm here to talk to you about Luca Contini. And before you think about saying who, don't bother.'

He grins. Turns to face me. 'The PF's laddie. Kicked his own bucket.' He spreads his arms. 'What's that got to do with me?'

'Nothing. Unless *you* set him up to take a drugs fall.'

He grins again. I wish he wouldn't, it's most unsettling.

'And why would I do that?'

'I don't know. But it's curious you were talking to him just before we busted the boy.' I take half a step forward. 'And I know my colleagues have already interviewed you about that but I don't actually give a rat's arse about you because I'm going to assume you *did* set him up. So all I want you to do is give me the nod. Then I'm out of here because I'm only interested in finding out if that boy was innocent. Nothing else.'

I deliberately step back, out of his space and out of range of his repulsive breath. A movement over to my left catches my eye. Steph's too, by her reaction. It's the woman who sloped off to the toilet, heading for the side exit. Her drink is still on the bar, G&T most probably. Interesting.

'So, James, what's it to be? Give me that nod, and you'll have one in the bank on my account.'

He stares at me. Raises his eyes skywards. Pretends to think. Meanwhile I'm wondering how hard to hit him. Then he gives me his answer.

'Fuck off, pig.' He jerks a thumb at Steph. 'And take piglet with you.' Steph stays relaxed, it would have been a monumental shock if our visit wasn't commemorated by some form of insult.

I sigh. Worth a try but being honest, this has panned out exactly as I expected.

'Have it your own way, Spider. It would've cost you

nothing to tell me, but as far as I'm concerned you're in negative equity. And one way or the other, I'll call it in.'

He wobbles his hands and makes a 'Woooo' sound.

I won't be demeaning myself by asking him to change his mind but I do give him a second or two, just on the off chance. But no. Steph and I exchange glances and I follow her as she weaves through the tables towards the door.

We're almost out when we pass an older bloke, slouched at a table by the wall. He's deliberately tapping a fingernail on his phone, it's lying face up. He catches Steph's eye, checks out the bar and spins the phone round. I watch as she reads what he's typed. They lock eyes then he hits the backspace key until the text is deleted. Steph tilts her head toward the street but he hits her with an enormous grin that says, *Behave yourself, lassie*. She taps the table a couple of times, like a snooker player acknowledging his opponent's shot, and carries on towards the door.

I wait 'til we're in the car before I ask her what he'd typed.

'"Everybody knows he set boy up. Was paid to do it."'

I'm happy now. 'Progress, Steph.'

I start the engine and indicate to pull out. 'Now all we have to do is find out who paid the nasty wee shite.'

Then I check the rear-view mirror. 'And more importantly, why.'

CHAPTER FORTY-NINE

SOPHIE GARDINER WAS WALKING down the stairs in her house when the doorbell rang. Without first checking who was outside she opened the door, and when she saw who was standing there she was stunned. No other word for it.

'Hello Soph. Can I come in?' He looked at her, added something else.

She didn't hear him. 'Sorry, what?'

'I made a big mistake breaking off our engagement. Can we try again?'

———

THEY SAT FACING each other in the living room. McLure was on the sofa, lounging back, left ankle resting on his right thigh. Sophie sat upright in an armchair, feet and knees tight together, hands clasped in her lap. Her initial shock at him turning up after several weeks' absence was beginning to subside. Now she was curious.

She was perfectly well aware his opening gambit 'I made a

big mistake leaving you' was utter bullshit. She could see it in his face and hear it in his voice. He wanted something from her, she was sure of it. And instead of flustering, she was surprised to find she grew calmer. She reasoned if she stayed quiet while he said whatever he had to say, she would have time and space to frame her response.

She was scared her voice might let her down so she coughed politely into her palm before asking, 'Cup of tea?' A masterstroke she thought, giving herself another few minutes' grace.

'I could murder one.' He rose at the same time as her but she put a hand out.

'No, I'll get it. You sit there for a minute. I have to pop to the loo.' She was pleased with that too, even more time to think.

———

ABOUT SIX MONTHS PREVIOUSLY, her mother had suffered a stroke. Since that day, Sophie had spent almost all of her spare time helping her father. Taking him shopping, cooking his meals, sitting with him as he visited his wife in hospital. Every day. She was under a tremendous amount of strain and had no spare time for Iain. After several weeks of putting him off, then not answering his calls and texts, she wasn't surprised in the slightest when he left a voicemail to say he was ending the relationship.

She suspected he'd been searching for an excuse and realised she'd presented him with a beauty; giftwrapped with a big red bow. Given her personal circumstances, at first she reckoned he had been callous but then discovered she didn't miss him. Not one bit. Her father was her priority and his welfare was paramount.

But Sophie and Iain had things to sort out so they arranged to meet up for a coffee. On her way there she examined her feelings to see if she might try to win him back but as soon as she laid eyes on him she knew they were dead in the water. Alexander, her younger brother, said it had been a narrow escape for both of them.

During their relationship she had spent most weekends in Kinghorn. One evening they'd gone out for a meal in a local restaurant. Iain drank too much and became garrulous, boasting about how wealthy he was and how he'd bought the house and the McLaren outright. Sophie rarely concerned herself with Iain's affairs but was intrigued, so, back at the house she kept the conversation and the drink flowing. He blethered on, dropping names all over the place, talking as much to the room as to her.

Then he let something slip, but it was half a sentence later before he realised. He made a half-arsed attempt to backtrack, failing miserably. But Sophie had noticed. Looking away quickly, she left a gap of two or three seconds before saying, 'Hmmm? What was that, Iain?'

'Nothing. Doesn't matter.'

Within minutes, Sophie affected a series of exaggerated yawns declaring it was time she went to bed. She filled up his glass with export-strength gin and left him sprawled on the sofa, a slack grin on his face, his arm wavering like it was too puny to bear the weight of his drink.

The following weekend, Iain caught a train over to Edinburgh to watch a Scotland rugby international. It was a corporate bash so Sophie had the house to herself for the rest of the day. She texted him just before kick-off to say have a great time. He replied with a line of beer emojis, a rugby ball and a clock showing twelve o'clock. She sent back a thumbs up, then walked through to his study.

She stood in the doorway, ran her tongue over her lips and wiped her palms on her jeans before crossing the floor to sit in his swivel chair. For a while she didn't move, apart from gently rotating the chair from side to side. Should she do this? Would Iain find out? Did she desperately *need* to prove there was any truth in what he'd said the week before when he was drunk?

Yes, she thought. I do.

She felt like a spy, lifting and examining every item on or around the desk. Placing them carefully back in their positions. It wasn't long before she found the filing cabinet key in a box of paperclips, and a green folded Post-it with the access password to the PC. Once it booted up she right-clicked the *Word* icon. The third file on the pinned list was *Recipes*.

That made her laugh; Iain struggled to open a tin of beans. The file contained a list of all his IDs and passwords so now she had free reign. She glanced up at the clock, the game still had half an hour to go. She checked her phone. Scotland were winning so she pinged him a smiley face and another thumbs up. She kept an eye on the screen until he replied a minute or so later with a line of foaming beer glasses.

Then she wasn't nervous at all.

For the next hour and a half, Sophie conducted a fairly exhaustive search of Iain's PC and his paper filing system until she was satisfied she'd discovered everything she needed to know. Sophie wasn't any form of computer whizz but she'd been planning this for a week so she'd been practicing on her PC at home. Before she viewed any files on Iain's recently opened lists on *Word* and *Excel*, she photographed them. Then before closing down she opened and closed all those files in exactly the same order so when she checked the lists and compared them to the photos, nothing had changed. Also, she hadn't saved or amended anything so the *Save* dates hadn't altered.

She was fully aware she would have left footprints on the system that could easily be found by someone with the right knowledge. Iain was certainly savvy enough but Sophie was banking on the fact that he actually considered her to be an idiot woman and wouldn't imagine she would ever be interested in hacking into his PC. And certainly not capable of such a feat.

In the evening she strolled through the village, trying to work out how she felt about being engaged to a ruthless serial blackmailer. The answer was strangely ambivalent, but also that the whole situation required careful thought rather than demanding an immediate explanation from him. In her gut she also felt her newfound knowledge, along with the documents and screenshots she'd saved to a USB drive, would eventually come in useful.

She just didn't know when. Or how.

———

Sophie put her empty mug down on the coffee table. She brushed a shortbread crumb off her skirt. 'So let me see if I've got this right, Iain. You made a big mistake breaking up with me, you want us to get back together *and* you'd like to stay here for a few days. It's a bit of a coincidence, if you don't mind me saying.'

He clasped his hands together and stared down at them. 'I can see how it looks, Soph ...'

Damn right you can.

He turned to face her. 'But it's not like that, honest.'

Honest? That'll be a first.

'I've been thinking about this for a while and the ... em ... situation I have at Kinghorn doesn't have anything to do with us. It's like you say, complete coincidence.'

Yeah, right. Maybe I'm not the brightest bulb but I'm not completely stupid, you arrogant patronising bastard!

She remained silent, thinking. Then, in a flurry, she placed the mugs and plates on a tea tray and stood up. 'As you can imagine, this is more than a bit surprising. So I'm not sure, I'll need time to think.'

'I'm kinda stuck, Soph.'

She took a couple of steps towards the kitchen then stopped. 'Maybe a hotel would be better for a couple of days?'

He flushed. 'Temporary cash flow problem, I'm afraid.'

Cash flow? Just put it on a credit card ...

And then the penny dropped.

You've been sussed out, Iain. The police, maybe? Or one of your marks?

'I'll put these away,' she said. 'Back in a minute.'

She walked into the kitchen and elbowed the door closed. She leaned against the sink, eyes on the door in case he followed her. Flashbacks came to her: him, bragging, drunk on his sofa; her, in his office, searching through files; images, documents, copied for safe keeping; and information she would be able to use when the time was right. She smiled, inside. Because that time was coming closer, she could sense it.

She pushed herself upright and breezed into the living room. Iain was over by the window, hands in his jeans pockets, looking out into the street.

'You have a visitor.' He grinned. 'Well, this'll be interesting.'

————

By the time Sophie opened her front door, Iain was on the sofa again.

A wave of cool air washed into the living room as a woman

appeared in the doorway. One step into the room, she stopped dead. 'What the fuck is *he* doing here?'

Iain's expression was half smirk, half sneer but his eyes registered surprise when Sophie said, 'Iain. Go out for a smoke.'

'But—'

'*Now*, Iain.'

He snared his jacket off a chair and marched out the room, slamming the door behind him.

Sophie watched him leaving. She'd always wondered why he wore a biker jacket because he'd admitted to her that he'd never been on a motorbike. She shook her head and turned round.

The woman stood with one hand on the back of an armchair, the other one on her hip. Her expression couldn't possibly have been misinterpreted.

Sophie lifted both hands in the air, palms facing away. 'Cath, you're my sister. You care about me, I get that. But trust me, I know what I'm doing.' There was steel in her tone.

Cath curled her lip. 'Whatever you say, Sophie.'

———

LATER THAT EVENING SOPHIE SAID, 'You'll have to go out tomorrow night, my nephew's bringing his new girlfriend to meet me.'

Iain didn't take his eyes off the TV. 'But I don't want to go out. Anyway, where would I go? Oh, lovely shot.'

Sophie glanced at the screen. She couldn't see the point in golf. A good walk spoiled, as someone had once quipped.

She tried another angle. 'It's just that I want to meet her by myself, I'm not sure how she'll be.' *With you here.*

They were both on the sofa. He leaned closer and laid his

palm on her thigh. She looked down at his hand, then at him. He smirked and moved it away. 'I'll behave, Soph. Promise.'

She lifted a magazine, opened it, flicked through a few pages. Iain being here was not what she wanted but she couldn't exactly throw him out. Not yet. She wasn't planning to let him weasel his way back into her life permanently but didn't see any harm in letting him think he could.

Sophie was a complex creature, often fragile and lacking in confidence. Life had been tough since her mother had taken ill. She tried her best to be strong when she was with her dad, and that was often, but summoning and portraying that strength took a lot out of her. It didn't come naturally so the minute she dropped him off somewhere or left him at his house she bottomed out and needed time to regroup. Sophie's job was her neutral zone; she was a receptionist in a small company. Nine to five, minimal responsibility, zero stress. The only situation where she was totally positive, always on top of her game, was with her voluntary work. She supported women and children who had escaped from abusive relationships. Sophie discovered she was perfect for the role: empathetic, undemonstrative and compassionate, precisely when these traits were required. She came home after every shift feeling invigorated, appreciated and most importantly, worthwhile.

But Iain turning up like this would become a major problem for her if she didn't maintain her equilibrium. She knew if she stayed on top of the situation and kept one step ahead of him, she would probably be fine. So far she was still in control, but the night looming ahead was critical. She was sailing into uncharted waters and couldn't be certain which version of herself would be at the helm.

But whatever else, Sophie wasn't naïve. Her relationship with Iain had lasted a little over eighteen months and she knew him inside out. Tonight, he would be angling for sex but she couldn't allow that to happen. Time to think and time to plan were absolutely necessary for her wellbeing both in the short and long term.

So she made up the spare room for him. He would argue, naturally, but she must hold firm.

Tomorrow might be different. No, she thought, it *will* be different. It was all a question of inner strength, control and timing. Especially if the point was fast approaching where the information she possessed about him and his criminal activities could be put to good use.

CHAPTER FIFTY

I'VE PULLED the team together in a briefing room on the second floor of our historic but dilapidated HQ. It's a decent room and for a change there's nothing wrong with the venetian blinds. That's because they're missing. Luckily, there's not much chance of us being blinded by the sun. For one, it's pouring down outside and for two, the brick wall of the adjacent building is only three feet from the window.

We're here to talk about the case that Tobias brought to my attention during his 'unusual crime' research. It concerns Mandy Westbrook, who has accused a man of assaulting and raping her. He is Kim Seung-Min, the prime and only suspect in DS Keown's allegedly sub-standard investigation. Kim is awaiting trial but continues to protest his innocence.

'Okay folks, listen up. I've discussed the case with Jeff and here's the deal. If I can convince him that Keown's investigation was flawed, he'll consider talking to her boss about going back to the Fiscal and asking for a review. Tobias, before we get right into it, for Steph and Andrew's benefit, talk us through the key elements.'

Tobias studies his notes for a moment then looks up, all business-like. 'Ms Westbrook lives in Dundee. She was visiting Edinburgh for the weekend and rented a flat, an Airbnb, on Willowbrae Road.' He's talking about a main route out of the city, heading east. 'She planned to hook up with friends in town that evening but instead, she started talking to Kim in a new bar in the Grassmarket. It's called GM2. This was at approximately seven thirty. She was with him for the remainder of the Friday evening until nearly midnight, cruising bars in that area and down the Royal Mile in particular.'

'She didn't meet up with her friends?' says Steph.

'No.'

'Do we know who they are?'

'We don't.'

'Why not?' asks Andrew.

Tobias shrugged. 'There is a note on the case file with reference to these friends. The decision was not to follow up. Ms Westbrook didn't meet up with them so they wouldn't be able to comment.'

'You're *not* serious?' I say.

'I am German. Naturally, I'm serious.' But he winks at me as he's speaking.

I shake my head. This is lazy policing by Deirdre Keown, and it bugs the hell out of me. Still, it's the first chink in her investigation. Here's hoping it's not the last.

Tobias picks up again. 'They took a taxi to her Airbnb. They were having consensual sex then things changed. He didn't have a condom and she told him they had to stop. No condom, no sex. He tried to persuade her, she still said no but he became violent. Hit her on the face, her stomach and her ribs. Then he raped her.'

Steph scowls and jots a few words on her pad. 'Did she fight back?'

Tobias reads from his notes. 'In her statement she said: "I wanted to fight him, honest I did but he was too strong. And he'd already smacked me about. So then I thought if I lie completely still, don't make eye contact, become just a limp body and don't react or respond to anything he does then maybe he'll lose interest. I don't know if it worked but he finished and climbed off me."'

'Then what?' I ask.

'"He was standing by the side of the bed, still naked, checking his phone. I was seriously pissed off when he did that and I lashed out, kicked him right in the balls. He went down, I grabbed my handbag and ran into the bathroom. I screamed that I was phoning the police. I heard him leaving and when I was told officers were on the way, I waited a few minutes then came out."'

We all fall silent; rape is a despicable crime. Steph and I are still quiet when Andrew asks, 'Tobias. Why do you think this case falls under Mel's "unusual" classification?'

Tobias is facing the window. He stares at the brickwork outside while he gathers his thoughts.

'I believe our colleague, DS Keown, based her entire investigation on hard evidence. And of course, that is what we must do. But I also believe if there are circumstantial elements which place that evidence in any doubt, we should examine these to see if the evidence remains solid. My view is that DS Keown discounted several aspects that are not evidence-based. But in my opinion, they are worthy of further consideration.'

He brings his gaze back into the room and addresses me directly. 'Because I am not one hundred per cent certain that Kim is guilty of this crime.'

I'm like a kid on Christmas morning, desperate to rip the paper off the major present. The one that's definitely a bike. But I desist and go for the boring pyjamas from Auntie Polly instead. 'Before we speak about that, does everything stack up forensically?'

Tobias flicks forward a couple of pages. 'Yes. The forensic medical examination of Ms Westbrook and subsequent biological analysis suggested that Kim had sex with her. His DNA was detected on her body. Semen, pubic hair and skin particles from in and around her vagina, and traces of saliva on her neck, her throat and the top part of her left breast. Plus, two head hairs with follicles were recovered from the bed linen. His clothes were cotton and denim, and although the biologist discovered trace evidence of textile fibres, she described them as generic. She compared them with samples of Kim's clothing that were seized when he was arrested but could not state categorically that they were a unique match. The report also mentions there were signs of early bruising to her jaw, her ribs and her shoulder, all on her left side.'

He looks up. Three pairs of eyes are glued to him.

'The final element relates to her underwear, you would call them pants?'

'That depends how big they are,' says Steph, deadpan.

Tobias raises an eyebrow and continues. 'Ms Westbrook stated that when she exited the bathroom, her dress was on the floor but she couldn't *find* her pants. It was assumed he had taken them as a trophy but they were not in his flat. However, a search was conducted and they were discovered in a communal waste bin adjacent to the building.'

'That's more than a bit odd, isn't it?' says Andrew. 'Why take them in the first place then drop them in a bin right next to where you live?' He jots down a note and catches my eye. I don't have to ask him to follow up.

My turn. 'Footprints? Fingerprints?'

Tobias shakes his head. 'Nothing apart from a smudge on a door handle that was inconclusive.'

'Not a complete surprise, I suppose. Some rentals are all laminate flooring and minimalist furniture. Plus, they might be cleaned from top to bottom every few days.' I motion Tobias to move on.

'Next, CCTV and digital forensics. It is beyond dispute that the couple were together for approximately four hours and twenty minutes that evening. There are multiple CCTV sightings in bars and on the route between the Grassmarket and the lower part of the Royal Mile, specifically The Canongate. Digital forensic analysis picks up Kim's mobile phone along the same route. The phone can be tracked along certain points between The Canongate and the Airbnb, and was stationary at the apartment at a time that matches the alleged assault.'

'Does the analysis suggest he then travelled from the Airbnb to his own flat?'

Tobias nods. 'Yes. And again, the phone can be tracked at the appropriate times.'

I tap a fingernail on the table top. 'I just want to make sure we all realise that the cell towers have tracked the journey the *phone* made but we can't assume it was in Kim's possession the whole time.'

Steph pipes up. 'Building on that, what was Kim's version of events? Because I'm assuming he's said something completely different.'

Tobias consults his notes. 'They were heading for the last pub on the Royal Mile. They had agreed to have one more quick drink because the pub was about to close but they stopped, they were kissing in a bus shelter. Then before they reached the pub, she pulled him into a lane called Cuthbert's Close. It is on the left of the Royal Mile, not far from the Scottish Parliament Buildings. In there, she performed oral sex on him.' He shakes his head then carries on. 'He said it was over quickly. Then he was surprised because she ran from the close.'

'*What*? Without saying anything?'

'No, she shouted to him that she would meet him in the pub. She needed to pee and he should get the drinks.'

Steph shakes her head. 'Let me guess, she didn't go into the pub.'

'He can't be certain about that because while he was ordering the drinks he discovered he'd lost his phone. He thought he must have dropped it in the close, so he went back but he couldn't find it. And although he asked the barman to watch out for her, she wasn't there when he came back. He assumed she had left and hailed a cab.'

'And there's no CCTV in that pub, is there?'

Tobias stares at me. 'No. But how did you know that?'

'Because, it's the closest pub to the Parliament buildings and I heard there was, how can I put it, "influence" exerted by certain MSPs, who frequent the establishment, to have all CCTV removed. So they keep their little skulduggeries and peccadillos private, if you get my drift.'

They do, by the gobsmacked looks on their faces.

'But back to Kim,' I say. 'What did he do then?'

'He waited for ten or fifteen minutes while he finished his drink then the bar was closing so he headed off home. It's about twenty minutes on foot.'

Tobias places his pen on his notebook and looks to me for direction.

'Thanks, Tobias,' I say. 'Right, I want to return to ... what were your words, "other elements"? Circumstantial. Not related to forensics.'

We all listen without comment as he explains his rationale and what he's discovered from examining the case files. And within half an hour of him finishing the four of us are heading out to talk to a variety of people.

CHAPTER FIFTY-ONE

My phone is wedged between my shoulder and my ear as I scribble down a few notes. Steph's on the line, bringing me up to speed with what she and Tobias have been up to. I nod, more than happy with what she's told me.

'Thanks, Steph. And you too, Tobias. Brilliant job. Let's pick up when we're all back in the office.'

I end the call and unfasten my seatbelt as I turn to Andrew. 'Time to speak to our man Kim.'

Kim Seung-Min buzzes us in and welcomes us at the door to his flat. He shakes hands with a firm grip and bows a little from the waist. He's wearing a smile like he's bumped into an old friend.

We sit at the kitchen table while he makes coffee for three. On the table are a couple of cardboard boxes containing flyers relating to Sir Robert Parker's charity. Andrew lifts one out and examines it. He flips it over to read the reverse then drops it back in the box.

Kim has dark hair as you might expect, and a diamond stud in his left earlobe. White shirt open at the neck, silver cufflinks, charcoal jeans and highly polished black shoes that click as he crosses the kitchen floor. I wonder briefly why he dresses so formally at home. Maybe he's been out or was just about to go.

Now seated opposite us, he looks at me expectantly so I kick the conversation off. 'I'm seeking authorisation to review the charges you're facing.' He opens his mouth to speak but I hold up my hand. 'I don't want to give you false hope, but we're definitely not here to cement the case against you. In fact it's quite the opposite. So we'd like to ask you some more questions to see if we can bring anything new to light.'

His natural smile falters. This has come right out of the blue and I can see he doesn't know whether to believe me or not. I could keep trying to persuade him but I figure if I crack on, that'll hopefully convince him we're on the level.

'I know you've been through all this with my colleagues but can you please talk us through your evening with Mandy Westbrook. Include everything you think might be relevant and leave us to judge whether it is or not.'

Here's what Kim has to say.

He was already at the bar in GM2 when Mandy came in. He didn't notice her at first then he spotted two lads eyeing her up, doing their best not to appear obvious and failing miserably. The place wasn't particularly busy. Kim was seated at the rectangular island bar, a couple of places away from a corner. She was sitting a similar distance along the adjacent side drinking a Cosmopolitan, and each time the sliding doors swished open she glanced over her shoulder. She took a sip every now and again, like she was killing time.

Eventually, she caught his eye just as someone new came through the door. She took another quick look before turning back to Kim. She raised an eyebrow, made a big deal of checking her watch, shook her head and drew a fingernail across her throat. Kim laughed and signalled a mind-if-I join-you gesture. She smiled and patted a spare barstool to her left, so he lifted his beer and moved over to sit beside her.

Kim said Mandy was friendly and outgoing, precisely his type. The fact that she was good-looking and sexy was a bonus as far as he was concerned. She told him she was supposed to be meeting a date but it was fairly obvious she'd been stood up. They chatted for a while and she admitted she was glad this man hadn't shown. Kim took that as a compliment.

So they were both on their own with no plans for the evening. After drinks in a host of different bars she began coming on to him.

I say, 'So the signals were clear enough?'

'Certainly, yes.'

'Forgive me, but there's something I'm curious about. Why do you frequent that area for your Friday nights out? I mean the Grassmarket, the Royal Mile, not exactly trendy are they? Why not the West End or George St?' I point at how he's dressed. 'More up-market, stylish. Places where the Edinburgh glitterati strut their stuff.'

'That is my Saturday night. I wear a suit, dress up. I like the Old Town on a Friday. Casual. Great buzz. Some pubs have live music. Lots of students, tourists. It's fun.'

Lots of pick-up options, more like.

I study Kim while he's talking and I can't help thinking there is nothing whatsoever about this young man that suggests he is guilty of assault and rape. His social life appears so uncomplicated, so relaxed. So modern. To be fair, he's early twenties so why not?

He carries on by saying their route was exactly as I'd just described, until she pulled him into Cuthbert's Close.

Andrew asks, 'Were you expecting that?'

'No. I was about to invite her to my flat.'

'Did you know where she was staying that night? Was she not expected home at some point?'

'She told me she was staying with her friend, who wouldn't be worried about her, who would know she was out doing her own thing. Apparently this was normal. For her.'

My turn. 'So where did you think you lost your phone?'

'I was sure I'd dropped it in the close. I left the pub to try to find it but it was too dark so I thought I would go back early the next morning.'

'Then, after she did a runner, you walked home. Why not take a taxi?'

'I am happy to walk if it is not raining. Nowhere in town is very far from here and I don't see the need to pay for taxis.'

Andrew flips to a different page in his notes. 'But then you found the phone on the staircase when you arrived home.' He looks up at Kim. 'How is that possible?'

Kim sighs. Screws up his face. Gives his head a shake. 'For me, it is a mystery. I said that to your colleague but she didn't believe me. How could anyone possibly leave it there? How would they know it was mine? Or where I lived? I could not answer. I had no proof that is what happened so I can see her point.'

Once more I find myself thinking, *he's accused of a violent sexual crime and yet he is so sanguine.* My shit-detecting radar is on full power. Something's not right here.

There's a lull in the conversation. Andrew is leafing through his notes, Kim's watching him and I'm still throwing all this around in my head.

'Kim,' I say. 'You're charged with an extremely serious crime yet you appear ... relaxed. Very accepting of the situation. Why is that?'

He draws in a deep breath, hunches up his shoulders, lets them drop again. 'Sir Robert believes I am innocent and tells me I should have faith in the justice system. I did *not* attack this woman. My solicitor will defend me in court and they will find the truth.'

Andrew comes in with a serious point. 'Forensic evidence retrieved from the Airbnb and from the woman's body tested positive for your DNA. That is compelling.'

Kim fixes him with a look. 'Yes. They found semen, hair, skin samples.' He laughs but without a trace of mirth. 'She gave me a blowjob so of course they found my DNA. It is not difficult to understand how that was possible. But I was never in that flat and I did not have sex with her.' He jabs a finger in his chest. '*She* had sex with *me*.'

We all ponder for a moment then I ask, 'What was my colleague DS Keown's reaction?'

'She laughed. Apparently I was being ridiculous.'

'Okay, Kim. Let's just say I can see how your DNA *was* on the lower part of her body. And I'm talking here about semen and skin samples. But what about the traces of your saliva on her neck, her throat and her left breast? She was obviously fully clothed all during the evening so how did it get there?'

Kim leans forward and slaps the table. 'Hah! That is an excellent question and it is a question I could not answer before. But I have thought about it a lot and now I know.' He pauses and we both give him *Come on then* looks. He takes the hint. 'You know we stopped in a bus shelter, yes? We were kissing. And a bit of ... well, you know?'

A bit of anything in a bus shelter is ancient history as far as I'm concerned but I nod anyway.

He's become more animated. 'We had been there for a few minutes, I think. Anyway, she whispered in my ear that she loves to be licked. *Everywhere.* And I thought, I can't do that in a bus shelter so we should go to my flat. Anyway, she pulled my head down on to her neck and so that is what I did. I licked her neck and her ear, and she held me there, tight. She was making pleasure noises but there were people passing so I stopped. Then she took her hand where I licked her and rubbed it on her throat and over her breast. You know, inside her dress? Like this.'

He sticks his right hand in his shirt to demonstrate. We didn't need the illustration but this could be another nail in the forensic evidence coffin.

'Did you think that was strange?' I ask.

'I meet lots of women. Most like to have normal sex, some want kinky stuff. That was just a bit unusual.'

The man's honesty is disarming.

'Were you drunk?' I ask.

He turns to face me. Waggles his left hand. 'A bit. Not too much.' His eyes drop. 'I did have a joint later but it was a long time after she left me.'

I don't have to check my notes to confirm this is the first we've heard about Kim having a wee puff. I manage to keep my tone on an even keel. 'When did you smoke this joint?'

And Kim's answer gives us the exact point when Mandy Westbrook's allegations are blown right out of the water and clean over the horizon.

I glance over at Andrew. He doesn't appear to have registered the look but he's nodding purposefully to himself. While we're driving back to the office, he explains what he's thinking.

'Sounds good to me, sunshine,' I say. 'Crack on, and keep me posted.'

It takes him a few hours but, as always, Andrew comes up trumps.

CHAPTER FIFTY-TWO

'WE'RE STILL CHECKING Kim's movements for later that evening, Jeff, so I don't have all the answers yet. I need more time.'

My boss has called me to his office to discuss case priorities. One of the best things about working with Jeff is he always does his best to stop pressure from his lords and masters from filtering down to his team. But there's a limit and I'm guessing we've just about reached it. He gave me the opportunity to prove my suspicions were correct and it's time for me to come up with the goods. Knowing him like I do, I'll only have one chance at this so I pick and choose my words carefully.

'We've talked to a number of people and studied the evidence: forensic, digital *and* circumstantial, and in my opinion it does not prove "beyond reasonable doubt" that Kim Seung-Min raped Mandy Westbrook.'

Jeff steeples his fingers in his lap. 'You believe DS Keown's investigation was flawed?'

'In certain areas, yes.'

'I'm listening.'

'A young woman, twenty-five, comes from Dundee to Edinburgh for the weekend. She has tentative plans to meet friends. Instead, she goes into a pub herself. Her friends aren't in that pub, she hooks up with a guy, stays with him the whole evening and doesn't contact these friends to explain why she didn't meet them. Unfortunately, DS Keown didn't check Mandy's story with them. In fact, she didn't speak to them at all.'

Jeff's eyes widen but I don't push the point. 'Then, whether you believe his story or hers, she has sex with him either in Cuthbert's Close or in the Airbnb. He rapes her, she calls 999 and *still* she doesn't contact her friends. In fact, her mobile phone records show no telephone calls, SMS or emails – outgoing or incoming – from when she boarded the train in Dundee on Friday at 14:25, to when she returned there on Saturday at 16:05.'

'None at all?' Clearly Jeff considers this to be outlandish behaviour from a person under thirty.

'Nothing.' I let that sink in before continuing. 'Now, to be absolutely fair to DS Keown, she and I are working this from completely different angles. She's been led by forensic evidence, while I'm ignoring it for the moment. Or at least trying to work out how it could have been manufactured.'

'And that's because you think this is case number four in a series of set-ups that are all connected?'

'I do.'

'What would Ms Westbrook's motive be for falsely accusing Kim of assault and rape?'

'I don't know.' Then quickly, 'Yet.'

I press on before he takes me further down that road. 'Forensic evidence "suggests" Kim was in the Airbnb, "suggests" he had sex with her, and "suggests" he assaulted and raped her.'

'And you're "suggesting" he wasn't, and he didn't.'

'Actually, no. It's the *lack* of a solid chain of evidence that makes me believe he wasn't there. Let's think about this. The last CCTV sighting of the couple is them heading down the Royal Mile, before Cuthbert's Close and therefore before the pub. Then they're not seen again. Her story is they took a taxi to the Airbnb on Willowbrae Road. He says she gave him a blowjob in the close, disappeared before he could pull up his trousers but said she'd meet him in the pub. Then she didn't show. He had no idea where she was, didn't see any sign of a cab, couldn't find his phone so he walked off home.'

'Does anyone remember him in the pub?'

'No. I spoke to the barman who was on duty. It was throwing out time. He says it's always carnage at that time on a Friday night.'

Jeff pauses. Fiddles with his ear lobe. 'I know that pub. There's no CCTV, is there?'

Clearly the rumours have reached his ears too. 'Apparently not.'

'Taxi companies?'

'No record of any journeys from the Royal Mile to Willowbrae at that time.'

Jeff shrugs. At the weekend, some cabs will work off the grid, not signed into their control, picking up fares off the street until they decide to call it a night.

'Any sightings at the Airbnb?'

'Nope. That part of Willowbrae Road is exclusively residential and there are no private cameras on the block. Nobody saw them arriving or him leaving or heard any ruckus going on. Neighbours say they hardly ever hear noise from adjacent flats. Solid traditional construction, apparently.'

Jeff leans way back in his chair and contemplates the ceiling. He addresses his next question to a light fitting. 'Kim said he walked home from Cuthbert's Close. So where's home?'

'East London Street. In the new development just off the north side of Gayfield Square.'

Jeff laughs because the Square contains the police HQ for Edinburgh City Centre East. 'More than a tad ironic, wouldn't you say?' He pulls up a Google Map on his screen. 'I know roughly where Cuthbert's Close is but which route did he take home? And if he was on foot, surely he's on CCTV somewhere. That would prove his innocence, would it not?'

I point out the route Kim said he followed. There are dozens of these Old Town closes running off the Royal Mile. Some are dead ends but Cuthbert's Close leads on to a back road that's tucked away behind the Royal Mile. Kim would have crossed that, then followed a series of lanes, quiet streets and public parks to bring him out at the end of London Road. Two minutes on foot from there through Gayfield Square and he's home and dry. Andrew took his mountain bike along all the routes Kim could possibly have walked, and spotted only one private camera. It was above the front door of a pub, concentrating on the pavement right outside.

I point at Jeff's screen. 'Here's the first sighting of him on CCTV at the junction of London Road and Elm Row, directly opposite Gayfield Square. Oh, and by the way, the road bordering the Square was closed off all that weekend. A BT contractor was upgrading their network as part of the city centre fibre broadband project, they've been working in the area for a while.' Then I leave him to figure it out. He's a sharp cookie, is Jeff, so he gets it straight away.

'Ah. It doesn't matter if he walked from Cuthbert's Close or came by taxi from the Airbnb, he would have ended up at the same point, the end of London Road. If he's a lazy git, he could have stayed in the taxi while it detoured all the way round to his flat but probably quicker to jump out there and walk the rest. So the CCTV sighting simply confirms he was at that location, not which route he took to get there.'

He pauses for a second to consider this then shakes his head. 'I'm sorry, Mel, but I'm still of the opinion that the key factors are the forensic evidence tying him to the Airbnb, *and* that we can trace his phone from the Royal Mile to the Airbnb then from there to his flat at East London Street.'

Jeff studies his screen as if for inspiration. 'The timings, do they check out? From the last CCTV sighting on the Royal Mile, to when he was picked up again, including all the nonsense in between. Did he have enough time to go to the Airbnb, assault her and catch a cab to London Road?'

Damn. I was hoping he wouldn't ask that. Regrettably, I have no choice but to answer, 'Yes. It was tight but the timings stack up.'

'And you believe she sent him to the pub as a distraction, to keep him out of the way for a while?'

'I do, yes. She would have known he'd discover his phone was gone and would have been pretty certain he'd go back to search for it. Wouldn't you?'

He drums his fingernails on the table for what seems like an age. 'Sorry, Mel, but forensically it's a slam dunk and that's why the Fiscal was willing to bring a charge. I happen to think Deirdre's probably called it right. I was prepared to be convinced otherwise but ...'

I'm beginning to feel a bit like David, if Goliath had pinched the wee man's slingshot and asked him *Now what, pal?*

Jeff carries on. 'I know we've worked cases where there's been no physical sighting or evidence of the perpetrator but we've still been able to secure a conviction through DNA, like someone spitting on the ground at a crime scene. But in this instance, Keown has much more than that.'

He's thinking again, and I decide to give him the space.

'As I see it, hard evidence is beating circumstantial hands down. So tell me anything else you'd like to pitch in with because I'm about ready to make a decision on this.'

I'm fairly certain I'm only playing out time but I go for it anyway.

'We spoke to the medical forensic examiner who saw Mandy, and also one of the senior nurses in attendance. They told us that during the exam, Mandy mentioned criminal compensation. Neither of them had ever experienced this before and they thought it might be down to trauma but when I asked, they both thought that Mandy wasn't particularly distressed.'

Jeff makes a face. 'Her timing was odd, no question. But people react in all sorts of ways in those circumstances. They can be angry, panicked, devastated, scared: you name it. But they can also be calm and rational.'

'Fair point, but another thing. When the doctor left the room, Mandy asked the nurse if she knew anything about civil damages claims. The nurse thought Mandy meant a claim against Kim but she was talking about his family.'

'You mean the ludicrously wealthy Sir Robert Parker?'

'Correct.'

Jeff stands up and moves behind his chair. He puts one hand on the back, twirls it round but stops it after one rotation. 'Did DS Keown talk to the medical team?'

'No. She didn't.' And *still* I don't actively criticise the original investigation. How restrained.

'Hmmm.' His expression suggests he's swallowed something particularly nasty. 'What about the SOLO?' He's talking about a Sexual Offence Liaison Officer. When a person has suffered sexual violence or harassment, they are appointed a SOLO who will interview them and be their point of contact to the investigating team. These are police officers who are specially trained to interview victims of rape or sexual crime.

'Interestingly, she didn't want to speak to the SOLO. Asked to speak directly to the investigating officer.'

Jeff's eyebrows do a little dance at that one. 'We insisted, I hope.'

'We did. And the SOLO said Mandy gave her statement right off the bat. She appeared to know precisely what she was going to say.'

'Are you reading anything into that?'

I make a face. 'Honest, boss, I *am* trying to give her the benefit of the doubt. But she did have plenty of time to think while we were organising her medical exam and pulling in a SOLO.' I pause for effect. 'But ...'

Jeff's eyebrows are at it again.

I carry on with my explanation. 'The SOLO also told us Mandy was offered a support worker from Rape Crisis Scotland. She declined. Didn't even want an information pack. And we offered to put her in touch with sexual health clinics in case she might have contracted an STI. Especially as he wasn't wearing a condom.'

'Also declined?'

'Yes.' I still can't tell if I'm winning so I keep going. 'And finally, when she was asked to attend the following day, simply to make sure no other injuries presented, she refused. Point blank.'

'But that makes sense, Mel. She'd be desperate to go home, surely.'

It's a fair point but as I'm almost out of shots, I don't admit it.

He sits down and sighs. He pulls his chair closer to his desk and sighs again.

Two sighs? I doubt that's positive. But I guess I'm about to find out so I watch him and wait.

I don't have to wait long. Jeff opens his mouth to speak but he's interrupted by a rap on his door. It opens and Andrew marches in.

'Sorry to butt in, boss,' he says to Jeff. Then to me, 'You'll want to see this.'

———

ANDREW GESTURES towards Jeff's monitor. 'May I?'

Jeff does a hand flourish and wheels his chair off to the side. Andrew bashes away on the keyboard, brings up a map of central Edinburgh and a video file ready to play. Then he turns to me, 'I take it you've talked about the route Kim took from The Canongate to the end of London Road?'

'That's right, we have.'

'What about how he got from there to his flat?'

That makes me start. 'No.'

'In that case, a little bit of background.' Andrew explains with the help of the map. 'We know the only point in Kim's journey home that he was captured on CCTV was here.' He uses a pen to point out the same place, the end of London Road directly opposite Gayfield Square. 'The street that borders the Square is one-way. It runs clockwise: west, through north, to east.' He doesn't bother explaining that the remaining side, the south, is formed by the top end of Leith Walk. That part of The Walk is called Elm Row.

Andrew moves the pen and taps the screen just off the Square on the north side. 'The most direct route from London

Road to Kim's flat, here, is along the *west* side of the Square, past the station.'

Jeff looks at me. 'I suppose one of us should ask the completely stupid question.'

Andrew says, 'No, boss. He didn't appear on our own CCTV.'

Jeff puts his hand to his forehead and shuts his eyes. 'What the bloody hell was Keown thinking? She's assumed that after Kim passed the London Road CCTV, he went directly to his flat and was inside two minutes later. But why did she not confirm it using the station's cameras?'

It's lazy policing again as far as I'm concerned. I keep quiet but inwardly I'm becoming seriously pissed off both at Keown's ineptitude and Kim facing these charges when his guilt is definitely being called into question.

Andrew continues. 'I spoke to Kim. He told me Leith Walk was still busy with traffic that night so instead of attempting to cross at London Road he carried on a bit further down Elm Row to the pelican crossing, here.' He pauses while it registers that this route would have deposited Kim nearer to the *east* side of the Square, meaning he travelled *anticlockwise* round the Square to reach his flat, well out of range of the police station's CCTV on the other side. 'Now this is only my opinion, but I think DS Keown was so far down the forensic evidence route that she didn't consider any alternatives. That may have clouded her judgement so she only looked at what she could see.'

'Meaning?' says Jeff.

Andrew's pen is on the screen again. 'If Kim had kept to the right on his way down to the pelican crossing, he'd have passed three cameras on the row of shops and pubs on Elm Row. DS Keown checked their recordings, Kim didn't appear so she assumed he was lying. But he didn't walk along the pavement in *front* of the shops to reach the crossing. He cut further over, next to the road, and was screened from the three cameras by trees and bushes.'

Andrew pulls a print from his papers. 'I've been back up there today and discovered another camera in the window of an outdoor clothing shop.' He shows us a still photo of Kim taken from behind, through a gap in the trees. He's waiting at the kerb.

Jeez, how much more has that woman missed?

'Anything else between there and his flat, Andrew?' asks Jeff.

'Not of Kim. But watch this.'

He brings up another file on the screen and leaves it ready to play. He speaks directly to Jeff. 'I checked the CCTV again because I couldn't believe Kim would have taken Ms Westbrook's underwear as a trophy and then dumped them in a communal bin a few metres from his front door. Height of stupidity in my opinion. It's possible I'm wrong but DS Keown's investigation concentrated on the time period *following* the point where Kim was spotted at London Road. I wanted to see if anything happened *before* that point. And I found this.'

He presses play. 'This is a view from the corner of the Square, across Leith Walk to London Road. Watch this guy here.'

As Kim had said, despite it being half past midnight, The Walk was still busy with traffic. A figure is moving quickly towards the camera, cutting through between the lines of cars. He's wearing a dark hoodie with a baseball cap underneath. The peak bobs about as he heads for Gayfield Square.

The camera viewpoint changes and Andrew explains. 'These images come from the station's cameras.'

The man appears again. He's striding along the west side

of the Square, keeping close to the front of the police station and directly beneath the camera. The angle changes and this time he's further along the pavement, heading towards Kim's flat. He walks closer to a communal bin, slows his pace slightly and drops something inside.

'Pause that for a moment, will you?' I say. 'Can we see what that was?'

'I've checked it several times. It's small and light coloured. Her underwear was found in that bin, so every reason to believe that's what it is.'

I nod, and Andrew presses play. The man steps off the pavement and crosses the street to avoid a section cordoned off by orange plastic barriers. Then we lose him. I start to speak but Andrew holds a hand up. Less than a minute later, we see our man retracing his steps, hands jammed in his pockets, head down, so the peak of his cap is pointing at his feet. Seconds later he passes the station before he turns the corner on to Leith Walk.

The film stops and we both look at Andrew, who shrugs. 'That's it, as far as the footage is concerned.'

I think he probably has more to say and I'm about to prompt him when Jeff jumps in. 'Two questions, Andrew. Do you have any idea who this man is, and why do you think he's important?'

Andrew clicks the mouse a few times, brings up a more detailed map on the screen. It shows the Royal Mile in the centre, Mandy's Airbnb at Willowbrae on the right and Gayfield Square on the left. The map is overlaid by a red squiggly line that connects the three areas, and there are blue markers with time annotations at various points on the line.

'I don't have an ID for our hooded friend in the video but I believe he was working in collusion with Mandy Westbrook to fabricate evidence against Kim Seung-Min.'

That makes Jeff and I sit up straight. In fact, we're too stunned to reply so Andrew carries on. 'I spoke to the digital forensic techs, asked them to check the cell towers again and extrapolate the route that Kim's phone took. Then I overlaid that with a street map. The red line on the map is the route he took. Now match that up with the timings. They show how quickly the phone moved from place to place, and where the delays were.' He runs his pen along the first section of the line. 'It moved from Cuthbert's Close to Willowbrae Road in eight minutes. And I think the reason Mandy disappeared so quickly after she ran out of the close was because she had an accomplice ready and waiting with a car.'

'The guy in the video?' says Jeff.

Andrew nods. 'Then, Mandy could have pilfered Kim's phone from his trouser pocket while he was otherwise engaged, and she took it with her to the Airbnb. The phone was in the flat for eleven minutes, long enough for her and A.N. Other to stage the crime scene. Then it moved again, this time to the end of London Road, taking another nine minutes. That's a total of twenty-eight minutes.'

I do my sums. 'About fifteen minutes *less* than the time Kim spent in the close, in the bar, and walking to the end of London Road.'

Neither Jeff nor I disagree with Andrew's rationale so far so I signal him to continue. 'The CCTV image proves Kim used the pelican crossing so surely he would have just walked to his flat along the east side of the Square? It's the quickest route.' He checks his notes. 'Now, remember he said he'd smoked a joint with two friends? I spoke to them this afternoon and their testimony would never stand up in court; they were wasted.'

'Please tell me they live on the east side of the Square?' I say.

'They do indeed. So now we can be almost certain of the route Kim took from London Road to his flat.'

'Is the delay while he was with his friends relevant?'

Andrew shakes his head. 'No. It's all about the route.'

'Why?'

He turns to Jeff. 'You asked why I thought hoodie man was important. The phone timings show it was stationary for three minutes on the other side of Leith Walk, opposite the Square. He had the phone, saw Kim heading away towards the crossing and took the opportunity to run through the traffic to get ahead of him. After we saw him dropping the item in the bin, he gained access to Kim's building somehow, left the phone in the stairwell and headed back to wherever he'd parked his car. And that's why Kim found the phone when he arrived home but he couldn't explain how it was there without sounding as if he'd made the whole thing up.'

I say, 'Did you find either hoodie man or the car after he left the Square?'

'No.'

Jeff stands up and moves over by the wall. He folds his arms. 'You've made a few assumptions in there, Andrew, and I'm not sure this is convincing enough to make a case against Mandy Westbrook.'

My younger colleague gives us a look that says, *I'm not quite finished yet.*

'We're not often this lucky but we might have caught a break here.'

Jeff moves away from the wall and peers at the monitor, while Andrew zooms the screen in. 'The icons on this map represent cell towers in and around the city centre. I don't mean to teach you how to suck eggs, but as you know, the techs use triangulation and signal strength to give us the approximate position of a phone. This icon here is a new mast on a building in Annandale Street, and from there to Gayfield Square is less than two hundred metres as the crow flies.' He taps another icon. 'The new mast is a replacement for this one but although the new one was up and running, they hadn't made the changeover yet. Both masts were running in parallel.'

I'm beginning to squirm in my seat, technical stuff can bamboozle me sometimes. 'Okay, I think I understand but how does that help us?'

Andrew smiles. 'Even with three masts nearby, the triangulation can be imprecise but an extra mast helps a lot.'

'Meaning the triangulation was more accurate?'

'Precisely. Have a look at this map.'

Andrew focuses in on Gayfield Square almost to the point where the image is pixelated. The streets that form the Square are blurred and the red line showing the phone's route is blocky. But the image is clear enough and the evidence is conclusive. The more detailed triangulation shows Kim's mobile was definitely carried down the west side of the Square. Kim and the phone may have coincided at the flat but they reached there by different routes. Only slightly different, but different nonetheless.

Jeff sits down again and says, 'You're right, Andrew, we did catch a break. I think we can be reasonably certain that Kim is not guilty of raping Mandy Westbrook.'

'Oh no,' Andrew replies. 'Not reasonably certain, *absolutely* certain. Because earlier, he told me something that was very interesting indeed.'

Andrew isn't normally one for milking a moment but he certainly does this time. Then he explains exactly what he's on about.

And when he's finished, I have to restrain myself from jumping up and doing a little jig round the room.

A few minutes later as we're both leaving Jeff's office, I say, 'See you tomorrow, boss. Once we're back from Dundee.'

Then I wink at him. 'And enjoy your chat with Deirdre Keown's gaffer.'

Jeff doesn't often swear but he's usually happy to make an exception in my case. And walking along the corridor, I repeat a sentiment I came out with a few days ago.

'Perfectly good investigation? My arse.'

CHAPTER FIFTY-THREE

LATER THAT DAY, Steph and I are in an interview room in a Glasgow police station sitting across the table from Frank Crolla and his brief.

Since Steph visited Phyllis Bruce-Mair and The Cross we've scrutinised Crolla's business accounts and tax returns with the help of Ellen, our forensic accountant. We've also had detailed discussions with HMRC tax and VAT inspectors. Ellen's overview makes it fairly conclusive that Crolla has been pulling the wool, with the willing assistance of Phyllis Bruce-Mair. They'll both go down unless they can cut a deal. Thankfully that's not my call, it'll be down to the Fiscal.

'Mr Crolla,' I say, 'how long have you been the proprietor of The Cross?'

'Nearly fifteen years.'

'And how long have you been a director of Cross Leisure?'

'Twelve.'

'Your co-director, Elaine Bartley, how well do you know her?'

'We've never met.'

I blink at him. 'Never?'

He shakes his head. 'No.'

'You don't have board meetings, AGMs, not even the occasional directors' night out?'

His solicitor places a hand on Crolla's arm, murmurs in his ear.

Crolla nods slowly then answers. 'The arrangements for all these things, including any associated paperwork, are not my responsibility. All I do is manage the bar and sign anything I'm asked to. Accounts, letters, minutes of meetings. Anything formal like that.'

I shuffle my papers for a few seconds, let the silence build. 'Would it surprise you if I told you Elaine Bartley was deceased?' I study his face, watching for any reaction.

'Not really.' It's like I've asked him how he likes his coffee.

'Why not, Mr Crolla?'

He spreads his palms. 'Because nothing surprises me about the way Cross is run. Not any longer.'

It's time for the heavy artillery. 'How long have you been using The Cross to launder money for Iain McLure?'

The solicitor whispers in Crolla's ear again and I discover my cannons are firing blanks. 'I don't,' he says.

'You don't?'

'No. I follow a strict set of business and cash management processes that were laid down by Mr McLure. These feed into the prepared accounts and I sign them. I have no latitude, no leeway. It's his way or no way at all.'

'But your name's on the license, Mr Crolla, so as far as I'm concerned what Iain McLure dictates to you is irrelevant.'

'As far as *you're* concerned.' He shakes his head and looks away.

'Are you in touch with Mr McLure?'

'No. I don't ever contact him. It's another one of his rules.'

'When did you last speak to him?'

'A few months ago, maybe?'

Then I show Crolla a series of documents. Till roll summaries, stock delivery notes, invoices, maintenance costs: the works. Ellen has annotated each one where they don't stack up. Crolla says he's familiar with them generally but can't confirm whether he saw these specific items.

I ask, 'How many of your customers pay by card?'

'Not many.'

'Do you discourage this method of payment?'

He sighs. 'Sometimes our systems are down and the card readers don't work.'

'Convenient.'

Deadpan. 'If you say so.'

I try a different tack. 'How many times have you had a VAT inspection?'

He thinks. 'Twice.'

It was hardly a difficult calculation. 'Where did these take place?'

'My office, at home.'

'Why not on the premises?'

He shrugs. 'Most small pubs don't have proper office space, we're no different.'

Then Steph cut in. 'I spoke to an HMRC inspector. He told me about the VAT inspection he was carrying out at your office during which he decided he wanted to visit the pub so he could get a sense of the place.' Crolla begins to squirm in his seat. 'And in particular, the four pool tables that were generating a significant amount of revenue. All in cash, naturally.' Steph sits back and folds her arms. 'So you both set off for The Cross but you didn't reach there, did you?'

Now Crolla's broken all eye contact. His solicitor is

throwing Steph questioning glances so she enlightens him. 'Your client insisted on taking his car and at a busy junction on Duke Street as the rush hour was kicking off, he somehow managed to crash into a bus travelling in the opposite direction.' The solicitor takes off his glasses and rubs his temples. 'Oh, nearly forgot the best bit. The lights were against Mr Crolla at the time.' Steph paused. 'But he still managed it.'

I guess solicitors are adept at keeping a straight face but this chap has his work cut out.

We continue until we've shown Crolla all of Ellen's documents. He gives more or less the same response to every one: 'Familiar, but I can't be certain.'

I sit quietly while I assess the interview. Frank Crolla hasn't exactly admitted The Cross is a money laundering operation but it looks like he's the patsy who has no choice but to do as he's told. In the absence of McLure, Crolla knows he'll take the rap and he seems to accept that. Which brings me neatly to my final question.

'The one thing I don't understand is why you are fronting this operation for McLure? Reading between the lines, you don't have any time for the man, you know he's a crook, he's the one who's making all the profit yet you're almost certainly going down for it. So tell me, Frank, why?'

At first he makes no response. Then a smile creeps across his face. He stays silent and stares at me.

I lean forward. 'Don't look at me as if I'm an idiot, Crolla. I know McLure's blackmailing you too, what I want to know is what he's got on you.'

And then he comes out with the magic words: 'No comment.'

'I thought I might be able to help you there, Frank, but obviously not.' I start packing away papers. 'Perhaps you'll remember that while you're doing time for fraud and money laundering.'

'If that's all I end up inside for,' he says, 'I'll take that any day.'

CHAPTER FIFTY-FOUR

'I HEARD HE WAS BACK, Auntie Soph. What's going on?'

Sophie cracked the top on a bottle of Sauvignon Blanc and poured herself a healthy measure. 'Nothing's going on, darling.' She patted her nephew gently on the cheek.

'Beer?' she said.

'Please.'

She pointed at the fridge. 'They're on the middle shelf.' She angled her head towards the living room. 'Get one for him too, please.' She held up the wine bottle. 'Now are you sure Lily wouldn't like a little glass?'

Kev shook his head. 'No thanks. She doesn't like alcohol, says it tastes horrible. She only drinks water.'

'Not necessarily a bad thing, Kev.' She took a tumbler from a cabinet and held it under the tap. 'Right, you take the beers and I'll bring these.' She put the two drinks on a tray with a few nibbles and followed him out of the kitchen.

'I'm not sure what I want to do yet,' Lily was saying.

'You're not going to uni then?' said Iain. He kept his gaze

on Lily while he reached up to take the beer from Kev, who promptly dropped onto the sofa next to his girlfriend.

'No. I don't think university will suit me. Possibly college, though. Maybe a course in new media or digital marketing.'

'I still don't know what I want to be when I grow up,' said Sophie. 'And I'm thirty-seven.'

Lily laughed. 'That's what my mum says.'

Sophie put the tray down and handed Lily her water. 'Are you sure that's okay?'

'Oh, yes. Lovely, thanks.'

Sophie sipped her wine. 'So what do your parents do for a living? Maybe there's something there for you.'

'My dad's a graphic designer so I guess that's an area I'm interested in.'

'And your mum?'

'She's a police officer, a Detective Sergeant.' Lily made a face. 'I definitely couldn't do her job. No way.'

Iain had been lounging in the armchair but eased himself upright. He swigged from his beer to stop himself jumping right in. 'That's interesting. A Detective Sergeant, you say?' His voice was a shade high and Sophie gave him an odd look.

But Lily didn't notice. 'That's right.'

Sophie lifted a dish. 'Nibble?'

Lily said, 'No, thank you,' but when Kev grabbed a handful and crammed them in his mouth she grinned at Sophie. Her amusement didn't last.

'So what sort of cases does a Detective Sergeant handle?' asked Iain.

Lily was perched on the edge of the sofa, her phone lay on a small pink backpack by her feet. She glanced down at it. 'I'm sorry, we don't talk much about Mum's job at home. Work's work and home's home, according to her.' She looked at Sophie and Kev, sending out a stream of Mayday signals.

'You okay, babe?' said Kev.

'She's fine,' said Iain. 'I was just making conversation.' He winked at Lily, who turned a shade of pink to match her backpack.

Sophie opened her mouth to speak but then he asked, 'What did you say your surname was?'

'Iain!' Sophie's expression was thunder. 'Stop interrogating the girl.'

'Jeez. I was only trying to be friendly.' He slumped into the cushion, picked up the remote and clicked on the TV. He shuffled about, struggling to get comfortable. His jeans were cutting into him, he'd obviously put on weight since he'd last worn them. The best laid plans, he thought.

A few years earlier, one of his latest marks had threatened to confess to the police about the activities he'd become involved in while on 'business trips' to Malaysia. It took all Iain's powers of persuasion to talk the man down and it was only when Iain showed him a draft email with jpegs attached and his mother's email address at the top that the man chickened out. From then on Iain left the man alone but he realised he'd been fortunate because the mark hadn't gone straight to the police, which gave him time to react. It dawned on him that he had no emergency bail out plans in place so he'd rectified that by making up a grab bag containing clothes and a variety of other personal items, including cash and fake ID.

Iain didn't have too many friends in Edinburgh but there was one woman he'd known for a number of years. They'd had a relationship of sorts until they both realised it would never have worked long term. She knew he wasn't exactly squeaky clean but she too had a dark side, so their relationship was strangely symbiotic. He asked her to keep the bag safe until he needed it. So after he'd shot out of the pub after witnessing the camera footage from Kinghorn and Dalmeny Street, he'd called her immediately.

But she hadn't been home, wouldn't be there until the next day and had always made it crystal clear that if things were bad enough that he was coming for the bag then under no circumstances would she put him up. Not even overnight.

So Iain had arrived at Sophie's the previous day with only the clothes he stood in, and attempted to bluff his way out of explaining. He was thankful Sophie hadn't pursued the point, she seemed to forget all about it once he collected the bag the following morning.

Now Sophie was watching him closely. Then she glanced at the TV. *Cricket?* She gave him one final glare then shook her head and switched her attention to Kev and Lily. 'Ignore him, you two. Right, how long have you been going out? Where did you meet? Come on, I want all the juicy details.'

Later on, she noticed Iain's eyes going back and forth between his phone and Lily.

What the hell's he up to?

———

THAT NIGHT SOPHIE lay in bed. The glow from the streetlight directly outside her window shone through the tiny cord holes in the blind, creating a vertical pattern on the wall. She was facing away from Iain, his burbling snores muffled by the duvet. They'd just had sex. He had taken charge like he'd always done, moving her around the bed, constantly changing positions. She imagined he fancied himself as some kind of porn star. She wasn't uncomfortable about that so she played along, like she'd been doing ever since she'd realised it actually gave her a degree of control.

Back in the beginning, as their sexual relationship was

245

developing, he'd pushed the boundaries. She was reasonably happy to satisfy his tastes but there were a couple of acts he'd encouraged her to perform and she'd told him no. Straight. He'd gone in a huff, of course, and tried it on again the following night. Still she said no. She liked him, she even thought she might love him, but it turned out she didn't. He wasn't her first sexual partner so she knew the sex should have been better, much better.

Lying there, she thought about their past life and accepted she had made a pact with the devil. Iain had simply been a route out of her humdrum existence, away from her tedious job and from mediating between her eternally squabbling siblings. He had money and didn't seem to mind sharing it with her. He was generous in that respect, the paradox in his behaviours had always bemused her.

Since he'd appeared the day before, she'd had plenty of time to consider her situation. The signs were obvious, he was in trouble. He'd arrived without any bags and with a 'temporary cash flow problem'? She'd asked him again why he couldn't go to his house and he'd snapped at her.

She knew she was pushing it but she had another go at him about why he was so interested in Lily's mother. And what was he checking out on his phone? He mumbled something about trying to be sociable but wouldn't meet her eye.

In different circumstances Sophie might have thought this was just Iain being Iain. But when she placed it alongside him turning up out of the blue and asking to get back together when it was as plain as day that all he needed was to keep a low profile, she realised the whole thing stank to high heaven. Given his interest in Lily's mother, there must be a connection between them. Was the DS investigating his blackmailing activities? If so, how did he know? And if that *was* the case then he wouldn't be hanging around for long, would he?

Then he'd be gone for good. On the plus side she would be shot of him but then she would miss the opportunity to exploit what she knew. It was a puzzle for sure; her problem was that she wasn't sure how long she had to solve it.

Not all that long as things transpired, but Sophie couldn't have known that.

CHAPTER FIFTY-FIVE

I HAVE to say that when I was younger Dundee was a bit of a dump but it's come on a bundle in the past decade or two. Andrew drove us in past Discovery Point, so-called because Captain Scott's Antarctic steamship is docked there. Right next door is the V&A Museum, which resembles an enormous concrete boat.

And now, in Tayside Police's spanking new HQ, having passed tinted windows with a view of the Tay Bridge, here we are in *Interview Suite C2*.

I'm observing the woman sitting across the table from us. I wonder what she's on.

She's fidgeting. Definitely jumpy. A tremor that might simply be a nervous tic. I know we're the police and even genuinely innocent people can become anxious when they're talking to us, but it doesn't take a genius to figure out this woman is hiding something. Truth is, we know perfectly well what that is but I'll let her stew for a while yet.

This is Mandy Westbrook. Following our discussions yesterday with Kim, and Andrew's revelations concerning the

CCTV, I've brought her in to talk through her original statement and to clarify a few points.

I'm not having this investigation fail on a technicality so because I *suspect* Mandy is guilty of falsely accusing Kim of assault and rape, and indeed framing him for these crimes, she's been booked in properly. She's been cautioned with attempting to defeat the ends of justice and offered access to a duty solicitor. Considering how scared she looks, I'm surprised when she tells me she doesn't want to be represented. But that's her right and, for the moment, I'm not about to dissuade her. When we reach the point where it becomes vital I'll strongly advise her to reconsider.

Mandy is twenty-five, dressed all in black, verging on skinny. Her hair is at least one day past washing and there are faint hemispheres of grime under her fingernails. I suspect she doesn't wear makeup, not because her hands are too shaky to apply it but because she needs to spend her money on other things. There are many different names for these 'things' but they fall under the general heading: narcotics.

So, here I am with this woman facing me and not only do I *know* something's wrong, I'm about to prove it. And that's all down to what Kim told Andrew yesterday.

'Mandy.' I leave it at Mandy. The pause, the lack of any follow up, means my use of her name is not to address her. Instead, it's a statement. With an accusatory tone. Its purpose is to further unsettle her.

It's working.

Her level of nervousness escalates like loan shark compound interest. I repeat her name, 'Mandy,' and metaphorically rub my hands as my takings increase.

She can't stop herself. 'What?' It's somewhere in between a demand and a wail.

'As things stand, Kim Seung-Min, the guy you accused of assaulting and raping you will be found guilty.'

'Good. He *is* guilty. He battered me and he fuckin' raped me. He did it! He *has* to go to jail.'

I turn to Andrew and put on my best confused expression.

'That was an interesting emphasis Mandy placed on the word *has*. "He *has* to go to jail". What do you think she meant by that?'

My sidekick plays along, carries on speaking as if she doesn't exist. 'It could be that he actually did do it.'

'Or?'

'Or, there's another reason he "has" to go to jail.'

'And what do you think that could be?'

'No idea. Let's ask her.'

We both face her and I say, 'Mandy?'

'*Stop saying Mandy!*' The woman is about to detonate so I keep silent and wait for the bang. She clenches both fists and waves them about. 'What the fuck are you on about? He has to, alright? He just *has* to.'

'There she goes with the "has to" thing again, DC Young.' I fiddle with a pen. It catches her eye so I stop. She doesn't look up at me, though. I must have morphed into DS Medusa.

So this time I address her directly, adding a sharp edge to my voice. 'You're beginning to sound a bit desperate, Mandy.'

She conducts a brief internal strategy meeting, revises her tactics and shuts up. She thinks it's a clever move but it won't make any difference.

'In my experience,' I say, 'most women who've been assaulted, like you claim you were, and who know the guy will be convicted, are relieved. Satisfied, even.'

Mandy is glaring at me. She's not sure where I'm going with this.

'I have your statement here.' I shuffle my papers around,

just for effect. 'By the way, as a matter of interest you've written your name as Mandy, not Amanda.'

'That's because my name *is* Mandy.'

'Figures.'

'Eh?'

I don't answer, I move on. 'These "friends" of yours. The ones you planned to meet but then didn't. Why didn't they check in with you? Find out where you were?'

'I ... em ... we don't have that kind of relationship. I said I might meet them but no sweat if I didn't. They were doing their own thing.'

'So you decide to have a weekend in Edinburgh. Not the cheapest of places to visit but you only had *tentative* plans involving this group of friends?'

'That's right.'

I turn to a fresh page in my notebook. Sit with pen poised. 'What are their names?'

Now I know what 'struck dumb' looks like.

'What?' she says.

'Their names, Mandy. What are their names?'

She shakes her head several times. 'They're just friends.' Then her eyes brighten. 'Not friends, actually ... friends of friends.' She's pleased with herself after that smart answer. It doesn't last.

I could ask her about when she contacted them to make arrangements but I know she'll lie about that too.

'During your medical examination you were offered the services of a support worker from Rape Crisis Scotland, but you declined.' I hold her gaze. Lock on. 'Why?'

Her eyes blaze back at me. 'I don't need any bloody social worker to hold my hand. I know what happened.'

She thinks she's on solid ground. Rehearsed ground. So I test her again. 'And that's why you didn't want anyone present, or even to be contacted? Because you're a big girl now.'

She juts out her chin. Says nothing.

The next point will be stronger coming from Andrew so I hand over to him. He says, 'You even declined an information pack covering sexual health clinics that can support you, including testing for sexually transmitted infections. I mean come on, Mandy. This is a guy you picked up, you're having sex but then he *rapes* you and he's not wearing a condom. He could have infected you with anything. Chlamydia, herpes, syphilis. Even HIV. Why would you *not* want to be tested?'

No answer. We're not even mildly surprised.

Now it's time for me to set up the money shot. 'In your description of him, you were asked to be precise. To describe him in as much detail as possible.'

Silence.

'In particular, with regard to his penis, you stated ...' I move my finger along a line of text. Again, just for effect. 'He was normal.'

I look at her. Still no answer. This is becoming tedious.

I change tack. 'You stated he was wearing jeans and a cream-coloured, casual, short sleeved shirt. Open a couple of buttons at the neck. Red check inside the collar.'

Still silent so I assume that means yes.

'The time you spent together, drinking in all those bars, making out in bus shelters; the way he was dressed meant you'd be able to give a fairly comprehensive description of him. Muscular arms, no tattoos: tick. Chest, buff: tick. Slim, no love handles: tick.'

Her eyes are darting all over the place. Thinking? Or panicking.

'It would be easy enough to judge his height,' I say. 'And even with his clothes on, you'd be able to guess his weight. So to give a full description, no details missing, all you need is that one, vital, statistic.'

Now Mandy's gaze is burning a hole in the brand new table. There is something different about her expression. The barely discernible shadow of impending defeat.

Things are warming up nicely. But frustratingly, I have to stop right there because if I go any further down this line of questioning I will compromise any additional charges I hit her with.

I terminate the discussion there. At the very least she'll be charged with wasting police time but this is looking more like attempting to defeat the ends of justice. I arrange to have her booked in while Andrew rounds up a duty solicitor.

I do believe we're on the home straight.

———

ANDREW and I are having a cuppa when my phone buzzes. He raises his eyebrows and I say, 'It's Steph.' I pop her on loud-speaker.

'Got a minute, boss?'

'Of course, Steph. What's up?'

'Iain McLure's gone off-grid.'

'Ah well, not too much of a surprise, is it?' I steeple my fingers. 'I'm guessing there's been no recent activity on any of his known accounts or comms?'

'No, but it's worse than that.'

I sigh. 'Go on, then.'

'I took a trip down to his Dalmeny Street flat to check the place out again and I spotted a miniature camera tucked into the top corner of the door frame.'

I bore right into Andrew's eyes. He screws up his face.

'It wasn't even the size of a drawing pin and it was cleverly hidden. And, to be fair, Andrew was only there on an initial enquiry so he wasn't expecting anything like that.'

It only takes a second for me to make the connection. 'Oh, no. Don't tell me.'

'Afraid so, there's one at Kinghorn too. More than one, in fact. I called Dunfermline CID and asked them to have a quick look to save me trekking over there. Same design but easier to hide on the front of a house.'

Bless her, she doesn't cast up that I missed it too.

'What do you want me to do, boss?'

I drum my fingers on the table, give myself a few more seconds to ponder. 'So, the cameras are motion sensitive, they auto-upload to the cloud and McLure is sent an alert, probably to his phone. Either that or he logs in regularly to check but somehow I doubt that. Anyway, he sees us snooping around, puts the whole picture together – no pun intended – and goes to ground.' I exhale. 'And the McLaren still hasn't been picked up by ANPR?'

'No. It's still in Kinghorn so it must be in the garage.'

Although it would be useful if we could prove the car was there, as things stand the only way we can do that is by gaining access. And for that we'd require a warrant. But there's no chance we'd get one without reasonable grounds because we only *think* McLure is a blackmailer. We have no proof.

'Ok, Steph, there's nothing more we can do for now. This man is extremely well prepared. He's off-grid and he'll know how to stay there. Sadly this has to drop down the priority list, which is bloody annoying but we'll have to switch our focus to other cases. So leave the flags on, for all the good it'll do us, run a quick check every couple of days and keep me updated.'

I put my phone down. She's right, of course. I can't really blame Andrew for not spotting the camera. Still, let's not allow logic to get in the way of me having a pop at the Boy Wonder.

'Think it's about time you booked yourself an optician's appointment, don't you?'

———

THREE HOURS LATER, there are four of us in Interview Suite C2.

Mandy's discussed her predicament with her brief, a surprisingly alert young man in a suit that's almost as snappy as Andrew's. He tells us Mandy is keen to cooperate, which is a plus. The last thing I want is a litany of no comments.

I go right back to my prodding. 'So, to quote Mr Kim, when you gave him a quick, fairly average blowjob that Friday night in Cuthbert's Close, it was to give you that last important piece of information ...'

'The sex happened in the flat. I didn't blow him in some manky lane.'

This isn't a surprise, she's making one last attempt to slide out from under. But her tone is flat. The volume, and therefore the conviction, isn't there. This is Mandy's last hurrah, the futile rearguard action of a vanquished force.

'Either way, not only do you know his penis size but you also have his DNA. Hairs, skin flecks, semen. And we both know what you did with that, Mandy, don't we? And none too gently, for obvious reasons.'

'I didn't ...' Her voice barely registers.

I harden my tone. 'Okay Mandy, I'll humour you. I'll give you one last chance.'

Her eyes light up, but all too briefly.

'If you pass, I withdraw the charges. You're out of here, and Kim goes down.'

But she can sense I'm holding four aces and so the light dims.

'You began having sex at the Airbnb? Consensual, at that point?'

She nods. 'Yes.'

'In the flat, lights on, clothes off?'

She thinks. Nods again. 'That's right.'

'Rolling around? Bit of foreplay? Maybe some oral?'

She hesitates, looking for the trap but can't spot it. 'Some of that. Yes.'

'And while all this lovely sexy stuff is going on, I'm assuming you're all over each other. Two naked horny people, up close and personal, having fun?'

One final nod, but it's a slow one. 'I suppose, yes.'

Now she's staring at me. She knows I'm getting there, but not when.

Not long now, Mandy. Not long.

'In your statement you stated that after he raped you, "He was standing by the side of the bed, still naked, checking his phone. I was seriously pissed off when he did that and I lashed out, kicked him right in the balls. He went down". Is that right, Mandy?'

She blinks. Wasn't expecting that.

'Know anything about testicular cancer, Mandy?'

She jumps a little, shakes her head. Definitely wasn't expecting *that*.

'Tell her, Andrew.'

My sidekick sighs, pretends to check his notes. Ratchets up the tension a smidge. 'When Kim Seung-Min was a young man, only eighteen, he contracted testicular cancer. With most cancers they treat the tumour, attempt to shrink it with radiotherapy or chemo, or operate to remove it. That's what they do with lung cancer, for example. But here's the thing, Mandy. With testicular cancer you can't remove the tumour, you have to remove the testicle.'

Mandy is chewing her lip as Andrew's story unfolds.

'Sadly for Kim he was incredibly unlucky. Three years later, same cancer, other testicle.' He pauses. 'Same op.'

Her eyes are glistening. She couldn't smile if you offered her millions.

Andrew continues. 'Testicular cancer patients might be offered implants. Some say yes, some say no thanks.' He paused. 'You've confirmed there was foreplay. You were both naked. The lights were on.'

Her cheeks are wet, she's crying. Andrew doesn't ask any of his final questions. One implant? Two?

Or none?

Everyone in the room knows she would have to guess.

I sit back, explain I'm giving her one more opportunity to cooperate fully. Then I formally suspend the interview and leave her with young Master Snappy Suit.

Over a sandwich in the unimaginatively christened Tayview Restaurant, Andrew and I wonder why Keown and her team didn't pick up on many aspects of Mandy's tale, particularly her mysterious absent friends, Kim's medical history and one or two other things we'll soon be asking her to confirm. But those are questions for Jeff and Deirdre Keown's boss. I'll be keeping well out of it.

I still have three bites of my BLT remaining when we're called to the interview suite. We change the point of attack. Andrew asks Mandy to tell us the whole story, this is how it goes: She was an escort for a relatively legitimate agency and was set up with the same man three or four times. Cash transactions only. He told her his name was Colin but probably it wasn't. She didn't care. She liked him and he appeared to like her. But Mandy's not completely stupid. She understood their relationship was professional and at best, short-term. They had sex of course, but all straightforward in comparison to what some other clients paid for.

The last time she and Colin met, he said he didn't want sex. He told her he had a proposition for her and gave her £500 cash just for listening. There would be another £1,500 for doing what he asked and a final payment of £8,000 at completion of the contract. Andrew asked what that meant. She said, 'When Kim goes inside.'

At that time Mandy had been clean for months but it was an enormous struggle. To some people, £10,000 isn't a tremendous amount of money but in her circumstances, it might allow her to escape Dundee and the downward spiral that was never more than a weak moment away. She agreed to do what Colin asked.

They travelled to Edinburgh one Friday evening, went to a bar up town where Colin pointed Kim out. They tracked him from bar to bar and Colin explained that Kim followed the same ritual virtually every Friday. He wasn't part of a group or even a couple, he simply cruised the same places, solo, interacting with people who clearly knew him. Kim was popular, handsome enough and easy to get along with, so it wasn't unusual for him to pick up a woman.

Mandy's job was to meet Kim once he'd had a few drinks, make sure he had a few more but to remain sober herself. Colin would be watching at all stages, partly for her protection. But if she became too drunk he would, in his words, dump her and she could kiss goodbye to the extra £1,500 plus the potential for £8,000 more. It was her job to get Kim to follow his normal circuit and to time it so they reached Cuthbert's Close just before midnight, when the last pub on the Royal Mile was heading for last orders. Then she was to lure him into the close, where she would give him a blowjob. She'd been stoking his fires for at least an hour and the session in the bus shelter was designed to achieve two purposes, to make sure the timing was right and to leave the poor lad practically at exploding point.

At this stage in Mandy's story, I become extremely sceptical. It's a long time since I was out on the pull and can't envisage how such an outcome, pardon the pun, could be even reasonably guaranteed. But Andrew's high-arched eyebrows mirror mine when she shows us images on her phone of how she looked back then. It's impossible not to notice the clothes she was wearing. Or almost wearing. A bloke would have to be gay *and* blind to resist a come-on.

Colin gave her a sterile glove to put on her hand immediately after the event. Its purpose was to protect any DNA she'd collected. He also provided a baggie for her to transfer Kim's semen into. I don't bother pressing her for details on how this would all work. When Mandy came running out of the close, unobserved by CCTV, Colin was waiting with a car to whisk her over to the Airbnb, where they set up the scene. This included a beer bottle that Kim had been drinking from; Colin had lifted it from one of the bars and left it on a bedside table for the police to find.

Their final act, nasty but necessary, was to make Mandy appear like a rape victim. She contaminated herself and her pants with Kim's semen and DNA, then Colin placed the pants into another baggie. Then he used a sex toy on her, he was deliberately rough. Finally, he hit her a few times on the face and body, hard enough to bruise. According to her, 'I've had worse, plenty times.' He didn't apologise, he just gave her the £1,500 she'd earned that night, repeated what must happen before she would collect the £8,000, and left.

She spreads her hands as if to say, *That's it.*

Andrew asks, 'Have you heard from Colin since?'

'Yes.'

That catches us by surprise.

259

'He called me the following day. He knew Kim had been lifted. He said he'd be back in touch when Kim went down. He promised I'd get my money as long as I kept my mouth shut.'

She gives us a detailed description of the man called Colin but we've only asked so we can tick a box. We stand zero chance of finding him because we have no idea where to search. Not even in which city. We'll run more checks on CCTV footage but I'm not hopeful.

'Okay, Mandy, we appreciate you telling us all that. What I'd like to do now is take you through the gaps in your account because I need to prove conclusively that Kim is innocent. You are not required to help us with this but it might be to your benefit in the long run.' I pause and look her right in the eye. 'No promises, though.'

'Kim didn't lose his phone,' I say. 'You lifted it from his back pocket while you were performing oral sex on him in Cuthbert's Close.' Mandy is no virgin, she's been turning tricks for years and to her, taking his phone and manipulating the evidence would be like robbing a blind man.

'You told Kim you'd meet him in the pub, but that was a distraction. To delay him getting home. Then you took the phone with you to the Airbnb, kept it there long enough for the alleged consensual sex, assault and rape then Colin drove it up to London Road to coincide with Kim arriving there on foot. You couldn't go with him because your job was to call the police and wait for us to arrive. The only thing you couldn't bank on one hundred per cent was that Kim would decide to walk home from where you left him. But it was a summer's night and you knew he doesn't carry cash and discovered he has a slight aversion to paying for taxis. And without a phone he couldn't call a cab even if he wanted to.

'*Colin* broke into Kim's block and left his phone there for him to find, making it look like Kim and the phone followed the same route as you, thereby placing him in the Airbnb. Colin knew we would never believe he'd lost it, and especially his story about it appearing like magic in the stairwell.'

I don't tell her about Colin's *big* mistake, that he carried the phone up the wrong side of Gayfield Square.

'This involved a lot of planning, Mandy. And money, assuming you ever received all the payments. What I want to know is, who's behind it all? And for what it's worth I don't think it's Colin, is it?'

She shakes her head. 'He, Colin, whatever his name is, made it crystal clear I was never to ask. Or else. And whatever you think of me, I'm not daft.' She smiles for the first time. 'So your guess is as good as mine.'

––––––

Down in the Custody Suite, just as we're leaving her, she asks, 'Will you be dropping the charges against Kim?'

I'm not able to keep the pity from my voice. 'What do you think, Mandy?'

Then we walk away.

Next on my to-do list is a courtesy call to Deirdre Keown. Although the chances of me being courteous are slim to negligible.

CHAPTER FIFTY-SIX

'O'KEEFE, it's time for your visitor.'

Emily placed a scrap of paper at her page and closed the book. This would be her first visitor. She'd instructed her husband to stay away until she was ready and on no account to even think about bringing in the kids.

As she followed the officer through locked doors and along corridors she wondered why this person had come to see her. She'd been told they were acting as a representative of the church committee, which was a surprise as she hadn't heard a word from them and neither did she expect to. So, as she was escorted into the visitor area she was already on the defensive.

Her visitor was seated at a table, facing away from the door. Emily walked round the other side and sat down. She knew this person but not all that well. 'I'm sorry,' she said. I don't understand. I mean, thank you for visiting me but ...'

'Why am I here?'

'Em ... yes. Is it to do with the committee?'

This time the response was a broad grin, followed by a low chuckle and a shake of the head.

Emily started to speak but something made her stop. Then it hit her. Her voice dropped to a harsh whisper. 'You! It was you?'

A full face smile now. 'Yes, Dr O'Keefe. It was me.' A pause. 'Or at least, I made it happen.'

Emily glanced towards the door. Two officers stood with their backs to her, deep in conversation.

'But ...' She shook her head, several times. It didn't help.

'You want to know why?'

Emily spoke through clenched teeth. 'Yes, damn you, why? Why did you do this to me? Why did you destroy my life?' She swept her arm round. 'What have I ever done to you to deserve this?'

The visitor stood up, the chair made a scraping sound on the tiled floor. 'Now I've given you the starter for ten, I'm sure it won't take you long to figure it out.'

Emily's throat felt like it was in a vice. She tried, but no sound came out. She looked towards the door again and flapped an arm. It felt like it weighed a ton and wouldn't follow her brain's instructions.

'Oh, Dr O'Keefe. They don't care about you. You'll probably find out they won't remember anything untoward about my visit except that you became terribly upset so I did the decent thing and offered to come back another day when you're feeling more like yourself.'

The visitor turned to leave then stopped. 'I do hope you enjoy your little break in here. Not quite a five-star resort in sunny Mexico but hey, you can't have everything.'

A pause. 'Oh, and by the way, I was in court to witness you being sent down. It was a thoroughly enjoyable experience, I'd never been in a courtroom before. I should say I did feel incredibly sorry for your mother, though. In a terrible state, she was.'

There was a moment's silence then Emily screamed. It would have shattered plate glass. *Then* the officers reacted. But they only began to really shift themselves when Emily kicked her chair aside and charged across the floor.

CHAPTER FIFTY-SEVEN

ANDREW and I are with Kim in his kitchen. The charity para-phernalia scattered about his table seems to have multiplied. Clearly he's working from home. He's a smiley guy anyway but now even more so.

'Kim,' I say. 'Can you think of any reason why anyone would want to falsify such a convoluted rape charge against you?'

He spreads his hands. 'No reason. I have no enemies ... I don't think.'

'An ex-girlfriend perhaps?'

He shakes his head, it won't be the last time. 'My relation-ships are usually brief. I am not looking for anything ... longer term.' Which is his polite way of saying, *One-night-stands only, thank you.*

'What about in respect to your father? Or to the charities?'

'I have spoken with him about that. There is nothing. No trouble, no major problems, no issues beyond the normal day-to-day matters. My father, he is a *good* man. Very honest, very trustworthy. Everything he does, he does in the right way.'

'Do you gamble?' It's always worth pushing the odd button here and there. But I'm taken aback when he laughs. A great big hands-on-the-belly laugh.

'I am from South Korea. Gambling is a way of life for us. Any of my countrymen who say they don't gamble is a liar.' He slaps his hand on the table. 'I bet you!' Then he laughs again, so I do too.

'Could it be something at home? In South Korea?'

In an instant Kim's mood switches to sombre. 'I was orphaned. An earthquake. All my family, we lived close by to each other. Everyone was taken. My parents, my sisters, grand-parents. Everybody. No one left but me.'

He pauses while I digest the incredible horror of his past. His eyes bore into the mess on the table as if he were trying to vaporise it. 'So I never go back.'

'I'm so sorry, Kim. That's unimaginable.'

I stay silent until he glances up. 'Thank you,' he says. 'Please, do continue.'

'So no one has anything against you. Nothing the police might be interested in?'

He strokes his chin with thumb and forefinger. Then shakes his head one final time. 'No. Nothing.'

I flip through a few pages in my notebook. 'When I reviewed the file concerning this case I came across a reference to a traffic related incident you were involved in. It was in November, would you like to tell us about it?'

He makes a face. 'It wasn't actually anything to do with me. Two cars collided ahead of me, the drivers became angry and were arguing. One of the men was older, I was concerned for him so I shouted to two of your officers who had just come out of a nearby shop. They calmed the whole thing down.' He stops there, as if to say, *That's all*.

'The officers' report stated you thought the younger man was responsible.'

He nods. 'That's correct, but witnesses who were better placed said it was the other driver. It appears I was wrong.' He looks at each of us. 'I didn't hear any more about it.'

I check my scribbles, the case notes confirm what he's just said. I'll contact Leo Contini to check what happened with this incident but I think it's a dead end.

I don't like dead ends. They annoy me. So on our way back to the station, I'm deep in thought. Because there's always a way round them. All I have to do is find it.

CHAPTER FIFTY-EIGHT

Tommy Jarvis was lounging about on the sofa in their rented flat checking the latest football scores on his mobile. The kids were asleep and his wife, Joanne, was beside him, immersed in a movie she'd seen several times before. Personally, he couldn't stand the sight of Julia Roberts.

His phone vibrated but he only picked up because of who was calling. 'Gary,' he said. 'It's late.'

Joanne heard Gary's voice but not what he was saying. Seconds later, Tommy leapt to his feet. 'I'll be right over.'

His wife ignored him. Barely a week passed without some drama kicking off. She heard him fishing his car keys out of the dish on the kitchen worktop then the front door slammed behind him.

Fabulous, she thought. The TV *and* the sofa all to myself.

———

Tommy peered at the footage on the laptop screen. 'How many times has she been at the house taking photos, Gary?'

'Four, as far as I can tell.'

Tommy thumped his fist on the table and the laptop bounced a little off the surface. '*Four?*' Then he was silent so Gary followed suit.

The woman Tommy was staring at, almost as if he hoped she'd turn and wave at him, was probably early twenties. Dark hair, glasses, carrying a small daysack over her right shoulder.

'Once or twice, she's maybe curious. Taking a couple of snaps to show her pals. Three times would be pushing it but who takes photos of the same thing four times?'

Gary winced in case his boss thumped the table again.

'No, Gary. This woman, whoever the fuck she is, is definitely involved. I just know it, feel it in my bones.' Tommy pointed at the screen. 'Move it on a bit.'

They watched as the woman continued along the pavement, aiming her phone at different angles towards the house. Then as she slipped the phone into her pocket she checked behind her, along the pavement then across the street.

Tommy half stood up, palms on the table. 'Look! She's making sure no one's watching her.' Without taking his eyes off the screen he asked, 'What times is she there?'

'Between five and quarter past.'

'Right. You and me, tomorrow night. We'll aim to be there by quarter to.'

This time he did slap the table. Hard. 'And we'll catch the bitch. Find out what the fuck she's playing at.'

———

BUT THE WOMAN didn't show up the following evening, nor the one after that. On the fourth day Gary told Tommy he was fed up, this wild goose chase was taking up all his spare time.

'I have to find this woman, Gary. Four hours, treble time, every night 'til we find her.'

Gary couldn't find a way to say no, so he agreed.

But after a week he told his boss enough was enough. Tommy wasn't stupid, he knew he'd pushed Gary as far as he could so reluctantly he called it quits.

And just in case Tommy changed his mind, Gary took the cameras down that very afternoon.

CHAPTER FIFTY-NINE

'Okay,' I say to Andrew and Steph. 'Here's where we're at. Mandy Westbrook has admitted to falsifying assault and rape charges against Kim Seung-Min. She was working with an accomplice. Colin, surname and identity as yet unknown. She stood to earn £10,000 in total, as long as Kim was convicted. And assuming Colin kept his word, that is.

'Now, our problem is still motive. We have no idea why Kim was set up and neither does Mandy. But this would have cost a lot of money. Fifteen k, ballpark. So someone wanted Kim in jail. Badly. But no matter, Jeff's given us the green light to follow up on all the other cases.'

I turn to Andrew for a progress update. His eyes are heavy. Yesterday was a long day for him. I left him working in Dundee, and I know he didn't get home until after midnight.

He talks without the help of notes. 'Mandy Westbrook's still in protective custody. We reviewed all the CCTV footage for that Friday night, trying to spot her with any other bloke that might be Colin or even if he was lurking somewhere in the background. No joy. Bryan Fraser sent me photos of every Colin processed by the Custody Suite in the past year and I showed them to Mandy.'

'Also no joy?' says Steph.

'None. Colin is almost certainly an alias.'

I hold up my index finger. 'We should also ask Bryan if he can think of anything at all that might conceivably be a reason for his mum's dog to be stolen, no matter how tenuous. Because I'm positive it's nothing to do with her.'

'Will do,' says Andrew. 'I also spoke to the Airbnb host, asked her to check her records for any single night bookings. I was hoping Colin might have booked in previously, stayed a night while he scoped out the place.'

'Am I sensing yet another "no joy" coming up?'

Andrew nods. 'She doesn't take bookings for single nights, it's a minimum of two. In the previous three months she rented to three parties for exactly two nights but they were all repeat customers. So that's a dead end, I'm afraid.'

'Thanks, Andrew.' I deliberately perk up before addressing the glum mood that's settled over the room. 'Let's not be too downhearted, people. By establishing that Mandy *did* set Kim up, we've stopped an innocent man from possibly being convicted and restored his reputation. We've also ticked off a lot of boxes and a big part of detective work is proving what *hasn't* happened, meaning our focus narrows down to what's left. And what's left is at least three other cases where again, the individuals involved possibly – no, make that *probably* – were framed. So let's pick up from there and bring our considerable collective intelligence and determination to bear.'

Steph shakes her head and tries hard not to smile. 'You're pushing it, boss.'

'I know. But I couldn't stand your miserable faces any longer. So come on, let's get on with it.'

'Onwards and upwards,' says Andrew. He winks at Steph.

'But be careful, it's a jungle out there,' she says.

'Oh, shut up, the pair of you.'

———

As a result of the discussion Andrew and I had with Kim, I'm just off the phone from Leo Contini. In relation to our cases the mist is beginning to lift.

Leo confirmed that Kim was witness to an RTC, a Road Traffic Collision, in November last year. A man called Peter Gardiner was charged and, get this, he's nearly seventy. *Seventy!* How the hell can you be so worked up at that age? Apparently, after an altercation at a junction in Leith he deliberately drove his car at another driver, a much younger man called Derek Parsons.

There were several witnesses. All bar one stated Gardiner was the aggressor. Kim was the only one who thought Parsons was to blame. But we know that Kim admitted he didn't see the original incident clearly, only the altercation that followed where Parsons was berating the older man at top volume. And as he told us, he alerted two police officers and pointed them at Parsons.

Based on the witness statements, if anyone was going to be prosecuted it should have been Peter Gardiner. But Leo told me his office chose not to prosecute Gardiner because it wasn't in the public interest and there were extenuating circumstances in favour of the man. On this occasion the Fiscal's decision was more about being compassionate than pursuing a conviction.

Then Leo had to field a number of interventions from the Gardiner family and their solicitor. They were incensed that Parsons wasn't charged, believing he was entirely responsible.

Leo was bemused by the family's reaction but thought they were simply trying to protect their father.

But I don't get it. Why were they so desperate to see Parsons in court when all the evidence pointed at Gardiner? Wouldn't you think they'd have accepted their father had dodged a bullet and let the whole thing die a natural death? No, there's something amiss here and that's why I want to follow up what might be simply a loose thread.

I definitely want to talk to Peter the pissed-off pensioner to hear his side of the story but first I've asked Andrew to contact Derek Parsons. As I'm deleting emails and dealing with other assorted crap, I hear Andrew talking to him. From what I can gather he's at home. I'm mildly curious as to why he's not at work when it's only just gone two, but no more than that. However, in the car, Andrew tells me Parsons didn't sound all that convincing when he said he was just taking some time off. I dare say I'll ask him myself.

———

THE BEST WAY TO describe Derek Parsons is slovenly. He's forty-two and if he tidied himself up he might even look his age. Battered slippers below a pair of jeans whose relationship with a washing machine is tenuous at best, and a tee shirt I wouldn't touch without the benefit of latex gloves. I glance around, the room suits him perfectly. A woman's touch isn't missing, it's non-existent.

And Jesus, this guy's in some state. It's a long time since I've seen anybody quite so nervous, especially when all we want to do is ask him about the RTC in which he was the innocent party. Sweat isn't actually dripping off him, but his face has a definite sheen to it. And his hands are shaking like this is the first day in a month he hasn't consumed a litre of vodka.

'Mr Parsons,' I say. 'Derek. You seem awfully nervous.' He's looking everywhere in the room apart from in my direction so I bide my time until eventually he comes back to me. 'We're not here to accuse you of anything. We're investigating another crime that the traffic incident is linked to, so all I want you to do is tell us what happened.'

For a fleeting moment he remains agitated then instantly calms down like the crazy woman in an old movie after the hero slaps her face.

'Oh,' he says. 'Okay.' Then draws in a deep breath. 'I was in the queue at the lights and the traffic ahead of me started to move. The old guy was trying to come out of Iona Street, you know how it's a staggered crossroads there?'

I know it well, pass it nearly every day. Parsons carries on. 'I suppose I could have let him in but he was being so bloody aggressive about it, jumping his car forward about a foot at a time. So I thought, oh sod off you stupid old git. Then things turned really mad because he tried to push through a space that wasn't there and bashed into my nearside wing. I couldn't believe it so I jumped out and I was walking round the front when, the next thing I know, he's driving straight at me. So I started shouting and slapped my hand on the bonnet of his car but still he didn't stop. It was bloody ridiculous. I dived out of the way and he drove straight over and hit a Mini coming in the opposite direction. Two coppers appeared but then the old guy gets out of his car and starts screaming at the Mini driver, waving his arms around and threatening all sorts. The coppers were doing their best to calm him down but then he took a swing at one of them. So they cuffed him and hauled him away.'

He stops there. I wait to see if there's more. There isn't.

'And that was it?'

He nods. 'Aye. Took ages to clear the junction, though.'

Andrew says, 'The witness in the car behind, did you know him?'

'I'd noticed him in my mirror while I was waiting. Oriental chap, driving a blue Mazda saloon. I spoke to him briefly while we were standing at the cars but no, I didn't know him. It was him that brought your mob in. He'd seen a police car parked and shouted to them as they came out of a shop.'

'And you'd never met Peter Gardiner before, the man who crashed into you?'

Parsons shakes his head. 'Definitely not! Crazy man. At his age too. They should take his licence off him.'

So now I have his version of the incident. It reflects what Leo told me so reasonable to assume it's accurate. But I'm not finished yet; Parsons is hiding something. I can feel it in my water. I glance over at Andrew, who gives me a broad smile and sweeps his arm in a small flourish towards our host.

'So, Derek.' I say, 'Where do you work?'

I've never seen anybody turn so red, so quickly. Amazing. And if he stuttered before, this time he can hardly put a consonant together. In fact, he can't speak at all so I give him a nudge.

'You're not taking time off at the moment, are you?'

Eyes down, miniature shake of the head. That'll be a no, then.

'Sacked?'

Another shake.

'Suspended?'

The smallest of nods.

'Okay, Derek. Why don't you tell us all about it?'

Over the course of the next ten minutes or so, Andrew and I take it in turns to tease out the full story. And when he's finished, for the first time since I heard about Luca Contini's death I can see how everything is beginning to link together.

It's a bit too early to wheel out the girls with the batons and the ra-ra skirts but I have them on standby. Because, after an interesting conversation with a sergeant in the custody suite, our next step is definitely a visit with Peter Gardiner.

CHAPTER SIXTY

ANDREW and I are in Peter Gardiner's house. We're sitting in a room to the rear that has a pair of wide patio doors leading onto the garden. It's been misty all day and the glass is steamed up.

There are many seventy-year-olds who are quite sprightly, but not this one. When I heard how he'd behaved at the RTC my curiosity was piqued, so I'd expected a feisty, grumpy old man with an axe to grind with everyone. But no, Peter looks his age and then some. He doesn't seem to be able to concentrate on us at all and I get the impression he'd much rather be having forty winks than visitors. Oddly, he's wearing a faded green tartan cap.

He's staring into middle distance and his daughter, Sophie, is huddled up to him on a beat up old settee wearing an expression that's fearful to say the least. She appears to be late thirties, early forties with pale, watery eyes. My overall impression is that her colour's been dialled down a few notches.

Her phone rings. 'Hi. Yes. Can you come over straight

away please?' The briefest of pauses then, 'Thanks, Cath.' She hangs up. 'My sister. She'll be here in a few minutes.'

Then she takes her father's hand in both of hers. The body language is crystal: *No talking until Cath arrives.* I wonder why Cath's in charge.

I spend the time checking out the room. It has a musty smell, it's maybe just old man. There's a faded wedding photo on a sideboard, I suppose it's Peter and his bride. Their hair-styles and dress scream 'The Seventies'. She has blonde hair in a feather cut. He's sporting a royal blue velvet suit with wide lapels and bell-bottom trousers that are no doubt concealing a pair of platforms.

I notice Peter is still wearing a wedding band but Sophie's behaviour and the emergency call she's obviously placed to her sister indicate mum is no longer around. Peter's maybe a widower or it could be his wife is in care.

On every wall there are framed family photos: infants, toddlers, teenagers and incongruously, a single picture of a line-up of adults. To hazard a guess, it's Mum, Dad and Sophie with Cath and two younger men. The group are in a walled garden, like you'd find in the grounds of a castle or a mansion house. The man standing on the extreme right, next to Sophie, has a face like fizz. I wonder what was up with him that fine day.

I watch as Sophie stands up, lifts a cloth from a radiator and mops up condensation from the window ledge. Then she fiddles with a freestanding device on the floor. At first I think it's a heater but I'm wrong, it's a dehumidifier. I notice Andrew is studying it too, then his gaze tracks across the windows, around the walls and up and over the ceiling. Before I can catch his eye, the door to the room is flung open and a woman bursts in. This'll be Cath, I expect. Sophie is only marginally less glum.

I introduce myself and Andrew. 'Cath Gardiner,' she says, and perches on the settee next to her sister. She doesn't offer to shake hands. Every movement she makes has a determined, functional edge to it.

Where Sophie is mousy, Cath is sharper, harder. It's difficult to tell if she's older or younger than her sister. Her hair is in a short bob that's too black to be natural and her clothes suggest she's come here from work. I notice she's wearing an engagement ring but it's on her right hand. What happened there, I wonder.

Sophie says, 'Cath, maybe we should call Nicholas or Alexander?' It's a plea, not a suggestion.

'Nonsense. Anyway, they're both working. I'll deal with this.' Then she glares at me, daring me to start.

I do but in my own good time. It's Peter I choose to address. 'I hear you were involved in a traffic related incident in Leith on the 28th of November, last year. Would you like to tell me what happened?'

It takes an age for his gaze to swing up and round to me. 'No.'

Okay, not the best of starts but let's give it another go. 'We know the Fiscal chose not to proceed with the case against you, and we just want to talk to you about what happened that day. We think there may be links into another case we're investigating.'

Then I smile, a little encouraging one. It's designed to help. But towards the end of my time on this earth, if I run out of smiles I'll regret wasting that one.

The old man sparks into life as if someone's plugged him in to the mains. He jumps to his feet and starts ranting at me, at Andrew, at the walls. He's not making any sense but the gist is clear. We've to fuck off out of his house and leave him and his family alone. None of this is their fault and can't we see it's everyone else we should be investigating?

'Especially that damned ...' He stops, dead in his tracks.

Now Sophie's standing beside him. She's clinging onto his arm, pulling his face towards her, desperately trying to sooth him. 'Shush, Daddy. Please don't upset yourself. I know it's not fair but things will be better soon.' Her bottom lip wobbles but she manages to hold it together.

I've no idea what she's on about and I'm pretty sure it'll be a waste of time asking her. I throw a *WTF?* vibe at Andrew but all he does is shrug. I think maybe the best approach is to wait and see how this all pans out.

Cath is standing in front of both of them, their three heads close together although Sophie has to bend down, and Cath is on her tiptoes. The two women may be sisters but they are completely different body shapes. Sophie is willowy, while Cath is short and solid. Cath puts her hands on her sister's shoulders and stretches up to whisper in her ear. Sophie looks at her with eyes a sick Spaniel would be proud of. She says, 'Come on Daddy, let's go through to the front room and settle you down,' then takes Peter by the arm and they both leave. As they cross the floor I notice the floorboards squeak like billy-oh.

I'm about to protest but Cath hits me with a *Don't you dare* death stare. Once the door closes behind them, she says, 'Listen. My dad's not fit enough to talk to you. And Sophie's had a tough time with everything that's happened. Other stuff to deal with too. Major stuff.'

She sits down. 'But I can probably tell you what you want to know.' She sighs, pulls down on every visible hem and cuff. 'My mum had a stroke back in September, a bad one. She'd been in hospital since the stroke and the day my dad was arrested, back in November, the hospital had phoned to tell him to get over there fast. Mum had had another stroke, even worse this time. He jumped in the car, became involved in all that nonsense, and when your lot tried to hold him I suppose he panicked and lashed out. So they cuffed him.'

I don't react. In circumstances like she's just described, by and large our beat coppers try their best to calm things down. But if the person won't listen and especially if they strike out then cuffs are the easiest option. It sounds harsh with Peter being elderly but there was possibly an element of keeping him out of harm's way too. They were in the midst of traffic, after all.

'Then,' she continues, 'when they reached the cells, it took bloody ages to process him. Apparently they stuck him somewhere and forgot about him. No one's admitting it but it's true.'

'Were you there?' I ask.

'I was already at the hospital with Sophie.' She glances at the door. 'I was right between a rock and a hard place. Although she's tougher than she looks, I couldn't send Soph. With it being Dad, she could easily have fallen apart. But I didn't want to leave her with Mum either.' She stops there, juts her chin out.

'Why not?'

Her eyes are like flint. 'Like I said earlier, she's had a tough time recently. Personal stuff. It's not my business to tell you.'

Which is her way of saying *Keep your nose out*.

I let her carry on. 'So I called my brother, Nick. He works split shifts so he went over.' Her brows come down. 'Oh, and by the way, if you're planning to ask me about the complete cockup with my dad at St Leonard's, don't bother. I've already put in a formal complaint about it although I'll be surprised if I ever hear anything.'

I don't react. Before we came here Bryan Fraser told me all about it and it's a definite sore point. According to him: 'At the time Peter Gardiner was brought in there was already mayhem in the station, the upshot of a protest march nearby. Some shit about oppressive regimes in Burma or whatever it's called this week. Loads of arrests. And yes, somehow he was overlooked. No phone call, no lawyer, his son here going absolutely ape-shit. Nearly arrested him too. It took a while to sort out'.

Cath's glowering at me. 'So Nick was up there for bloody ages trying to get Dad out of the cells and over to the hospital in time. But they were too late.'

My next question is definitely on the tricky side but fortunately Cath's in full rant mode. She tells me what I want to know. 'Mum fell into a coma while my dad was still locked up.'

'How is your mother?'

She studies the floor. 'Not good. Persistent vegetative state. She'll need permanent care until ...'

The pause lasts a few seconds then Andrew digs a bit deeper. 'So the reason your dad lost his temper and lashed out was because he was desperate to be at your mum's bedside?'

Cath throws her arms wide. 'Is that so difficult to believe? Because my dad's life has been wrecked. My parents aren't that long into retirement and all their plans, all the places they wanted to go and all the things they wanted to do, that's all gone down the pan. He's stuck in this never-ending cycle of hospital visits, knowing Mum won't recover and at the same time knowing she might linger on for years. And what's cutting him up the most is he never had the chance to say goodbye properly.'

She stands up, walks away a few paces then spins to face us. 'And it's not only Dad. We're all suffering. After Mum had her first stroke she was able to communicate although she had terrible trouble speaking. I think we all hoped it was just an episode and she'd recover.' She examines her fingernails. 'Or maybe we were kidding ourselves, not brave enough to face the fact she could easily have another stroke that could leave her worse off.

'The doctors tell us there's not much hope of recovery.' She snorts. 'Actually, no hope at all. But then they say it might help if we talk to her. Stories, memories, normal day-to-day crap. "Hi Mum, how are you today? Work's been a bitch but hey ho." But my dad can't do it. He can't speak to her without falling apart. Can't even get a few words out, and it's killing him.'

She glares in our direction but it's not at us. We just happen to be here.

'He told me a few weeks ago he wished she would die so she doesn't have to suffer any more. But really, it's Dad who's suffering. And I get that. Me 'n Soph, we both do. God forgive me, but I wish she would die too. Then Dad can grieve. It'll take a while but he'll recover and get at least part of his life back.'

She collapses into an armchair, facing us. Silent.

There's a decent pause then Andrew, bless him, kicks things off again but changes the angle slightly. 'When your dad hit the first car, there was a witness in the car behind. Do you know him? Or does anyone in your family?'

'Oh aye, the fine upstanding citizen? An old man, in a terrible state, being shouted at by some arsehole, and *he* brings the bloody police in.'

Andrew doesn't react, simply repeats the question. 'Do you know him?'

'No, of course I don't. Why would I? Never seen him before, interfering bloody do-gooder. Why the hell are you asking me about him anyway?'

'He was charged with an extremely serious crime but we've discovered the accusation was false.'

'So? Who cares? It's got bugger all to do with us. Is that

what you've come here for? Do you not think my dad's suffered enough, what with Mum in a coma and then being kept in the cells all day when it wasn't even his fault?'

I'm just about to say I don't give a shit whose fault this incident was when Cath jumps to her feet. 'Right! If there's nothing else, I want to go and see how Dad is, give Soph a hand. Because you've got a flamin' cheek coming here and harassing him, especially the way he was treated before. But what do you care?'

I've no doubt there's more she wants to throw at us but she leaves it there, marches over to the door and opens it wide. Her meaning couldn't be clearer if she had a big red flashing neon arrow pointing through the gap.

As I'm climbing into the car, everything suddenly seems much clearer. I can't help sympathising with Peter Gardiner and his family but I have the distinct feeling I'll be charging either him or one of his offspring fairly soon.

CHAPTER SIXTY-ONE

'What are you looking at, Cath?' asked Sophie.

Cath ignored her sister, she was more concerned about making sure the police officers had gone. When she had closed the front door behind them she went into her father's living room but moved directly to the window. It's not that she wasn't concerned about Peter's welfare, it's that he'd have to wait until she was good and ready.

'Cath!'

'Oh, shut up Sophie, will you?'

'But ...'

'Just be quiet for a minute, I need to think.'

She could see the roof of the officers' car over the top of the privet hedge but it stubbornly refused to move. *What the hell are they playing at? Hanging about outside ...*

Sophie was still twittering on but now her tone was definitely narky. Cath spun round. 'Listen! *You* called *me*. So let me deal with this but I want to make sure they've gone first.'

Then she heard an engine starting and when she glanced out, the car was moving off. She watched as it completed a three point turn and drove off down the street. The male cop was driving.

But Sophie wasn't letting go. 'Big talk as usual, Cath. Deal with what? What've you done apart from involving that ...'

Cath took a couple of quick steps towards her sister. She glared at Sophie, jerked her head in her father's direction and made a *Zip it* motion across her mouth. But Peter was staring at a wall and didn't notice. Cath breathed out as Sophie got the message and fell silent.

Then Cath walked quickly to the door. 'I have to make a call then I'll be straight back in.'

This time it was Sophie who ignored Cath.

———

'I'm busy right now. What do you want?'

Cath didn't react to this gruff greeting; it wasn't unusual. 'The pigs have been here asking questions.'

'That's what pigs do. What sort of questions?'

Cath lifted the same cloth Sophie had used earlier, wiped up a line of condensation along the bottom edge of the window. 'About that traffic thing he was involved in at Iona Street.'

'Okay. So why are you phoning me?'

'Because I know they spoke to you too.' She hesitated before pressing on. 'Have you got yourself involved in all this? Because if you have, I'll ...'

A snort came down the line. 'You'll what? End our cosy little arrangement? Go off and find somebody else? Oops, I nearly forgot, no one else will have you. That's right, isn't it Cath?' There was the briefest of silences on the line. Then, 'Anyway, I told you, I'm busy. Phone me later.'

Cath looked at her phone. 'Bastard!'

CHAPTER SIXTY-TWO

'I'm off to see Jeff. Something's up.'

Andrew speaks over his shoulder. 'What makes you think that?'

'Not sure. He called, wants to see me for a "chat". That's a bit wishy-washy, isn't it?'

And it's true, Jeff's always extremely precise, knows exactly what he wants. I tap on his office door and walk in. And instantly I know that something is, most definitely, up.

In the room, sitting next to Jeff *behind his desk* is your friend and mine, DS Deirdre Keown. Files are lying open on the desk and she's writing in an A4 notepad. She clicks the top of her pen with her thumb and lays it down. Then hits me with a broad but totally insincere smile.

I drag a chair over. This is *not* going to be good news.

'I'm going off on secondment,' says Jeff. 'To PSNI. There's a major anti-corruption initiative going on over there.' By PSNI he means the Police Service of Northern Ireland. 'It's a development move that's been on the cards for a while but I wasn't expecting it quite so soon.'

I feel like I've been punched in the stomach.

Then the frosty one's smile evolves into a smirk when he follows up with, 'Deirdre is taking over from me as from next week. We've started the handover and I'd like your input. Your fake crimes, what's the latest?'

I look down, work out which one is the wrong foot and start off on that. 'Being honest, we were struggling but the false rape allegation against Kim Seung-Min put us on the right lines.'

Deirdre's glare must be bouncing off my skull but now's not the time to worry about upsetting her so I soldier on. 'Talking to Kim, I discovered he witnessed an RTC last November. It was caused by a pensioner, Peter Gardiner, who attempted to crash through a stationary line of traffic but hit a car being driven by an IT manager, Derek Parsons. There were several witnesses but strangely, Kim was the only one who thought Gardiner wasn't at fault. Two uniforms were attempting to calm the whole thing down when the old man took a swing at one of them so they brought him in.'

Jeff's taking it all in but Keown has a *Jesus, this is some story* face on. I keep talking.

'The old man had been in a tearing hurry, trying to reach the hospital because his wife had suffered a bad stroke. But there was a cockup at the Custody Suite and he was kept in the cells far too long. By the time he was released, Mrs Gardiner was in a coma. She hasn't come round and, according to his daughter, she's not likely to either.'

'That's terrible. Poor guy,' says Jeff.

I can see he's about to hit me with a 'But', so I hold up my index finger. 'The Custody Sergeant on duty that day was Bryan Fraser, it was *his* mother whose dog was stolen. The poor woman was badly injured when the van drove over her. Then, for some peculiar reason, Gardiner's solicitor tried to put pressure on Leo Contini to charge the other driver, Derek Parsons—'

'Ah. And it was Leo's son who was framed, we think, for dealing drugs?'

'That's right. And I just found out that Parsons was arrested recently, suspected of grooming a minor.'

All the way through I've been deliberately addressing Jeff. I can't help it, he's my boss. Keown is clearly not happy so she butts in. 'Could you direct your report to me, Melissa, because I'll be making any decisions about how or *if* we progress your cases once Jeff moves on.'

Ah hah! Major strategic error there, you stuck up cow!

I don't imagine Jeff will have liked that and I'm bang on. He says, 'Actually Deirdre, for the remainder of this week you're still a DS. You don't take over 'til next week so pull your claws in.'

I figure punching the air would be OTT so I settle for the tiniest of demure smiles instead. But I risk a glance and she's absolutely livid. I'm chuffed Jeff slapped her down, and I'll just have to deal with whatever shit she dishes out in the future.

Jeff leans forward, elbows on the desk. 'So, let me make sure I've got this right. The Gardiner family wanted Parsons to be prosecuted but Leo Contini said no, and we know what happened to his son. Parsons himself has been charged with grooming a minor, and Bryan Fraser's family has been targeted to the extent of his mother being the victim of what, aggravated robbery?' He taps a fingernail on the table. 'Mel, I'm struggling with two of them. Parsons first, why would someone frame him? He didn't cause the RTC.'

'No he didn't but the family are adamant he did. When I spoke to Cath Gardiner, she's Peter's eldest, she swore blind her dad wasn't responsible. As far as they're concerned the whole thing was Parsons' fault although God knows why.'

'Okay, but what about Kim? Where does he fit in?'

'He called the uniforms over and that's why the RTC escalated.'

'So you think these four people, including Kim, have been targeted because they all contributed in some way to Mr Gardiner being carted off to the cells. And that meant he missed the chance to talk to his wife before she slipped into a coma.'

I pause. When my boss puts it like that it all sounds faintly ridiculous and I'm tempted to say, *You're right. Just ignore me. I'll go away and find something productive to occupy my time.* But then I remember Mandy Westbrook's confession, Celia Fraser suffering terrible injuries attempting to save her pet, Derek Parsons being accused of the most vile of crimes, and not forgetting poor Luca Contini feeling so devastated he took his own life.

So I puff my chest out and take a breath. 'Yes. I *do* think that's why they were targeted.'

Then Keown pipes up. 'So the motive is revenge?'

I face her for the first time. 'Yes.'

'By Peter Gardiner?'

I shrug. 'He's seventy and doesn't appear to be a well man. So it's possible but unlikely.'

'Who else then?'

'I'll look at his children first.'

'But it's hardly a strong motive, is it?

I sigh. 'On the face of it, it's hard to disagree with you ...'

'But?'

'But the powerful motivator is how the sequence of events has ultimately destroyed Peter Gardiner's life. Dreams in tatters, has to visit his wife in hospital every day, no chance she'll recover, and it's reached the point where he thinks it would be better for the whole family if she died. So yes, I accept the motive is thin but I do believe it's possible one or more of the Gardiners decided to seek revenge on all the people who, one way or another, stopped their father reaching the hospital in time to talk to his wife.'

'So, four different crimes,' says Jeff. 'Four people, all targeted in different ways and their lives destroyed, ruined, wrecked – call it what you will.' He ponders for a moment. 'I think you're right, I can't see the motive being anything else but revenge. What's your next move?'

I hadn't realised I'd been holding my breath. 'I intend to interview, under caution, all five Gardiners and see what shakes out. I'll bring them all in at the same time so they won't have a chance to collude. Then hopefully, I'll know for sure. But I'll keep you posted.'

And before the gargoyle gives me any more grief, I add, 'Both of you.'

'Could either of the sons be involved in this rape case?' says Jeff.

I shake my head. 'It doesn't seem so. They don't even closely match Mandy's description of the Colin guy, and there's no evidence of another woman being involved so that leaves the daughters in the clear. I'll be asking them all for a DNA sample but I expect it'll be to rule them out.'

Jeff stands up and strolls over to the window. He gazes down at the street. 'So if the Gardiners didn't set up these fake crimes themselves they must have either relied on favours, possible but highly unlikely, or they hired people to do their dirty work. But that wouldn't have been cheap, would it?'

'I've been thinking about that and it certainly would not. Stealing the dog: a couple of neds at what, a few hundred quid? Parsons: his company can't find any security breaches so that sounds as though he was hacked. That would have meant paying a specialist costing what, a few thousand? Then setting up Luca Contini, another grand or two? And finally, Kim. If they *were* actually intending to pay Mandy the ten k, and I have my doubts, the whole lot comes to around fifteen, twenty k. And it would all be in cash.'

Keown pipes up again. 'Any unusual transactions on the father's accounts?'

'Nothing. No suspicious cash withdrawal patterns. No money like that going out, especially to his offspring. We'll check their accounts next.'

Jeff says, 'Thanks, Mel. And your blackmailing case? Any progress yet?'

'Not in finding McLure, no. He's done a vanishing act.' I sense rather than hear Keown shaking her head but I ignore her. 'But we think we know where he lives and what car he drives. We're fairly sure the car's at the house, but unfortunately he is not. However, I am virtually certain that Francis Crolla, the nominal owner of Cross Leisure, is laundering money for McLure through the Cross business.'

'What proof do you have?' says Keown.

'A report from Ellen, our forensic accountant, which proves the business accounts don't hold water.'

'How so?'

'For example, stock orders against inventory don't tally. The daily summary sheets from the tills show inflated prices for a range of purchases, and invoices have been doctored. Ellen made a couple of test calls to suppliers and has uncovered a few major discrepancies that warrant further investigation. We're also in discussion with HMRC. I've put pressure on Frank Crolla so I want to see what that produces.'

'And what does Crolla say?'

I sigh. 'In his head, he's hiding behind a technicality

whereby he does whatever McLure tells him. He has no leeway on how he operates the pub or manages the finances. But he's the business owner so he's screwed. However, I'm convinced the real reason is McLure is blackmailing him too.'

'But you can't prove that?'

'Not yet, Deirdre. Give me time.'

———

LATER, I spot Jeff wandering through the office, heading in my direction. He stops and chats to colleagues along the way. Eventually he reaches me. He takes a casual glance around but no one's in earshot.

'Just to say, Mel, I haven't a clue why this secondment has happened at such short notice. And it utterly defeats me why they've chosen DS Keown to cover for me. It doesn't make sense and, between you and me, I've made the point she's not the best person for the job but it fell on deaf ears.'

'No worries, boss. It is what it is.' God, I hate that bloody cliché but, like him, there's nothing I can do about the situation.

'If I might make a suggestion?' He makes it clear I can't stop him even if I want to. 'It would be to your advantage if these two major investigations were a good bit further along before your new DI takes up the reins. Otherwise, I'm not sure how much latitude you'll be given.' He inclines his head a little. 'If you get my drift.'

'I do, indeed.'

He stretches, turns to leave. 'Night, Mel. See you tomorrow.'

I watch him as he picks his way across the floor. He holds the door open for a couple of colleagues who are calling it quits.

I sigh. That's another day done and although I appreciate the heads-up from Jeff I didn't have to be Mystic Mel to pick up clear vibes from Keown this morning.

What the hell, I'll worry about her later.

CHAPTER SIXTY-THREE

Sophie drove straight home after the police visited her father's house.

'What's wrong, Soph?' asked Iain, yawning. He'd been napping when she walked in.

She held her jacket folded over her arms, protecting her body like a shield. 'Nothing.'

He moved to the edge of his chair. Leaned forward, elbows on his knees. 'I can tell by your face that something's up so what is it?'

She hesitated, but who else could she talk to? 'The police came to Dad's house today. They were asking all sorts of questions about Mum's stroke and the time Dad was arrested ...'

'He was *arrested?* Jesus, Soph. When? And what the hell for?'

'It was only a stupid traffic thing but he was all upset and ... they arrested him, and he was stuck in the cells for ages, and Nick had to go and get him out, and ...'

Sophie fumbled in her bag for a tissue as her eyes brimmed

up. Iain had been about to laugh at her father's predicament but that stopped him. He moved over beside her.

'And what, Sophie?'

She blew her nose, pulled out a fresh tissue and dabbed at her eyes. 'He was on his way to the hospital because Mum had another stroke and the delay meant he missed her. She was unconscious, in a coma by the time he arrived. Anyway, this detective was asking if we knew the people involved because there's a link to other crimes. I don't really know, it was Cath who spoke to her. I was with Dad.'

Iain's eyes narrowed. 'Her? A female detective?'

Sophie sniffed. 'Yes, Iain. There *are* female detectives these days, you know.'

'What was her name?'

'What?'

'Her name, Sophie. What was her name?'

'She was a Detective Sergeant. Melissa somebody. Can't remember her surname.'

Iain couldn't believe this. How was it even possible that Sophie couldn't add two plus two here? He was nervous about confirming his suspicions but he had no choice. He fought to keep his tone level. 'Was it Cooper? Melissa Cooper?'

Sophie peered at him. 'That's right. Do you know her?'

He was amazed. *What planet is this bloody woman on?*

'Maybe. I know a few cops. I've probably come across her while I was researching a feature.' He jumped to his feet. 'I'm just off to the loo.'

Sophie stayed where she was, watched him as he marched out the door. She heard him climbing the stairs, two at a time.

Researching a feature, Iain? When? She couldn't remember the last time she'd seen his byline anywhere, never mind a feature involving the local police.

CHAPTER SIXTY-FOUR

THE SPREADSHEET I'm working on is boring beyond belief. I can't comprehend how anal you must be to create something quite so tedious.

Then my screen lurches ever so slightly; I wonder if I've actually drifted off.

But no. Turns out it's Andrew's bum that's caused the movement. He's perched it on the corner of my desk.

'Can't you see I'm busy with these incredibly interesting crime stats?' I say.

He doesn't answer me so I sit back, fold my arms, glare at him. 'Andrew. You're wearing your superior, verging on smug expression. What do you want?'

'All the time we were in Peter Gardiner's house something was bugging me.'

'And?'

'And now I know what it was.'

CHAPTER SIXTY-FIVE

DCS THORNTON TURNED AWAY from the window as his subordinate walked into his office. 'Come in, DS Keown. Close the door behind you.'

He pulled a chair away from the meeting table and indicated a place opposite him. Before she even sat down he said, 'I want you to do something for me.'

This was an unusual situation for both of them. Compared to the DCS, Keown was low down on the food chain and Thornton rarely got his hands dirty if he could avoid it. Normally he would communicate with the lower ranks through a Detective Chief Inspector, but this was delicate. Too much of a risk.

'And what would that be ... sir?'

He let his gaze drop to her breasts. Her blouse was tight across the front but it was a good fit so the buttons weren't being pulled by the pale green cotton. He saw she wasn't displaying any cleavage. Disappointing, but exercise for his fertile imagination.

He looked up again. Her expression appeared completely

neutral but then her right eyebrow lowered slightly and the shake of her head was so imperceptible he couldn't be certain she'd actually done it.

'DS Cooper's investigation into this alleged blackmailer, how is that coming along?'

She frowned, eyes narrowed. 'I couldn't say for sure. I haven't completed the handover with Jeff Hunter yet.'

He couldn't read her, didn't know if she was lying.

'But you take over from him next week officially, yes?'

'Yes.'

'Right, first chance you get, tell Cooper to pull the plug on the investigation. I don't care where she is with it, shut it down. Immediately.'

Then he stood, leaving her staring up at him. His expression was tight. She didn't know if she should risk questioning him, then realised she couldn't simply say 'Yes, sir' and walk out as if she'd been sent for a box of printer paper.

'And what reason should I give, sir? Because she's bound to ask.'

He put his index finger to his lower lip. 'Oh, I don't know, let me see. Resources over-stretched, don't have the time, higher priority cases. Take your pick. And if that doesn't work, you're her boss so tell her to obey fucking orders. I don't care how you do it. Just make sure the investigation ceases.'

———

Minutes later, standing at the lift, she wondered precisely why a Chief Super was interfering with a DS's investigation. She had her suspicions, but the involvement of a blackmailer certainly had her juices flowing. Thornton was her senior officer but she certainly felt no allegiance towards him. No, she would have to play this incredibly carefully.

One thing's for sure, no way am I taking any fall that comes along. The flak will either go up the line, or down. As things stood, she didn't know which option was preferable. But, either way, it would definitely be to the benefit of Acting Detective Inspector Deirdre Keown.

CHAPTER SIXTY-SIX

'It's me,' said Mark Thornton.

Iain McLure chuckled. 'I know who it is, you complete tool. Jesus, what fuckin' idiot promoted you to that level? Anyway, what do you have for me?'

'I've fixed it. Permanently.' Not strictly true but the Chief Super knew that to offer anything less was nothing short of career suicide.

'Explain. I require, let's say, reassurance.'

'I've taken Cooper's boss out of the picture. His replacement will not be supportive. Cooper has been told to shut the case down.' This second lie sounded more plausible somehow.

'And what makes you think Cooper won't be able to talk him round?'

'Not him, her. And they hate each other.'

'And you lot are in charge of upholding the law? God help us.'

'Well, whatever. It's fixed. You don't have to worry any longer.'

Damn. That was a mistake.

'But that's the point, I do worry. That's why I'm always a step ahead.'

During the pause, Thornton's phone bleeped.

'That's a message from me, by the way,' said McLure. 'You might want to delete it, once you've digested the contents.'

As usual, it wasn't Thornton who terminated the call. When he looked down at his phone he discovered McLure had sent him a PDF and before his nerve failed him he tapped the icon. When he saw what it was, he was glad he hadn't eaten recently.

The document dated back to when he was a Detective Chief Inspector, it had been instrumental in securing promotion to his current rank. Thornton was the author or, to be absolutely accurate, the author of two slightly different versions of the same document. It concerned Police Scotland's orchestrated response to County Lines drug dealing. 'County Lines' is the term used to describe a form of organised crime where criminals based in urban areas pressurise vulnerable people and children to transport, store and sell drugs in smaller county towns.

Version one was for internal consumption at high level, but once the content was signed off he'd taken it home and made subtle but important alterations to create a second version. It was the content and actions from version two that were executed operationally. His bosses had no reason to suspect that the initiative they had authorised had not been fully implemented by Thornton and his operational units. The changes he'd made were in the detail but they swung the focus away from people who rewarded him handsomely to protect their interests. It now appeared that McLure had links with the same people.

He studied the document and was aghast to find it was the original with the alterations highlighted in red text. He laid his phone face down as if it would explode on contact with the desk.

Who on God's earth gave McLure that file?

But Thornton knew in his heart it was a stupid question. He'd screwed over too many people, shit on too many colleagues as he bulldozed his way up the career ladder. No wonder some of them would be only too keen to see him coming to grief. If this ever came to light, the eventual outcomes of at least three Scotland-wide investigations would be cast in doubt and every initiative, project or even case he'd ever been involved with or in charge of, would be compromised. As would the reputation of the service.

Prosecutions would inevitably follow so Thornton was fully aware this wasn't only about his career, it was about his life. And McLure was in the position where he could work Thornton like a ventriloquist's dummy.

Mark Thornton stared at the back of his phone for a long time. If nothing else happened he'd bought himself a few days' breathing space until Keown was able to shut down Cooper's investigation into McLure.

Until then he would simply have to wait. And hope.

And pray.

CHAPTER SIXTY-SEVEN

'LISTEN,' says Peter Gardiner. 'I fail to see why you've dragged me in here. Like I told you before, I don't know anything about these cases you're investigating and neither do my children.' He glares at his solicitor. 'For God's sake sort this out, will you?'

It's just after nine a.m. and we are questioning Peter Gardiner on suspicion of attempting to defeat the ends of justice. This will be a full-on day because we've also brought in Peter's offspring on the same basis. I can't run the risk of them colluding, so we have each of them in separate rooms. Oldest first, they are Catherine, Sophie, Nicholas and Alexander. It was Andrew who pointed out the Russian theme; way over my head, I'm afraid.

One of the main logistical problems was finding five duty solicitors who would be free at the right times but as usual Steph's done a marvellous job organising things and they're all lined up.

Andrew's working with me but we've agreed that I'll do the

bulk of the interviewing, while he'll be monitoring their behaviour closely and taking notes to keep me right.

We're talking to Peter first, but it's hard to imagine he's behind these crimes. He's far frailer than a man his age should be and when I saw him at his house he didn't seem quite with it. But today he's sharp enough. There's colour in his cheeks and his eyes have a spark to them.

'Let me lay things out for you, Mr Gardiner,' I say. 'We have Derek Parsons, involved with you in an altercation following a road traffic collision, and before we know it he's accused of using online chatrooms in the attempted grooming of a minor. I believe he was framed but I can't prove it yet.'

Peter's shrugs, looks at the wall to his left. 'I don't even know what a chatroom is.'

'Next there's Kim Seung-Min. He alerted our officers to the incident. Three weeks ago, Kim was accused of assault and rape but we know the accusation to be false. The woman involved has admitted she was promised a large sum of money to set him up.'

'Don't know the chap, never met him.'

'Then you were held for far too long at St Leonard's. No one doubts you were unfairly treated but the custody sergeant's mother's dog – bear with me here – was abducted. The woman is only a couple of years younger than you and in attempting to save her dog, she was dragged under the van. She suffered terrible injuries: broken leg and fractured pelvis. In fact she's still in hospital. Her *granddaughter* is having counselling, she's only twelve. Added to that, the family were sent disgusting threatening videos suggesting their pet was going to be bait for fighting dogs.'

Peter's no longer such a healthy colour. I press on.

'But then it turned up safe and sound a few weeks later. So again, Peter, this appears to be a set up. Not a real crime.'

I give him time to respond but he shakes his head. I don't let up.

'And finally, the teenage son of the Procurator Fiscal was accused of dealing drugs. At first I thought he'd been set up too. Payback because the Fiscal intended to prosecute you for causing that traffic incident. But then I find the case against you was dropped on compassionate grounds because all you were trying to do was reach your wife's bedside as quickly as you could. Most people would think they'd struck it lucky there, but not your family. No, *your* family urged your solicitor to attempt to divert the blame onto Parsons, but the Fiscal refused because he had half a dozen witnesses prepared to testify that you were responsible.'

I pause, wait for a reaction. Nothing. I lean forward, forearms on the table. 'Putting the two things together, I think Derek Parsons was targeted because someone was totally convinced *he'd* dodged a prosecution, when in actual fact *you* did. And because the Fiscal didn't do what your family wanted him to, his son was framed for dealing drugs.'

Peter snorts at that. 'Here's another way to look at it. Maybe he wasn't set up, maybe he actually *was* running drugs?' Peter spreads his hands, palms up. 'And if he was, I hope he gets what he deserves.' He stops there, folds his arms, glares at me.

I wait a few beats before I reply. 'I'm guessing, Peter, that you're not aware that this teenager, Luca Contini ...'

Peter's brow comes down. 'Contini?' He thinks some more. 'I remember the name. Wait, is he the boy who ...?'

I nod. 'Yes, Peter. As a direct result of being framed, Luca Contini died. Suicide. That's why we're determined to prove his innocence and find out who's behind all this.'

'Well it's not me, I can tell you that for nothing.'

There was a tremor in those words so I think he's probably

telling the truth, but there are a few more buttons I can press first.

'Here's what I do know, Peter. That traffic incident kicked off a chain of events that meant you didn't reach the hospital on time before your wife lapsed into a coma. Now that's desperately sad and I do feel for you.' Peter's eyes well up but I'm in no mood to let him off the hook. 'But there is one thing that was bothering me about this whole saga.'

His eyes are sharp. 'Was?'

I nod. 'I just couldn't figure out why you, or anyone in your family, would be pursuing a vendetta against all these individuals. Parsons, Kim, the Fiscal, our custody sergeant. None of them were responsible for your wife having a stroke. So then I was left wondering, was this solely about the fact that tragically, you didn't reach your wife on time? One incident? That seemed unlikely to me.'

Peter turns to his solicitor. 'How many times do I have to tell her I don't know about any of this apart from the traffic thing in Leith and the complete cockup at St Leonard's?'

I wait 'til he's facing me again. 'DC Young?' I say.

Peter shifts his attention as Andrew taps his pen on his notebook. My colleague comes way in from left field. 'The room at the back of your house?'

'Oh, don't get me started on that!'

'On what?'

'Bloody disaster. Wish we'd never done it.'

'Done what?'

'Had that extension built. Like I said, bloody disaster from start to finish. Bloody cowboys.'

Andrew nods. 'Cowboys? You mean TJ Construction? Headed up by Tommy Jarvis?'

'That's him. Aggressive prick.'

'Tell me, Mr Gardiner, did you know Tommy Jarvis's

house was burned down in the early hours of Sunday the 3rd of April?'

Peter blinks, rapidly, as Andrew moves on. 'And did you also know that his house insurance was cancelled, not by him, meaning he and his family are homeless and have lost practically everything they own?'

At first Peter appears thunderstruck but then an enormous grin illuminates his face like a floodlight hitting centre stage. A second later he starts to laugh until I think his septuagenarian bladder might give out.

Eventually he subsides. I worry he might be about to kick off again, when Andrew taps his pen once more. 'Mr Gardiner, according to the hospital your wife suffered her first stroke in September of last year.' I feel bad we have to be so blunt but that doesn't half wipe the smile off his face. 'TJ Construction told us the extension was started over six months prior to that, late February, and wasn't finished when she became ill.'

'What do you mean "wasn't" finished. Bloody thing's *still* causing problems.' He's waving his arms around. 'Leaking windows, condensation, cracks inside and out. Buggers won't come back and fix them. Even when they do appear they find some bloody excuse not to finish what they're doing. You've no idea the stress—'

He stops, dead.

Andrew jumps in. 'Yes, Mr Gardiner? What were you saying about stress?'

Peter stays silent.

'Do you think the stress might have contributed towards your wife's stroke?'

'How would I know, I'm not a bloody doctor.'

I tell you what, he's a big fan of the word 'bloody'.

'So,' I say, 'if we add Tommy Jarvis to the list there are now five people affected by strange events, alleged crimes or false accusations and all five are linked to *your* family. That's why we're talking to you all today. You can see there's a pattern, can't you?'

His solicitor stirs for once. She puts a hand on Peter's arm but he shrugs it off.

'Yes, of course I can. I'm not bloody stupid. But how many times do I have to tell you, I don't know about any of this. It would take brains, money, criminal connections. I don't have any of those. And neither do my children.'

Outside, Andrew and I agree that perhaps Peter Gardiner *isn't* streetwise enough and *doesn't* have enough free cash or the right connections. But could he be wrong about his offspring?

———

NEXT, we have Cath. Peter's eldest is forty, single, but the ring on her right hand suggests a broken engagement.

'That's a lovely ring,' I say.

'Thanks.'

'Had it long?'

'None of your damn business.'

This is Cath. Hard, aggressive, blunt. Takes no prisoners. She manages a betting shop over in Muirton, an area in North Edinburgh that's nowhere near as bad as it once was but possibly still not the place I'd choose for a gentle evening stroll.

Cath dresses provocatively. Brassy, you might say. She's on a decent salary but her bank account is almost always down to double figures by the end of the month. And mostly cash withdrawals too. It's a reasonable place to start.

'Cath. Most of your regular expenditure is in cash, that's unusual these days isn't it?'

'Is it?'

'And you appear to spend your entire salary every month.'

She shrugs. 'There's no pockets in a shroud.'

'The cases we're investigating will have been financed in cash. Can you account for where your money goes?'

She strokes her chin and stares up at the ceiling. Then comes back to me. 'No.'

'You don't save anything?'

'What's the point in a savings account? You get fuck-all interest these days.'

Time to poke her from a different angle. 'Are you angry about the way your father's life has turned out?'

She gives me a hostile glare for that one. But no reply.

'You know Tommy Jarvis don't you?'

This time she does reply, with the most offensive swearword in the English language.

'Ever visited his house?'

'Oh, aye. I pop round for afternoon tea most Sundays.'

'Did you know it was burned down recently? Deliberately.'

She says no but her expression tells me she's lying, and she doesn't care that I notice.

And this is how it goes for the next half an hour. Dripping sarcasm, gives nothing away, doesn't ever reply 'no comment' but as good as.

I have nothing else to prod this woman with so I leave it there.

———

SOPHIE IS thirty-seven and if Cath has a polar opposite then her younger sister is it. She gives the impression of being perpetually sad. The fire in her eyes has subsided, if it was ever there. I recall what Cath said about Sophie being tougher than she looks but I've yet to see any sign. She works as a receptionist in her uncle's company but it's difficult to imagine her in a public-facing role.

It's clear she's devoted to her dad and is probably shouldering his emotional burden in addition to her own. Maybe that's why she appears worn down.

I'm not ruling her out as a suspect, that would be stupid. But I wouldn't put my last pound on her being the guilty one. I remember her being upset in Peter's house and I don't think it will take much to kick her off again. So I launch straight in.

'Sophie, I heard you've had a tough time recently.'

She gasps, opens her mouth but no words come out.

'What's been happening to you, Sophie?'

She turns to her solicitor and just stops short of grabbing his sleeve. His expression says *Move on, DS Cooper*. It was worth a try.

'Tell me, what do you do with your spare time?'

She blinks. I smile, to encourage her.

'I look after my dad.'

'Anything else?'

'I volunteer.'

'Where?'

'I don't think I'm allowed to tell you.'

I smile again. Keep my voice quiet. 'We're the police, Sophie.'

She squirms a bit in her chair. 'Okay. I volunteer in support of abused women and children.'

'That's a tough gig. How long have you been doing that?'

'Six or seven years.' She lifts her chin. 'I get a lot out of it.'

'And how did you become involved?'

'Through the church.'

I look at her.

She blinks again. 'Our Lady and All Saints.'

As she warms up, the interview becomes less like pulling

teeth. Sophie becomes more willing to answer our questions but rarely elaborates without us nudging her. When we finish, I still have an open mind about Peter's second child. But it's ajar, rather than right back on its hinges.

———

APPARENTLY THE GARDINERS took a break from procreating because Nicholas is thirty-one, six years between Sophie and him. But *he* hasn't been hanging about, married with four kids already. Funny thing is, he dresses like a teenage version of himself but doesn't quite pull off the image.

My starting point is he did time for aggravated assault when he was only nineteen, in his second year at St Andrews.

'You didn't finish uni, Nicholas?'

This particular Gardiner sports a permanent glower. 'No. Stuck up bastards kicked me out. Couldn't have a jailbird mixing with the upper classes and all their rich foreign pals.'

I check my notes. 'And you're a delivery driver?'

'Anything wrong with that?'

I can glower with the best of them but I can't be bothered. 'No, Nicholas. Nothing at all. But you have five Highers. Straight A's.'

He shrugs. Now he *does* look like a teenager. 'So what? They're no use if I can't even get an interview, never mind a decent job.'

I wonder if he'd like tomato ketchup with those chips on his shoulder.

'Anyway,' he says, 'there's little point asking me stuff because I'll tell you something for nothing, I don't like the cops.'

I give out a short, harsh laugh. 'Guess what, Nicholas, I won't be standing for president of your fan club any time soon.'

He is startled. Clearly he didn't expect such cheek. 'I'm asking you "stuff" because we're investigating several crimes that are linked. And the link is your family. Maybe one of you, maybe all five, who knows. And that's what we're aiming to find out.' This time I do glower at him. 'Okay?'

He shrugs again, glances away. Tries to affect an air.

I know the answer to this but I ask anyway. 'What does your wife do?'

'Nails.'

I point my pen at his face. 'It's dead easy being a smartarse, Nicholas. For example, I could be the type of smartarse that throws your sorry carcass in a cell overnight until you feel like being a bit more civil.'

His eyes are down, he blushes. 'She's a freelance beautician. Specialises in manicures. Nail art, eyebrows, things like that.'

'Does she ever freelance at Boutique KSM?'

He's back on me. 'I think you already know she does.'

I do indeed. And that she trains and mentors women who Kim helps. So perhaps Nicholas is not as divorced from these crimes as he'd have us believe.

―――

I CHECK THE CLOCK. Opposite us is the youngest of the Gardiner clan. Alexander is twenty-nine and the definition of flash. The clothes are top end Hugo Boss, and his blond hair looks like it's razor-cut every other day. He's possibly the most smiley member of the family, but I wouldn't trust him as far as I could spit a caramel.

He owns a penthouse flat down at Ocean Terminal and clearly he's bright. He runs a company that designs apps, with several FTSE 250 clients on his portfolio and a string of business awards that would shame the crew in *Dragons' Den*. Money goes to money as they say, and to prove the adage we discovered he'd won seven figures on the lottery last year. And get this: he tells us, matter-of-fact, that he didn't share any of it with his siblings.

'You make your own luck in this world,' he says. 'And you shouldn't expect a free ride just because you're related.'

'Even your father?' I've decided I definitely don't like this guy.

'He needs to get his act together. Sort himself out. And the others are soft for running about after him.'

It's times like this when police officers should be allowed to slap suspects around. But only for a few minutes until we feel better.

'Have you fallen out with your family, Alexander?'

He traces his fingernail along a jagged gouge in the table. 'No.'

'The reason I ask is because *close* families normally help each other.'

'Do they?' he says, his lip curling.

I move on to relate the litany of fake accusations and crimes along with their consequences to utterly innocent people, but he does not *give* a shit.

'If they caused Dad to arrive late at the hospital they deserve all they get.' A little thundercloud drifts over his horizon when I mention Luca Contini's death but he soon recovers. 'What goes around, and all that.'

I thump both fists on the table, causing him to jump involuntarily. Then I hit him with a snarl that wipes the supercilious look off his face. 'An innocent boy has died. You might not care about that, but I do.' I'm desperate to add *you slimy little turd,* but I display monumental professional restraint for once in my life.

Despite the phoney Joe Cool demeanour he's momentarily derailed. So I follow up by sticking a printout under his nose and pointing at it. 'Can you explain to me why you withdrew £40,000 in cash during this three week period?'

He stares at the paper, pauses, then he's back on an even keel. 'Maybe I had a hot date that weekend. Who knows? I have plenty of money. More than you, that's for sure.'

'Let me rephrase the question for you, Mr Gardiner. On what – did you spend – £40,000 – in cash – recently?' I glare at him. 'And don't give me any crap this time.'

'Poker.'

'Poker?'

'That's right, poker. High rollers, in a private club, up town.'

He sits back. Gives me a brief smile that doesn't go anywhere near his eyes. He thinks he's got me, that there's nowhere I can go with that.

He might be right. But not if I've got anything to do with it.

CHAPTER SIXTY-EIGHT

No MATTER how many facelifts they give our beloved HQ down here in Leith, there's a growing sense amongst the inhabitants that it's not long for this world. Capital budget constraints are keeping us here but I often wonder if the constant outlay on refurbishment stacks up against the cost of a new building. Having said that, the occasional silver lining does brighten up our day and the room we're in is a case in point.

It's the smallest of three operational incident rooms that are fitted with brand spanking new technology; a wall-to-wall, floor-to-ceiling interactive whiteboard that duets with a Smart-Table. Right now, the four of us are clustered around this futuristic wonder. A thing of beauty with a surface like a giant iPad, two metres by one. Using it as the interface I can create text, tables and diagrams, or download and manipulate maps or images then project them on to the wall. I can move them around, resize, and draw connecting lines in any colour that takes my fancy. And I can save, print or email either segments or the entire wall to another wall or to a PC. I'd hated the training course with a passion, but now I'm a complete convert.

After this morning's round of interviews, Andrew and I pulled our thoughts together before bringing in Steph and Tobias. Now we're studying the data, arranged in a table that summarises our discussions with each member of the Gardiner family – a five by five matrix. Five Gardiners across the top, and five crimes down the side. Symmetry and balance: lovely.

'Okay, team. Here's where we are. Andrew and I will be going into another round of interviews this afternoon so we need to sense check everything we have so far. Steph, Tobias. Any questions, comments or observations, just shout. Especially if something doesn't stack up. Okay?'

The left column contains Peter's data. I tap it and his mug shot appears on the wall. I move a laser pointer around the table while I summarise the salient points relating to the senior Gardiner.

'Tommy Jarvis caused Mr and Mrs Gardiner a lot of heartache, and no small amount of stress. Mrs Gardiner suffered her first stroke and was hospitalised. Several weeks later, another stroke. Much worse this time. Peter was trying to get to the hospital, in a hell of a rush as you can imagine. But three people, one after the other, conspired to delay him. *He* crashed into Parsons. Then Kim called two PCs over to the scene. Peter was arrested and held at St Leonard's. He didn't reach the hospital before his wife fell into a coma so he was denied the chance to say goodbye. Finally, Leo Contini refused to prosecute Parsons, so he was dragged into the melee.' I pause for a breath. 'Then, in the days and weeks that followed, all of those five people were victims of crimes that threaten to destroy their lives. Our job is to prove one or more of the Gardiner family is responsible.'

Steph is first up. 'Do we really think Peter is capable of either committing or arranging the five crimes?'

'We suspect not,' says Andrew. 'He's physically too frail and mentally, sometimes he's not firing on all cylinders. He has no criminal connections and, because we can't find any suspicious payments or withdrawals from his accounts, that suggests he didn't pay anyone to carry them out. Plus, he did seem genuinely surprised when we told him about Tommy's house burning down.'

'Although,' I add, 'that was possibly the best piece of news he's heard in ages.'

Tobias lifts his hand. 'But, he could still be responsible if he was working in collusion with one or more of his children. He wouldn't need to pay them, would he?'

'You're right, he wouldn't. Now considering Peter, and assessing means, motive and opportunity, he has the motive because he's the most directly affected. If he has the means he's keeping it well hidden, but we don't think he's capable of taking the opportunity.'

Nods of assent all round. Peter Gardiner might appear to be the obvious link to all five crimes, but none of us actually believe he's our man. And even if we did, we have no evidence to back it up.

I bring Cath Gardiner's photo up next and immediately Steph pipes up. 'Hang on a minute, I know her.'

'You do?' I'm surprised, and my face must show it.

Steph half stands up to lean closer to the photo. 'Not *know*, exactly. But I definitely recognise her.' She drums her nails on the table top. I'm about to say we'll come back to it later when she snaps her fingers. 'Ah-hah! She was in the pub when we went to talk to Spider Kilbride. As we walked up to the bar she disappeared off to the loo. When she came out she left by the side door.'

I clap my hands together and give her a double thumbs-up.

'Terrific spot, Steph. Can you follow up on that, please?' I tap Cath's data and add a potential relationship with a known criminal to the 'Opportunity' field.

Then I pick up again. 'Assuming she wasn't standing next to Spider by pure coincidence, what is the relationship? We know from her bank accounts that she's on a reasonable salary but her balance is more or less zero by the end of every month. So does she owe money? Is that why she only uses cash? Does some of that cash end up in Spider's pocket? And is there any connection to Leo and Luca Contini, bearing in mind we're almost certain Spider set Luca up on the drugs bust.'

Andrew lifts a hand. 'I hate to disparage the entire population of Muirton and its environs, but could the person who broke into Tommy's house be a customer of either that pub or Cath's betting shop?'

'And could that be the same for the little shits who stole Celia Fraser's dog and drove over the poor woman?' says Tobias, much to our collective surprise.

I add these thoughts to Cath's data so we can all read it. 'So Cath has the motive, and possibly the opportunity if we can prove her relationship with Spider.'

'Next, Sophie. While she's not exactly axe murderer material we can't afford to ignore her. She gives the impression of being meek and emotionally unstable, but is she? Clearly she's devoted to her father but if that's the case, why wouldn't Cath let her go to St Leonard's to get him out and take him over to the hospital? That struck me as odd, especially when Cath then said she couldn't leave Sophie with her mum either. I mean, if she's that emotional and apparently helpless, how come she volunteers to support abused women and children? She must experience some harrowing stuff in that environment. Finally, her sister says Sophie has been dealing with, quote unquote, "major stuff".'

'And you want to know what this major stuff is?' says Steph.

'Indeed I do.'

I pause while she makes a note.

'Now, finances. Unlike her sister, Sophie actually *has* savings but they're untouched. No unusual withdrawals from any of her accounts either.'

Andrew taps the table. 'We spoke earlier about Cath maybe having criminal connections because of where she lives and works, could there be a similar link with Sophie and her voluntary work?'

'Meaning?'

'Most of those women have abusive partners. Might Sophie's work bring her into contact with the type of person who could carry out these crimes?' He spreads his hands. 'Tenuous, admittedly.'

'I'll drop it in; maybe her reaction will tell us what we want to know.' I finish typing and study Sophie's data. 'She has the motive and, like Cath, possibly the opportunity. Financially, she has the means but hasn't touched her savings.

'Next, the sons. Nicholas Gardiner has a record. An aggravated assault charge when he was nineteen, which resulted in him being kicked out of uni. But I'm pretty sure DNA will prove Nicholas wasn't Mandy's accomplice. The description doesn't match. He hates the police, blames the judiciary system and St Andrews for his life going down the pan. But he does have a connection to Kim because his wife's a beautician, works for Boutique KSM.'

'Motive and possible opportunity for Nicholas too, then?' says Andrew.

'Yes. But with four kids under ten I doubt he has the means.'

No disagreement, so I move on again.

'And finally, the delightful Alexander, the baby of the family. Arrogant prick. He doesn't match the description of Mandy's accomplice either, but he definitely has the money. Independently wealthy through his business and, jammy bastard, a seven-figure lottery win last year. Clearly there's family tension here because he didn't share any of it with his siblings. He criticised them, saying they were soft for running about after his dad and thinks all Peter needs is a good kick up the backside.'

'Sympathetic, or what?' Obviously Steph's not a fan either.

'So he's arrogant, cocky, smart, an extremely successful businessman even before he won the lottery, and ruthless as far as his family are concerned. And yet ... he thought the victims deserved whatever they got if they caused his dad to be late reaching the hospital.'

'What is his business, boss?' asks Tobias.

'They design apps. Why do you ask?' I give him a second while his brain cells tick over.

'Because Derek Parsons is accused of grooming a minor online. He is said to have used his work laptop, which was stupid especially as he leads an IT team. If he's innocent and we assume he is, although we haven't proved it yet, then someone hacked into his employer's systems. Alexander's company may design apps, but he and his employees will probably have computer science degrees and experience in many other applications. So it's possible one of them was the hacker.'

Tobias doesn't say much but when he does he's usually worth listening to. I give him a pointed look before adding this to Alexander's data.

He smiles back. 'Yes boss, I'll check them out.'

'He also withdrew £40k in cash from his account, said he spent it playing poker.' There's a groan from round the table. 'Yes. I know. Dead end.'

'Maybe not, I'll put out feelers.' says Andrew. 'Although I'm not hopeful.'

'And to summarise Alexander, less of a motive, definitely has the means. But, opportunity? Nothing jumping out at me apart from possibly the IT angle.'

I fall silent while we scan the whole family's data on the wall. I highlight the new points we've raised. There's some general discussion but no one has any important changes to make.

'Okay. Just to make sure we've got these new points covered. Steph. Any links, financial or otherwise, between Cath and Spider. What reasons might there be for her using only cash? And, can you dig up anything on Sophie. Especially around this so-called "major stuff"? Tobias. Take a closer look at Alexander's staff. Particularly, could any of them be our hacker? And talk to Derek Parsons' employer. Can they recheck their security for any obvious breaches? And Andrew, we need to know where Alexander plays his poker.'

I check my notes. 'I'm going to push all of them a little further on their possible criminal connections, see how they react. Especially Peter. He'll want to protect his children, so he might slip up.'

I'm last to leave the room and as I stride along the corridor I begin to feel confident something conclusive will shake out in the next few hours. By the time I catch up with Andrew near the interview rooms, I've got my game face on.

'Ready to go, boss?'

'Damn right, my boy. They've got away with this for long enough.'

CHAPTER SIXTY-NINE

THE POLICE SUSPECT OUR FAMILY. *It was only a matter of time.*

They think the responsibility for these so-called crimes lies at our door. And, broadly speaking, they are correct. What is interesting is they have only cited five of these happenings, it appears they still have not discovered the existence of the doctor. I find this both amusing and ironic because she played a key role. And she, of all people, deserves to suffer. As they all do, of course, but the doctor more than most because she could have done so much to help in the early days. But she didn't.

Although she was adapting well to her incarceration, my recent visit, as intended, will have set her back immeasurably. Now she knows who is responsible for her predicament but no one is listening to her.

The police officer who led my interview, I suspect with the others too, is clever. Her questions are insightful, incisive. She knows what she is searching for. The only saving grace is that she does not, as yet, know precisely where to look.

Her younger colleague doesn't contribute much but he listens, observes, analyses. I fully expect that after the interviews she asks him his opinions and she will pay close attention to what he says. It is abundantly clear they are a close-knit pairing, a strong opponent.

Because we are all being kept apart, and I confess I didn't see that coming, I only know what the detective has asked me. Where she has prodded and probed, the questions she has posed in order to seek out the truth. To counter her, I know where the gaps are in my account, where she might insert her scalpel in order to expose the truth that lies beneath this skin of lies and deceit. She will be doing the same with the others but probably in different areas, in different ways, and comparing answers to use against us.

It is a few minutes past two. We are only part-way through the day so there is more to come. Will they find the answers they are searching for? I would be surprised if they didn't, so I must defer the inevitable for as long as possible. But how? Distract, lie, obfuscate, delay? Possibly even hope for a procedural error on their part. In truth, however, that is most unlikely.

Ultimately, it will not matter. What was done, was done for the most principled of reasons and I do not care what the law says. People have suffered because they deserved to, and it is my intention to prolong that suffering for as long as I am able.

Ah! Voices from the corridor outside. Are they going past?

No.

CHAPTER SEVENTY

'You see, Peter, I believe the catalyst for this series of events was the ongoing building work at your house. Or, more accurately, the stress this caused to you and your family, which possibly resulted in Mrs Gardiner having a stroke.'

It's six o'clock and Peter's been in this room virtually all day, while Andrew and I have moved between the interview rooms, the office and the staff kitchen. Peter's definitely tired, I'm beginning to flag too but I'm buoyed by the fact that we're nearly there. Peter doesn't know that yet but he's about to find out. If all goes to plan, this will be the last interview today so I press on.

'You stated earlier, and I quote, "I don't know anything about these cases you're investigating and neither do any of my children". Is that still your position?'

If he possessed the energy he'd probably throw his hands in the air but he settles for an extended sigh. 'Yes, DS Cooper, that is still my position.'

I sit back. 'DC Young? Over to you.'

Andrew scrapes his chair a little closer to the table. 'Since we left you this morning, we've conducted two interviews with each of your sons and daughters—'

'Two?'

'Yes, Mr Gardiner, two. And we've cross-checked a number of statements you've all made. We believe one of your family, maybe more than one, is responsible for five other families suffering dreadful events, all of which were life-altering. And we're very close to proving which of you it is.'

Possibly a mild exaggeration but let's not worry about that for the moment. Andrew's bold statement has the desired effect, Peter is biting his lip and seems to have difficulty finding a comfortable position.

Andrew keeps things moving. 'Now, with regard to these events, you also stated, "It would take brains, money, criminal connections. I don't have any of those. And neither do my children". Unfortunately you're mistaken, Mr Gardiner. Or deluded. One of the two.'

Peter folds his arms, tight. His brow is down so low his glasses move.

Andrew checks his notes. 'Let me ask you, Peter, what's the relationship between Cath and James Kilbride? Goes by the nickname "Spider".'

Peter winces. Only a slight movement but we both catch it, and he sees that we did. We wait while he picks his words. 'There is *no* relationship between *my daughter* and that crooked little bastard.'

'But she knows him?'

'Of course she *knows* him. He's in and out of the betting shop all day long. But that's all, there's no relationship.'

'A connection then?' Andrew smiles. Too late, Peter sees where this is going.

My colleague makes a big show of writing in his notebook. 'Cath Gardiner … connection with known criminal.'

327

'Oh *come on.*' Peter turns to his solicitor. 'Can he *do* that?'

Before she can reply, Andrew says, 'Ms Gardiner has already explained the extent of her relationship with James Kilbride. Now what about your son, Nicholas? Aggravated assault? Inside for a year but still ... impossible for him not to be adversely influenced by other inmates. Then there's Sophie ...'

'*Sophie?*' It's a full-on shriek from Peter this time.

Andrew ignores him. 'You know she volunteers?'

'Of course, but ...'

'Specifically she volunteers to help and support abused women and children, not a job I could do at all. So here's our next question, is it even remotely possible that she might have come into contact with partners of those women? Men who could be violent, dishonest, crooked?'

'I don't know, you'll have to ask her.'

'We already have, Mr Gardiner. Remember you said no one in your family has criminal connections? It now seems Sophie, Cath and Nicholas do. Don't they?'

Peter starts to speak but Andrew cuts him off. 'Oh, and returning to Nicholas for a minute, he also has a connection with Sophie's volunteer work.'

'How?'

'Because his wife provides training for some of those women, to help them back on their feet. It's organised through Sir Robert Parker's foundation.'

Peter's lip curls. 'Does she? I didn't know.'

Andrew is in quick. 'How is your relationship with your daughter-in-law?'

Peter looks away. 'It's fine. As long as we're not in the same room.'

Andrew throws a glance in my direction. I reckon he's about to fly a kite so I keep a close eye on Peter.

'Does your strained relationship with Nicholas's wife have

anything to do with Alexander's lottery win and the fact that he didn't share any of it with his family?'

That definitely hits the spot. Peter is throwing out tells like rose petals at a Hindu wedding. Andrew waits, doesn't push it, lets Peter have the floor. 'If that bloody woman had just shut up and given Alexander the chance ... but no.' He heaves himself out of his chair, catches a heel and almost falls before tottering back to the table and grabbing the edge. 'He's done well with his business, he was comfortably off already but anyone who lands that amount of money needs time to come to terms with it. We all stood off him ... but not her. No, straight in. Grasping greedy little cow. Wanted him to set Nicholas up in business, put money in trust for her kids. Aye, and bearing in mind neither Catherine nor Sophie *have* kids. And neither does Alexander for that matter.'

He takes his glasses off, pinches the bridge of his nose. 'She should have kept her bloody nose out. It was none of her business.' He sits down again but the chair is still set away from the table. He sticks his legs out. 'Anyway, Alexander eventually blew his top. Told her in no uncertain terms she wouldn't see a penny of his money. Fell out with his brother too because Nicholas sided with his missus.' He snorted. 'No question who wears the trousers in *that* house.'

He pauses for a couple of seconds. He's calmer. 'Things totally fell apart after that. His mother and I stayed out of it. Sophie kept quiet, of course. And Catherine ... well, Catherine said her bit then walked away. Alexander kept all his money to himself and that's the way it is. Can't say I blame him in the slightest.'

'Do they still speak?' asks Andrew.

'Alexander and Nicholas? Not in civil tones. But as for his sisters, Alexander's their baby brother, isn't he? Can't do a thing wrong in their eyes.'

Andrew pauses there, lets that sink in. 'He gambles though, doesn't he? Plays poker.'

Peter nods. 'So I gather. Pretty good at it too, from what I hear.'

'He's smart, obviously.'

Peter nods. 'But so is Nicholas. Five straight A's and an unconditional acceptance for St Andrews.'

'Hmmm, and Cath manages a small business.'

Andrew smiles at Peter. 'So there we have it, Mr Gardiner. Brains, money *and* criminal connections. Not in short supply at all, are they?'

CHAPTER SEVENTY-ONE

'WE DON'T HAVE ENOUGH to charge any of the Gardiners, do we?' says Andrew.

It's the following morning. We're all back at the table and everyone's waiting for me to make the call.

I rub away a mark on the surface. 'No. We don't.'

I study my notes, find my list of outstanding points. 'Right. Let's take one more spin round the dance floor, see what's what.' I tap the point of my pen on item one. 'All five have agreed to a DNA test?'

'Yes,' says Andrew. 'Meaning they're innocent or they're confident they won't be caught.'

I turn to Steph. 'Cath's fondness for dealing mainly in cash?'

'I had a quick word with Ellen, the forensic accountant. As we thought, there's absolutely nothing we can do. Cath withdraws money frequently from her account. Standard amounts, between forty and a hundred pounds. From the same ATMs most of the time. How she spends it is simply untraceable unless she tried to spend a wedge of it anywhere, like on a car.

But money laundering rules and regs would stop her doing that.'

'Financial links between her and Spider?'

Steph shakes her head. 'Sorry, boss. Still looking at that, and at Sophie's background.'

'Tobias, what about Alexander's staff?'

'There's nothing there, I'm afraid. He has fifteen employees: eleven software engineers, three in marketing and business development, and one office manager. None of them have a criminal record.'

'And Derek Parsons' company?'

'When we first told them we suspected Mr Parsons was set up, they ran an internal check on systems accesses and user profiles. Didn't find anything but to quote them, they're "not systems security experts."'

'Would they be willing to check again, in more detail this time?'

Tobias holds his hand up, rubs the pads of his thumb and forefinger together. 'It would be too expensive. And they don't see the point as they're in discussion with Mr Parsons about reinstating him.'

'Without more concrete evidence we're probably stuck but we're a long way from giving up. Steph. Keep looking into Cath and Spider because if he has something on her, and we can find out what it is, we could possibly go after him a bit harder. Same with this "major stuff" Sophie is supposed to have gone through. Her bosses and colleagues in Social Services probably won't comment, but ask them anyway. And can you also talk to friends and colleagues from her day job. Tobias, have one final word with Derek Parsons' employers. See if there's *anything* they're prepared to do that won't cost them the earth. And Andrew, it would certainly be helpful if we could find out where Alexander plays poker.'

He nods. 'Nothing's come back so far, boss. But I'll keep trying.'

I wait until they all stop scribbling, then save the file and power down. We can access the data remotely if necessary. Then I set off to update Jeff and discover he's been called out to a double murder inquiry so goodness knows when he'll be free.

Bloody typical, that is.

CHAPTER SEVENTY-TWO

As far as Iain McLure was concerned, today was going to be a good day. As things stood he only had about £200 to his name but the next couple of hours would see him back on easy street.

Of all the issues he was facing the least important were his existing bank and credit card accounts, which were no more than a front for his journalist persona. He hadn't touched any of them since he'd discovered the police had visited his house at Kinghorn six days previously. He knew they would easily have found the accounts and would be monitoring any activity so he hadn't even accessed them online. No, as far as he was concerned they were a write-off. He had other accounts they wouldn't be able to trace.

Then there were his assets. His flat in Leith, the house in Kinghorn and the McLaren. It was looking like he'd have to abandon the flat, but he would be able to withstand the loss. Again, it was a front although if things had panned out perfectly he'd have sold it eventually.

The house was a different proposition, worth four or five times the value of the flat. It wasn't in his name but the complicated ownership mechanism he'd set up meant there was a reasonable chance he'd earn a decent amount from the eventual sale although his solicitors would undoubtedly hike up their fees considerably to cover not only the extra work they'd have to do but the nature of it.

Finally, the McLaren. He loved that car. It was a real statement and his ego was boosted every time someone stopped to gawp at it. But there were other McLarens, other cars, and once everything was sorted out he'd replace it.

He shook himself out of his reverie. All the pieces were in place to rejig his finances. Sophie was at work so he had the house to himself and undisturbed use of her PC. He'd played around on it for a couple of days and performed some basic research to give him a head start on what he was about to do.

Once he was finished, all his money problems would be solved meaning he could concentrate fully on the longer term. And whatever that was, he'd be moving on. This day was always going to come, it was only a matter of when. He'd often wondered if the authorities would catch up with him and if this was what he'd end up having to do; desert one life and start again, albeit not exactly from scratch. The fact he was still in the game left him feeling pleased with himself because, apart from a small amount of luck, the real reason he'd never been caught was mostly down to meticulous attention to detail and always being prepared for when something would upset the applecart of his cosy criminal life.

The cameras he'd installed at both properties had done their job, offering a level of security and advance warning that had proved crucial. Even if he'd been at home when the police called he'd never have answered. The blinds were permanently closed for good reason so unless they'd battered down the front door he would have watched them on his app until they gave up and went away.

He settled himself at Sophie's desk and powered up the PC. A photo appeared of her and her father, huddled together on a bench down by the beach on what was clearly a cold and windy day.

Sadly, no more Sophie, he thought. He'd surprised even himself when he suggested they should be married, ridiculous romanticism that hadn't ever played a part in his life. But even if they had become Mr and Mrs McLure, if it became necessary for him to move on and leave nothing behind him then he would have. In a heartbeat and without a second's regret. Iain's view was that, like all women, Sophie had her uses but was ultimately dispensable.

As soon as she'd gone out he'd walked to a shopping area containing a range of discount stores including one that specialised in unlocking mobile phones, repairing cracked screens and a range of other services the high street stores couldn't or wouldn't provide. These shops had a well-earned reputation for not asking too many questions, perfect for his requirements.

Iain walked out with a basic refurbished smartphone with four Pay-As-You-Go SIM cards from four different providers, all pre-loaded with £5 worth of credit. They sat on the desk in front of him, ready for use.

He opened a Notes file he'd hidden deep inside the PC's folder structure, it contained text and links to reference articles. He clicked a link with the heading: Update.

A few years previously he'd met an IT student whose focus was heavily towards the dark side. She was already creating her own public image: hardworking, diligent, studying hard for her exams. Truth was, she could pass the course in her sleep, paid little or no attention in class but was always seen to be typing copious notes into a laptop while the lecturers blathered on. These were nothing to do with her studies, she spent practically every waking moment compiling hacking or malware code. Her ambition was to make a fortune either exploiting the internet or selling her services as a White Knight, helping organisations to stop people like her from infiltrating their networks, systems and databases. Poacher turned gamekeeper and vice versa.

Iain made her a proposition. Teach him how to protect his identity online and how to move his accounts and their contents around while remaining completely undetected, even to the extent of outwitting her counterparts in the police and other financial institutions. Furthermore she was to remain on call at a moment's notice, ready to advise him of security enhancements and crucially, advances in the art of remaining incognito. His pet student didn't think the project was much of a challenge but was content to pocket the generous annual retainer he paid her.

Earlier, Iain had left her a simple coded voicemail including Sophie's home number. Less than thirty minutes later she returned his call with an ID and password to a page on one of her private websites. He pasted the information on that page into the Update file and digested the content. It all made perfect sense.

On her recommendation he downloaded a recently released browser specifically designed for surfing the web anonymously. Unlike mainstream browsers that leave electronic footprints a blind man could follow in a fog, this one would leave zero trace and wouldn't collect, store or report any information about his online activities.

On separate browser tabs he navigated to the login pages of each of his three alternative accounts and typed in the user credentials. These accounts, registered under false identities, held a little over half his assets. He was ninety-nine per cent certain the accounts would be invisible to the police. But giving undue consideration to the remaining one per cent was what had kept him several steps ahead of any authorities who'd paid him even the slightest attention in the past.

And although Mel 'bloody' Cooper was far from the first to come looking for him, he had bad feelings about her. He needed to distract her for long enough to help him vanish permanently with the majority of his money, and that would require some thought.

On three more browser tabs he set up new bank accounts in different countries, none of which would even contemplate sharing their clients' financial data with their counterparts in the UK. Apart from the email address field, which was still blank, he completed the account applications to the point where he would click Submit. From past experience, he knew these banks would be ready to accept money transfers within minutes.

His final preparatory step was to register with a website that generated random email addresses comprised of obtuse names and domains. These addresses were required to open the three new bank accounts but the addresses would remain valid for only one hour before being deleted permanently.

Everything that Iain had done up until that point was perfectly legal, anyone with the knowledge and resources could have done the same. But that legality was about to be stretched, at least in the eyes of UK banking regulations.

He wasn't nervous, he'd performed these steps several times before. He wiped his palms on his jeans and went to work, typing quickly and smoothly.

On the email address website, he clicked an icon with the word 'Generate'. An address appeared on screen, which he copied and pasted to the email field of the first bank account application. He'd already input the telephone number of the first SIM card on this account so when the bank sent a One Time Passcode or OTP, it went to the burner. He used the OTP to complete the application for a new account in an Albanian bank.

Then he switched to the tab for one of his hidden accounts, and logged in. The account opened immediately, it hadn't been frozen. If the police were monitoring it, a flag would be raised and Cooper would be alerted. But he was relaxed. The browser he was using guaranteed anonymity and what he was doing would not be reported to Sophie's service provider so his location would remain unknown. Still, he wasn't prepared to take undue risks. He set up a transfer for the entire balance from this account to the new one. Again, his old bank generated an OTP and he used that to authorise the transaction. Then he cancelled the old account.

He breathed in and flexed his fingers. One down, two to go. Working at the same speed, there was no need to go any faster, he repeated the process twice more and transferred the balances from his other two accounts across to the new one. Once he'd finished, all his old accounts were empty, closed and cancelled.

He picked up the burner, flipped the back off and extracted the SIM. He deliberately placed the tiny card at the far end of the desk and put a new one in the phone.

He typed the number of that SIM into his personal details for the Albanian bank, used the generator to create another email address, updated the fields for account number two and hit Submit. Moments later he had a second new account, this time in the Caribbean. His money whizzed its way electronically halfway round the world and the minute he saw the credit, he closed and cancelled the Albanian account.

He repeated this process once more. He set up a third account in Lebanon, transferred the balance from the Caribbean and cancelled that account.

He reviewed everything he'd done using a handwritten tick list, which he shredded. Only the account in the Lebanese bank remained, containing all his money. Tomorrow he'd open an account in a British bank, online access only, and transfer some working capital from Beirut; modest sums over the next few weeks that wouldn't excite curiosity. In a few days he'd apply for a credit card and then he'd be back in business full time. He had set up a P.O. Box in the West Midlands, his old stamping ground, and would have the cards sent to that address. He'd pick them up when he moved there, probably in the next couple of days. He intended to stay in a budget hotel for a week until he sorted himself out, leaving poor old Sophie and the bitch Cooper flailing about in the dust.

Then he performed an array of computing housekeeping tasks. The browser didn't retain cookies or temporary files so he didn't have to worry about traces being left on Sophie's PC. He used the option for Deep Uninstall to remove it then he ran Sophie's anti-virus on its most powerful Scan, Detect and Remove function. He waited patiently while that cycled through three times. After each scan, the PC shut down and restarted automatically. He made a quick visual check, checked the history for Sophie's browser to make sure it was clean then shut down the PC one last time.

Finally, he cut the three used SIMs into minute pieces and flushed them down the toilet. He fitted the fourth one in the burner, it would be his new number after he moved on.

He took a beer from the fridge, drained it where he stood then carried a second one into the living room and sat on the sofa. He picked up the remote and clicked the TV on. He heard a few solid clacks and a polite murmur of appreciation from an audience.

'Snooker. Perfect.' He settled down to watch, wondering what Sophie would be making for his dinner.

CHAPTER SEVENTY-THREE

I⒯'s Monday morning and my backside has hardly warmed my seat when Keown's on the line. *Come up when you have a minute.* I'm not daft, the subtext is clear so I go straight away.

I tell the team, 'I'm off to see the "Boss".' I waggle my fingertips around the term to demonstrate my feelings on the subject. On the plus side I've stopped referring to her as Frosty Knickers. Not that I've had a respect implant you understand, it's just that I might come out with it at an inopportune moment. Better if I desist.

'I've reviewed your caseload, Melissa.' She pulls a sheet of paper from a pile to her right and studies it. 'These *mystery* crimes you're investigating, give me an update.'

Jeez, she can hardly help herself but I don't react to the slight dig. 'We interviewed Peter Gardiner and his four children and we have a definite pattern.'

Keown doesn't interrupt as I lay the events out in chronological order beginning with Tommy Jarvis and the building works as the root cause of Mrs Gardiner's first stroke.

'It's clear,' I say, 'that at least three of the Gardiner siblings share the same motive. Revenge for their mother being in a coma and the pain their father continues to suffer because he was, in their eyes, prevented from reaching the hospital while she was still lucid. Peter Gardiner has the same motive but it's more personal. I'm keeping an open mind but I can't imagine it's him.'

'Imagine?'

I close my eyes for a second, refrain from sighing out loud. 'The Gardiners have various possible connections to criminal elements in North Edinburgh. One daughter, Cath, appears to be an associate of a known criminal, Spider Kilbride. He might have her in his pocket. The other daughter, Sophie, volunteers with Social Services so that's another possible link. One of the sons, Nicholas, has done time for aggravated assault but it's his younger brother Alexander who's of most interest to me.'

'Explain.'

'Several weeks ago, he drew £40k in cash from his bank. Technically, he can't account for it, his excuse is he plays poker in a high rollers' game. He runs an IT business so we're checking out his employees, it could be one of them has skills related to computer hacking.'

'There are a lot of words in there like "possible", "appears", "could be". None of it is conclusive, is it?'

I have to admit she's right. Bummer. But I plough on. 'I'm certain I'm on the right lines. There's a link missing, all I have to do is find it.'

Deirdre stays silent for a while, staring down at her desk, fingers tweaking her bottom lip. I imagine she'd like to rubbish the whole thing but there's simply too much there. I perform an internal fist pump. Prematurely, as it transpires.

She puts the paper down and sits back, examining me as if I were a behavioural puzzle she's pondering over. 'Okay, Melissa. Whatever your opinion of me, I'm not stupid. I can see there's *something* worth investigating but in my view it's not worth the resources you're throwing at it. There are higher priority cases that require our attention so convince me about this one or I'll be pulling the plug.' The clear message is *And that's the way it is.*

But before I can speak, she says, 'This is how it's going to work. I have some questions for you and if you don't give me the right answers ...'

I can't believe what I've just heard. That's not the way we do things in this team. Jeff ... I stop myself. Jeff's no longer in command, it's this jumped up bitch. And there's sod all I can do about it.

'Fire away.' My tone and my expression both declare, *If you must.*

She lifts the paper again and turns it over. 'Do we have any hard evidence against the Gardiners? Not circumstantial, not gut feeling, not possibles. Solid evidence.'

I can already see where this is heading and I have no choice. 'No, we don't.'

'Can we place any member of the Gardiner family at the crime scenes?'

'No.'

'Any definite links between a family member and an offence? Technological, financial, electronic footprint?'

'None so far.'

'DNA?'

'Waiting for results.'

'Any other forensic evidence at all?'

I shake my head.

'Money transfers unaccounted for?'

'Only Alexander's £40,000, supposedly his poker stake.' I don't bother mentioning Cath's ATM withdrawals. Small fry.

'Comms links, phone, SMS, email?'

'No. Nothing.'

'No one else you can question?'

I can't even come up with a decent lie. 'No one.'

'You've proved Kim Seung-Min is innocent, though?'

What the hell am I supposed to say to that?

She waves a hand, glosses over it. 'Yes, I don't know why I missed that. Mind you, the investigating team I had working for me were useless.'

I shudder. Bang out of order, Deirdre. *Bang* out of order.

She makes a big deal of letting that single sheet of paper float down onto her desk. 'Well, Melissa, not looking good is it? Now, where are we?' She brings up the calendar on her PC. 'I'm being generous here because I'm out for the next day and a half so I'm giving you until close of business tomorrow, Tuesday, by which time I expect you to have made an arrest. If you haven't, I will have no choice but to back burner the case and move you on to higher priorities. And that's non-negotiable, by the way.'

I'm so frustrated I could scream. This is not how Jeff would have handled it. *Bloody Jeff. Northern Ireland. Wait until I get my hands on him.* But I have to say something positive.

'I'm sure I can have it all squared away by then.' I suppose I might as well be optimistic. But it's as if I hadn't spoken at all.

'Next. Tobias Hartmann. I have to rebalance resources so I'm transferring him to another team. Immediate effect.'

'What? But I need him.'

I'm damned if I'll whine but that was close. However, I've left the door open for the obvious follow up. Shit!

'Need, Melissa? And what exactly do you "need" him for?'

'His analysis skills are proving incredibly useful, which has helped us move the Gardiners case on.'

'But you've just told me that's nearly squared away.' She smiles, the bitch is enjoying herself. 'So is it ... or not?'

Shit! Fuck!

'It is.' I can see check coming but hopefully I can dodge around for a while and avoid mate. Wrong.

'In that case you *don't* need him, and I do.'

The near-whine is back. 'But I was planning to move him across to help with the blackmailing case.'

But I'm blindsided. Again.

'Ah yes, that. It doesn't appear as though you have any firm evidence against this man, McLure. And anything you do have is pure conjecture. A rumour spread by a dying man whose motives are unclear and if the case ever goes to court we'd have to call him from beyond the grave. The Chief Super spoke about it at this morning's briefing, he says stop unless you can move on McLure this minute. He and I both agree it's *another* waste of resource.'

'Look, Deirdre ...'

No smile this time. 'It's "Boss" to you, and make sure your team know that too.' She turns to her keyboard. 'That'll be all.'

Check mate?

Over my dead body.

CHAPTER SEVENTY-FOUR

I CHARGE into our office and don't stop for anyone or anything.

The team are all there, which saves me hunting them down. I go straight to my PC and check the small incident room is free. It is, so I reserve it for the rest of the day. I'm not supposed to do that but today, I don't give a shit.

I grab everything off my desk that might be of the slightest use and stand up. 'Andrew, Steph, Tobias. Doing anything you can't put down?' Triple shakings of heads. 'Excellent, come with me.'

While I'm setting up the SmartTable and the wall, I explain. 'We have thirty-six hours, tops, to move the Gardiner case along significantly. And by that I mean if we don't have enough evidence to make an arrest by this time tomorrow, the case is toast. I can probably push the deadline out but I'll have my knuckles rapped, I expect.'

Andrew says, 'Keown?'

I nod. 'Yes, and you're supposed to call her Boss.' They throw me some curious looks but nobody comments. Banter usually stays within the team, it's only me who occasionally takes it across a boundary. 'She put me right on the spot, asked a long list of questions and I had to answer no to practically all of them. We need a different approach.'

Andrew stands up and drapes his jacket carefully over a spare chair. Smart lad, this could be a long haul.

I pick up a laser pointer. 'We're going to try something I've used before a couple of times, it's called the five whys. Believe it or not, although it's based on a business problem solving technique, I first heard of it at a talk by a crime thriller writer. We had a long chat about storylines and how they had to hold water. He explained how he uses the five whys to test out his plots.'

I point up at the wall. 'Those are all the facts of this case. Some are stronger than others, some are still to be proven. We're still working on a few of them but Keown's imposed a deadline so time's running out.' I hold up my index finger. 'Naturally, I don't agree with how she's handling this but I'm stuck with it so if we don't catch a break today all our work will be wasted. And I'm not having that.'

'So how does this five whys thing work, boss?' asks Steph.

'Study the wall, pick any point you like and ask me *why* I think it's true. Once I give you my reason, you ask *why*. I explain and you ask why again. And you keep asking why until I have no more answers to give. It's designed to force us, me in particular, to drill deeper into every fact or supposition than we've been before. You don't stop asking why until it's absolutely, and I mean *absolutely* exhausted. It's three against one and I have to be able to defend or justify every single point on that wall.' I look at each of them in turn. 'Okay?'

I pull my chair closer to the table. 'Go.'

They're tentative at first, not sure where to start. They give up a little easily on asking *why* so I have to insist they keep pushing me. Then it begins to click and they start zeroing in with the whys. Occasionally they ask many more than five and we discover elements we thought we had ticked off properly but we hadn't. One of the rules is I can't say things like, 'I don't piggin' know why, do I? Move on'. It's not allowed. That's how the technique works.

We take a break about an hour and a half later. I'm doing well. I've successfully argued every point but stopping for a while will recharge our batteries.

But nearly two hours later I'm drained, emotionally rung out. We've scored off over ninety per cent of all the points on the wall. Crimes, suspects, victims. Motive, means, opportunity. Facts, assumptions, proof. Who might be guilty, and who might not. You name it, we've dissected it.

Then as I'm about to run up a white flag Andrew discovers the flaw, the minute gap in my reasoning. We all pause, stare at one another. It's only the merest glimmer of an answer but it's there. And like a tangled ball of string, we know if we tease it, work at it, gently tug at it, we might, just might be able to unravel what was a carefully constructed pattern of lies, deception and trickery.

Now I am elated, excited. Our energy levels go through the roof as we attack the case and everything we had held up as truth and fact. We ask *why* with total conviction. We drill deeper and faster, and we dump existing theories as if they were square wheels.

It's well into the afternoon before I power down the wall and we leave the incident room.

We all know what we have to do and we're on it.

And only time in the shape of Deirdre Keown's ludicrous deadline is against us.

But I am stone cold certain this case is all but over.

CHAPTER SEVENTY-FIVE

It's NOT YET nine and Andrew will shortly be arriving in Dundee. He's off to eyeball Mandy, who's still in protective custody. He has one key question for her and to prove our theory it's vital that he witnesses her reaction.

I stop by Steph's desk, hand her a piece of paper. 'See if you can track down a bank account in this name or something similar.' She reads what I've written, tilts her head. The name is familiar to her but not in that combination. Then she gets it. Smiles. 'Leave it with me.'

Half an hour later I take a call from an analyst who specialises in CCTV footage. I dropped by his desk this morning while he was still on his first coffee. He says, 'I've emailed you a selection of images. Think it's what you're after but I'll hold while you check them in case you need me to clarify anything.'

I don't have any questions. The images tell me exactly what I was hoping for. Result!

Then my phone rings. I listen for a minute. 'Brilliant,

Andrew. Just what we wanted to hear. Yes, if you could tidy up and come back here ASAP. See you soon.'

'Were we right, boss?' asks Steph.

'We were bang on. And now all I'm waiting for ...' I glance up to see Dave Devlin heading my way. 'Ah, perfect timing! Here comes my favourite beat copper.'

He grins at me. 'I bet you say that to all the boys.'

'Take a pew, Dave. And thanks for coming in. There's something I'd like your help with. Grunt work, I'm afraid. I'm looking for some warm bodies with a bit of intelligence.'

He finds that funny. 'I'm not sure about the intelligence but I have four of my finest specimens standing by.'

Once I've talked him through it, he sighs. 'What's the old saying, Mel? The impossible I can do straight away, miracles take a wee while longer.'

I laugh. 'You'd better crack on, then. I'm in a bit of a hurry for this.'

Dave's still on his way across the floor when another call comes through. 'He what?' I pause. 'Oh, does he? Right, I'll be straight down.'

Well, this'll be interesting.

Less than ten minutes later, I ask the solicitor sitting diagonally opposite me, 'And you're okay with this? You've advised your client this is the right thing to do?' She replies yes to both questions.

'Okay, Peter. Let's make sure I understand. You are responsible for all these crimes. All five of them are down to you, yes?'

'That's correct.'

'You arranged them all by yourself, you weren't working in conjunction with anyone else.'

'No one else in the family. Just Spider Kilbride.'

'Ah, yes. Spider. So you paid him and he made all these bad things happen?'

'Yes.'

'What, everything from stealing a dog to burning a house down and hacking into a company's IT system in order to frame someone for grooming?'

'Yes. Everything.'

'And to pay Spider, you borrowed £40,000 in cash from your son, Alexander.'

'That's right.'

'What did you tell Alexander the money was for?'

He shakes his head. 'Can't remember. I made up an excuse.'

'And Alexander didn't say something like, "Hey, Dad. Tell me again why you need £40k in cash?"'

He makes a poor attempt to stare me out then all he can manage is, 'No.'

I tilt my head slightly. 'Tell me, Peter, what have you got against Spider?'

'What do you mean?'

'I mean, I know he's not exactly squeaky clean but why are you dragging him into this? Implicating him.'

'Because he's ... he's a criminal. Scum.'

I stand up, gather my things together. 'I know that, Peter. But he's lowlife scum and certainly not capable of the range of crimes we're investigating in this case.'

He rises part way out of his chair, slaps his hands flat on the table. 'But wait! Where are you going? You're not arresting me?'

I look down at him. 'Before I arrest you, I have to pop back to my office first.'

'Eh? What for?'

'To check whether I'll be charging you for lying on a grand scale, wasting police time or taking me for a complete idiot.'

I pause as I reach the door. 'I might even go for all three.'

———

AT MY DESK, I check my watch. So much still to do, so little time left. I call Andrew and divert him to talk to one of our suspects. I tell him to apply pressure if necessary, at this stage I don't give a damn how tight the thumbscrews are.

My next call is to a computer science analyst. I ask him what I thought was a straightforward question about computer hacking and after a long-winded explanation I tell him to cut to the chase. The answer isn't exactly what I was hoping for but it'll do. Things are still moving in the right direction.

Next I speak to a local Social Services team lead. She says no, what I'm suggesting is highly unlikely. Ah, well. Some you win ...

———

IT'S TIME FOR A BREAK. My head's spinning and I'm ravenous. So I grab a sandwich from the Italian deli across the street, go for a stroll in the fresh air and let all these threads float around like spiders' webs on a hot summer morning.

As I walk and munch, another idea comes to me. I ring Steph and ask her to make a call to the planning department at Edinburgh City Council.

———

LATE IN THE afternoon I hear my first disappointing news of the day. Dave calls. 'No joy so far, but we'll be back at it first thing in the morning.'

This means I'll fail Keown's stupid deadline. I'd better keep a low profile and pray she doesn't come looking for me.

CHAPTER SEVENTY-SIX

'WE'RE CLOSE, GUYS,' I say. 'So bloody close.'

It's eleven o'clock the following day. Steph and Andrew are with me but Tobias is missing. Keown carried out her threat and transferred him to another team. I'm certain she only did it for spite, but there's nothing I can do now. I was beginning to rely on his input, and there's no doubt he'll be a big loss.

As things stand, we have most of the evidence we need to crack the Gardiners' case but, agonisingly, there are still a few key pieces missing.

I didn't sleep well last night, too much rattling around in my head. Andrew called me late in the evening to tell me the thumbscrews had worked. He'd found out where Alexander Gardiner plays poker, which forges another solid link in the chain. I'd gone to bed planning to pick up the threads this morning but I was still spark awake at half one. So I gave in, padded off downstairs to find my notebook and scribbled away for another hour.

Steph comes over to tell me she's had to admit defeat. She's unable to prove any link between Spider Kilbride and Cath

Gardiner, despite Peter pushing us in that direction. I always felt it was tenuous so we'll have to leave it for now. I could have dragged Spider's arse in here for a light grilling but I can think of better ways to waste my time today.

Tobias called from his new HQ. In his own time he'd been to Derek Parsons' company to ask again if they could run any other security checks but they gave him short shrift. Sometimes there's only so far we can push. I thanked him for all his work and promised we'd all catch up for a beer once we'd put this case to bed. Ever the optimist, that's me.

Steph's phone rings. She peers at the number but picks up anyway. Andrew stands up. 'Coffee, anyone?' He glances down at Steph but she's focused on the call. As I move to join Andrew, Steph thrusts her free hand in the air and clicks her fingers like mad.

A couple of minutes later she thanks her mystery caller and punches the air. She explains, and now we have the answers to two of our remaining questions. But it's too early for backslapping, I'm still waiting for Dave Devlin to come up with the goods.

Steph picks up her phone again. 'I'm fed up waiting for the Council to ring back. I'm away to rattle their cage.'

Steph on a mission is unstoppable so we leave her to it and head towards the staff kitchen. Two minutes later she marches into the room with more good news. This day is definitely looking up.

I stir my coffee with some gusto. 'Come on, Dave. I really need you to come up trumps.'

And, two hours later, the man in question is standing in front of my desk wearing a grin that could advertise toothpaste.

CHAPTER SEVENTY-SEVEN

KEOWN BEGINS TALKING at me as she storms across the room. 'DS Cooper, what time is it?'

Time you stopped being a pompous cow is the answer that springs to mind, but I can't be arsed with her so I go on the attack.

I sweep my arm round in an arc, indicating the room full of people who are all watching her like hawks. 'Are we going to have this conversation here?' My voice is surprisingly devoid of emotion.

My direct challenge to her lack of decorum doesn't even make a dent. She has clearly decided to hang me out to dry, in public. 'It's almost two o'clock and as per my direct instruction, I was expecting an update from you, which I should have had *first thing.*' She folds her arms and tries to stand even straighter. 'Now clearly that didn't happen, so obviously you haven't solved the Gardiners' case.'

The room is a wasteland of movement or sound. No conversation, no clacking keyboards. Nothing. All my colleagues are straining to hear how I'm going to counter that.

I hold my nerve, think, and phrase my response carefully. There will be no weasel words and definitely no whining. 'I expect that case to be completely tied up by the end of the day. We're off to arrest ...'

She slaps a file down on my desk. 'No, you're not off anywhere. If I set you a deadline, you *will* adhere to it. And correct me if I'm wrong, that deadline was close of business *yesterday* by which time you said you'd have things squared away. And the fact you have not reported progress to me by the allotted time clearly means you haven't done your job.' She points at the file. 'So you will put the Gardiners' case on the back burner until I say otherwise and you will transfer your attention *immediately* to this.'

I have had enough. I will not stand for this. She thinks she's humiliated me but I can read the mood of the room. Steph and Andrew are facing her, throwing out defiant vibes. Everyone else has turned away. They may be rooting for me but they don't want her to see that. I walk slowly out from behind my desk and move to a point just inside her personal space.

I speak so she's the only one who can hear me. 'We *have* made significant progress on a number of fronts, to the point where I'm ready to move. *Right* now. The last detail was only confirmed a few minutes ago and if I wasn't having to stand here and justify myself to you, in full view of all my colleagues might I add, I'd be on the road already.'

Given the expression on Keown's face, it's possible I'm the first person ever to have spoken to her like that. And before she has time for a response, I hit her with a follow up.

'Now, I know we haven't been working together long but I'd like you to consider this. I'm an experienced DS and I don't need anyone holding my hand. You can rely on me to keep you in the loop but I will not be knocking on your door to update you every time a suspect farts in the wrong direction. That is not the way I work.' I pause for half a second. 'Boss.'

Having said my piece, I take a step back. I expect fireworks but no, it's ice. She sticks a finger in my face. 'You listen to me, *Detective Sergeant*. I don't give a flying fuck how *you* work. You'll do things my way or I'll have you transferred out so fast your feet won't touch. I'm ordering you to drop the Gardiners' case this minute and change your focus to that one.' She points at the file again and holds her arm out so we can both see her wrist. 'And here's another deadline. Report to me how you plan to proceed by 16:00 latest. Do you understand me?'

I want her out of here so I say, 'I understand you.' Flat tone. Zero sincerity.

'Good.' She taps her watch glass. '16:00, and not a second later.'

Then she marches away. I'm tempted to toss her case file into the confidential waste but I'm not entirely stupid. I wait until the door slams shut behind her then turn to Steph and Andrew. They're both smart enough to listen and stay quiet.

I dish out detailed instructions on what I want them to do next. Then they gather up their stuff and head on out. I'd love to go with them but like I said, I'm not stupid.

Time will tell how closely I'll follow Keown's directive but the bonus is she didn't mention anything specifically about my team.

Then I check to see which interview rooms are free.

CHAPTER SEVENTY-EIGHT

I HURRY along the corridor to meet Andrew waiting outside interview room one.

'How did it go?' he asks.

I flap a hand around. 'Ach, I was in and out of Keown's office so fast she probably didn't notice I was there. Anyway, I told her what I was planning to do with her bloody case so she's off our backs for now.' I point at the door. 'But as far as this is concerned, we have to produce a result tonight. Even then I still might be in bother but I'll worry about that later. Right, let's go in.'

At the table, I move swiftly through the formalities and go straight into my first question. 'Can you account for your movements on the evening of Thursday the fourteenth, two weeks ago?' I could have chosen any Thursday, that date was entirely arbitrary.

'I'm ... I'm not sure.'

Affected confusion. I don't buy it. 'How about last Thursday, the twenty-first?'

Silence.

I come over all dramatic, and sigh. 'On both of those dates, in fact most Thursdays, do you play poker in The Cumberland private members' club on Abercromby Place?'

'If you say so.'

'I'll take that as a yes.'

'That's up to you.'

'How long have you been a member there?'

A shrug. 'Six years, maybe seven.'

'And do you always play with the same people?'

'People come, people go.'

'What are their names?'

'It's a *private* members club.'

'I appreciate that, but it's not illegal to play poker.'

'Still, I would be breaching confidence and it would be against club rules to discuss other members' personal details.'

I find that quite funny, considering. 'I'm pretty sure that after we're finished here your membership will be revoked. Unless being squeaky clean isn't necessarily a prerequisite for joining that club.'

I pull out a sheaf of photos, A4 size. They all have sequential coded identifiers with date and time stamps printed across the top. I lift the first one, place it on the table and rotate it with the tip of my finger.

'This is a CCTV image taken from the corner of Antigua Street and Gayfield Square. I'd like you to look at this person here, jogging through the traffic towards the Square. Do you know who this is?'

'No.'

An unnaturally quick response, not unexpected. I push the next image forward. 'This is the same person, walking down the west side of Gayfield Square towards the police station. Do you know who this is?'

'No.'

Another photo. 'Now the person is approaching from the opposite direction. Do you know who this is?'

For the first time, the solicitor pipes up. 'DS Cooper, my client has given you the same answer twice. I cannot see how changing the angle of the photographs will make any difference.'

I've worked with this solicitor before and I think I can push this a bit harder without her hackles rising.

'You might think that's a fair point but this is the most important angle. See that cap? It's pulled down low across the face ... unnaturally low, don't you think? But even so, I'd like your client to answer my question. Do you know who this is?'

A sigh. 'And for the third time, no. I don't.'

'In that case, I'll tell you. This is a chap called Colin.'

I'm pleased to see that my explanation has created a palpably relaxed atmosphere on the other side of the table. The perfect time for me to screw that up. 'Or so we were led to believe.'

I bring out another photo but keep it facing towards me. 'Ever heard of forensic gait analysis? No? That's good, my chance to show off. This is another still shot of "Colin". It's taken from a distance so it's not the best. However here he is again captured from the front with his cap down low, remember? Now, we employ some incredibly smart people with even smarter software that allows us to analyse a person's gait. The way they walk, in case you don't know. And we used the software to compare the gait of this person, who we thought was Colin, with these people here.'

I lay down a series of images, five individuals captured as they exited the station. There's a camera at the corner and it catches all five, at different times on the same afternoon. They're all walking towards the lens.

I carry on with my explanation. 'Our software has calculated there is a minimum 90% probability that Colin's gait, and the gait of this individual here, are identical. In other words, they are almost certainly the same person.' There's a gasp from across the table and it's not from the solicitor. *She's* totally spellbound as I gradually reveal just how much we've worked out. 'So that's how the London Road timings were so precise and how it was possible to gain access to the flat so the phone could be dropped on the stair.'

I leave my words hanging for a moment before continuing. 'You've stated you don't know the person walking through Gayfield Square, the one who's wearing the cap. It's meant to be Colin but that's not the case. Would you like me to tell you who it is?'

Total silence. I feel cheated but it doesn't last. I pull one of the photos towards me, it's the third person leaving the station. I tap the image. 'This individual and Colin are one and the same.'

And now our suspect has a question. 'Have you ...?'

'Made an arrest?'

But I don't answer. I gather my papers together and push my chair back. 'Interview suspended 16:34. For the benefit of the recording, DS Cooper has left the room.' I look across the table. 'DC Young will be staying here. You are not free to go.'

Then I walk out, leaving two people wearing utterly baffled expressions.

CHAPTER SEVENTY-NINE

LILY WAS CHANGING to go out when her phone pinged.

Change of plans babe can you come to the flat? Gonna be leaving from here xx

She slung the phone onto the bed and screwed up her face, because of the change rather than the inconvenience. Truth was, it was easier for her to get to Kev's flat than it was to meet him up town especially as he'd moved in to his new place and it was on her bus route.

She moved in front of the wardrobe mirror to put on some lip gloss. She felt guilty she hadn't told her parents Kev had moved. She'd meant to but he'd only been in the flat a week and her mum had been incredibly busy so she hadn't managed to find a good time to tell them. She knew they weren't totally sold on him but she hoped they'd come round. He'd been such a fool, lying about his age to impress her. Honestly, she thought, what was he thinking?

She lifted her phone off the duvet and sent the simple response:

ok x

———

LILY WAS WALKING along the landing towards Kev's door, when it opened. His was the last door on the top floor. She broke her stride and put her hand on the bannister as a large figure appeared in the doorway.

'Oh!' She was caught by surprise. 'Hi. I was expecting Kev.'

McLure was shrugging into a leather jacket, a dark green holdall sat on the threshold. He grinned at her and stood to one side. 'Sorry, didn't mean to startle you. I only popped in to say hello but I'm just heading off.' He gestured with his left arm. 'In you go, I think he's in the kitchen.'

'Okay, thanks.'

Lily twisted half sideways to pass him. She reached for the door handle but he was there first. 'I'll get it,' he said, beginning to pull the door closed behind him.

The kitchen was on the right towards the rear, past the living room on one side and the bedroom on the other. Both were in darkness. Lily walked to the end of the carpeted hall and as she reached the doorway, she heard the lock catching on the front door. The kitchen was a galley affair so it was immediately obvious the room was empty. Then Lily sensed she wasn't alone after all. She smiled as she turned round.

CHAPTER EIGHTY

INTERVIEW ROOM two is a few metres further along on the other side of the corridor, I knock and enter. Steph is on this side of the table. She stands up. 'Boss?'

I don't say anything, just turn so my face can't be seen by the duty solicitor or his client. I wink at her, make sure she's picked up the positive vibe then sit down at the table. 'Could you do the needful please, DC Zanetti.'

Once Steph's finished I launch straight in. 'You've already stated that on the date in question, the 3rd of April, you were at home all day but unfortunately there's no one who can corroborate your story.'

'That's right. I live on my own.'

'I'm going to show you some photographs. As you will see they are all date and time stamped.' I spin the first one into the middle of the table and point at the bottom right corner. 'This is a still image taken from a CCTV camera positioned above the concourse at Haymarket railway station. I'm sure you're familiar with the station but to be clear, it's on the main line for all trains travelling from the north of the country.'

'I'm not stupid, I know where Haymarket is.'

I give out my version of a sweet smile. 'Just making sure.'

I point at a figure standing near the top of an escalator. 'Do you recognise this person?'

There's a definite pause. 'It's hard to say. The photo's not all that clear and I don't have my glasses with me.'

I push another photo away from me. 'Perhaps this one will help, we've zoomed in a bit.'

There's a sharp intake from the other side of the table.

'Is that better?' I know it is.

'It ... em ... looks like me.'

'Thank you, that's what *we* thought. Not at home all day after all, were you? Now, in these next pictures you're with someone.' I push out another two stills. 'You'll see from the time on these images that you spoke with this person for over eleven minutes. Can you tell me who she is?'

The pause is longer this time but I'm a patient girl.

'I'm sorry, I've forgotten her name.'

I place my palm delicately on my chest. 'Oh dear, that's a pity. But fortunately, I already know.' I tap the photo. 'This is Mandy Westbrook. You met her off a train from Dundee and after you finished your conversation she caught the next one to Edinburgh Waverley. We're not sure what she did in the following couple of hours, but we do know that later that evening, she met a man called Kim Seung-Min whom she later accused of assaulting and raping her.'

The solicitor conducts a brief whispered conversation with his client. I wait until their attention is back on me.

I change tack. 'Did you drive a white Volkswagen Polo in Edinburgh that night, in the vicinity of The Canongate?'

'No comment.'

'Were you with Mandy Westbrook at any time later that evening or night?'

'No comment.'

'Were you with Kim Seung-Min at any time that evening or night?'

'No comment.'

'Did you drive a white Volkswagen Polo from Willowbrae Road to London Road at twenty-five minutes past midnight?'

'No comment.'

I exhale, lay my pen down on my notepad, rest my palms flat on the table. 'Clearly, your solicitor has advised you it is your legal right to answer "No comment" to all questions but you're not doing yourself any favours. Perhaps you've never been in this position before but I have, hundreds of times. To me, "no comment" doesn't mean "no comment". It means "I could answer but the reason I'm not going to is because I have something to hide". So I'll make things easy for you. You might think this is a fishing expedition but I should advise you I know *exactly* what you're guilty of.'

I turn to give Steph a look and she responds with a nod. She knows to keep her entire focus on the other side of the table. I flip over a page in my notes. 'You *did* meet Mandy Westbrook again that evening, when you picked her up in your car from the lane that runs parallel to Cuthbert's Close. From there, you drove Mandy to her Airbnb on Willowbrae Road. Throughout our investigations we were led to believe Mandy had an accomplice, a man by the name of Colin. We have proof that Colin didn't ever exist. But if there *was* no Colin then who did all the things he was supposed to have done? Who assaulted her? Who set her up as the victim at a rape scene? Who transported Kim's mobile from the Airbnb to London Road and then, crucially, to the stairwell where it was, in quotes, "found"?'

I pause. 'Did you do all these things?'

'No comment.'

'Yes, I thought you might say that. But here's a general knowledge question for you.' I bring out my stack of photos again. 'Ever heard of forensic gait analysis?'

After I've repeated the same preamble as earlier, I place two images side by side. *Colin* walking towards the camera on Gayfield Square and a person leaving the station at Queen Charlotte Street.

Now I can administer the *coup de grace*. 'Our analysis suggests there is a minimum 90% probability that these two photos are of the same person.'

I sit back. 'In fact, the man we thought was Colin is actually ... *you*.'

I turn my attention to the solicitor. 'I expect you'd like time to talk with your client. So while you do that, interview suspended 16:58. For the benefit of the recording, DS Cooper and DC Zanetti are leaving the room.'

CHAPTER EIGHTY-ONE

'Sorry,' said Kev, 'I had to get something from the bathroom.'

Lily noticed the slight catch in his voice and the warmth spreading to his cheeks. She reached up to touch his face then put her arms round his waist, ran her hands down over his back pockets. She both felt and heard the little packet crinkling.

She stood up on her toes and kissed him. She took one step away then turned and held out her hand. He took it and they stepped into the bedroom. The room was in darkness and they left it that way while they kissed again, for longer this time. Lily sat down on the bed and just as Kev bent to sit beside her, they heard the click and were dazzled by the ceiling light.

Lily screamed. Kev shot upright and whipped round so quickly he almost overbalanced.

CHAPTER EIGHTY-TWO

Back in room one I nod at Andrew who leans over and presses the button. 'Interview resumes. For the benefit of the recording DS Cooper has entered the room.'

I study our adversaries across the table. 'This won't take long.'

Then I take a breath and gather myself. 'Kim Seung-Min, I am arresting you for attempting to defeat the ends of justice. You are not obliged to say anything but anything you do say will be noted down and may be used in evidence. Do you understand?'

Kim folds his arms. 'I trust you have evidence to prove that.'

'Oh, I'm confident I do. Because as a result of sterling detective work by a dedicated team of analysts, I've discovered gaps in your story. First, the suggestion that Mandy Westbrook performed oral sex on you in Cuthbert's Close that evening. To provide the necessary DNA evidence for the alleged rape scene, the act would have had to take place because Mandy needed a fresh semen sample to take to the Airbnb. But personally, I've always had my doubts about that because although I'm no prude, wouldn't there be a certain amount of pressure to perform?'

I hold up my hands in defence. 'I know, I know. You're a virile young man, but why take the risk when you have a tight deadline. Plus, why not provide said sample a little bit earlier in the evening and enjoy yourself while you're working?'

I produce a fresh set of images. 'In this job we need the occasional bit of luck so when our analysts revisited every single pub in the Grassmarket and on the Royal Mile, would you believe that after all this time the Mitre Bar would still have internal CCTV footage from that night? Turns out that every time they called us in to investigate fights or vandalism or whatever, they were having to hold back loads of DVDs. So last year they installed a super-duper system with huge digital storage capacity. Lucky for us, unlucky for you.'

Now I spread the photos across the table. 'Here you both are, sitting together. And this is where you leave the bar, separately, to go downstairs to the toilets. Note the time, please. This is you walking along the corridor ... entering the ladies' loo ... and emerging, having had some fun, fourteen minutes later. No pressure at all, job done.'

I leave the photos there. Kim continues to stare at them, as if he can somehow alter the evidence.

I carry on with my tale. 'It's a pity we didn't notice this first time around but in our defence, we *were* only attempting to confirm your route and the timings, not what you were doing while you were having drinks. I do apologise.'

Kim glowers at me but I don't care.

'Now, as you may be aware, the *alleged* assault and rape of Mandy Westbrook is one of five related crimes we're investigating. One of the others, at least, involves computer hacking ...'

Kim shuts his eyes.

'Hey,' I say. 'You've guessed it. Transpires one of the worlds' major sources of hacking expertise, and at bargain basement prices too, is your homeland.'

Kim's solicitor looks at me strangely until I explain. 'It's amazing what one learns in the course of one's job. Practically since the dawn of broadband, South Korea's network has been significantly more advanced than ours with speeds that are God knows how many times faster. So it's no surprise that, in general, their citizens' expertise is much further round the curve than poor backwaters like the UK. And with all that talent comes skills that are on, how can I put it, the side of the bad guys.' I indicate Kim. 'And by the expression on his face, my guess that he tapped into that expertise, for at least two of the crimes he's charged with, is right on the money.'

The smile I'm wearing falls firmly in the extremely satisfied category.

Kim turns to the solicitor and then to me. I'm not surprised by what he says next. 'I am solely responsible for all these crimes. You don't have to consider anyone else.'

'Ah, Kim. How gallant. How misguided. Because you are one of two people I am interviewing this afternoon.'

He blinks and is about to speak when I hold up my hand.

'Interview ends. The time is 17:10.'

CHAPTER EIGHTY-THREE

'HAVING FUN, KIDS?' said Iain McLure from the doorway. 'Mind if I watch?'

Kev took a couple of paces towards him, pointed at the door. 'Get outa here, you pervy old bastard. Or I'll ...'

McLure stepped in and knocked Kev out with a single punch. He fell back against the bed then slumped heavily to the floor. Lily stared down at her boyfriend. She was shocked rigid, unable to speak. McLure seized her arm and hauled her upright. He pulled open a cupboard door; the space was about four feet square. Bare floorboards, an aluminium stepladder, a couple of cardboard boxes and a grey plastic toolbox.

He pulled Lily right into his face. 'Where's your phone?'

She flinched, eyes wide, unable to speak. McLure gripped her arms at the elbows and shook her. 'Where's your bloody *phone*?'

'In my bag. Out in the hall somewhere.' She tried to back away. 'Please ...'

He spun her round, pushed her further into the cupboard.

She clattered into the ladder, put her hands up as it began to topple. 'Ow!'

He jerked her towards him again. 'Not a fuckin' sound from you or I'll hurt you. *Get it?*'

She nodded, a barely imperceptible move of her head, tears streaming down her cheeks.

He glared at her. 'Don't move.' Then he leaned down and manhandled Kev into the space. When the younger man's body was half inside, McLure grabbed his legs and flipped them over. Kev groaned.

McLure opened the toolbox lid and rummaged about. He found a couple of white plastic cable ties, used them to fasten Kev's wrist to the ladder then kicked the toolbox out into the bedroom. He glanced around the cupboard and smashed the wall light with his elbow. Shards of glass and filament pattered down onto the cardboard boxes.

He took a step closer and pointed at Lily. 'Remember, not a sound from either of you. Mind you, no one would hear you anyway.' He hammered his fist on the wall. It was a solid old tenement building and the cupboard backed onto the bathroom so it was completely internal to the flat. Not soundproof, but not far off.

He made a fist. 'Any noise, any noise at all and believe me, you'll both regret it.'

He slammed the door shut behind him and locked it. He stuck the key in his jeans pocket and strode out into the hall. He flicked off the bedroom light and pulled the door closed.

He took his jacket off and wiped his forehead. Lily's backpack lay on the carpet. He ripped the zips open until he found her phone. He powered it down, tore the back off and removed the SIM. Kev's phone was charging in the kitchen and McLure gave that the same treatment.

He found a glass, jammed it under the cold tap and sluiced it down. He dragged the back of his hand across his mouth then leaned over the sink, fearing he might throw up.

'How the *fuck* am I going to get out of this?'

CHAPTER EIGHTY-FOUR

REGRETTABLY, *it's the end of the road.*

My solicitor's advice was that I should reply 'No Comment' from the beginning of the interview but we have come to a point where it is better that we bring this whole escapade to its natural conclusion.

I have to say I was only slightly surprised when the detective revealed the photographs of me talking in earnest with Mandy Westbrook. I have never underestimated DS Cooper and this demonstrates my assessment of her intelligence was correct. She has been a worthy opponent.

So when I do switch to 'No Comment' it's not because I don't want to answer her questions. I could do so quite easily, for the game is up. The adventure is over.

Then Cooper explained her rationale and everything she said was 100% correct. I had indeed heard of forensic gait analysis, but I presumed it was in the realm of science fiction. An error on my part alas, and I couldn't prevent myself from gasping audibly when she showed me the two images and proved I was indeed the fictitious Colin.

So my solicitor and I have had our little chat, for all the good it will do me. There are a few more elements of this tale still to be revealed and I am sure I will hear DS Cooper's summation before long.

The door opens.

It is time.

CHAPTER EIGHTY-FIVE

'FEEL like tidying up a few points for me?'

'Which ones, for example?' says Sophie Gardiner.

I've just advised her she's been arrested, quoting precisely the same words I used with Kim not half an hour ago. At this point, she doesn't know that.

'You chose to use Mandy Westbrook partly because of her background as a call girl and also because she was vulnerable and rather needy. But how could you be certain she would stick to her story and not give you away once we worked out her part in the plan?'

Sophie shrugs. 'Mandy may not be the brightest but she's a part-time prostitute with an addiction to certain drugs, and what that means is she is a compulsive and convincing liar. It comes second nature to her, she doesn't even notice she's doing it half the time. So I briefed her and she invented her own little world in which this adventure could take place. To Mandy it was real and she played her part to perfection. Plus, there was the money.'

'Two thousand pounds? She kept the story going for a measly two grand?'

'No, that was another element she kept from you. She would earn *six* thousand if she maintained the deception, no matter how things panned out.'

I shake my head. You just can't tell with people, can you? 'Moving on to the car you were driving that night with Mandy, and with Kim's phone in your possession. A hire, wasn't it?'

She gives me a wry smile. 'Congratulations, DS Cooper. I didn't think you'd even look for a hire.'

'I'll spare you the details, but our systems came up with the goods. And once we narrowed it down to a hire, all it took was a few calls and a couple of visits to the rental office. An extremely observant and helpful chap recalled a man renting a white VW on the day in question.'

Once more she appears amused but only until I say, 'They don't see too many South Koreans in there, apparently.'

Silence.

'Yes, Sophie. Your lover and partner in crime *was* in the room along the corridor, but now he's on his way to the cells.'

We are definitely *not* amused after that little bombshell.

'So, Sophie, that's everything tied up for that particular crime but as you know we're investigating five in total. So I'd like to talk about a house being set on fire. You know, the house belonging to Tommy Jarvis?'

More silence.

'And don't think I can't make it stick because I most certainly can.'

'And *how* do you propose to do that?'

'One of the few mistakes you made along the way was to seriously underestimate Edinburgh City Council's Planning Department web portal, and how much of your information it retained while you were sussing out the layout of Tommy's house after he built the new extensions. If you'd only checked it a couple of times like some of his nosey neighbours did, you wouldn't have stood out. But eighteen times over the course of a fortnight, Sophie? *Big* mistake.'

She's looking down, in more ways than one. But I'm on a roll. 'Finance, though. That was a major problem for us. We couldn't find the money trail anywhere. None of your family's bank accounts revealed any large cash transactions. And it didn't come from Kim, we checked his accounts too. But then something your sister mentioned ...'

Her head jerks up. '*Cath?* She gave me away?'

I shake my head. 'Not intentionally, no. But she did say there was major stuff going on in your life and my colleague here eventually worked out what that was. DC Zanetti?'

Now it's Steph's turn. 'Once I put together everything we knew about you, Sophie, there were only a few possibilities left. And one of those was a broken engagement. So I trawled through newspaper announcements and eventually I found this, published in *The Scotsman*, 11th of May last year. Steph reaches into her folder, pulls out a sheet of A4 and lays it in front of Sophie. There's one block of text on the page and despite herself, Sophie reads it.

Then Steph says, 'He must be a generous chap, this Iain McLure. He breaks off the engagement but still leaves you a large sum of money in an account in your soon-to-be-married name: Sophie McLure. But not much in it now, is there? Especially given the amount of cash you've withdrawn from it in the last few weeks.'

Sophie picks up the paper, crumples it and throws it on the floor. 'He might be generous but he's a bastard. That money was a pay-off to salve his conscience. I've-dumped-you-but-this-demonstrates-what-a-magnanimous-chap-I-am.' Her smile is at the watery end of the scale. 'But at least I spent it on a worthwhile cause.'

'Hardly,' I say. 'I'll come back to Mr McLure in a minute but one thing that's always baffled me is when your father had that altercation with Derek Parsons, how did Kim manage to be right there in the traffic queue? Because that's *too* much of a coincidence.'

She slings me a look that says, *You're not very bright are you?* But she can't resist telling me anyway.

'Kim was just going about his normal business that day when the whole thing unfolded right in front of him. He only called the police over because he was concerned about my father's welfare. In his culture the elderly are respected and treasured. You might already know this but Kim is an orphan. He lost his entire family in a disaster and he feels that spiritually an important part of his life was snatched away from him. He had always imagined he would take care of his grandparents and parents, to continue to learn from them and benefit from their wisdom and their humanity. So when he saw Parsons shouting at my father, he could see Dad becoming more and more distraught and was absolutely appalled when they arrested him. He tried to speak to the officers but they wouldn't listen.'

Sophie's voice caught at that point. She ran the back of her finger below her eye before continuing. 'Kim was so disgusted by what had happened he was telling anyone who would listen. Then someone mentioned I worked with the Foundation and he sought me out. We met up and talked for hours. I told him everything. All about the building works, my mother's strokes, Dad being kept in the cells all day. And how his life has been more or less destroyed because of what they had done to my family. I said I wanted them all to suffer, and I was gobsmacked when he agreed and offered to help me. The question was how? So we came up with the ideas together.'

'So the rape case against Kim, it was all a smokescreen?'

Sophie nods. 'At first, I was happy to go along then his plan grew arms and legs and I tried to talk him out of it. But he said we had to divert attention well away from him, make him a victim like the others.' She shrugs. 'It nearly worked.'

I almost can't believe what I'm hearing. 'But setting him up like that was incredibly risky. He could easily have been convicted.'

'No. I told him if that had happened, I would have come forward. He didn't want me to do that but he couldn't have stopped me.'

We all fall silent then she says. 'What were you going to ask about Iain?'

'We're investigating him for another crime but he's AWOL. Do you know where he is?'

'Will it help me and Kim if I tell you?'

'Probably not, Sophie.'

'In that case, you can sod off.'

————

I KNOCK on Keown's door and enter. Time for me to fess up.

'Boss, just a quick ... Wow!'

'Pick up your jaw, Melissa. I *do* have a life away from the office, you know.'

It's incredibly difficult but I'm doing my best not to stare while I compare the plain vanilla Deirdre Keown: smart skirts, pumps, neck high blouses and hair tied back, to the glamorous version standing at her whiteboard with a marker in her hand. Clothes at well over a month's salary, hair like a L'Oréal commercial and made up to the nines. And cleavage. Jeez! I'd have to wear two push up bras to even come close and I'm not exactly Olive Oyl.

'Sorry, Boss. You look … em, nice.'

'Melissa. If my date tonight tells me I look "nice", he'll get a kick in the nuts for his trouble. Now, what do you want?'

'Thought I should give you an update. I've closed the Gardiner case. Signed and sealed, two arrests.'

She takes two steps towards me, holding the marker like a stiletto. 'The Gardiner case? Jesus, Cooper. I *had* hoped we'd be able to work together but clearly …'

My phone goes off. It's buzzing like a Geiger counter in my hand. I don't have to check it to know who it is. Conor set it up to buzz in different rhythms depending on who is calling me.

It's Callum, and he *never* contacts me at work. I have no choice but to stammer out, 'Sorry, I have to take this.' Keown is gripping the stiletto marker as if she wants to crush it to death.

'Callum?'

He speaks. Clipped phrases. I listen.

Then I tell him to hold. I say to my boss, 'My daughter's missing.'

CHAPTER EIGHTY-SIX

I GLANCE up at the wall, ten past seven. 'When was she supposed to be home?'

'It's Wednesday,' says Callum. 'She's always home by six.'

My husband is teaching Lily to cook for whenever she eventually flies the nest, and every week they work together to concoct a new dish. She just *loves* these one-to-one sessions with her dad. They're set in stone and there's no chance on earth she'd miss one voluntarily.

'Where did she say she was going?'

'Meeting Kevin up town.' A pause. 'Not sure where.'

I do my best to remain in cop mode and suppress the panic-stricken-mum alternative. 'And she's not answering her phone?'

'No. Straight to voicemail.'

'So either it's off, there's no signal or the silly girl has forgotten to charge her battery. Again. Okay, tell me what you've done already.'

My husband's voice is clear and calm but I do detect an edge. 'I waited 'til quarter past six then left a message on her voicemail. And I've texted and WhatsApped too, but she's not been live on there since 16:58. I've checked our landline to make sure it's working, and I've spoken to Conor to see if they've been in touch at all. I've also checked to see if she's live on Messenger. I'll keep refreshing but it's a long shot.'

He's right. The cool kids are far more likely to be on Insta-gram or Snapchat but those platforms don't show when users are active on line. Less 'Big Brother' but not helpful for us. And while we're on that subject he adds: 'I've put out an Insta-gram post too.'

'What about Paula? Those two are usually joined at the hip.' Then I remember Lily's best pal has dropped out of the social scene. Callum's answer confirms that, but I'll message her to let me know immediately if Lily surfaces. Who knows, our daughter may not be speaking to us for some stupid teenage reason. But I doubt it, that's not Lily. She'd give us both barrels then hug us to death.

'Gimme a second.' I put my hand over the phone and say to Keown. 'Can you call Andrew? Ask him to meet me outside with a car.'

She nods and turns away.

It's too early to panic but never too early to be worried, it's part of the job description for any mother. This is when I wonder yet again if I should have installed tracker apps on their phones. Being a good democratic family we'd discussed it but the kids shot the idea down in flames. I'd suggested to Callum we could put them on covertly but he gave me one of his best pained expressions and vetoed me on that one.

'Have you tried Kevin's number?' I ask.

'Yes. It goes straight to voicemail too.'

Then I realise that despite the time we spent with our daughter's boyfriend the other Saturday we don't know much about him. Name, phone number and home address, and that's about it. 'Right, leave it with me. I'll go to his flat, hopefully they'll both be there.'

I'm sure there's a perfectly acceptable reason why neither of them is answering their phones but I'd rather not conjure up that image.

I'm heading for the corridor when I hear, 'Mel.'

I nearly give myself whiplash. *Mel?*

Keown says, 'My phone will be on, so call me when you find her. And if she hasn't turned up in a couple of hours, tops, call me anyway. You'll need help.'

A golf ball has lodged itself in my windpipe so I nod, flap a hand in her direction and hurry out of her office. On my way to my desk I call the control room sergeant. I don't know who's on duty but turns out it's Ronnie Murdoch. We're old pals.

'Ronnie, it's Mel. My daughter's *very* late home but there's a chance she's at her new boyfriend's flat. I'm on my way there now and hopefully this is a false alarm. At this stage I don't have cause to run a trace on their phones ...'

'I can make that call, Mel. Give me the info so I'm ready as and when.'

I read out Lily's number and Kevin's details and hear him tapping at a keyboard, one finger at a time. 'Okay,' he says. 'Keep in touch, I can escalate if necessary.'

'Will do, Ronnie. Thanks.'

Keown and Ronnie are in the same position as I was when I first checked Kevin out. He's not part of an active investigation, either as a witness or a suspect so we can't use our systems to locate him. He's an innocent citizen as far as we know, just going about his normal life. And although in my head Lily is missing, she's only about an hour and a half overdue and there's probably a perfectly legitimate reason why she hasn't come home. None of them will wash with me of course, but we still can't mobilise the troops to track her down. Not yet. But

Keown's given me a time when she'll step in with her authority, and Ronnie has a certain autonomy as the late shift sergeant. For the moment I'll do what I can but if push comes to shove I'll be calling them.

Downstairs, I find Andrew waiting in the car. The passenger door swings open as I jog across the pavement. I tell him the address and he pulls away. He says Steph's waiting to hear from us so I call her on loudspeaker and ask her to meet us there.

As we're driving along I fall silent. Something's bugging me, nibbling at my subconscious but I just can't grasp it. I focus on not thinking, hoping whatever it was will drift in again.

It's not long before we're driving along a cobbled street with three and four storey tenements looming on both sides. These probably date back over a hundred years and it appears the vapid amber street lighting hasn't been upgraded since.

We're double parking when I see Steph's car nosing out of a side street. Andrew flashes his headlamps. Now the three of us are standing on the pavement, staring up at the building. Only a couple of windows are showing lights.

'It's flat 2F2 but that could be to the front or the rear of the building.' I march over to the door and shine a torch on the access panel, checking out the nameplates. Three of the buzzers have no buttons, just holes like pulled teeth. 2F2 does have a scrap of paper behind the Perspex but it reads Anderson, not Moffat. I hit the buzzer anyway, wait about half a second then jab at all the others at least twice each.

CHAPTER EIGHTY-SEVEN

McLure stood at Kev's living room window, arms folded, staring out over the distant rooftops. There were no tenements directly opposite. At ground level, the area was dark for a good distance over to the left. He didn't know what was in there and he didn't care.

Throughout his blackmailing 'career' he'd never hurt anyone. Not physically, at any rate. He simply used people's vices against them. Their failings, weaknesses, egos and ambitions all provided him with openings and all he did was exploit them. They were all willing to pay, and some paid handsomely to avoid their sordid secrets being revealed to their families, their colleagues, their rivals or the media.

That's what he did and it had never troubled his conscience. Not once. Extortion was a white collar crime and every single one of his victims deserved everything they got.

But today he'd crossed a line. Several lines. He looked down at his hands, his fingers were trembling. Was it the shock of hitting Kev, or being aggressive towards a teenage girl? For him, this was a severe departure from the norm and it had stopped him dead in his tracks.

He jumped when three floors below, a vehicle's door slammed. It was a car, double parked, an illuminated sign on its roof. It was half hidden below a tree so he couldn't make out what it was. He felt a slight tremor as the door to the tenement crashed back on its hinges, and running footsteps sounded in the stair.

Then four young women all dressed up for a night on the town fanned out onto the pavement below. Shrill voices, cackling laughter, they piled into the taxi. Seconds later it pulled away, heading up town.

McLure leaned forward, his forehead in contact with the cool glass. He had just closed his eyes when he heard a sharp noise. He listened, then the sound came again. An aluminium ladder screeching across bare floorboards.

He stormed into the bedroom. There was yet another crash from inside the cupboard. From a metre away, he bellowed, 'I told you, keep it quiet in there. No one can hear you anyway.'

'Fuck you, you prick!' yelled Kev.

McLure practically bounced up to the cupboard door, dragging the key from his pocket as he moved. He paused for a heartbeat, then hammered on the door. '*I fuckin' warned you.*'

Then he jammed the key in the lock.

CHAPTER EIGHTY-EIGHT

ONE OF THE occupants speaks to me via the tinny intercom. 'Yeah?'

'Pizza!' I turn to Steph and make a face. The door buzzes and we're in. By the time I wheeze up the two floors, Andrew has knocked on 2F2. A faint glow appears in the fanlight, it's struggling to penetrate decades of grime.

We hear a key being fumbled into the lock but the door stays closed. A female voice calls, 'Who is it?'

It's not Lily's voice. So what gives?

I hold up my warrant card to the spyhole but I'll be surprised if the woman inside can read it. 'Police. Open up please.'

There are a couple of clicks, the door opens and a woman peers out at us. Her hair is damp and she's wearing a washed out towelling robe.

I fear the worst, but I ask anyway. 'I'm DS Cooper and these are my colleagues. Does Kevin Moffat live here?'

She pulls the robe together at her throat, shakes her head. 'No, I live on my own. I only moved in at the weekend.' She looks at each of us in turn. 'He could have been a previous tenant but I don't know.'

While I'm hauling out my phone to double-check the address, Andrew asks, 'Are you renting too?'

She shakes her head again. 'No. I bought it. My first place.' She hesitates, risks a small smile. 'Since the divorce.'

After a brief conversation we're back at the car, right next to a pair of communal wheely bins. Neither of the lids can close, there's rubbish spilling out from everywhere. Did I make a mistake when I noted down Kevin's address? No, I remember repeating it to Lily.

Steph has her iPad open, checking the landlord register for Edinburgh. When the woman bought 2F2 it was rented out so if the landlord was legit we should be able to find him. That turns out to be a big if. She also gave me the name of her solicitor but that's no use to me until morning. And I can't afford to wait anywhere *near* that long.

And *still* there's something playing tag with my mind. *What the hell is it?*

I haul open the car door. 'Let's go to my house. We can work better from there and it means Callum will be in the loop. Steph, give me your iPad. I'll do another search for Kevin.'

We set off and as Andrew turns into our cul-de-sac I slap the iPad's cover shut. 'Damn! The same crap I found the first time. Stupid photos of drunk people. Nothing we can use.'

Andrew gives me a quick glance, doesn't comment. Under different circumstances he'd have given me serious earache for checking up on my own child.

As we pull onto the driveway, Callum hurries out to meet me. We hug briefly before I ask, 'How's Conor?'

He inclines his head towards our son's bedroom window,

there's a flickering light behind the blinds. 'Trying not to worry, but ...'

'Me too. I'll pop up and see him. Take these two inside, we'll use the dining room.'

I trot upstairs. Conor's door is open but I tap on the frame as usual and go straight in. He's sitting on his bed. 'Hello, wee man. How's you?'

He stands up and comes towards me. 'Fine.' It was a decent attempt, but his voice gives the game away.

I sling my arm around his shoulders, realising it won't be too long before I'll have to hug him round the waist. He seems to be growing an inch a day at the moment. I kiss his cheek. 'Don't worry, pal, we'll find her. Now, I know your dad's already asked you ...'

'No, Mum. I don't know where she is.' He sniffs, and drags his sleeve across his eyes. 'And I've searched *everywhere*, honest.'

I smile and hug him again. It's the online world. He's searched everywhere without leaving his bedroom.

Then my subconscious kicks in once more and ... 'Ah hah!' I concentrate for a few seconds then clap my hands. 'Gotcha!'

Conor looks at me sideways. Has his mother lost the plot?

I tug at his sleeve. 'Come on, son.' I head for the stairs, he's right on my heels.

'I know how to find Kevin's new address,' I say to the others. They all start in with the questions but I ignore them and snatch my phone off the table. The call connects. 'Dave? Mel Cooper here. My daughter's missing and I think you'll be able to help.'

After I explain what I want, I hang up then turn back to face the music. Callum is in first. 'You asked your *colleagues* to check up on your daughter's boyfriend?'

I straighten, stick out my chin. 'Once we find her you'll be

BE SURE YOUR SINS

glad I did.' It's not easy to look down your nose at someone who's a head taller than you.

Apart from righteous indignation, he has nowhere else to go so he makes do with a glare. I'm in no mood to apologise, but I explain so everybody knows where we're at.

'The only reason I checked Kevin out was he told her he was twenty-eight, ten years older than her.' I glance at Callum. 'Like *any* mother would. But because I couldn't use our systems, I asked Dave Devlin to put out feelers. Ever since you phoned me earlier, something's been niggling away at me but it wouldn't come. 'Til now. I've remembered Dave spoke to a pal of his, a copper who lives in the same street as Kevin and his stepmother.'

My phone rings. 'Dave. Hi.' I make a scribbling motion. Andrew hands me his notebook and pen. I sit down at the table, jot down a few words. 'Thanks, Dave. Yes, I'll shout if I need any more.'

I study the address. Rotate the notepad so Andrew and Steph can read it. Tap my finger on the page. 'Ring any bells?'

'Shit,' says Steph.

'Interesting,' says Andrew.

'What?' says Callum.

Conor doesn't say anything. Like his dad, he has no idea what's going on.

I grab my bag. 'This'll never work over the phone, it'll have to be face to face.'

CHAPTER EIGHTY-NINE

'I TELL YOU WHAT, you've got a fuckin' nerve. Why the fuck, exactly, should I help *you*? With *anything*?'

I breathe in, do my best to remain calm. This will go nowhere if I start shouting and screaming. Violence might help but it's further down my list of options.

'Like I said, Cath, my daughter hasn't come home. I'm trying to find her and she could be at your son's flat ...'

'Stepson.'

I close my eyes. The violence option moves one step closer. 'Your *stepson's* flat. Has he moved recently? I just need his new address, that's all.'

'Ah. So let me get this straight. You treat my father like crap, put my family through hell, arrest my sister and accuse her of all sorts of shit. And now you're standing on my doorstep asking for my help.' She laughs out loud. 'What a fuckin' cheek.'

Before I can reply, I hear a man chuckling. I glance up at a window in the house next door. He's leaning out, pointing a phone at us.

Cath cranes her neck. 'And you can fuck off too, Craig, you nosey bastard.'

'What? And miss the cabaret? Don't think so, Cath.' He puts two fingers on the screen, obviously zooming in.

I'd thought it best to speak to Cath on my own, didn't want to arrive mob-handed so I'd asked Andrew and Steph to stay in the car. Cath's is the end house on the block. There's a side street off to my left and I see Andrew is moving slowly along the pavement, holding his phone to his ear.

I turn back to Cath. 'Do you think we could go inside?'

She folds her arms, moves her slippered feet into a wider stance. She's two steps higher than me and uses it to her advantage. 'Do I have to let you in?'

I sigh. She's on her last warning. 'Technically, no. But I was hoping ...'

'In that case you can stay out there while you beg me for help.'

I've had enough. I clench my fist and put my foot on the bottom step. 'Now listen to me you f ...'

Then from behind a pair of strong hands take a firm grip of my upper arms and guides me gently backwards. Andrew leans in close and murmurs, 'Go sit in the car, Mel. I'll deal with this.'

I glare at him. Then I notice his expression is telling me not to argue, so I don't. As I'm walking along the path I hear Cath saying, 'Hey, Craig. Make sure you catch this in case pretty boy here beats me up.'

I climb into the car. It's facing away from the house so it's awkward for me to see what's happening but not even a minute later Andrew gets in the driver's side. He guns the engine, pulls the car round in a fast U-turn and accelerates away.

'Where are we headed?' I ask.

'To St Leonard's, to see Sophie Gardiner.'

I'm buggered if I'm going to ask him, but I've never been able to bite my tongue. 'Go on, then.'

'Cath and Kevin fell out a few years ago after his dad did a runner. Kevin blamed her and the two of them haven't spoken since. So Cath doesn't have any contact info for him—'

'This isn't another my-auntie-is-actually-my-mother story is it?'

'No.'

'But Sophie's in touch with him?'

'She is.'

'And how did you find all this out so quickly when the bitch wouldn't give me the time of day?'

'There was a car parked on that side street with a personal plate: SP11 DER. Did a PNC check and it does indeed belong to our man Kilbride. So I asked Cath if she fancied being the subject of a drugs raid with all her neighbours watching.'

In the back seat, Steph sniggers. 'Nice one, *pretty boy*.'

CHAPTER NINETY

'AND HOW *WAS* CATH?'

Sophie has dark patches below her eyes and her clothes appear to be hanging off her but she still manages to squeeze out a smile. She twists a strand of hair round her finger. 'Is Kev in any trouble?'

'I don't know, Sophie.' I say. 'I hope not. But all I want to do is find Lily, and to do that I have to find Kevin. If everything's okay, neither of them is in any trouble.'

'He's really keen on her, you know.'

Sophie's eyes are flicking all over the place. I have to tread carefully here but I'm also desperate to find my daughter. I lean forward and clasp my hands. 'Kevin's contact details, Sophie. Please?'

She looks at me as if I'm speaking Swahili. 'I don't know them off the top off my head, I'll need my phone.'

And, of course, we'd have taken possession of it when she was booked in. Andrew moves quickly, leaves the room. We wait in silence, this could take a while. The phone will have been sealed as evidence related to Sophie's crimes. They'll have to find it, there'll be paperwork, signatures, the works.

I close my eyes, try to zone out. I want to pull up an image of Lily but I can't place her in any context that's not …

Andrew is back. He sits beside me, phone in hand. The screen is flashing as it powers up. 'What's the code, Sophie,' he asks.

She holds her hand out but Andrew shakes his head. 'I can't let you use it. Tell me the code.'

She blinks, focuses on the table top, traces a jagged line with her fingertip. 'Four three six zero.'

The phone lights up again. I lean over to watch. Andrew taps *Contacts*, swipes a few times, taps *Kev Mob*. I read the number. It's the one I have so I'm not hopeful.

Voicemail.

He taps the screen, the call connects. Same result.

Sophie says, 'Straight to voicemail?' She frowns. 'That's definitely not normal. Kev's phone's never off.'

I pick up my pen. 'He's recently moved house, hasn't he? What's his new address?'

'It's on Montgomery Street but I don't know the number.'

'*What?*'

'I'm sorry, I've only ever been there once. I went with him to view it a few weeks ago. When we came out it was dark.'

'Jesus, Sophie. Montgomery Street's about a mile long. You must have some idea.'

She stares past me. 'I can't … oh, wait, it's opposite the kids' playpark.'

I'm familiar with the street. That park runs for about two blocks. 'Can you be more specific?'

'I can't, no. Like I said, it was dark. We walked along to Easter Road and Kev put me in a taxi.'

'Which floor, Sophie?' asks Andrew.

'Top.'

Steph hands me my coat. 'You go, boss. I'll tidy up here and catch you up.'

I'm almost at the door when Sophie says, 'DS Cooper, I think Lily's a lovely girl. I really like her and I hope she's okay.'

What?

I phrase my next question carefully. 'What do you mean, you really like her?'

'Because I've met her, of course.'

'You've *met* her?'

'Yes. She was at my house. Kev brought her over to meet me. Iain was there too. Although he was a bit of a dick, as usual, asking her all sorts of personal questions.'

The clanging of alarm bells means I hardly hear my next few words.

'Iain McLure has met my *daughter?*'

Sophie clamps her hand over her mouth. But her eyes tell me my tone has scared her.

Steph's already swiping away at Sophie's phone. She puts it to her ear. Shakes her head. 'Iain's number's unobtainable.'

'Shit!' I say. Then, over my shoulder, 'Come on, Andrew. Let's move.'

CHAPTER NINETY-ONE

Deirdre Keown's phone rang, it was on the bedside table. She stopped what she was doing, leaned over and picked it up. 'I have to take this.'

As she slipped off the bed her lover pawed at her breast but she swatted his hand away.

'Yes?'

She was silent for a while, eyes focused on her painted toenails. 'Where are you?' She reached down for her clothes. 'I'll be there in ten. I can coordinate support from my car.'

Without warning him, she clicked the switch to bring on all the room lights. Detective Chief Superintendent Mark Thornton swore and shielded his eyes with his right hand. 'What the hell's going on?'

He watched her as she dressed quickly and efficiently. She checked in the mirror as she buttoned her blouse, ran her fingers through her hair and dropped a necklace and her phone into her handbag.

'You could at least tell me who you're leaving me for.' All that was missing was the petted lip.

'That was Mel Cooper. Her daughter hasn't come home, she might even be in danger. I told her if the girl hadn't surfaced in two hours she should call me. I'm going to help, pull strings if necessary.' She glanced at him. 'I won't be back by the way. I've gone off the notion.'

His expression suggested he'd figured that out for himself. 'So what did Cooper say? Where is she?'

'She's heading for the boyfriend's flat. It's possible the girl could be at risk from, believe it or not, Iain McLure.'

Thornton practically leapt off the bed. 'Give me a minute, I'll come with you.'

She paused, one arm in her jacket sleeve. 'Why?'

He hesitated. 'In case you need more clout.'

He was zipping up his trousers so he didn't see her perform a little fist pump. 'Okay, Mark. But don't take all night.'

CHAPTER NINETY-TWO

Andrew and I haven't even warmed the car seats when Steph calls. Apparently Sophie had been about to say something to me but we'd shot out the door before she had the chance. Steph tells me what it was, and now we have a change of plan.

Andrew goes back inside and I'm heading off to try to find Kevin's flat somewhere on Montgomery Street. Dave Devlin's been alerted and he'll meet me there with the cavalry in tow.

I drive along Montgomery Street and stop at this end of the park. Dave and two cop cars arrive within a minute, blue lights flashing. It's a big wide street but we make an excellent job of cluttering it up. We pick the first tenement with any view over the park. Six of us are spread out along the block, checking nameplates, hitting buzzers, asking questions, sprinting to the next door.

I'm running along the pavement when one of the PCs shouts, 'Boss! Boss! Did you hear that?'

I stop. Make a face. 'Hear what?'

She holds a hand up. Officers are shouting at intercoms all over the place.

'*Quiet, you lot!*'

I've never heard a female with such a commanding voice before. Impressive.

Then there's a yell from way above us. 'Muuum!'

Is that Lily?

'Muuum! Help!'

It *is* her, definitely.

Then, like a bunch of Stepford Wives, we all walk off the pavement and look up. I can't see her. I expect her to be hanging out of a fourth floor flat but there's no sign.

Then I see a hand waving out the gap at the side of a tilted window. It's a small hand. A woman's hand. She's banging the other one on the glass. The light in the room behind her reveals her silhouette.

It's my daughter.

We pile along the street until we work out which tenement the window belongs to. I stand out on the pavement providing reassurance while the others disappear inside like rats up a drainpipe.

She shouts that Kev's spare key is on the lintel above his door and I relay that to the troops before one of them breaks a shoulder. Then she yells, 'He's not here, Mum. The Iain guy. He's gone.'

I don't answer. I just nod and smile and wave. But I say to myself: *I know that, darling.*

Once the team are inside the flat and confirm the pair of them are safe, I desert my post and hurry up the stairs. I meet Lily on a landing. She throws herself at me, then promptly breaks down. I hold her until she stops crying.

We walk back down and sit on a low wall outside. She calms down enough to tell me about being locked in a cupboard, and their plan to escape. Kevin told her the access hatch to the loft was in the ceiling. Problem number one: he's cable-tied to the lowest rung of the ladder. But he reckoned Lily could climb up into the loft and try to attract attention from a Velux window set into the roof. Problems two, three and four: the cupboard was pitch black, the ceiling was almost four metres high and Lily had to confess she'd never climbed a ladder before.

It took a while but he persuaded her she had to go for it. He told her if she pushed up against the hatch it would fall into the loft. There was a torch on the floor within a hand's reach. He would be able to help her until she was about five steps up but then she was on her own. Lily had been scared McLure would climb up after her but Kevin said there were lots of boxes and packing crates up there so she was to close the hatch and pile the whole lot on top.

But she'd only reached the second step, knees wobbling like jelly, when she stopped. 'Wait a minute. Can you hear him in the flat?' Earlier, when Kevin had called McLure a prick, Lily had nearly fainted. The last thing she'd wanted was him coming back in but she couldn't hear any noise so she told Kevin to shout again. He did, but this time with far less conviction.

But McLure didn't come. Lily stepped off the ladder and put her eye to the keyhole. The key was in the lock. Then, the oldest trick in the book, she raked about in a box, found sheets of brown wrapping paper, slid them under the door, poked the key out and prayed it didn't bounce too far. It didn't.

Back in real time an ambulance is here for Kevin. The medics want to make sure he's not concussed. He has nasty cuts on his wrist from the cable ties, but they're superficial. He's going to be okay.

I'd called Callum. He's hotfooted it into Montgomery Street. Conor has even discarded his uber-cool persona to come with his dad, but not quite enough to greet his sister with any more than a lukewarm one-armed hug.

They go home without me. I need to catch up with Andrew and Steph. I've already missed one call from them.

They have some news.

CHAPTER NINETY-THREE

IAIN McLURE WAS SITTING on a bench on the main concourse at Edinburgh Waverley Station. He didn't even register the whirring clack and rattle of the mechanical departures board updating. If he'd been in good humour he might even have derived some childish enjoyment from watching it, or maybe even celebrated that the traditional model had valiantly fought off competition from silent LED upstarts. But he didn't need to look at it to confirm the last train to Birmingham had left from platform 8, with him on the wrong side of the barrier.

He had a little less than half an hour to decide on his next step. That was when the last train left for Kinghorn on the other side of the Forth Rail Bridge. He lifted his holdall and placed it next to him then folded his jacket and lodged it in between the handles. The leading edge of his iPad was poking out of the side pocket, he slapped it down then pulled the zip across. There was no point in checking again, the story it told wasn't going to change.

———

When McLure had heard Kev calling him a prick and he'd put the cupboard door key in the lock he knew he had two choices. If he opened the door he was scared he'd lose control so the alternative was far preferable: get the hell out of the flat. He stepped quickly out into the hall, lifted his holdall and charged out the front door. He closed and locked it behind him and when he reached the pavement, he tossed the key into an overgrown garden. Then he walked the few hundred metres to London Road, hailed a cab and took it to Princes Street before descending Waverley Steps to the station.

In the cab, he checked the times for trains to Birmingham New Street but in truth, anywhere south of the border would have done. He was amazed when the live timetable said there was a delayed train set to depart in twenty minutes. That would give him time to withdraw enough cash for the ticket and grab a sandwich, while spending the minimum amount of time in the station. That was his plan. And you know what they say about plans.

The ATM in the station ticket hall rejected his with-drawal. Insufficient funds in his account. *Bollocks! I transferred a grand in there yesterday.*

He tried again. Same result.

He tapped the button for Print Recent Transactions and it explained clearly what was wrong. The £1000 had been cred-ited, but that morning there had been a debit for the same amount. *What the f...?*

With no time to worry about the whys and wherefores, all he could do was to transfer more money. It would credit instan-taneously. He moved over to a flight of three steps in front of a door that hadn't been opened in years. He sat down, opened his iPad, tapped the banking app and typed in the login details for the Lebanese account he'd set up from Sophie's PC. Then he hit Enter.

Nothing happened.

He scrolled up and saw the error comment in red type: Username or password invalid. Please retry.

He wiped his hands on his shirt, took a breath and typed in the details again. Carefully.

Another login failure.

This cannot be happening.

Perhaps he'd been too gung-ho, working from memory. Truth was, he didn't believe that for a second but he checked the details stored on his phone.

That's what I typed. Definitely.

He juggled the phone and iPad on his knees and made a third attempt. This time he enabled the View password option. He checked and double-checked the details across the two devices. They were identical. But he stopped before hitting Enter. He knew that three failures would lock him out of the account. He wasn't sure for how long but he wouldn't get his access back tonight, that was for sure.

He checked the time, only ten minutes until the Birmingham train left.

Hand trembling, he tapped the screen.

Username or password invalid.

'Shit! Shit! And double-shit!'

The temptation to smash the iPad off the tiled floor was almost irresistible but instead, he dropped it into the pocket of his bag and moved out onto the concourse. At that time on a midweek night there weren't too many people about so there were several free benches where he could sit to consider what was, undoubtedly, a serious predicament.

He didn't have enough cash to travel any distance by train. He couldn't withdraw from the ATM, and the bank's helpdesk was closed for the day. He checked the coach station timetables but the overnight buses to Birmingham had long gone. Even if hotels accepted cash these days, and he didn't know if they did, a room in Edinburgh in the tourist season would be way beyond his means. He had a credit card on order, for all the good that would do him. He couldn't go back to Sophie's and there was no one else he could call on for help, not without a ridiculous explanation to go along with his request.

All in all, he was screwed and he knew it. The only option was to hide out in Kinghorn. He had no idea if the cops were monitoring the house but he very much doubted it. He would be taking a risk but what choice did he have? No, Kinghorn it was. He'd sneak in under cover of darkness and work things out from there.

'May as well go and buy a ticket,' he muttered.

'Sorry, didn't catch that?'

He checked out the young woman who'd just spoken to him. She was blonde, hair in a ponytail, fit – in more ways than one. She smiled at him.

Jeez. A hooker. That's all I fuckin' need.

Then an idea occurred to him but as soon as it popped into his head, he jettisoned it. He couldn't afford her either. He flapped a hand in her direction. 'Sorry darlin', I'm not interested.'

Still she smiled at him. He was about to tell her to try elsewhere for a punter when she asked, 'Are you Iain McLure?'

'*What*?'

'I said, are you Iain McLure?'

'What if I am? But more importantly, who the fuck are you?' He grabbed his holdall and jacket and stood up.

The woman made a stop signal with her hand. 'I'm Detective Constable Zanetti and I'm arresting you—'

McLure guffawed. 'You're kidding, right?' He looked her

up and down, and took a step towards her. 'You're about half the height of fuck all, now get out of—'

Quite how he ended up with his cheek and eye socket scraping the tiled floor, and his wrist in an extremely unnatural position between his shoulder blades, he would never know.

A pair of gleaming black shoes below charcoal grey suit trousers stepped into his eye line. He was hauled to his feet. The woman held his right arm; she had fingers like steel rods.

DC Andrew Young was smiling too. 'In your case, sir, size *doesn't* matter. DC Zanetti, you were *saying?*'

'Iain McLure. I am arresting you under suspicion of several counts of extortion. You are not obliged to say anything but anything you do say will be noted down and may be used in evidence. Do you understand?'

McLure placed a palm against his forehead. 'I only have one question. How did you know where I was? I mean, no one knew I was coming here.'

His holdall had fallen to the ground in the struggle; his jacket had slid off the top and lay next to it. Steph snapped on a pair of gloves then bent down and picked up the jacket. 'This is how we found you, sir.'

'What? But loads of people wear jackets like that.'

'You're right, sir.' Steph turned the garment inside out and held the label towards him. 'But you're the only one with a tracking device sewn into the lining.'

He gawped at her. 'Sophie?'

'I couldn't possibly comment, sir. Now would you like to come with us?'

CHAPTER NINETY-FOUR

As soon as Callum drives off with the kids and while the medics are still loading Kevin into the ambulance, I jump in the car and head for the Custody Suite at St Leonard's. Steph's updated me with the fantastic news from Waverley and I've called Keown to divert her.

I pull into the car park behind the station just as Andrew and Steph are escorting a man into the building. I assume it's McLure, I've never laid eyes on him until now. I'm manoeuvring into a tight space when a black VW Golf appears and double parks, completely jamming me in. It's Keown. There's a shocker, eh?

And that's when a weird thing happens. The passenger door of her car swings open and out steps DCS Thornton.

The two of them march across the car park and I follow on, trying to work out this little conundrum.

I arrive downstairs at the booking-in area to find McLure standing in front of the Custody Officer. I'm still wondering why the Chief Super is slumming it when the man himself leaves Keown's side and pushes through to the counter. He speaks briefly to the officer behind the desk, then to Andrew. He completely ignores Steph. Her expression suggests she'd like to knee him in the balls. Andrew pauses for a second before nodding and moving a few metres off to the side. Steph stays where she is until Andrew walks over and tugs at her sleeve.

The next move catches everybody by surprise. DCS Thornton takes McLure's elbow and guides him into an office over to our right. The walls are reinforced glass so we are able to observe what's going on, while pretending not to.

Thornton moves in extremely close to McLure and they speak, head to head, for at least five minutes. From time to time their gestures are incredibly theatrical: arms waving about all over the place, exaggerated shrugs, wide-eyed disbelief – you name it. Everyone out here is staring, wondering what the hell is going on. We can't hear what either of them is saying although the tones and volume occasionally penetrate the glass. No one knows what to do. Apart from wait.

Then McLure shakes his head, folds his arms tight and rocks back on his heels. I don't know whether this is defiance or refusal, but the Chief turns away. He looks as though he's bitten into something particularly nasty.

He opens the door, clearly thinking the conversation is over. It isn't, and now that we can all hear him McLure seizes his opportunity. No one misses the punchline. 'If I'm going down, Thornton, you crooked bastard, *you're* going down too. And serves you fucking right.'

The scene remains on freeze-frame for not far short of an eternity. Then Thornton moves to the far corner of the room and faces in to the wall, pulling out his phone on the way. Andrew steps into the office and escorts McLure to the counter. The spell is broken and we all begin moving and speaking again.

Keown appears by my side and taps my arm. 'DS Cooper. Come with me, please. Quickly.' Then she marches towards Thornton, who still has his back to us.

I fall in behind her. I take in the skirt, the heels, the whole overt sexy look. Then I spot Thornton's midnight blue suit with the pale coloured button-down shirt and the expensive shoes. And ace detective that I am, I figure out *precisely* who my boss's date was this evening.

At about the same time, Thornton turns and puts a hand up. 'No, Deirdre. Wait ...'

She stops right inside his personal space and I pull up by her shoulder.

'Detective Chief Superintendent Mark Thornton,' she says, 'I am arresting you under suspicion of conspiracy to defeat the ends of justice. You are not obliged to say anything but anything you do say will be noted down and may be used in evidence. Do you understand?'

And all the cops in the room are rooted to the spot yet again, resembling a hallelujah choir caught in freeze-frame.

As everyone gradually breaks free from their collective catatonic state there's a queue at the counter. McLure and Thornton are being processed in parallel. Andrew, Steph and Keown finish up at pretty much the same time and I decide I'll head back to the office.

Then my boss steps in front of me. 'DS Cooper. My car. Now!'

CHAPTER NINETY-FIVE

I CANNOT BELIEVE MY EARS. 'Seriously, Boss. Do we have to do this now? Here?'

But she doesn't answer. She walks outside to the car park leaving me to trail along behind like a guilty schoolgirl caught smoking behind the bike shed.

I slam the car door closed and turn in my seat. 'Listen, if this is about the Gardiners' case ...'

'It's not only about *that* case.'

'Okay but can we leave this 'til tomorrow and then you can give me my bollocking? Because I have a stack of paperwork waiting for me and I'd like to go home to see how Lily is.'

'Mel. As far as I'm concerned, the paperwork can wait 'til the morning, and you can go home as soon as we're finished here.'

Aw, jeez. The bitch is going to suspend me. For disobeying orders or some shit.

But: *Mel? She called me Mel. Again?*

I twist further round until I'm sideways on the passenger seat. 'What is it with all this "Mel" crap? Sometimes it's DS

Cooper, other times just plain Cooper. At best, it's Melissa. And now "Mel"? Are you messing with my head or what?' I slump back, fold my arms. 'If you're planning to suspend me then bloody get on with it, will you?'

'And why on God's earth would I suspend you?'

I realise she's laughing. Not sarcastic, not sneering. Not quite tears down her cheeks, but genuine laughter all the same.

'Mel. If my boss had told me to drop the Gardiners' case when I was as close as you were to solving it, I wouldn't actually have *told* her to fuck off. But I definitely would have kept working at it and worried about the inevitable shit later on.'

'But you've been such a ...'

'Cow?'

'Or similar.'

She shrugs. 'Yeah, sorry about that. I suppose I should explain.'

'If you wouldn't mind.'

I twist round again but she's off on a tangent. She addresses the windscreen. 'You've solved or helped to solve three major investigations. First, closing the Gardiners' case was excellent work. Congratulations. Second, at the same time as finding your daughter, you brought McLure down too. And third, you helped me finally nail Thornton.' She glances at me. 'And for that you have my eternal gratitude.'

My brain is beginning to tick over. 'The Chief wanted the McLure case dropped. He put pressure on me by going through you. McLure's a blackmailer, but the Chief ...?'

'McLure has been blackmailing him for years and years. It started with something minor but Thornton is an arrogant, greedy, corrupt individual who screwed up people's lives so he could clamber all over them on his way up the ladder. Gradually, the blackmailing became more serious and to stop McLure dropping bombs on Thornton's career, and on his personal life, he was forced to start interfering with investigations. Criminal cases collapsed, clean-up projects were derailed, and when Thornton reached DCS whole initiatives were downgraded. A lot of crooked people made a pile of money as a result. McLure was able to capitalise on that by twisting the knife into Thornton so McLure earned money on the deals too. Lots of money, in fact.'

'So how long have you been building the case against the Chief?'

She stretches her arms, leaves one hand resting on the steering wheel. 'Years. And you've no idea how many times I've nearly given up.' She draws in a deep breath and exhales. 'But now, at last, I've got him. The bastard!'

We're silent for a while but this isn't hanging together for me. 'Deirdre, was it an official investigation?'

'Does it matter?'

'No, but you were sleeping with him. I don't think I could do that if it wasn't ...'

'Personal?'

I nod.

She drops her hand down and scratches her knee. 'Thornton's always had affairs, everybody knows that. If it has a fanny and a decent pair of tits ...' She glances down at herself and laughs again, but there's no mirth this time. 'I was getting close, you see. But from where I was, on the outside, I was nowhere near close enough.' She breathes in, gives another loud exhale. 'So being in possession of the necessary attributes, I used them.'

'You said you were gathering evidence, but how? I'm surprised he wasn't really careful.'

'He was *obsessively* careful. Until recently.' She shakes her head. 'I was toiling, and I thought I was going to have to give up. But then you came along.'

'Me?'

'Yes, with your investigation into McLure. And as you got nearer to him, he ramped up the pressure on Thornton. Then Thornton started to make mistakes. I guess in days gone by, blackmail would be in person or by letter, and latterly by email. But McLure's been delivering all his recent threats by phone. WhatsApp and the like. And Thornton's biggest mistake was he didn't delete any of the incriminating documents McLure sent him. Like I said, arrogant.'

'But surely his phone would be locked. How did you break into it?'

'He was never off that bloody phone so it was just a question of watching, constantly, building up a picture.' She smiles to herself. 'And it's amazing what you can pick up when you're pretending to be sleeping. You know, post-coital bliss and all that.' She glances over at me. 'That would be *faked* post-coital bliss, by the way. Anyway, eventually I sussed his security code and tested it while he was in the shower. Uploaded the offending documents, and Bob's your mother's brother.'

I don't know what else to say so I settle for, 'Phew!'

Then I take a risk. 'So how long had it been going on?'

'What, the sex?'

'Well, yes.'

'Mind your own damn business.'

We both laugh at that.

'But why the total bitch persona,' I say. 'Because, talking to you now, like this, the real Deirdre seems quite different.'

She sighs. Pauses. Shuffles her bum to bring herself upright. 'Initially, it was all about keeping people away. I'm not vain, not really, but I know men are attracted to me. And you know what they're like, a few of my colleagues began hitting on me. So I had to stop them, and playing the sour-faced bitch from hell was my solution. Bit of a sledgehammer, admittedly.'

Then she laughs again so I have to ask. 'What's funny?'

'The irony was, one of my female colleagues saw I was knocking the guys back and made the wrong assumption. So I decided to be a bitch to everybody and it just became a habit. And the strange thing was none of my bosses even batted an eyelid.'

'So will you stop now?'

'No. But it doesn't matter, I'm done with policing. I'll be handing in my notice as soon as the investigation into Thornton is complete. I'll stay to make sure no one screws up. Or worse, lets him off the hook.'

I draw in a breath to speak but she cuts me off at the knees. 'And don't come out with any shit like "That would be a waste" or "You're a good copper". Because I'm not. Maybe I was at one time but my heart's not in it any more. That's why I made such a pig's ear of the rape case with Kim what's-his-name.' She looks at me. 'Sorry about that. You did well to pull it out of the bag.'

We're silent for a moment but I have one more question to ask. I hesitate, then ask it anyway. 'You said it was personal?'

She nods. Stares out the windscreen. Nods again. The silence lasts a while.

'When Thornton was a DS, twenty-odd years ago, a female PC was seconded to his team. She was young. A newbie. Blonde, attractive and a bit ditzy. He screwed her, then he screwed her career. Boasted to all his mates. They assumed she was easy but when she refused them all, too late unfortunately, they treated her like shit. And he was the worst of the lot. She raised a formal complaint, it was brushed under the rug, things became worse if that's even possible and eventually she broke. Took her own life.'

This time I daren't ask.

'Her name was Jill.' She reaches for the ignition. 'Jill Keown.'

Then she stops, dead. No further explanation. No more questions. She starts the engine. 'See you tomorrow, Mel.'

I'm back outside. I shut the door. I can see Steph walking towards me but then I hear the passenger window humming open. Deirdre leans across the passenger seat.

I bend down to look inside. 'Yes?'

In a low tone, she growls. 'Not a word, Mel. Not a fucking word. You do *not* want to make an enemy of old Frosty Knickers.'

Then she winks at me.

She makes her final statement at top volume, deliberately so. 'My office first thing, Cooper. And make sure that report's finished or I'll have your guts.'

She sits upright and zooms off. I watch the window closing as she disappears out of the gates.

'Everything okay, boss?'

I turn and smile.

'Tickety-boo, Steph. Everything is just tickety-boo.'

EPILOGUE

IT'S JUST BEFORE ten o'clock, I'll be heading off to court soon to watch Iain McLure being sentenced.

I gaze out into the office. It's quiet, Steph's the only person in sight. She's over by the filing cabinets, surrounded by paperwork, humming away to herself. She's talented in many ways but the poor dear couldn't carry a tune in a shopping basket. Such a shame, for anyone within earshot.

It's all change around here. Mark Thornton's demise created a massive gap in our senior management structure so, temporarily, we've been moved up a notch. Jeff's back from his stint in Northern Ireland, and is now Detective *Chief* Inspector Hunter. I'm covering his job. DI Cooper? I'm not sure about that, but let's see how it goes.

The excellent news is Andrew's been substantively promoted to Detective Sergeant. And not before time. He's on holiday for the next couple of weeks with his new girlfriend. He hasn't told me anything about her yet, partly because he prefers to keep his cards close to his chest but mainly because he knows how much it's bugging me.

Tobias is back in Germany. I called him last week and although he's pleased to be home after his sabbatical, he doesn't rule out the prospect of working with us again. He was a superb addition to the team, and I'd have him back in a flash.

Deirdre Keown hasn't yet left the service. Between the evidence she gathered and the stories McLure was all too willing to relate, the case against the Chief Super should be a slam dunk. It's not a question of *whether* he'll be found guilty, it's more about how long he'll be put away for. But she's staying, for the time being anyway, as a visible reminder that everyone should keep their collective eye on the ball.

Personally, I'll be sorry if she resigns. She's not a bad copper, it's simply that her focus was elsewhere for a while. I did invite her along to Tobias's leaving do. She just smiled, said, 'Behave yourself, Mel,' then told me to shut the door on my way out.

My phone pings me a reminder: *McLure – Court.*

I'm reminded of how events had unfolded following his arrest. While our forensic colleagues were gutting the house at Kinghorn, they discovered a safe in the basement. It provided a wealth of treasure, including a computer hard drive that had belonged to Francis Crolla at some point in the dim and distant. Detailed analysis of the contents is going to put him away for a long time, in an area of the prison specially reserved for the likes of him. And I'm not talking about dodgy pub owners.

On the subject of computers, Sophie Gardiner's PC also provided material that, paradoxically, was both delicious and frustrating. Clearly the woman had been highly suspicious of her former fiancé, which is probably why she had keylogger software installed on the machine. Then, when our pet forensic accountant, Ellen, followed a trail of financial transactions that she termed 'significant' it came to an abrupt halt at an account in a Lebanese bank. An account with a zero balance, I should add. Not long after that, over the course of a month, several Edinburgh charities were handed sizeable windfalls. All donated anonymously.

I quizzed Sophie purely for my own interest and although she denied any knowledge of the keylogger or these windfalls she was lying through her back teeth. Which isn't easy while you're smirking for Scotland.

Talking about Sophie, the prosecution involving her and Kim Seung-Min hasn't yet been brought to court. It's taking time to pull all the threads together. But I bumped into Leo Contini recently and he thought they'd be lucky if they were given anything less than ten years each. His office had been astounded at the complexity of the five stings, especially how quickly the two perpetrators had pulled them together.

Then, only last week, Dave Devlin related an item of news that kicked off a Mexican wave in our HQ. Tommy Jarvis finally overstepped the mark. He was found guilty of harassment and threatening behaviour towards a young woman who lives about ten minutes' walk from his house. The reconstruction project had started and one day he discovered her taking photographs. He completely lost the plot, screaming obscenities and pushing her around before smashing her phone with the heel of his boot.

That was bad enough, but then things became a whole lot worse for Tommy when we discovered film clips and stills of the woman on his phone. The court heard she was an architectural student, the photos were for her third-year university project. He was fortunate not to end up inside, but it's pleasing to me that he now possesses a criminal record. Some people would say that's well overdue.

———

Twelve years. Even with good behaviour McLure will spend at least eight of them locked away.

As I walk down the wide flight of stone stairs from the courtroom, I reflect that a few more years on top would have been nice. But hey, you don't always get what you want.

As I approach a landing, an elderly gentleman is coming towards me down a different set of stairs. We've both been in the same courtroom, it had two exits. He's possibly well into his seventies, but sprightly and smartly dressed. His leather soles click on every step and I slow down to allow him onto the landing first. I'm in absolutely no hurry.

He glances up at me as he comes off the last step. Then he smiles and gives me a little wave, like a salute. He doesn't stop but I do. One hand on the polished bannister, I watch him as he reaches the foot of the stairs and strides on out towards the daylight. He doesn't look up again.

———

In my office, I find the piece of paper I'm searching for. I make a call, ask my question, then wait.

The woman comes back on the line. 'Sorry to keep you hanging on. Could you just confirm that name for me, please?'

I repeat what I told her a few minutes ago.

'I'm very sorry,' she says. 'But according to my records we've never had a patient by the name of Rhys Harding at this practice.'

I thank her, and end the call. Just for the hell of it, I ring the other number I'd written down all those months ago. A solicitor's office up in George Street. Surprise, surprise, they haven't heard of Mr Harding either. And they certainly haven't ever employed anyone called Dawn McDermott, the 'solicitor' who advised me that poor old Rhys had passed away.

HARRY FISHER

The smile on my face takes a good minute to fade. I
chuckle, shake my head then crumple up the paper and throw
it at the confidential waste bin. Wonders will never cease, a
direct hit!

I sigh. There's plenty I could be getting on with but I sit
there without moving. I'm just enjoying the peace and quiet.

I hear footsteps approaching and I snap back into the land
of the living.

'Got a minute, boss?' says Steph.

'Of course. What is it?'

She waggles a folder in my direction. 'I've been tidying out
some paperwork and came across a case that was near the
bottom of Tobias's original list, one we didn't ever investigate.
Involves a GP, name of Emily O'Keefe. She was treasurer on
her church committee and embezzled £50,000. Her sentence
was two years. She's been in for seven months already, and I'm
told she'll definitely be serving the full term. Not a model prisoner from what I hear.'

Then I see a look I'm familiar with. I think she learned it
from Andrew. Or maybe even from me.

I sit back. 'I'm assuming there's a bit more to it than that.'

'There is. I've been doing a bit of digging, Dr O'Keefe was
the Gardiner family's GP.' She pauses. 'And, she and Sophie
go to the same church.'

There's a moment's silence between us, then I stretch out a
hand. 'Pull up a chair, Steph. Let's find out if the good doctor
might be innocent victim number six.'

I open the file. Glance out the window at the sunshine on
Leith. Today is turning out to be a good day. A very good day
indeed.

ACKNOWLEDGMENTS

To everyone who encouraged me and helped turn a jumble of assorted ideas into this polished work, you have my deepest gratitude.

Specific thanks go to many wonderful individuals who gave freely of their time, expertise, advice and opinion.

For offering your expert advice: my niece Dr Anna Wight, Alan Moir, Alison Bruce, Alison Cusiter, Andrew Crosbie of www.crime.scot, Carol Nicholson, Colin Watson, Dagmar Grant, Dave Cowie, Duncan Smith, Fraser Burr, Graham Morrison, Jackie Cunningham, Julie McDonald, Mark Cochrane, Mark Ewan, Nathan Lamb, Ross Cunningham, Ray McCulloch, Shui Lee and Stuart Murray.

For helping to shape and improve different versions: my beta readers Chris Livingston and Karen Hart; and Debbie Mitchell, Janice McKinlay and Nicky Jenkins. A special thank you to my cousin, Joyce Nisbet, for your many brilliant suggestions and for continuing to be so encouraging and complimentary about my writing efforts.

To Adrian Hobart and Rebecca Collins at Hobeck Books

for having faith in me and my writing, and for all the work you do in the background. To my editor, Helen Gray, who has eyes like scalpels and works in such a collaborative manner. And a photo credit to Maurice Dougan for providing the street sign image on the cover.

I must admit to playing fast and loose with legal timescales and court procedures to fit the storyline. Any errors that remain are entirely down to me.

And finally, my amazing, wonderful wife, Shiona. Where do I start? For binning my first idea – it would never have held water; for reviewing the early drafts; for working with me through the final draft by reading it aloud, word by word; for helping me to shape and reshape this work by finding and fixing literally hundreds of tiny imperfections that improved the final version immeasurably. For everything, quite simply: THANK YOU. I love you. HTM.

ABOUT THE AUTHOR

Harry Fisher is originally from Leith (the port of Edinburgh) but lives in Aberdeen with his wife, Shiona. They're both into travel, outdoor activities, wine and food. They share their home with their crazy Hungarian Vizsla – his job is to stop them seizing up completely.

Prior to self-publishing his debut crime thriller, Harry had never written a word of fiction. So he just launched in – cold turkey for authors. *Way Beyond A Lie* is set in Edinburgh, with themes that are bang up to date: identity theft and cybercrime. During two Free Book Promotions in 2020, it was downloaded 2,700 times over five days.

His second book *Be Sure Your Sins* is #1 in the DS Mel Cooper series. Also set in Edinburgh, it involves six events that happen to six people that destroy six lives. It's not a sequel but *Way Beyond A Lie* readers told Harry they loved Mel and her sidekick Andrew Young so, easy decision, they got their own show.

Due spring 2022 is #2 in the DS Mel Cooper series *Yes, I Killed Her*. A story of the perfect murder – with a twist. Then another one.

Harry loves talking to readers about crime writing. Covid has meant that online has become the norm but he'd far rather meet people face to face.

f

WAY BEYOND A LIE

'An excellent debut novel.' *****

'Engaging crime thriller filled with suspense, intrigue and peril!' *****

'I do hope we can expect more of the same from the talented Mr Fisher.' *****

'EXCELLENT ... All I'll say is READ IT!' *****

'Characters realistically described, and sadly all too prevalent in today's society!' *****

'You never quite know where it will go next!' *****

'A beautiful twist in the very last line.' *****

**Your wife goes missing. She leaves no trace.
You have no idea where she's gone.
How would *you* try to find her?**

When Ross McKinlay's wife, Carla, vanishes during an afternoon shopping trip he's left bewildered and grief stricken. As Ross uncovers the reasons for his wife's disappearance, his life begins to unravel. He's determined to find her. He needs answers. But the deeper he delves, the more confused he becomes and the closer he edges towards danger.

As Ross is soon to discover, he isn't the only person looking for his wife.
One man wants the truth.
Another wants blood.
Who will find her first?

The prequel to the DS Mel Cooper Series, Harry Fisher's fast-paced story of love, friendship, fraud, intrigue and murder will keep you guessing until the last page.

HOBECK BOOKS – THE HOME OF GREAT STORIES

We hope you've enjoyed reading this novel by Harry Fisher. The prequel to this novel, *Way Beyond A Lie*, is also a Hobeck book. The second book in the series is due out in 2022. If you would like to find out more about Harry's writing please visit his website: **www.harryfisherwriter.com**.

If you enjoyed this book, you may be interested to know that if you subscribe to Hobeck Books you can download *Crime Bites*, a free compilation of novellas and short stories by the Hobeck team of authors: **www.hobeck.net**.

Included in this compilation are the following:

- *Echo Rock* by Robert Daws
- *Old Dogs, Old Tricks* by AB Morgan
- *The Silence of the Rabbit* by Wendy Turbin
- *Never Mind the Baubles: An Anthology of Twisted Winter Tales* by the Hobeck Team (including all the current Hobeck authors and Hobeck's two publishers)
- *The Clarice Cliff Vase* by Linda Huber
- *Here She Lies* by Kerena Swan
- *The Macnab Principle* by R.D. Nixon
- *A Defining Moment* by Lin Le Versha

Also please visit the Hobeck Books website for details of

our other superb authors and their books, and if you would like to get in touch, we would love to hear from you.

Hobeck Books also presents a weekly podcast, the Hobcast, where founders Adrian Hobart and Rebecca Collins discuss all things book related, key issues from each week, including the ups and downs of running a creative business. Each episode includes an interview with one of the people who make Hobeck possible: the editors, the authors, the cover designers. These are the people who help Hobeck bring great stories to life. Without them, Hobeck wouldn't exist. The Hobcast can be listened to from all the usual platforms but it can also be found on the Hobeck website: **www.hobeck.net/hobcast**.

Printed in Great Britain
by Amazon